SIZZLING NIGHTS
WITH DR OFF-LIMITS

BY
JANICE LYNN

SEVEN NIGHTS
WITH HER EX

BY
LOUISA HEATON

MILLS &
BOON

Janice Lynn has a Masters in Nursing from Vanderbilt University, and works as a nurse practitioner in a family practice. She lives in the southern United States with her husband, their four children, their Jack Russell—appropriately named Trouble—and a lot of unnamed dust bunnies that have moved in since she started her writing career. To find out more about Janice and her writing visit janicelynn.com.

Louisa Heaton lives on Hayling Island, Hampshire, with her husband, four children and a small zoo. She has worked in various roles in the health industry—most recently four years as a Community First Responder, answering 999 calls. When not writing, Louisa enjoys other creative pursuits, including reading, quilting and patchwork—usually instead of the things she ought to be doing!

SIZZLING NIGHTS WITH DR OFF-LIMITS

BY
JANICE LYNN

Published in Great Britain 2016
By Mills & Boon, an imprint of HarperCollins*Publishers*
1 London Bridge Street, London, SE1 9GF

© 2016 Janice Lynn

ISBN: 978-0-263-91513-6

Our policy is to use papers that are natural, renewable and recyclable
products and made from wood grown in sustainable forests.
The logging and manufacturing processes conform to the legal
environmental regulations of the country of origin.

Printed and bound in Spain
by CPI, Barcelona

Dear Reader,

Sometimes a story idea hits and just takes off. Emily and Lucas's story was that way. Occasionally couples who are meant to be together let life pull them apart and blind them to their true feelings. That's what has happened with Emily and Lucas.

Lucas is hesitant to take his dream job because his ex-wife works at the hospital—but how can he turn down an offer to make real advances in brain injury research when that's his life's passion? Emily was his best friend once upon a time. Surely they can make peace and have an amicable work relationship? Only once he spends time with Emily he wants much more than just a work relationship with his ex. He wants *her*.

When her ex buys a date with her at a charity bachelorette auction Emily is reminded of all the things that made her fall in love with Lucas to begin with. Only this time around she isn't young, naïve, and blinded by visions of happily-ever-after. This time she won't let him anywhere near her heart. Only what if he's had it all along…?

I had so much fun on Emily and Lucas's journey to healing and happy-ever-after. I hope you enjoy their story as much as I did. I'd love to hear what you thought of their romance at Janice@janicelynn.net.

Happy reading,

Janice Lynn

To Reesee. Love you to the moon and back!
Love, SMOM.

Books by Janice Lynn

Mills & Boon Medical Romance

The Nurse Who Saved Christmas
The Doctor's Damsel in Distress
Flirting with the Society Doctor
Challenging the Nurse's Rules
NYC Angels: The Heiress's Baby Scandal
The ER's Newest Dad
After the Christmas Party...
Flirting with the Doc of Her Dreams
New York Doc to Blushing Bride
Winter Wedding in Vegas

Visit the Author Profile page at
millsandboon.co.uk for more titles.

**Janice won The National Readers' Choice Award
for her first book
*The Doctor's Pregnancy Bombshell***

**Praise for
Janice Lynn**

'Fun, witty and sexy… A heartfelt, sensual and
compelling read.'
—*Goodreads* on
NYC Angels: The Heiress's Baby Scandal

CHAPTER ONE

No. No. *No.* Her ex-husband *hadn't* just made an outlandish bid for Emily Stewart's Manhattan Memorial Children's Hospital Traumatic Brain Injury fund-raiser bachelorette date.

Lucas couldn't. Wouldn't.

Oohs and aahs were sounding around the hotel ballroom as the auctioneer expressed his excitement over the enormous leap in the bid. Emily just wanted to cry, *Noooooooo.*

She'd never dreamed of putting in a clause that said if her ex-husband lost his mind, bid and probably just won, her donated "date" was null and void. Then again, when she'd first volunteered with the fund-raiser, she'd not seen Lucas in five years. She couldn't possibly have expected him to show up at the auction, much less bid outrageously for her bachelorette number.

What she'd expected was her boyfriend to buy the date.

The reality was she'd been worried Richard would be her only bidder.

If only he had.

Why had she let Meghan convince her to do the auction? Standing on a stage letting men bid on a date with her was not her thing. Still, it had been for a great cause she believed in and she hadn't had the heart to say no despite fear of humiliation and embarrassment.

But if she'd known Lucas would show up and bid on her, no way would she have agreed to participate.

Ugh.

If she had one of those auction number thingies, she'd bid on herself. Could a girl do that?

White-knuckled, she forced a smile to stay on her face, but her cheeks were starting to hurt. Then again, that could be from her gritted teeth rather than her fake smile.

She dug her fingers into her palms and pretended everything was just fine, as if the man who'd once ripped her heart to shreds hadn't just bid a ridiculous sum to go to dinner with her.

He hadn't eaten with her when it hadn't cost him a thing except his time. Why would he want to now? After all these years? For that matter, why had he even taken the job at Children's? Manhattan was big enough for the both of them. Barely. Their paths should never, or at least rarely, cross. They'd been apart five years and, although she occasionally heard his name or saw a photo of him come across one of their few mutual acquaintances' social media page, she'd not seen him in person since the day their divorce had been finalized.

Until this past month.

Now she saw him every time she worked.

The auctioneer resumed his rapid-fire words, calling for another bid. Emily's gaze went to Richard, silently pleading with him to outbid Lucas. He might not have Lucas's millions, but the bid was far from being outside his reach. Why wasn't he stepping up, letting Lucas know she was his?

One of the auction volunteers walked over to stand near Richard, encouraging him to up the ante. But rather than do so, he shrugged and said something she could only make out bits and pieces of from where she stood on stage.

What she caught was that the auction was "all for fun" and "for a good cause."

Cheeks on fire, forced smile glued in place, heart pounding out of her chest, Emily wanted to disappear. Richard made a good living. He could afford to bid higher. As her boyfriend, he should be bidding higher.

"Anyone else, folks? Come on, just look at her. Imagine a night out on the town with this gorgeous woman on your arm." The auctioneer turned his attention back to the rest of the crowd, trying to entice a new bidder into the ring. As if anyone else was going to cough up that much money to oust Lucas's high bid when her own boyfriend wouldn't. Ugh. This was humiliating.

"Going once," the auctioneer warned. "Going twice."

Her cheeks were so hot maybe she'd just spontaneously combust. Then sharing a meal with Lucas wouldn't even be an issue.

"Sold to the lucky gentleman holding number 146," the auctioneer crooned.

Great. Lucas had just won her date.

Emily walked across the stage to where the other auctioned-off women waited while the next bachelorette took center stage. In just a few minutes Emily would have to have a photo taken with her ex-husband. She'd have to stand next to him, smile at the camera and pretend she wasn't dying on the inside.

Thanks to his winning bid she had to sit through a meal with him across the table.

How dared he do this to her? Hadn't he caused enough havoc already to last a lifetime?

No.

Just no.

She was not having a meal with her ex-husband. Just the thought made her want to barf.

She'd play nice for the picture, but she would make a matching donation to the charity and wiggle out of the date. Although, Lucas had certainly been generous enough that doing so would make a painful dent in her savings. Still, the charity and avoiding time with her ex-husband were worthy causes.

Why? she wanted to scream at him from across the crowded luxury hotel ballroom. The hundreds of attendees might as well have not existed. All she saw was Lucas, smiling so nonchalantly, as if he hadn't just done something so absolutely wrong. Dressed in his tux, he was so handsome she wanted to shake her fist and yell it wasn't fair that he looked even better than he had when he'd been hers.

Their divorce hadn't left him any worse for wear. She'd been the devastated one who'd had to pick up the shattered bits of her heart and pretend her whole world hadn't fallen apart.

Her whole world had fallen apart.

But she'd survived, was stronger for the life lessons learned from her marriage to Dr. Lucas Cain.

Why had he drawn attention to himself, to her, by bidding such an out-of-the-ballpark amount for her date?

Why, when she'd finally put the pieces of her life back together, did he show up to throw rocks at her glass house?

She had made a good life at Children's, was dating and liked said boyfriend who'd not won her bid. Richard Givens, a pharmacist who worked near the hospital, was everything Lucas hadn't been.

She glanced Richard's way, saw him laughing at something someone at their table had said. Exasperation filled her. He'd just lost a date with his girlfriend to another man and he was laughing? Ugh. He wasn't worried. Why should he be? He didn't know Lucas was her ex-husband.

No one at Children's did.

Not wanting any reminder, she'd changed back to her maiden name and they'd never heard Lucas's name on her lips. Not until three weeks ago when he'd started in a medical director position at Children's pediatric neurology department. The department she worked in and loved. Maybe she could ask for a transfer.

Not having to see him would be worth giving up her beloved nursing position at Children's. Almost.

Anger flared.

How dared he show up where she worked and make her consider transferring positions when she'd already left one job to escape reminders of the biggest mistake she'd ever made? She'd left the hospital where they'd met during the end of his neurosurgery fellowship.

She should have known better than to marry Lucas.

She had known better.

Her parents had warned her. Her friends had warned her. His parents had warned her. His friends had warned her. No one had thought they should marry. She was too young, Lucas wasn't ready to settle down, they were too different and from too-different lifestyles. She'd been an ordinary middle-class girl from Brooklyn. Lucas had been born with a silver spoon in his mouth and had never had to stress over anything.

But she'd paid no heed. She'd been in love and thought she'd found her happily-ever-after at twenty-one.

She'd just graduated from her nursing program and had been at the hospital for only a few weeks when the most handsome man she'd ever seen had stolen her breath with his quick smile, mischievous eyes and quick wit. They'd had a whirlwind romance, then married and settled into her little apartment close to the hospital, because she'd refused to move into his parents' Park Avenue penthouse as he'd apparently thought they would. No, she had not wanted to start out her marriage living with her in-laws, whom she'd met only a couple of times. She'd planned to prove all the naysayers wrong over the next fifty-plus years.

She'd been the one proved wrong.

Wrong when Lucas had become less and less enamored with their marriage no matter what she'd done to try to keep things smooth. She'd not expected a lot of his attention. He'd been in the midst of his fellowship, after all. But she had expected him to occasionally make time for his young wife, who'd loved him so much. Near the end, she'd barely seen him, had wondered if he'd even noticed she'd moved out of the apartment as he'd asked her to.

He must have. He'd immediately filed for divorce. For irreconcilable differences and abandonment.

Who'd abandoned whom?

She'd given him her heart, had put all she'd had into making her marriage a success, and he'd discarded her like yesterday's trash.

She'd sunk into a deeper and deeper depression, but nothing had ever hurt the way the demise of her marriage had, the way he had pierced her heart and bled it dry. Now that she'd carefully nurtured herself back into some semblance of a living, breathing person, had he come back to take shots at her a second time?

She wouldn't let him.

Her insides seethed with bitterness.

He couldn't steal her happiness or her peace of mind.

Only, from the moment she'd found out who had accepted the department position, her peace of mind had become a war zone. But it was a battle she would fight and win. She wouldn't give him so much power over her. Not ever again.

She'd planned to avoid him, to not interact any more

than absolutely necessary to effectively perform her job duties.

Apparently, Lucas had other ideas. Like a date he'd very publicly paid too much money to beat Richard to secure.

While the current bid came to a close, Emily glared at her ex-husband, wondering if you could hate someone you used to love more than life itself.

He was no doubt considered quite the catch. She knew better. She knew his flaws, knew that behind that handsome exterior beat the heart of a man incapable of loving another human being, of a man incapable of being there when his wife had needed him.

A man who hadn't been there on the worst night of her life.

Had he been at the hospital working, at his parents' or out partying with his buddies when her world had crumbled? Either way, he hadn't been at her side in that emergency room.

"Lucky you, girl!" Emily's best friend, Meghan, whispered. "I can't believe Dr. Cain just bought your basket. And for that price? You must be giving off some major pheromones or something because for a few minutes I thought he and Richard were going to come to blows."

Emily had never thought that. Lucas had never fought for her. He'd never fought for anything in his whole life. He wanted something and it just fell perfectly into place in his perfect life. She was probably the only mar on his stellar record.

And Richard, well, he was a nonconfrontational beta kind of guy, so she hadn't been too surprised when he'd let Lucas win the bid. Disappointed, but not really shocked. He would find paying such an exorbitant amount for something he did several times a week for free as a total waste.

Emily would have been highly impressed had Richard

stepped up and rescued her from Lucas's bidding clutches. A knight in shining armor to her damsel in distress. Too bad. She'd have enjoyed Richard putting Lucas in his place.

To be fair, Lucas had raised the bid a stupid amount and Richard didn't have a deep trust fund to line his pockets, but the bid hadn't been out of his financial reach. Not by a long shot. Still, he worked hard for his money, was someone whom Emily could relate to. Richard was the same as her, an ordinary person living an ordinary life. She liked it that way.

"You can have him," she muttered under her breath to her fellow pediatric neuro nurse.

"Are you blind?" Meghan's expression was incredulous as they exited the stage to make room for the bachelors to be auctioned off. "He's the hottest thing to hit Manhattan since the term Big Apple was first coined."

Stepping a few feet away from the stage, Emily wrinkled her nose. Looks could be so deceiving. "He's not my type."

"Girl, he is every red-blooded female's type." Meghan waggled her perfectly drawn brows. "Tall, dark and handsome."

"To each her own, because he isn't mine. I prefer Richard."

This time it was Meghan's nose that wrinkled. "Richard is boring."

Emily frowned. "Richard is loyal, handsome, intelligent, kind—"

"You deserve so much better than the likes of Richard," her best friend assured her. Meghan had never understood her attraction to Richard, always claiming that she felt he stifled Emily.

"Not to me, he isn't." She'd had excitement and the fast lane while married to Lucas. She didn't need parties and a revolving-door social life. She liked going home to her apartment after her shift ended, cooking a light dinner for two, discussing their day and occasionally going for a walk or perhaps to a show.

Richard was calm, predictable, stable. Totally to her taste in men.

Totally and completely the opposite of Lucas.

"You can't tell me Richard is even in the same league as Lucas Cain."

"You're right, he's not. Richard is way above it."

Meghan gave her an odd look. "You been drinking?"

Emily laughed. "Because I find the man I'm dating more attractive than some new doctor at the hospital, you think I'm inebriated? Richard is my boyfriend. Why wouldn't I find him more attractive than Dr. Cain?"

"Do you?" a familiar male voice asked from behind her.

Every cell in Emily's body did a nervous jump to attention, making her legs weak, making her hands tremble, making her heart race. Not wanting to look at him, not wanting to have a conversation with him, she turned to face her ex-husband.

Up close he looked even better than he had from across the room. Why, oh, why couldn't time have taken its toll and marred the physical beauty of his face?

He told you to leave. He filed for divorce. He's a cold, heartless jerk who means nothing to you.

Even so, her hands shook and her stomach threatened to hurl the appetizers she'd consumed earlier. "Do I what?"

"Find the man who bid against me more attractive?" His blue eyes twinkled with the same old arrogant mischief. He knew that he was handsome as sin, that women fell to their knees when he so much as bestowed a smile upon them. He couldn't fathom her finding any man more attractive. The jerk.

"Of course I find Richard more attractive, Dr. Cain." She put great emphasis on her formal use of his name. "He and I have been dating for almost ten months."

"Ten months?" He raised a brow as if impressed as his gaze took in everything about her. "Some marriages don't last that long."

Her breath lodged in her throat and she dug her fingernails harder into her palms. Mentally, she called him every rotten name she could think of.

"You're right," she agreed. "Too many people get married who shouldn't. Probably because they're too young to know any better or one of them wasn't committed to the relationship to begin with. My guess is that when those people become involved in their next serious relationship, they are a lot choosier."

The arrogant look in his eyes flickered just a little, as if she'd delivered a damaging blow and won that round. Good. He needed taking down a peg or two.

"I bet you're right." He turned to Meghan and gave her a smile so charming that it was a wonder she didn't swoon. "Hi, I'm Dr. Lucas Cain. I work at Children's with Emily."

Ugh. He sounded so nice, so polite, and Meghan was tripping over herself trying to form coherent sentences. He'd always had that effect on women. Even her.

But that had been in the past. These days her sentences were freaking pieces of grammatical art. She'd been inoculated against his sexual mojo.

Well, mostly. He was a sexy beast and her body wasn't dead. Good thing her mind knew better and ruled.

"Me, too," Meghan practically stuttered. "At Children's. I mean, I work at Children's, too."

Lucas's brow lifted. "On the neuro floor with Emily?"

Hearing her name on his lips caused tightness to squeeze Emily's chest. Darn him that he was here creating chaos in her world, not to mention making a blabbering idiot of her best friend.

Meghan nodded, still stammering and stuttering. "I've taken care of a few of your patients."

He flashed one of his most potent smiles and Emily had to forgive her friend. When he was more handsome than anything Hollywood had ever put on the silver screen, how was Meghan supposed to resist? Her friend didn't know he had a heart of ice and a soul as black as coal.

"Ah," he said. "That's why you look familiar."

Emily wasn't buying that he hadn't known who Meghan was. No doubt he knew everything about her best friend.

Meghan's lashes swooped downward. "I guess you heard what I was saying about how you looked."

Her best friend was flirting with her ex. Not that Meghan knew, but still. Gag. Gag. Gag.

Just take Emily out and push her in front of a taxi driver right now. She couldn't take any more.

"If you'll excuse me, I need to go find a ladies' room." She went to move past Lucas, but the photographer chose that moment to appear.

"Hello," the overly friendly guy said, smiling and motioning for Lucas and Emily to pose. "Get together for a photo for our website."

Emily clenched her teeth and moved one step closer to Lucas.

The photographer frowned. "Smile. Look happy. You just brought in more money than any of the others."

There was that. Raising money for a good cause did make her happy. She sighed and focused on the help that would be provided to her patients' families because of Lucas's generosity.

Surprisingly, he looked a little hesitant. Lucas off guard.

Now, that was something new. Still, he put his arm at her waist and smiled for the camera.

Trying to ignore the fact that he was touching her, Emily curved her lips upward.

The photographer's flash went off a couple of times.

"Thanks." The photographer turned to Meghan and her winner, who'd joined them. "Your turn, Pretty Lady."

Meghan curled up next to the stockbroker she'd gone on a couple of dates with.

Which moved everyone's attention off Emily and Lucas.

Her throat suddenly tight, she glared at him. "Congratulations. You're such a winner."

CHAPTER TWO

THAT HADN'T GONE anywhere near the way Lucas had mentally rehearsed his first encounter with Emily outside the hospital.

Then again, what had he expected? He should thank his lucky stars that she hadn't made a scene.

The look she'd given him said she'd like to have smacked him. Or worse.

"I think you two got off on the wrong foot." Meghan rejoined him after the photographer had snapped a few shots of her and her date winner. The brunette frowned after Emily. "I don't understand how that's even possible. Emily gets along with everyone. She's the sweetest, kindest person I know."

They hadn't gotten off on the wrong foot, but they'd ended that way.

He closed his eyes and inhaled a deep breath, catching the faintest whiff of Emily's perfume still on the air. She'd always worn the light vanilla scent. He could never smell anything even close to the fragrance without being haunted by memories of the past.

Lately, most everything had his mind filling with Emily.

Ever since he'd been offered the position at Children's, he'd been confronted with memory after memory. Probably because he'd known taking the job meant coming face-to-face with his biggest regret.

To head the department, oversee research in traumatic brain injury, play an active role in the decisions being made that would impact how things were done on the pediatric neurology unit—Children's had offered him all that and more. The position was his dream come true.

He'd still hesitated.

Because of the woman walking away from him.

Just as she'd walked away five years ago.

Not that he hadn't deserved her leaving. He had. He just hadn't thought she'd walk away from their marriage, no matter how bad things got.

He'd been wrong.

But Emily had been right to leave. She'd been so unhappy, crying more often than not. Marriage to him had rapidly done that to her. He'd thought she was depressed, needing counseling, but when he'd suggested as much, she'd burst into tears. That night had been the night she'd packed her things.

His wife leaving him had hurt like hell, but he had gotten over it, had moved on and made a good life for himself.

But seeing Emily again had been tough. More so than he'd been prepared for. He wasn't sure quite what he'd expected of her, but the cold shoulder he got every time he walked onto the unit just had to go.

No, he didn't expect her to do cartwheels that he'd joined the hospital where she worked, but he was a good pediatric neurosurgeon and was now medical director of her unit. What had happened between them was a long time ago, water under the bridge, they'd both moved on. He was happy. She was happy. There was no need for awkwardness between them.

That was why he'd bid on her date.

Mostly.

As Emily's bid had proceeded, he'd grown more and more annoyed with the man she'd arrived with.

The man she'd been comparing him unfavorably to.

The man who'd acted as if bidding on Emily was an inconvenience.

Emily was too good for the guy.

He supposed it could be argued that she'd been too good for Lucas, too. She probably had been.

Besides, the guy must make her happy, since she'd defended him to her friend. Something Lucas had failed miserably at.

Regardless, the man's reticence to bid had irked. As he'd watched her on stage, the insecurities that only someone who knew her as well as he had would recognize flittering across her lovely face had brought out something protective.

So much so that he'd placed a bid. Then another, then, when her foolish date had hem-hawed on his last bid, Lucas had more than doubled the amount.

Probably not his brightest move.

But the guy needed to be hit over the head with the news that a date with Emily was worth every penny.

The realization hit Lucas hard.

He watched her retreating backside head out of the ballroom, appreciated the curvy lines of her body beneath the sleek lines of her formfitting emerald dress. Once upon a time, he'd slept with her backside snuggled into the curve of his body, spooned so close every breath he'd taken had been filled with her. Now he didn't have the right to even stroke his finger over the silky smooth skin of her cheek.

Lucas swallowed. Where had that thought come from?

He hadn't bid on Emily because he wanted a date with her. He didn't. He only wanted a chance to clear the air between them.

Maybe he'd been led to Children's so he could set the past right, could mend his relationship with Emily to where they could be friends, or at least amicable coworkers.

When Emily joined Richard at their table, his expression was sour and she cringed on the inside.

"Who was that man?"

She supposed she should have been prepared for his question, but it still caught her off guard. She'd run back to Richard to escape Lucas, not talk about him.

She bent, kissed her date's cheek. "No one, dear."

She wasn't lying. Lucas was no one. No one of any importance. Not anymore. Not ever again.

"He's interested in you." Richard didn't sound pleased. No wonder. Lucas had just upstaged him and their colleagues would be curious.

She sat in her chair and scooted closer to him. "He's new at the hospital and just drawing attention to himself."

Richard didn't look convinced. What he looked was annoyed. "By paying that crazy amount for you? Why would he do that?"

The money meant nothing to Lucas. He had paid too much. But did Richard really have to sound as if he found the idea that a date with her could possibly be worth so much as unfathomable? Shouldn't he find time with her priceless?

"It was for charity," she reminded him, irritated by his insensitivity to how she might take his question. "You said so yourself."

His expression pinched, Richard straightened the napkin in his lap. "I saw him talking to you a few minutes ago. Should I be worried?"

She laughed. "No. His type appalls me. Besides, all the bachelorettes took photos with the winning bidders. What did you want me to do? Refuse?"

Not that she wouldn't have liked to have done just that.

Richard's eyes narrowed beneath his wire-framed glasses. "You labeled his type in those few short minutes?"

"I've encountered him before." Ha. Wasn't that the understatement of the century? "He's a pediatric neurosurgeon in the department where I work. Actually, he's the new head of the department. He started about a month ago."

Twenty-two days.

Not that she was counting.

Emily shot a nervous glance toward where Lucas still stood with Meghan. They were both looking her way. Seeing her looking at them, Lucas lifted his glass in salute.

The jerk.

Emily rolled her eyes, grabbed Richard's hand and moved her chair to where her back was completely to Lucas. She didn't want him anywhere near her line of vision. She just wanted to forget he was even there.

Which later proved impossible even after Richard had quit talking about Lucas. He'd finally relaxed, quit suggesting she'd encouraged Lucas, and they were enjoying a slow dance. The emcee's boisterous voice cut in.

"Folks, it's time for our bachelors and bachelorettes to share a dance with their lucky high bidders." Applause went through the ballroom, but Emily didn't clap. Instead, she clung to Richard.

"Did you know they were going to do that?" He sounded aggravated, as if she'd somehow arranged the dance.

"No." She shook her head, wondering if she could make a mad dash toward the open double doors leading into the hallway. She could hide, freshen up in the ladies' room. "Maybe he won't come over here."

No such luck. Not that she had much hope of Lucas staying away. His new life mission was to irritate her as much as possible.

"Hello, Emily. I'm here to claim my dance." His gaze shifted to Richard's. "If that's okay with your date?"

She cringed. She did not want to dance with Lucas. Nor did she want to further upset Richard.

Hello. He'd been the one to let Lucas have the high bid. Couldn't he have spared more cash to have ensured she didn't spend time with any other man? Then again, Lucas might have just kept bidding higher and higher. Money meant nothing to him, except during the time when they'd been married and he'd been forced to live within their means rather than his parents'.

Maybe she was being overly sensitive of Richard. Maybe. Being around Lucas had her on edge, making her more critical than she should be.

She liked Richard. He was calm, soothing. He never rocked the boat, never made her question herself. Usually. Why was she letting Lucas disrupt her nice, content life? Letting him make her question a man she sincerely liked and had previously never fought with?

Her annoyance with her date was Lucas's fault, not Richard's. She needed to remember that.

Her gaze met Richard's. *Just say no*, she mentally pleaded. *Tell him to get lost. That I belong to you. That you refuse to share me. That I'm the love of your life and you'll never let another man take me into his arms.*

Richard didn't do any of those things. He just gave an

exasperated sigh, stepped back and practically handed her to Lucas on a silver platter.

"Go ahead. All the others are," he said by way of justification.

So much for Richard going all macho and staking his claim. Not that she was the type to want the drama, but he could have at least issued some type of "she's mine, hands off" warning.

"He's a real winner, Em," Lucas teased as they stepped out onto the dance floor. "I see why you find him so attractive."

"Be quiet," she ordered, placing her arms around his neck. The feel of his body next to hers, the smell of him, the utter maleness of Lucas Cain, the memories of the past that hit her full force, almost had her forgetting about not making a scene and dashing out of the ballroom.

But she couldn't run away from him forever. She might as well find out what it was he wanted from her so he'd leave her alone. She didn't fool herself that he didn't want something.

Once upon a time, she had been what he wanted. That time hadn't lasted, had been more a tiny vapor that disappeared almost as quickly as it had appeared.

What was it these days that filled his dreams? That he wanted enough to come seek her out after all this time?

Had she accidentally taken a favorite shirt five years ago or something that he'd decided he just had to have back?

Too bad, so sad. Any clothes of his she'd accidentally taken had been donated to a local homeless shelter long ago.

Except for one shirt.

Memories assailed her.

Memories of going through a duffel bag she hadn't used in a long time and finding a T-shirt he'd bought at a concert they'd attended at Madison Square Garden. They'd been happy, dating, in love, laughing continuously, totally enamored with each other, believing nothing could ever come between them.

How wrong they'd been.

She'd shredded the T-shirt into pieces, hoping she'd feel better after doing so, but had only felt just as tattered as the bits of material.

"I'd have never let another man win your bid back when we were dating."

"No, probably not," she agreed, still fighting the urge to flee his arms. "But you'd have gift wrapped and hand delivered me after we were married."

Touching him was torture. Like being burned alive. Like having a vise on her heart and it squeezing until every last drop bled forth.

"That's not true." His body stiff, his feet stopped moving for a few beats before resuming their dance. He looked torn, but then, rather than argue his point, he just sighed. "Let's not talk about the past anymore, Emily. Not right now. Let's just enjoy the song."

His capitulation surprised Emily. Before, he'd never have given in just to keep the peace. That had been her job. But he was right. They shouldn't talk about the past. The past was just that. The past. Done and gone forever. Best thing they could do was forget the past. It was what she'd been striving toward for five years.

She couldn't have said what song was playing prior to his calling her attention to it. A slow tune about second chances and new love. Ha. Emily never planned to fall in love again. Sure, she wanted someone to love her and to love, but she never planned to experience the craziness she'd had with Lucas.

That had been overwhelming, intense, too much for a heart to take when things fell apart.

She wasn't so naive as to think relationships lasted forever. Not anymore. Just look at most of the people she knew. Separated. Divorced. Achingly single.

Give her good old dependable Richard.

Sure, he didn't light any fires or even smell half as good as Lucas, but he wasn't a stick of dynamite burning at both ends, either.

"You smell nice, Emily."

Not something she expected to hear Lucas say. She misstepped and probably scuffed the black Italian leather dress shoes he wore. She didn't care. If she stomped his toes a dozen times, he deserved each and every smash.

"I don't know what you expect me to say." She didn't look up at him, just kept her eyes focused above his shoulders.

Her gaze collided with Richard's unhappy one.

Great. Trouble in paradise. Well, not paradise, but… trouble in Just Okay Land?

She inhaled sharply, then frowned at how her senses were overcome by Lucas. How could she have forgotten how good he smelled? Not that he wore cologne. At least, he hadn't in the past. Did he now? Maybe the light spicy scent was his aftershave? Or maybe his bodywash? Or maybe some expensive and pheromone-filled fragrance that guaranteed to drive women wild?

Not that he was driving her wild. He wasn't. Crazy did not equate to wild. Just…well, he smelled nice, too. And felt strong and solid next to her. Yes, her heart was beating wildly, but that really was just crazy.

"Honestly, I don't expect you to say anything. Nor did I mean to say it. The words just slipped out, but they are true.

You do smell good. You always did." His breath brushed against her temple with soft, moist heat that prickled her skin with goose bumps. Why was he holding her so close? Why was she letting him?

She took a step back to put distance between their bodies. She hated that she reacted to him in any way.

If only every nerve cell in her body had quickly bored with Lucas.

"I didn't ask you for the walk down memory lane." The last thing she wanted was more memories. "You're the one who has instigated all this. You have no one to blame but yourself."

"That's true." His palm rested at the curve low on her back and pulled her close to him as they moved gently to the music. "I am the one who instigated our dance."

Emily's eyes narrowed. Had he bribed the emcee to announce the date-winner dance? Looking at him, she knew he had requested the dance.

"Why?" Did she even want to know? Probably not, but at least if she knew what he was up to, she could prepare a defense. She needed a defense.

"I could beat around the bush, but that's never been my style."

No, he'd always been blunt about whatever was on his mind. Like when he'd told her to move out of their apartment, for instance.

"This job at Children's is important to me."

His job. Of course this was about his job.

"I want everything to go as smoothly as possible, for nothing to stand in the way of my accomplishing the greatest good for our patients."

"You think I'd stand in the way of our patients getting good care because of you? How dare you imply that I'd ever not put my patients' needs before our petty past." She

quit dancing. Probably because her feet felt heavy as con-
crete blocks. Her jaw dropped somewhere near the base-
ment floor of the high-rise building. She stared up at him,
wishing she could erase the past month, erase his having
reentered her life. She'd been fine without him. She'd been
good, healthy, content in her Just Okay Land relationship.

Lucas's gaze didn't waver from hers. "I don't think
you'd intentionally do anything that would put our patients at risk."

"You think I might do something unintentionally?" she
asked incredulously.

"No. What I think is that how you feel about me influ-
ences how you respond in front of our patients and coworkers. That could be problematic. That's why I bought
your date, so we could talk and forge some type of friendship between us."

"You're crazy." He was crazy. Crazy to be at Children's.
Crazy to be at the fund-raiser. Crazy to have bid on her
auction. Crazy to be on the dance floor with her in his
arms. Divorced people didn't do this. She was sure of it.
"You and I will never be friends."

"We at least need to forge some type of coexistence.
There's too much tension and you run every time I come
near."

"Perhaps you failed to get the memo, but I don't like
you. Of course I leave when you're near."

"You think others haven't picked up on the tension between us?"

Why would anyone have paid attention to how she reacted to the new doctor? Before tonight. Now, after he'd
bid such a stupid high amount, she suspected lots of people would be watching them to see if any sparks developed on their "date."

"I don't want you here," she snapped, wondering if

anyone would notice if she stomped her high heel into his toes. His absurdity deserved a little pain. A lot of pain.

"I understand that," he clarified. "Knowing you were at Children's was my only hesitation. A mistake from five years ago shouldn't stand in the way of my dream job. I want to make peace with you."

She laughed. A louder than it should have been, close to hysteria laugh. "Let me get this straight. You bought my date because you want to make peace with me because of your dream job?"

His jaw worked back and forth. "Something like that."

Her hands went to her hips. "What if I already had my dream job and you pursuing your dream job is ruining mine? Why should I have to give up my dream job so you can pursue yours?"

"It's not as if I expect you to give up your job, Emily. Listen to what I am saying. I want us to coexist, maybe become friends." As if to prove his point, he pulled her back to him and began to sway to the music. She let him for the sole reason that standing in the middle of the dance floor with her hands on her hips squaring up to the man who'd just bought her date was just asking for people to stare. Anyone paying the slightest attention to her and Lucas was the last thing she wanted. Already, Richard couldn't take his eyes off them.

Obviously, Lucas didn't see a thing wrong with what he was saying. Or doing. That he was turning her world topsy-turvy. He thought it was okay to slow dance with his ex-wife and suggest they become friends. *The nerve.*

She closed her eyes, prayed she'd wake up and find the past month had just been a bad dream. "I cannot believe this."

"Why is it unbelievable that I want us to be friends?"

"We can never be friends," she hissed.

"Why not?"

"We were never friends to begin with."

"We were."

She shook her head. "You were never my friend."

"I'm sorry to hear that, because once upon a time you were my best friend."

His words gutted her and every cell in her body weighed down with lead, making movement almost impossible.

"Why couldn't you have just stayed in the past?"

"Because Children's offered me the position of medical director of the traumatic brain injury unit."

"I was here first." Even to her own ears her words sounded whiny and childish.

"I'm sorry that my being at Children's is problematic for you."

Two apologies in less than a minute. Wow.

"I'm not trying to force something on you, Emily. I just want the opportunity to make peace to where there isn't tension on the unit."

"I'm professional enough that I can hide my tension."

He sighed. "Then do it for me, please, because apparently I'm not."

"I owe you nothing," she stated.

"Then do it for our patients. I'm good at what I do. This position gives me the opportunity to do more. Let me."

As if she could stop him.

No hospital would give up a talented pediatric neurosurgeon just because a nurse, no matter how good she was, used to be married to him.

"Please."

Her gaze lifted to his and his sincerity surprised her. He didn't need her approval. They both knew it. So why did it matter? Why was he saying please? She didn't want to think he'd changed. She needed to keep him categorized in the "bad guy" box.

"None of this matters. What I think, what I want, doesn't matter," she reminded him. "You want this position, it's already yours. Just because I was here, loving my job and my life without you in it, doesn't matter to you. Nothing does except you getting what you want."

"This isn't just about me getting what I want. It's about doing the right thing, about what's best for all involved."

"Me coexisting with you is what's best for all involved?"

"You know it is."

She knew no such thing. Just being in his arms was driving her crazy, the feel of him, the smell of him, the sound of his voice. Okay, so her mind and body had gone a little mushy, but that was nostalgia, right? He'd been her first lover, her husband, her fantasy. Once upon a time, he'd been the center of her world and she'd have done anything to make him happy.

Her body had had a momentary lapse in memory, had responded to his spicy male scent, the feel of him against her, and, yes, she'd melted a little. A lot. But that was just old chemistry rising to the surface.

All she felt for him now was loathing.

Liar.

She squeezed her eyes shut and took another deep breath before meeting his gaze again with steely resolve. "This is ridiculous. You are ridiculous."

"Your heart is racing against mine, Emily."

He was right. Her heart was racing and was next to his, but what that had to do with anything, she wasn't sure. When had they moved so close that her body fully pressed against his as they swayed to the sultry beat? But she wasn't alone in being affected by the other one's presence. His heart was racing, too.

"Hearts race for a lot of reasons. Fear being one of them." Was that why his raced? She couldn't imagine Lucas ever being afraid of anything.

"Fear?" He looked taken aback. "I never gave you a reason to be afraid of me. Never."

He meant he'd never hit her or physically abused her in any way. He hadn't. The ways Lucas had hurt hadn't left visible scars, just jagged ones on the inside.

"Not any reason that could be physically seen." Emotionally, he'd beaten her to a pulp. She needed to remember that, to focus on how getting involved with him had devastated her whole world. She couldn't coexist with him. Not without severe consequences.

"You weren't the only one hurt by our marriage falling apart."

His words stung. He'd been hurt, too? Somehow she couldn't bring herself to believe him. He'd lost interest in her, in their marriage, long before the night he'd told her to leave.

How could he have hurt by losing something he'd no longer wanted? By losing something he'd not even known about because he hadn't wanted to know?

Hadn't wanted, period. Had accused her of depression when in reality she'd been… No. She wasn't going there. She wasn't.

She glanced around the dance floor. No one was paying much attention to them. No one except Meghan, who gave her a thumbs-up when their gazes met.

Oh, Meghan, if you only knew.

She resumed scanning the crowd. Her gaze connected to Richard's again. She was going to have to do some explaining when she returned to the table.

Resentment built up in her and threatened to spill free.

"If you hurt, too, then why are you here opening up

old wounds, Lucas? I've healed, am happy and could do without the twisted walk down memory lane."

She felt more than heard him swallow.

"I told you why I'm here."

"You and I will never be friends, Lucas. Leave me alone."

With that she stepped out of his arms and made her way back to where Richard waited. Richard, who clearly had a hundred questions waiting to spring from his mouth.

She didn't want to explain why she was upset about a shared dance with a man she worked with.

She bypassed the table and headed to the little girls' room.

Oh, yeah, she was happy.

CHAPTER THREE

"HI, CASSIE. I'M DR. CAIN," Lucas introduced himself to the little girl he'd be doing surgery on soon if all went as expected. He'd spent a lot of time reviewing her medical records. She'd been diagnosed with a noncancerous brain tumor that had been increasing in size despite treatments to shrink the mass.

His true love within his field was traumatic brain injury, but he dealt with a lot of brain tumors and other brain maladies, too.

"Hi," the six-year-old answered, staring at him with big brown eyes that filled with uncertainty and a lack of trust.

No doubt over the past few months she'd been poked and prodded, tested and treated repeatedly to where she felt on constant guard long before his being asked to consult on her case by Dr. Edwards.

"What're you doing there?" He gestured to the puzzle she worked on.

She resumed scanning the puzzle pieces. "My mom says I need to do more puzzles. That it will keep my brain sharp."

"Your mom is a smart lady." He sat down at the table next to her. "Can I help?"

She shrugged. "If you want to. I'm not sure all the pieces

are here. It's just a puzzle I found here, but it wasn't put together when I started."

Here being in the hospital playroom. A large room equipped with kid-sized tables, video game stations, toy centers and table activity centers.

He sat at the table, seeming to search for a place to fit the puzzle piece he'd picked up. In reality, he studied Cassie, watching her movements, her facial expressions, how she moved her hands, her body. How she grimaced repeatedly when she tried to focus on what she was doing, how she squinted her eyes and had a slight tremor to her movements.

"Does your head hurt, Cassie?" The answer seemed obvious, but sometimes asking a child an obvious question, even one he already knew the answer to, could help break the ice. He wanted Cassie to trust him.

"Yes, but sometimes not too bad."

Her headaches were the first symptom that had clued her parents in to the fact that something wasn't right with their little girl. Never had they imagined they'd be told she had a brain tumor the size of a golf ball. Fortunately, Cassie's tumor wasn't cancerous, but, due to the size and the fact it was growing, she'd begun to have more and more problems. Visual changes, hearing changes, speech changes, motor-skill changes. She'd started falling for no reason other than poor balance. Because the mass was taking over vital brain tissue and causing increased pressure in her head.

Although it would be tricky due to where it was located within the brain and the amount of tissue it encompassed, Cassie needed surgical excision of the mass.

Lucas was the doctor who was going to perform the surgery.

"Are you going to take my blood?"

At the child's suspicious question, he shook his head. "No, I'm not here to take your blood, Cassie."

"I don't kick and scream," she told him, not looking up from her puzzle. "I used to, but I don't anymore."

"That's good to know, but I'm not going to take blood."

She cast him a dubious glance. "What are you going to do?"

"Right now? Help you put this puzzle together and talk about your headaches."

She shrugged. "Sometimes it feels like my head wants to blow up."

No doubt.

"I'm a pediatric neurosurgeon. My job is to make your head stop hurting."

The child looked up and squinted at him. "Can you do that?"

He nodded. "I've consulted with the neurologist you've been seeing, looked over your imaging tests. It's not going to be easy, but, yes, I believe I can make your headaches go away."

The child glanced toward her mother, who was sitting in a rocking chair watching their interaction. Looking tearful and tired, the woman nodded.

"I'd like my headaches to go away," the girl said.

"Me, too." He told the truth. Unfortunately, a lot of his cases weren't things he could correct or effectively treat. Once he removed the tumor, Cassie should get great relief.

Of course, nothing about brain surgery was ever that easy.

With removal of her tumor came a lot of risk. A lot of worry about what type of residual effects she'd have from his having removed a portion of her brain. Her tumor wasn't small and hadn't responded to the chemotherapy meant to shrink it. There was a chance Cassie would be permanently brain damaged after the surgery, that she wouldn't be able to do the things she currently did.

There was an even bigger chance that, at the rate her tumor was growing, the mass would take over her good tissue and cause more and more damage and eventually death.

Those were things he'd discussed with her parents in private already. They'd wanted to schedule surgery as soon as possible. He'd wanted to meet Cassie, to interact with her and to do a consult with a trusted pediatric neurosurgeon colleague to be sure he agreed with how Lucas intended to proceed with Cassie's care and predicted outcome.

He popped a puzzle piece into place. "Let's see if we can get this thing figured out."

She nodded and handed him another puzzle piece.

Emily stopped short when she entered the hospital playroom and saw Lucas sitting in one of the small chairs at a table where Cassie Bellows worked on a puzzle.

Emily took all her patients to heart. Cassie was no exception. Emily had instantly felt a connection to the little girl and her parents.

Especially Cassie's mother. Maybe because the woman was the same age as Emily. Maybe because of the gentle spirit she sensed within Cassie.

She'd known Lucas had been consulted on the case, knew that he'd likely do surgery on the child.

What she hadn't known or expected was to walk into the playroom and see a highly skilled pediatric neurosurgeon sitting at a child's table helping his patient put a puzzle together.

She'd worked in this department for years and that was one sight that had never before greeted her. If someone had told her she would see that, never would she have believed that neurosurgeon would be Lucas.

Lucas might have gone into pediatrics, but he'd given her the distinct impression during their marriage that he didn't like kids. Too bad he hadn't let her know that before…before… She sank her teeth into her lower lip.

He laughed at something the child said, then popped a puzzle piece into place, earning a "Good job" from Cassie. The girl studied the connected pieces and quickly found another fit.

Lucas high-fived her, compensating when the little girl's movements were off from a sure smack of their hands.

Old dreams rattled inside Emily's chest and her eyes watered. A metallic tang warned she'd mutilated her lower lip.

Darn him. She didn't want to see him being nice. How was she supposed to keep him behind those "bad guy" walls she'd spent years erecting if he went around acting like a good guy?

It was an act. Had to be. He didn't even like or want kids. Not that he'd ever said he didn't like kids, but he'd reacted so poorly when she'd told him she wanted to have a baby. He had said point-blank he didn't want children and for her to stop talking about it. If only she could have. By that point, he had taken anything she said to him the wrong way, and she'd quit talking to him. Talking had led to crying and crying to arguing and arguing had led to more and more distance between them.

Currently, distance between them was what she desperately needed.

Having him at Children's was pure torture. Every time she saw him, she was taken to the past. She just wanted to forget the past. All of it.

Especially the end and the heart-wrenching events that had followed the night she'd left Lucas.

If only she could forget.

Why was he putting a puzzle together with Cassie? He didn't have to interact with the child. All he had to do was examine her, talk to her parents, get surgical releases signed and then do brain surgery. No. Big. Deal.

No interaction required.

He needed to stick with the program of how he was supposed to behave.

Instead, he played with the little girl while her mother watched them as if he were a superhero. If Lucas cured Cassie with minimal negative effects of removing the tumor, she supposed Mrs. Bellows would find her views justified.

Emily knew better. He wasn't a superhero, he was…

She stopped.

He was an ex-husband who was apparently a phenomenal pediatric neurosurgeon, and perhaps even a nice guy to his patients if the vision before her could be believed.

Which she still didn't quite buy.

But Lucas was right about one thing.

If she was going to stay at Children's, she had to let go of the personal. She couldn't let patients like Cassie and her parents pick up on her animosity toward Lucas.

What if she caused them to doubt him? What if her feelings toward him somehow influenced a patient in a negative way and delayed or prevented needed care?

She'd told him she was a professional. She was. But even professionals could have broken hearts blinding them from time to time.

She couldn't allow her personal biases about Lucas to bleed over to her patient care in any way. Not and remain proud of the type of nurse she was.

She'd not seen him since Saturday night at the fundraiser. She'd managed to slip back into the ballroom and convince Richard she'd developed a headache and would like to go home. He'd looked relieved.

The headache had served as reason to send him home, as well. That hadn't left him looking relieved. Quite the opposite.

He'd acted as if he suddenly wanted to stake his claim.

Perhaps she should have let him stay.

She cared about him, had been thinking they'd have a nice life together. He never made her cry.

But that night she hadn't even been able to tolerate the idea of Richard kissing her. Nor had she been able to stomach the idea of him kissing her since.

She wasn't sure she'd ever want him to again, because just-okay-ever-after might not be good enough, after all.

Darn Lucas and the turmoil he'd caused. Saturday night and last night she'd dreamed about him, dreamed about the past. Not the tears or fights, but about the one part of their relationship that had been magical.

Sex.

She'd had no previous experience and sex had never been as mind-blowing since. How good things had been between them could only be credited to his skills. He'd made her feel amazing, loved, completely over the moon and satiated.

One touch of his hand had made her squirm with desire. One kiss from his lips had made her need him with a ferocity that had never failed to surprise her. One time with him and she'd been hooked like an addict with a potent new fix.

He'd been her drug.

Only, not long after their marriage, he'd bored of sex with her. Had he actually cheated on her?

She didn't think so.

Despite their flawed marriage, she didn't think he'd

taken their vows that lightly. He'd told her to leave before he'd gone that far. Maybe she was being naive, but she truly didn't think he had.

In the days since their divorce, she didn't fool herself that he'd been abstinent. He'd enjoyed sex too much for that.

Darn him that just seeing him sitting and playing with a child had somehow morphed into thinking about sex. She wouldn't be having sex with Lucas. Not ever again.

Which was a shame in some ways, because he'd certainly made her feel things physically she'd not felt since. Richard really wasn't the guy for her. She needed to look for someone else, someone who wanted the same things out of life that she did, but was also good at sex.

Did such a mythical creature exist? So far her experience had been one or the other, but never the twain had met. She'd thought so with Lucas, but everything had fallen apart and left her devastated. So much for young love.

"You want to help with our puzzle?"

Emily blinked. Darn. He'd caught her staring at him and no wonder with how long she'd stood watching him, reminiscing about the past. Oh, yeah, Lucas being at Children's was affecting her professionalism, and she hated it.

"Sorry." Sorry she'd gotten caught. Sorry her cheeks were on fire. Sorry her mind had wandered. Sorry she couldn't be immune to him. Sorry her body flushed when he was looking at her as if he somehow knew what she'd been thinking. "I need to check on Cassie. She's due a vitals check."

The child looked at her suspiciously. "Are you going to take my blood?"

Focusing on her patient and doing her best to ignore the man watching her, Emily shook her head, hating that this was always the first question Cassie asked. Poor kid. "No.

I'm going to take your temperature, your blood pressure, your heart rate, your oxygen saturation. Those kinds of things. But no needles."

Cassie digested her answer, then lifted her little chin bravely. "I don't cry anymore when my blood is drawn."

"That's a very big girl," Emily praised, wanting to wrap her arms around the child. "But it's okay to cry sometimes."

Cassie blinked. "Do you ever cry?"

She'd cried an ocean's worth of tears over the man sitting across the table from Cassie. Until Saturday night after she'd returned home from the TBI fund-raiser, she'd not cried in a long time.

She'd watered up on the anniversary of the day she'd left, but even then she'd managed to choke back the tears and keep herself distracted from the grief she knew she'd carry to the grave.

Unfortunately, a few days later, she'd broken down and cried bucketfuls. That had been the last day she'd cried. Maybe she'd always cry on that particular date. Oh, how much she'd lost.

"I used to cry a lot," she answered honestly. Lucas had hated her tears, had begged her not to cry, but usually that had left her only more tearful. "But I rarely cry these days."

Just when her ex-husband showed up and rocked her world by saying he wanted to be her friend. Right.

Lucas's gaze was intense, so much so it bore into her. She ignored him. Let him think what he wanted. She'd wondered if hormones had played into her constant tears, but perhaps Lucas had been the real cause.

"These days, what makes you cry, Emily?" Lucas asked, his fingers toying with the puzzle piece he held. Did he know she'd cried Saturday night? Did he want her to admit how much he'd affected her? Truly, he triggered strong emotions whether they were of happiness or sadness.

"Sad movies," she answered flippantly. No way was she getting into a discussion about what brought on her tears.

"Me, too," Cassie piped up and began to talk about a movie where a dog had died and she'd cried.

While Lucas watched, Emily removed the thermometer from the supply tray she carried. She took the girl's temp across her forehead, took her blood pressure, clipped the pulse oximeter over the child's finger and completed her vitals check.

Then she took her stethoscope and listened to the girl's heart and lung sounds and jotted them down on a notepad she kept in her pocket. She'd record them into the computer electronic medical record when she returned to the nurses' station.

"Is there anything you need, Cassie?" she asked.

Wincing a little, the little girl shook her head. "Just to finish this puzzle."

Emily glanced down at the three-fourths completed puzzle. "Looks like you're making good headway."

"Dr. Cain is helping."

"I'm not much help," Lucas quickly inserted. "Cassie is the puzzle master. I'm just riding on her coattails."

Emily's throat tightened. She didn't attempt to speak. Why bother? There was nothing to say even if he was kind to a child.

She fought to keep from frowning. *Professionalism*, she reminded herself. *Professionalism*.

Ugh. She had to get him out of her head.

Which had been a lot easier when he'd been out of her sight. Now that he was working at Children's, she was going to have to learn a new strategy to keep Lucas from ruining her hard-earned peace.

Work. She'd focus on work.

She turned to Cassie's mother, smiled. "Anything I can get for you, Mrs. Bellows?"

The woman shook her head and thanked Emily anyway.

Without a word to Lucas, she headed out of the room. Lucas joined her in the hallway seconds later.

"I'm sorry."

That made three apologies. Seemed Lucas's vocabulary had definitely expanded over the past five years.

"For?" she asked, not sure what it was that had him saying a word he used to be unable, or unwilling, to say.

"Saturday night."

Her heart raced within her chest, using her lungs for punching bags and leaving her breathy. "There were so many things you should be sorry for about Saturday night. Enlighten me as to which you refer specifically."

"All of it."

She ordered her hands not to shake and her feet not to trip over each other. "All of it?"

"Well, not the buying your date part," he amended, flashing a good imitation of a repentant smile. "I'd like to take you to dinner, Emily."

He wanted to take her to dinner. Flashbacks of the past hit again. He'd pursued her hot and heavy, had asked her out repeatedly until she'd said yes. Not that she'd not wanted to say yes to the handsome doctor, but she'd planned not to fall into the trap of dating the doctors she worked with. Ha. That hadn't turned out so well.

"Perhaps you misunderstood how the date works," she said, just because he waited for a response. "Part of what you won is that I am supposed to provide you with a meal."

"I'd rather provide you with a meal, but beggars can't be choosers. Would tomorrow night work?"

Beggars couldn't be choosers? What did he mean by

that? Whether or not she agreed to coexist with him really didn't matter a hill of beans in his achieving his career goals. He had to know that. She frowned. "Maybe we should just make the 'date' a lunch one."

He shook his head. "I work through lunch most days and just grab a few bites of something when I can."

So did she, most days.

"Okay, fine. Tomorrow night," she agreed for the sole reason that the sooner she had her "date" with him, the sooner she had that behind her and wouldn't have it hanging over her head like an executioner's ax.

"Really?"

Why did he look so surprised? Then again, he didn't know she'd gone to the TBI fund-raiser chairman and requested to purchase her date and void her obligation to Lucas. The woman had denied her request with a laugh that said she thought Emily was silly for even asking.

"Let's get this over with."

His smile made his eyes twinkle. "What time can I pick you up?"

She did not want to be seen with him in public, but she supposed most of her friends already knew he'd bought her date. Several of them had asked how it felt to be bought by the hospital's hot new doctor. Ugh.

"I'll meet you at Stluka's." She told him the address of the bar and grill that was not too far from her apartment.

"Sounds great." He smiled and Emily's brain turned to mush. Pure mush. Lord, help her. She didn't want his smile affecting her, didn't want him to smile and her nerve endings to electrify with old memories.

That was all that was causing the zings through her. Old memories and not that he was knocking down bits and pieces of the protective wall she'd erected between them.

Maybe she was being too hard on herself. Lucas was

a beautiful man with gorgeous eyes and a quick smile. Plus, she knew what those long fingers, that lush mouth, his hard body, were capable of. She knew.

Darn. She needed Lucas repellent. Or Lucas resistant spray. Or something. Anything to give her the power not to respond to his utter maleness.

She didn't want to respond to him.

He represented the worst time of her life.

He represented the best time of her life, a little voice reminded. Only, that time of joy had been short-lived and she'd spent years recovering from the aftermath.

CHAPTER FOUR

EMILY ARRIVED AT Stluka's right on the dot of seven. Although she'd been ready and nervously pacing across her tiny apartment for the past hour, she'd refused to arrive early. She would not have Lucas thinking she'd been eager to spend time with him.

She wasn't.

She just wanted this over. Which didn't really explain why she had a nervous jittery feel in her stomach. Maybe that was normal when dining with one's ex-husband.

The perky blonde hostess greeted her with a huge smile and welcomed her to Stluka's. "Are you meeting someone or just want to hang at the bar?"

At that moment, a man stood from a bar stool, turned, met her gaze.

"I'm meeting someone. He's already here."

The girl followed Emily's gaze and gave an impressed look. "Lucky you."

Lucas joined her, but Emily wasn't sure if he overheard the girl's comment. If so, he didn't acknowledge her admiration.

"We're ready for our table," he told the hostess.

Smiling, she grabbed a couple of menus and motioned for them to follow.

The place was packed, just as it usually was, so the

fact they were immediately being shown to a table surprised Emily. Then again, there was no telling what Lucas had tipped the girl to have a table ready for them. Money talked.

"What are you thinking?" he asked as they walked toward a semiprivate booth.

"Nothing."

"Your expression went sour. Surely I haven't already done something to ruin your evening. I'd hoped you'd enjoy tonight."

"I'm not here to enjoy my evening, Lucas. I'm here to fulfill an obligation."

"And determined not to enjoy one moment of having to endure my company?"

"Something like that," she admitted, which garnered a low laugh from him.

He let her slide into the booth, then joined her. The hostess handed them the menus.

"Your waitress will be over in just a few minutes."

Lucas scanned the menu. "It all looks good. What's your favorite?"

She glanced briefly at her own menu. She did not want to make small talk, but the night would pass quicker if she at least attempted to interact.

"I like their cedar-plank salmon."

"Sounds good. That what you're getting?"

She nodded. "The apple-stuffed duck is really good, too."

"I'll order that, then, and share."

"I don't need you to share your food with me. I'll have my own."

"Maybe I was hoping to try the salmon and the duck so I'd know which I preferred for next time."

Next time. Would he be on a date? Have some young

woman with him who wasn't so prickly, wasn't so five years ago.

"Suit yourself."

Their waitress came, took their order, then disappeared.

"Tell me, Emily, how did you end up in that bachelor/bachelorette auction? Even though it was for a great cause, I will admit, I was surprised to see your name."

She bristled. "Why? Think no one would bid on me?"

"I bid on you."

"It would have been better if you hadn't."

"Would you have agreed to dinner with me if not for the auction?"

"No."

"Then it was best that I bid. Besides, your guy was ticking me off that he barely upped the bid each time someone bid."

Yeah, there was that. Speaking of ticked off, Richard had not been happy that she'd canceled their plans that evening so that she could go out with Lucas. Actually, he'd been downright surly.

"That's why you jumped the bid out of his ballpark? Because he was barely upping the amount?" She'd just been happy that Richard had kept bidding against the strangers who'd been bidding prior to Lucas putting an end to all other interest.

"You deserve someone who sees your worth, Emily."

"Yes, I do, which doesn't explain why *you* bid on me." She immediately wished she could retract her words. She didn't want to argue with Lucas. She wanted to make it through dinner and go home unscathed from spending time in his company.

"Ouch."

"The truth often hurts."

"True." He took a sip from the glass of water the waitress had set on the table. "If I was completely honest, I'd admit that I didn't know I was going to bid, until I actually did."

He hadn't meant to bid on her? She wasn't sure if that made her feel better or worse that he had.

"Like I said, you shouldn't have." She unfolded her napkin and put the cloth in her lap. "All it's done is cause problems."

"How so?"

"Richard is my boyfriend. He isn't thrilled at what you did. Nor is he thrilled that I'm out with you tonight."

"He could have bid higher." He took another drink of water.

"He could have," she admitted, wondering why she was defending Richard. He could easily have afforded to bid higher and he should have. That he hadn't irked her. Never would she have let another woman win a "date" with her man when she had the means to prevent it. "But Richard is way too practical to spend that much money on dinner with me. Why should he when he knows he gets to spend time with me for free?"

"You like practical?"

"I love practical," she immediately answered. She did like practical. Impractical made her feel out of control and that was something she never wanted to be again.

Lucas coughed as if his water had lingered and gone down the wrong pipe. "You love that guy?"

She wanted to lie. She wanted to say she was madly in love with Richard. She wanted to be able to tell Lucas that, yes, she had moved on past him and given her heart to another.

Instead, she told the truth.

"Richard is a great guy." Despite how surly he was over Lucas. Then again, Lucas was a handsome doctor; under

different circumstances that didn't involve a past relationship that had ended in divorce, Richard would have
every right to be surly. Maybe she should tell him who
Lucas really was. "We have a lot in common and I enjoy
our relationship."

At least, she had right up until Richard had let Lucas
walk away with the winning bid without even putting up
a fight. Now she found herself questioning everything.

Lucas's gaze didn't waver from hers. "But do you love
him?"

Did she love him? Not in the way Lucas meant. Not in
the way she'd loved him. She'd never let herself love that
way again. She knew how much that kind of love hurt.

"I don't think my feelings toward Richard are any of
your business."

"You don't." He leaned back against the booth seat and
studied her. "You're not in love with him."

At first she thought he sounded smug with his claim,
then she realized he was saying the words as much for
himself as he was to her. Which had her wondering why.
Why would Lucas care if she was in love with Richard? He
hadn't come to Children's because of any lingering feelings for her. He'd come because he'd been given a medical director position that was his dream job.

"What do your parents think of him?"

"They like him." Mostly. Part of her knew her parents
were just glad she was out and dating, that she was rebuild-
ing a life for herself. Plus, Richard was a pharmacist, a
good man with a steady income, and he came from a similar background to Emily. They liked that about him. They
liked that he wasn't Lucas. They'd die if they knew she
was out with him, that he'd come to work at Children's.
Her mother would be trying to get her to change jobs im-

mediately. Her father would, dear Lord, her father would likely come after Lucas if he knew she was within ten feet of the man who'd broken his little girl's heart.

"How about you?" she asked, wanting the conversation to turn away from her and Richard, to turn away from her parents and how they, probably rightly so, felt about Lucas. "Anyone special in your life?"

He shrugged. "I date from time to time but am currently not seeing anyone."

"Maybe you'll meet someone at Children's and sweep her off her feet and live happily ever after."

Why did the thought of him meeting someone and her having to watch that relationship blossom make her physically ill?

"I'm not looking to meet anyone, Emily. I'm at Children's because of the career and research opportunities being there provide me. Nothing more."

Nothing more. As in, she shouldn't get any ideas he was there because of her. Ha. As if. She knew better than that. He'd expressed himself loud and clear on that one over five years ago. "What type of research opportunities?"

His eyes lighting, he told her about a new procedure he and a colleague had been developing to reduce intracranial pressure post head trauma. His passion for what he was doing, what he hoped to achieve, impressed Emily. Lucas loved what he did and wanted to make a difference in his patients' lives. Darn him. She didn't want to like anything about him, but she admired his passion.

"You couldn't do that at where you were before?"

He shook his head. "Dr. Collins is still the medical director and shot me down every time I wanted to use the procedure."

Dr. Collins. A grumpy old man who was so antiquated

he must have come with the building. No wonder a progressive neurosurgeon like Lucas had sought other career opportunities.

"At Children's you get to make the final call of whether or not the procedure takes place?"

"I'm just waiting for the right patient."

"What's the advantage over traditional procedures to decrease ICP?"

"It's less invasive and less risk of post-surgical complications." He explained the procedure and continued to do so after their meal arrived, pausing only to brag about how good the duck was.

Surprisingly, Emily found herself enjoying listening to Lucas.

"I didn't know you were so interested in research."

He shrugged. "It's always been a dream."

"I never knew that."

"We didn't talk about my school and work much."

"We didn't talk much about anything," she reminded, more sarcasm than she'd meant coming out in her tone.

"That's not how I remember things. At least, it wasn't that way in the beginning. We'd spend hours just talking."

La. La. La. La. She fought to keep memories from rushing into her head. Memories of lying in Lucas's arms, naked, sated, and talking about anything and everything. Much easier to keep him at a distance if she only remembered the endless tears and screaming matches they'd battled through.

Seeming to realize that she was throwing up walls, he forked a piece of his duck, then held out the loaded utensil. "Here. Taste."

She shook her head. "I know it's good."

"Humor me so I won't feel guilty when I ask to try your salmon."

She did not want him to feed her, nor did she want to feed him. "But I…"

"Emily, please."

Please. The word on his lips undid a knot holding her emotions back. She leaned forward and took the bite he offered.

The sweet yet tart flavor of the apples next to the tender duck had Emily sighing. The salmon was her favorite, but the duck dish ran a close second.

"That's good."

His gaze dropped to her plate.

"Oh, all right." She forked a piece of the flaky pink meat and proffered her fork.

His gaze locked with hers, his mouth closed around her utensil, then he smiled. A real smile that reached his eyes and was full of pleasure.

Emily fought to keep her eyes open, hating the weakness surging through her. She didn't want to respond. Not in any way, shape or form.

But sharing his food, sharing her food, had her gulping.

"Amazing," he agreed, and she assumed he meant the food and not the starburst of feelings shooting through her. Why, oh, why couldn't she be immune to this man? She should be immune. He'd hurt her so badly, he shouldn't have any control over her feelings anymore. Not any.

"This was a really bad idea." She hadn't meant to make the admission out loud.

"Why?"

"You're my enemy."

"Your enemy?" He shook his head. "That's not who I am, nor how I see you, Emily."

"How do you see me, Lucas?"

* * *

Lucas studied the one woman he'd given his name to and who had held more power over him than any other. His wife. Ex-wife, he corrected.

"I see you as the most beautiful woman on the inside and out that I've ever met."

She was. If only her sadness hadn't taken over their relationship. If only he'd been able to understand and help her through whatever had changed within her. Him. He'd been what had changed her. No wonder she'd jumped at the chance to leave.

Emily's eyes closed and she shook her head. "Don't say things like that."

"Things like what?"

"Things you shouldn't say to me."

"Why shouldn't I tell you how beautiful you are?"

"Because you quit making me feel beautiful long ago."

Her words stunned him, shocked him, but maybe they shouldn't have. He and Emily had fallen apart. He regretted that he'd played any role in her not seeing the beauty so evident in everything about her. "I am sorry, Emily."

"I don't want your pity. It was a long time ago."

"I don't pity you. I pity myself at what I lost." His admission shocked him almost as much as hers had. He did regret that he hadn't been able to make Emily happy. When he looked across the table at her, saw the depth of emotion in her eyes, heard the sincerity in her voice when she spoke, he was filled with longings for her laughter, for her to smile at him the way she used to, before they'd married.

"Can I interest you in dessert?" the waitress asked, filling up Lucas's water glass.

Emily shook her head. "I'm full, but thank you."

Lucas found himself wanting to order dessert just so he could prolong the meal, could prolong his time with Emily, but he declined, also.

"Thank you for dinner. Everything was delicious," she told him so formally he cringed.

"You sound as if you're done."

"I am."

"The night doesn't have to end, Emily." At her look of horror, he elaborated. "I didn't mean we should have sex."

Although, he didn't find the idea nearly as horrific as she obviously did.

Because he still wanted her.

The realization was an earth-shattering one.

He still wanted Emily.

"Whatever you meant, my answer is no."

"You aren't curious about what I had in mind?"

She shook her head. "I just want this obligation over."

Which put him in his place.

The waitress set their check on the table, and when Emily went to grab it, he beat her to the ticket.

"You're not paying for our meal."

"But the fund-raiser…"

"Doesn't matter. You're not paying."

"But…"

"Emily, please don't argue on this one. Just let me feel like a man by paying for my date's dinner."

"But I'm not really your date."

"Sure you are. That's what I won. A date with a beautiful bachelorette to raise money for a great cause."

She glanced down at where her hands rested in her lap, then shrugged. "Okay, if that's what you want."

What he wanted was Emily.

She was his ex-wife, not a woman he was trying to woo or get to know better. He already knew Emily better than any woman in his life. Only, he didn't know her at all. Not anymore.

But he wanted to know her. Everything about her.

He finished his fresh glass of water, then nodded. "Yes, that's what I want."

When they'd split, he'd not been thinking clearly. He'd been spoiled, a kid still in many ways, focused on becoming a doctor, and when he'd had free time, he'd wanted to unwind, to hang with his fellow residents, his lifelong friends, to enjoy life and being young, not sitting inside the tiny apartment they'd called home and staring at the four walls. Or fighting, which was all they'd seemed able to do once they'd said I do.

What he should have been enjoying was Emily, but how could he do that when she'd cried almost nonstop, when he'd looked into her eyes and seen such horrific sadness that he hadn't been able to stand it?

She'd once been so bubbly. Within minutes of meeting her during his residency program, he'd become enamored with the perky nurse who knew her stuff and had the most enchanting smile and big green eyes he'd ever encountered. He'd been intrigued, asked her to go for coffee, and, although he could tell she was similarly intrigued, she'd refused.

He'd asked again the next day. And the next. And the day after that, too, even when he hadn't been working.

That day she'd said yes for the following day, if he was available. Although he'd had to do some major shuffling, he'd made himself available.

Over coffee they'd talked, laughed, ended up going for a walk in Central Park, and coffee had turned into dinner. She'd told him she'd said no not because she wasn't attracted to him, but because she'd just started at the hospital a few months before and really wasn't interested in becoming involved with someone who also worked at the hospital. When it had come time to tell her good-night, their kiss had been intense. He hadn't wanted to go, but she wouldn't let him stay.

Over the next few weeks, he'd spent every spare moment with her and quite a few he hadn't had to spare. The demands of his residency program, his family obligations and wanting to be with Emily nonstop started taking their toll. He pretty much gave up sleep, felt exhausted more often than not and knew he couldn't keep burning his candle at both ends. He'd thought if they married, it would ease the strain on several counts.

He'd been wrong.

She'd been trying to be the wife she'd thought she should be, but she hadn't connected with his family or his lifestyle, had insisted she live within her means instead. With each day that had passed, her smiles had become less and less frequent until they'd completely been replaced by tears.

He'd kept telling himself it would get better once he finished his residency, that he just had to bide his time.

Then she'd started talking about wanting a baby.

They'd been married less than a year. She would burst into tears within minutes of seeing him. He was in a medical school residency program. All they'd done was fight and have makeup sex. He'd talked with his parents and they'd accused Emily of being a gold digger, of trying to tie herself to his inheritance forever by having a baby. He hadn't believed them, not really. If Emily had been after money, why would she have insisted they live in her tiny apartment? To live within her income rather than the lavish lifestyle his trust could have provided? If his money was what she'd wanted, why was she so sad all the time? Because he'd have given her anything. He'd tried, had wanted to, but no matter what he'd done, it had been wrong. Being married to him had clinically depressed Emily. Not that she would admit it or agree to get help. How was that supposed to make a man feel? That being his wife made her ill?

He'd found himself backing away from their relationship. He'd barely been able to find time for the things he'd had to do, she'd cried all the time, and she'd been thinking about throwing an innocent baby into the mix?

If he'd been with Emily, he'd wanted her and had feared that she might end up pregnant on purpose. He'd started spending more time at the hospital, doing research, spending time with his parents, especially his mother, who'd been reeling from losing her mother a few months into his marriage to Emily, spending time with his friends, anything and anywhere to where he and Emily hadn't been alone, to where they couldn't have been intimate.

At first she'd gone with him to the things she could, had tried to keep up with his crazy, fast-paced schedule. Eventually, she'd quit, opting to go home. And do what? He really didn't know. Just that the emotional rift between them had kept dividing until it had reached mammoth proportions over just a few months.

And yet, for all the past, he wanted her even now. Just without the golden rings to choke out everything good between them, without that stress they'd put upon their once fantastic relationship, without the tears and the fights. He wanted what they'd had those first few months they'd been together and she'd been his best friend, his confidant, the person who had brightened his life in so many ways.

So long as they didn't put the expectations upon each other their wedding vows had burdened them with, they should be just fine.

In his mind, it all made perfect, logical sense, but when his gaze met Emily's across the table, he knew his logic and her logic weren't anywhere near on the same page.

CHAPTER FIVE

EMILY WANTED TO SCREAM. Why did Lucas keep staring at her that way?

A way that had her questioning his motives.

A way that made her think he wanted to have her for dessert.

As if.

He paid for their food by tossing down a couple of large bills that no doubt made their waitress's night.

"No change? Really?" The young woman smiled hugely. "Thank you."

"Thank you for dinner, too," Emily added, standing. "I need to be going. I have to work tomorrow."

She needed to get away from Lucas. Seeing his kindness, his generosity, to the waitress bothered her. Not that she didn't want him to be generous. He could certainly afford to and generosity was a good thing. She just didn't want to witness any more "good guy" behavior. Nor did she want to make any more comparisons between Richard and Lucas. Richard was a "to the exact recommended percentage only" tipper and would have been appalled at what Lucas had given to the young woman. Just as he was appalled at how much Lucas had bid for tonight's "date."

"I'll walk you home."

"No."

"Emily," he began, but she shook her head.

"Lucas, you aren't going home with me."

"Walking you home and going home with you aren't the same thing."

"Either way, I walked myself here and I can walk myself back."

"You offend my gentlemanliness."

"Too bad, but you aren't getting anywhere near my apartment."

"Is being around me that bad?"

Why had his voice sounded off when he'd asked his question?

"Being around you isn't good."

"I'd like to prove that you're wrong about that," he said as they stepped outside Stluka's and onto the sidewalk. Although the street wasn't that crowded, at the end of the block they could see the hustle and bustle of Broad Street. "I think our being around each other could be good for both of us."

She paused walking. A man behind her excused himself and went around her as she glared at Lucas. "Why would you possibly think that?"

"We had a lot of passion and strong emotions between us that we were too young to deal with and we let our relationship fall apart. Life has thrown us back together for a reason."

"You're crazy."

"Yeah, maybe I am, because right now all I can think about is how much I've missed spending time with you. I suppose there are a lot of people who'd say that's pretty crazy."

"For the record, I'm one of those people. The only reason I'm spending time with you is because you won the auction. Don't mistake my being here as anything more."

"I don't believe you, Emily. I feel the vibe between us."

She glanced down the street, considered making a run for her apartment. How dared he call her bluff?

"You're still as attracted to me as I am to you."

"I'm not attracted to you at all. Whatever vibes you think you're picking up on all have to do with the past, Lucas. There's nothing between us in the present. Nothing at all. Good night."

Head held high, she walked away, praying her feet didn't trip up and make her land on her face because she felt his gaze on her retreat.

Some of Emily's patients truly broke her heart. Jenny Garcia was one. The four-year-old girl had been rushed to the emergency room after she'd been abused by her mother's drugged-out boyfriend. The child had sustained multiple injuries including broken ribs, a busted lip, blackened eyes and bruises all over her tiny body. She'd also suffered from a concussion and brain injury that had the emergency physician opting to admit the child onto the unit where Emily worked.

Lucas was the physician assigned to her case and he'd shown up on the floor just minutes after Emily got the unconscious girl checked onto the unit.

"How bad is she?"

"She's pitiful," Emily admitted, her eyes watering. No, she was not going to cry. She wasn't. She would not lapse into crying in front of Lucas. She was beyond that life phase.

"Some people shouldn't have children."

Some people didn't.

Emily flinched. Nope. Not going there. La. La. La. Not allowing those thoughts to enter her head.

"I agree." She handed him the computer tablet with the girl's information pulled up.

His wince tugged way deep inside Emily. Lucas sighed, then raked his fingers through his thick hair. "Where's the mom?"

Emily shrugged. "I've not seen her. One of the ER nurses said she was there for a while, but that she didn't stay."

"How could anyone leave their child after something like this happening?" Lucas asked, truly looking shocked.

Emily had had the same thought when the ER nurse had told her the girl's mother had left. Emily tried not to judge, but sometimes it was darn hard not to.

Lucas nodded. "Go with me to check her?"

Emily didn't want to go anywhere with Lucas, but she couldn't refuse the unit's medical director.

When his eyes touched on the child in the hospital bed, his disgust emanated.

"There are several consults already in the system besides yours," Emily told him. "The ER physician just felt having you look over her brain scans and getting her ICP down was the most imperative once they had her otherwise stabilized."

"She's going to need surgical repair of some of her injuries."

Emily nodded. "Jeremiah Franklin reset a bone and closed a few wounds prior to her transfer to the floor. He plans to take her back to surgery once you feel it's safe for him to do so."

"Noted." Lucas did a neuro check on the child from head to toe so he could assess the extent of her injuries. Emily had already completed a similar examination but watched Lucas's highly efficient but gentle exam. The child was unconscious and yet, still, his touch was nurturing and caring.

The girl moaned in pain, the sound barely above a tortured whimper.

"I'll kill the guy myself if he ever shows his face here."

Emily nodded. She felt the same. The absolute protectiveness Lucas was showing over the child stunned her, though.

He'd have made a great father.

A tortured whimper escaped her own lips at her thought and she turned away.

"I'm sorry, Emily. I shouldn't have said that out loud."

Forcing herself to face him, she shook her head. "No, for once, we agree on something. I'd like to introduce him to my dad's baseball bat."

A small smile toyed on Lucas's face. "I've heard about your dad's baseball bat."

Emily's gaze flickered to the child. "Yeah, well, too bad she doesn't have a dad with a baseball bat to have protected her from the world's bad guys."

"Agreed." He touched her shoulder, then let his hand fall away as if realizing he shouldn't be touching her. "I'm off to get prepped for surgery to release the pressure in her head. Pray all goes well and I have her back to you before your shift ends."

With more wires and bandages than she'd left with, Jenny returned to the unit about an hour before time for Emily's shift to end. She got the child settled, with all vitals checked and recorded.

Lucas looked over the information in the computer, then went to the girl's room and found Emily standing next to the child's bed and holding her hand.

His heart squeezed at the image, at the compassion on

Emily's face. The look that said had this been her child she'd have protected her until her dying breath.

Once upon a time, Emily had wanted a child. His child. Did she plan to have children someday still?

As much as she'd talked about having a baby and starting a family, he was surprised she hadn't already.

Any child would be blessed to have her as a mother.

If only they were meeting now for the first time, without the past between them, how different would things be? Would he be looking at her right now and admiring her beauty, her compassion, her heart, and wondering at the emotions she elicited within him?

Would he ask her to dinner and commiserate over life's injustices that a child would suffer such a cruel fate? Would they bond and hold hands, hug each other, share their first kiss? Would they—

"Oh, sorry, I didn't see you there." Emily interrupted his thoughts, pulling her hand free from the child's and moving away from the hospital bed. "She's resting peacefully at the moment and her ICP pressure has improved a lot from prior to surgery. You used your new procedure on her. It seems to be working."

"So far, at any rate. She has a long way to go to recovery."

Emily nodded. "If you'll excuse me, I'm going to go check my other patient."

Lucas watched her walk across the room. Just as she made it to the door, he stopped her. "Go to dinner with me, Emily."

He hadn't known he was going to ask her, but more than anything he wanted her to say yes.

"I can't," she told him. "I already have plans."

"With the pharmacist?"

Not meeting his gaze, she nodded.

"Will you understand if I don't say to have a good time?"

Her gaze lifted to his. "Not really."

He sighed. "Go, Emily. Have a good time. The best."

Emily didn't have the best time. Richard was quiet, sulky, wanting her to pay penance for having dinner with Lucas the night before. She kept having to remind herself that Richard wasn't the problem. Lucas was.

She smiled across the dinner table, forced herself to listen to him recount a story one of his pharmacy customers had told him that day. She hadn't had to force herself to listen to Lucas the night before. She'd soaked up every excited word he'd said. He'd talked with such passion about his career, about the new procedure and the research he planned to do at Children's.

"Emily?" Richard cleared his throat loudly. "I asked what you thought about that."

"Sorry." She was even more sorry because she had no clue what he was referring to. No matter as he launched back into another recount of the tale. Emily tried to remain attentive to what he was saying, but instead her thoughts drifted back to Lucas.

Where was he? Still at the hospital or had he perhaps made plans with someone else?

Why had he asked her to go eat? They'd worked together amicably enough that day. She hadn't run off when he'd shown up on the unit, which was what she gathered his purpose in buying her bachelorette date had been. What would be the point in going to eat a second time?

Her phone buzzed in her purse that sat in the chair beside her. While keeping her gaze trained on Richard, she slid the purse into her lap and removed the phone. With a quick swipe of her finger she opened the screen, glanced down and hit the message button. She didn't recognize the number, but she knew who the message was from.

You look bored.

How do you know? she typed back.

Just hungry and ended up at the same place as you.

Hard to believe that's coincidental.

Yet it is.

"Emily, am I boring you?"
She glanced up at the man across the table from her. "Sorry, I had a message I needed to answer."
"Work?"
Heat flooded her face. "Yes, someone from work."

Oops. Sorry. Someone looks upset. Guess I better quit bothering you.

Yes, you should.

You should have said yes when I asked you to dinner.

Why?

Because you'd be having a better time.

With you? I don't think so.

We should test that theory. Don't make plans with him tomorrow night.

Leave me alone, Lucas.

Please.

Ugh. There was that word again. When had he learned to use it so proficiently?

"Everything okay?" Richard asked, causing her to glance up from her phone.

"Yeah, just had a long day today."

"Anything you want to talk about?"

"No," she admitted, realizing she didn't want to tell Richard about her day.

"Were you out that late last night? No one forced you to participate in the fund-raiser," he reminded her, his voice full of condemnation. Again.

"No, I wasn't out that late last night, and no one forced you to let someone else win my bid."

Ouch. Had she really just said that out loud? She hadn't meant to. She'd meant to keep her feelings quietly under wraps. Even if Lucas had pointed it out. Even if Lucas was probably watching her argue with Richard.

Richard's lips compressed into a tight line. "If you'd wanted me to buy your bid, you should have told me."

Practical. Logical. Infuriating.

"Really? I shouldn't have to tell you that I wanted you, the man I'm dating, to win my bid."

His voice had taken on a truly confused tone. "Then how was I supposed to know?"

"You shouldn't want me going to dinner with another man."

"I don't want you going to dinner with another man, but you went anyway."

"Then you should have bought my date so I wouldn't

have had to." She pushed her plate away. "I'm tired and ready to go home."

He frowned but put his napkin down. "We can leave as soon as I pay the bill."

"Good. Great. The sooner the better."

Why, oh, why did it bother her so much that he tipped their waitress to the exact penny of the recommended amount?

She'd barely had a couple of conversations with Lucas and he'd already managed to make her question her relationship with a man she'd been quite content with.

Content?

Since when was life about just being content?

When did she stop wanting happily-ever-after and the full-blown fairy tale?

She knew. She'd stopped believing, stopped dreaming, when her marriage to Lucas had fallen apart.

She fought to keep from looking around the restaurant to spot Lucas. Where he was didn't matter.

She and Richard walked back to her apartment in silence. She turned to him. "I'll just say good night down here."

"You're not letting me come up?"

She shook her head. "It really has been a long day."

"This isn't working for me, Emily."

She blinked at him. "What do you mean?"

"I mean, you going on dates with other men and then sending me home. I'm supposed to be the man in your life."

He was right. He was supposed to be the man in her life. Only, she wasn't sure she wanted him to be. Surely she deserved better than just the status quo.

"I think you need to reconsider or we need to consider taking a time-out from our relationship."

What? "If I don't invite you upstairs, we're through?"

He didn't answer, just stared at her with an expectant look on his face that was answer enough.

Well, at least he was making this decision easy.

"You're right. We do need a time-out from our relationship."

Surprise flittered across his face. He'd thought his ultimatum would result in an invitation into her bed?

"If you've set your sights on that doctor, Emily, you're wasting your time. You're throwing away a good thing for a man who's never going to take someone like you seriously."

"Someone like me?" He made it sound as if she weren't good enough for Lucas, as if she were lucky Richard found her appealing.

He shrugged. "You're not in his league."

Ouch.

Emily's lips curled into a forced smile. "Thanks for an enlightening evening and for making what could have been a difficult moment into an easy one. Goodbye, Richard."

Emily was assigned to Cassie and to Jenny the following day. Cassie had continued to decline, but Jenny was holding her own. It would probably be a couple of days before the four-year-old regained consciousness, which was probably a good thing. Perhaps some of her injuries would have subsided a little.

"Her vitals remained good during the night."

She turned to the man entering the room. The man she'd lain in bed and thought about way too much the night before. Shouldn't she have been thinking about the man she'd just ended things with instead?

"Yes, she's stable."

"That's good news." He examined the unconscious little girl, then turned to Emily. "Give me more good news."

"Pardon?"

"Tell me you didn't make plans for tonight."

Emily sighed. "I'm not going to go to dinner with you, Lucas. There's no point."

"Is there a point to you going to dinner with the pharmacist?"

"Richard has nothing to do with why I won't go to dinner with you," she answered honestly. "I'm no longer seeing him."

Lucas's gaze shot to hers and he studied her so long that she found her feet wanting to shuffle beneath the weight of his stare. Instead, she found the strength to step away from him.

"I'm going to check on Cassie."

"I'll be there when I've finished my chart notes on Jenny."

"Take your time." Maybe she'd be finished and not have to see him again.

"Are you going to go out with Dr. Cain tonight, since you and Richard are history?" Did Meghan have listening devices hidden in the patient rooms or what?

"No, I'm not going out with Dr. Cain. We had our auction date. Tonight, I'm going to stay home and cook."

Meghan wrinkled her nose. "You're crazy, you know."

"I enjoy cooking."

"You could go to the movies with Amy and me."

"No, thank you. I'm cooking because I want to."

To keep her mind occupied she'd enrolled in cooking lessons not long after her divorce was final. Yes, she'd burned more than a few meals prior to figuring out what she was doing wrong, but she had learned. Excelled even. Cooking had been great therapy. Mainly, she'd discovered, as long as she didn't get lost daydreaming about Lucas, her meals had turned out decent. Decent had gone to good. Something she'd detested had gone to something she enjoyed and found therapeutic. As time passed, she'd quit dreaming about Lucas altogether.

Emily left the nurses' station and checked on her patients. Lucas stopped her just outside Jenny's room.

"Are you really going to cook your dinner tonight?"

He sounded so incredulous that she winced. Okay, so she hadn't been able to cook when they got married. That wasn't a sin. There had been lots of things she could do. She'd just grown up in a house where the majority of meals had been takeout and she'd never mastered much more in the kitchen than use of a microwave.

"I can cook." She glared at him, hoping no one was in the hospital hallway to see them, but afraid to look around to check. "I'm not a stagnant person, you know."

"I didn't think you were."

"Then you shouldn't sound so surprised that I've learned to do things I couldn't do so well a few years ago."

"You always were a quick learner." He didn't say more, didn't say to what he referred. He didn't have to.

Emily's brain went there anyway.

Or maybe it wasn't her brain, but her body.

Her body seemed unable to not go there when Lucas was near.

"Prove it."

"Prove what?" she asked, not following him.

"That you can cook."

"I know what you're trying to do. You're just trying to get me to invite you to dinner."

"You're right. That is what I'm trying to do. What are we having?"

"Chopped liver," she said without thought, hating that he was once again keeping pace beside her.

"Chopped liver?"

She almost let a laugh escape from her lips. Almost.

"Oh, yeah." She knew he didn't like liver, that he hated it. "Plus broccoli."

"I see you remember all my favorites."

Glancing toward him, she smiled sweetly. "But of course."

He stared at her a minute, then surprised her by the easy smile that slid onto his face. "I'll come hungry."

"I didn't invite you to dinner," she reminded him.

"But you're going to because you want to prove to me what a great cook you are now."

He had her there. She narrowed her gaze at him in dislike. She did want to impress him with the fact that she wasn't the same person she'd been five years ago. Stupid pride.

"I'm eating at nine. I'll eat without you if you're late."

CHAPTER SIX

LUCAS COULDN'T SAY the smells that greeted him were the best he'd ever smelled, but they weren't bad.

Immediately after letting him into her apartment, Emily disappeared. She didn't tell him to make himself at home, just opened the door, motioned him in without a smile or a look that said she was glad he was there, then disappeared.

He assumed to the kitchen.

She probably wasn't glad he was there. He'd practically begged for the invitation. Something he didn't quite understand. He'd only wanted to make peace with Emily, to be able to function at the hospital without undue awkwardness between them. Now he wanted to be with her because he liked being with her. Which wasn't in his plans at all, but that didn't seem to have stopped him from pushing for an invite to taste her cooking.

Or from feeling ecstatic that she and the pharmacist were history.

He closed the apartment door behind him and checked out her living room. The comfortably decorated room was a far cry from the hovel where they'd lived when they'd been married. It had taken everything she'd made for them to scrape by.

He'd looked at things differently than she had. He'd been in school, not some lazy bum seeking handouts from his family. Sure, his family hadn't been pleased that he'd married Emily, but they'd never cut off his funds. Plus, he'd had his own money from his trust his grandparents had left him. Maybe he'd taken that for granted. But the reality was, the money had been his and there'd been no reason for him and Emily to struggle financially.

Only, Emily had insisted she made more than enough for them to get by and had refused any help. He'd given in, for the most part, because he'd thought she'd eventually see sense. She hadn't and he'd resented the change she'd imposed upon him.

Or, more likely, he'd hated that she'd been the one supporting them financially. He'd wanted to take care of her, but she'd refused to let him help to the point of being unreasonable, in his opinion.

All because his parents had accused her of being after his money and she'd been determined to prove them wrong, even if it had meant cutting off her nose to spite her face.

How much had the stress of carrying the financial load played into her depression?

He walked over to a shelf, picked up a photo of her parents. He wasn't sure how old the photo was, but they looked exactly the way he remembered. Then again, just because it seemed as if it had been forever since he and Emily had been married, really it hadn't been that long ago.

Five years since a judge had decreed their divorce final.

His hand shook as he set the frame back onto the shelf.

Her living room color pattern was very neutral, very pleasing to the eye. Creams, earth tones, with a few jewel-toned throw pillows tossed on the sofa. She had a few knickknacks scattered about the room, but overall it was a clutter-free look.

Without one trace of her former life.

Not that he'd expected there to be. Just that he noted there wasn't.

Then again, did his own living quarters boast anything of his life with Emily?

No. At least, they hadn't before a few weeks ago when he'd dug out a box of things he'd been unable to bring himself to throw away. Inside the box had been a photo-booth strip they'd had taken in Atlantic City on their one and only trip there. They'd labeled the weekend as their honeymoon.

He'd wanted to take her on a real honeymoon, somewhere exotic, but instead they'd stayed in a cheap budget motel, eaten junk food, lain around on the beach, played in the water, ridden rides and had sex as if they'd been in heat.

Not the honeymoon he'd wanted to give her or that he'd ever imagined, but he could recall few times in his life he'd been happier. When Emily had been happier.

Once upon a time, being with him had made her happy.

His stomach clenched at the memories.

Tired of being in the living room by himself, he followed his nose to where he'd find Emily. The apartment wasn't very big, so it was easy to find where she stood at a stove.

She still wore her apron, but that was where her resemblance to a fifties housewife ended.

Her hair was pulled up high on her head with a few loose tendrils that hung past her shoulders. Her makeup was subtle but perfectly accented her big green eyes, high cheekbones and pouty, all-too-kissable pale pink lips. Beneath the apron was a pair of jeans that showed off long, slender legs and a T-shirt that matched her eyes. All she needed was a television crew filming her and she'd be a cooking show megastar.

He'd certainly tune in week after week to see what new concoction she'd dreamed up.

"It's almost done," she told him, picking up a glass of wine and dumping its contents over a dish on the stove top. "I was just finishing."

"You didn't have to go to any trouble. I really wouldn't have minded takeout."

"I cooked for me, not you."

He glanced around the small but efficient room. A vase with a few colorful flowers sat in the middle of a table. Two expensive-looking plates with ringed napkins in the center and perfectly laid out silverware to the sides sat opposite each other. He'd have bet money she couldn't properly set a table back when they'd been married. Had she looked up how to on the internet or was this another newly acquired skill?

"What are we having?" he asked, eyeing what she was doing. "Liver, broccoli, asparagus and peas?"

"You always were a good guesser." Her eyes twinkled with merriment.

"That's a lot of greens."

"You're a doctor," she reminded him with a sugary sweet fake smile. "I figured you liked eating healthy. Greens are good for you. If you'll have a seat—" she gestured to the round table that sat four "—I'll serve dinner."

Something about the idea of sitting at her table with her waiting on him struck him as wrong. "I don't want you to serve me, Emily."

"It's no problem. You're my guest."

Reluctantly, he sat down in the indicated chair and watched as she picked up his plate and piled on large portions of each dish, put a sprig of green to the side of the meat and set it before him.

She then prepared the second plate, a much less full one, and put it on the table opposite where he sat. "Can I get you something to drink?"

"I should have brought us a bottle of wine." He hadn't brought anything. No wine. No flowers. No anything. He hadn't been thinking. Not about anything but the person's company he wanted. Emily's.

"It's just as well you didn't," she assured him. "I have no desire to drink something that lowers my inhibitions and makes me not think as clearly."

"Especially around me?"

"Lowering my inhibitions was never something you had a problem with."

"You said no that first night and quite a few after."

"Barely." She laughed, a low sound that was more self-derision than humor.

He regarded her for long moments. She didn't look at him but stared at her plate. Her cheekbones had the slightest bit of blush on them, accenting their height and the beauty of her face. When her gaze lifted to his, the intense color of her green eyes beneath darkly fringed lashes stole his breath.

"You want me to tell you I'm sorry I wanted you so much?"

"I don't want you to tell me anything." Her voice was too calm. "I just want you to eat your food."

"Fair enough," he agreed, wondering at the ache that had settled deep into his gut when he'd yet to even take a bite of her specially prepared meal. "Let's talk about work, then. What's your favorite thing about Children's?"

"The kids." She forked a piece of meat, liver no doubt, and popped it into her mouth. "Mmm, that's good."

Lucas would never believe that anyone could make eating liver look sexy. Emily had. Who knew it was even possible?

He picked up his fork, but, rather than take a bite, he toyed with the food. He really didn't like liver. "What about the kids?"

"Everything about them." She gestured to his plate. "Not hungry?"

"Not very."

Her eyes sparkled. "A shame to let good food go to waste."

He agreed. He didn't believe in being wasteful, but he wasn't mentally psyched up to take a bite of liver just yet, either.

So he forked some broccoli and took a tentative bite.

The garlic and butter flavor lightly coating the vegetable surprised him. "This isn't bad."

Her brow arched. "Did you think it would be?"

"Broccoli has never been my favorite dish."

She blinked innocently. "Really?"

"Really." He ate all his broccoli, then eyed the asparagus and liver.

"Sometimes in life we learn to like things we once didn't and vice versa."

"Are we talking about food or how you feel about me?"

"You tell me." She pointed her fork at his plate. "Try the asparagus. It's delicious."

No doubt.

He cut a piece of the long green stalk with his fork. "Here goes."

The butter cream sauce on the asparagus really was delicious. He ate every bite she'd put on his plate.

"Now, for the main dish," she encouraged. "The meat is exquisitely tender and flavored with my own special sauce."

Based on the other two dishes, no doubt he'd have to revise his lifelong claims that he didn't like liver to that he only liked liver prepared by Emily.

She'd taken things he hadn't liked and prepared them in ways that made him reverse his opinion. He could admire that she'd done that. Really, he should applaud the cooking talent she'd acquired since she'd last prepared a meal for him.

Not surprisingly, the meat was as tender as she'd claimed and the flavor was quite good. Not dry and chewy as he remembered his previous trials with liver.

He clapped his hands together. "Bravo."

Her cheeks flushed. "You like it?"

"You meant for me to, right?"

"I suppose."

"Am I going to regret eating this later?" he asked, taking another bite.

"I don't know. Are you?"

"No rat poison or anything that's going to put me in the emergency department?"

"Would you deserve it if there was?"

He had to think about that one for a minute. Mainly because he wondered if she thought he deserved it? Still, despite her quick comeback, he knew she hadn't done anything to him. She wouldn't hurt a fly.

"Maybe I would."

Emily sat quietly eating her food and staring at her plate rather than look at him.

"I'm sorry I hurt you, Emily."

She dropped her fork.

"I'm sorry for a lot of things," he continued, trying not to wince at her pale face. "Especially how sad you became during our marriage. I regret that I ever played any role in you not being happy."

Her gaze lifted to his.

He waited, not trying to hide his sincerity, not surprised at her look of disbelief. Or was that disgust?

She obviously wanted to scream. She practically did. "No. You can't do this to me."

Not understanding her anger, he asked, "What?"

She pushed her plate away from her and shook her head. "You can't come in here apologizing and acting like you regret how we ended."

"I do regret how we ended." More than she'd ever know or believe, he regretted everything that had gone wrong between them. "I've always regretted how we ended."

"Bull." She pushed herself away from the table and walked over to the refrigerator. She pulled out two individual glass servings of what appeared to be pudding with a dollop of whipped cream on top.

Which didn't exactly fit with the theme of their meal. He loved pudding. Always had.

He had a vague flashback of pushing her away after she'd attempted to make pudding that had turned out to be a clumpy mess instead of anything close to edible.

Not that he'd cared about the pudding, but the broken look in her eyes had about killed him. When she'd started crying yet again, he hadn't been able to stand it, had wanted to take her in his arms and kiss away the tears in her eyes, had wanted to tease her, spread the liquid concoction on her lips and suck it off until they both forgot about everything except each other.

Instead, they'd fought. Badly. He'd stormed out of the house and gone to stay the night at the hospital doctors' lounge. That had been the end.

The night he'd told her if she was that unhappy, she should leave.

She had left. Because she had been that unhappy. He had made her that unhappy.

When he'd come home the next day, she'd been gone and the tiny apartment had never felt more lonely, more claustrophobic, more cheap and distasteful.

He hadn't meant his words. He'd not wanted her to

leave. He hadn't wanted her to be unhappy, either. No matter what he'd done, he hadn't been able to make Emily happy.

Pride had taken over and bad had gone to worse.

What an immature idiot he'd been.

A selfish, immature idiot who'd driven away the best woman to ever come into his life. She'd been a likable person. A good person. Honest, wholesome, real, a ray of sunshine on a cloudy day.

A person unlike any he'd ever known.

"I really am sorry things turned out the way they did, Emily. I'm also sorry if that truth upsets you."

"I'm not upset," she obviously lied. Not looking at him, she shrugged. "Life turned out the way it was supposed to."

"Do you believe that?" Because he wasn't so sure. Instead, he wondered if the way they'd ended had left them both with too many unresolved emotions to really ever move on. Then again, perhaps it was only him who felt that way. Maybe she really was happy now and he should just leave well enough alone. So why couldn't he?

"Yes, I do."

"I'm not so sure," he admitted, surprising himself at his honesty, surprising himself by standing and moving to stand near to her.

Emily closed her eyes, bit into her lower lip and felt tortured. Why had Lucas come over to her? Why wasn't he eating his darn pudding?

"Do you remember the first time we kissed?" He bent close and his words seduced her ear, her body, her mind.

Seriously, did he think she'd forgotten their first kiss?

"I do," he continued, so near she could feel the warmth of his breath. "We were standing outside your apartment door and I leaned down to press my lips to yours. Your mouth was the sweetest thing I'd ever tasted and I couldn't get enough. You set me on fire."

Her brain was on fire. So was the rest of her. Hellfire because he was torturing her with past memories. She'd loved him so much, wanted him so much.

But that was long ago.

"What does it matter if I remember?" she asked incredulously, shaking her head. "All of this is crazy. I don't understand why you wanted to eat at my house, because we both know it wasn't so you could try my cooking."

"Your cooking was great," he assured her, still close to her, too close. "I want the friendship we shared, Emily, before everything went wrong between us. I want to kiss you again. I want to do a lot more than just kiss you. I want all the good there was between us without the golden rings of death to choke out that goodness."

What was he saying? That he wanted them to be friends with benefits? Was he asking her to be his friend while calling their marriage "golden rings of death"? He really was crazy.

"You want to be my friend?" she quipped, her brain still reeling at what he was saying. At the fact that he'd just said he wanted to kiss her again. That he wanted to do more than just kiss her. Darn him. She didn't want to think about Lucas kissing her, doing more than just kissing her.

He was so close, he could kiss her.

The thought had her wanting to back away from him. The thought had her wanting to turn to him and satisfy her curiosity. Had Lucas really kissed the way she recalled him kissing her or did her mind play tricks on her?

"Have you lost all your other friends?"

His lips curved upward in a wry grin. "You know better than that, Emily. I'm a good friend. A very good friend."

Perhaps he had been to his other friends. Not to her. To

her, he'd been a mostly absent friend. Although, he probably meant sexual friends.

"Sex?" She rolled her eyes and moved away from him, sitting down at the table and picking up her pudding. "That's what all this is about? Why you outbid Richard? Why you are interfering in my life when I can't stand you? Because you want sex?"

"I told you, I didn't intentionally go to the auction to bid on you. And if the idiot who let me win your bid wasn't willing to fight harder for you, then good riddance. He didn't deserve you, either." He followed her lead and sat back down at the table, too. But rather than pick up his pudding, he leaned toward her. "I don't believe you can't stand me. I think you want me. Sex was very good between us."

Her lips twisted with bitterness. "Did you think so? I got the impression you bored of sex with me very quickly."

"Never."

"Then you have very different memories from mine."

That seemed to throw him. He stared at her a moment, then took a spoonful of his pudding and closed his mouth around it. "This is good."

"Of course."

Her sarcasm wasn't lost on him and he arched a brow in question.

"You changed the subject," she accused.

"You want to talk about my memories of sex between us?"

No. Yes. Maybe. Depended on what he would say.

"Let me tell you. I remember a woman I couldn't get enough of whom I married and still couldn't get enough of. A woman whom I was so obsessed with that I wanted to be with her rather than doing all the things I needed to be doing, like studying and preparing for my next day's patients, or doing the things my parents needed of me.

A woman I'd rather spend time with than sleep or eat or anything else."

The blood drained from her face and she felt cold all over. "I never asked you to put me before anything. I knew you had to study."

"Saying that and living it are two different things. You expected me to be the husband you thought I should be. You cried all the time, Emily. No matter what I did, I felt I never could do enough, could never make your sadness that you'd married me go away. Knowing how unhappy you were made me miserable, too."

"You regretted marrying me from the moment we said I do."

He didn't immediately deny her claim.

"It's true, isn't it?" Her voice broke as she pushed for a response. She closed her eyes, shook her head. "Allowing you to come here was a mistake."

"I asked myself a dozen times why you did. Why you and the pharmacist are no longer together. Reality is we needed to talk, Emily."

Restlessness hit her and she couldn't stay seated in her chair a moment longer. She jumped up and moved across the kitchen.

"Despite our past and the way things ended, you're as curious as I am to see if the heat is still there. You want to know if you'll melt at my fingertips if I touch you."

"No." She grabbed hold of the countertop and white-knuckled the edges. She didn't want to know those things. Not really. She just… Oh, help her. Curiosity was going to kill her.

"You could have said no to cooking for me," he reminded. "Why didn't you?"

Why had she agreed to let him come to her apartment? Had she just wanted to see him? To spend time with him?

She let go of the countertop, turned away from him.

He stepped over to her, put his hands on her shoulders. "Upsetting you isn't what I want. What I want is to make you feel good, to make you happy. It's what I always wanted but could never seem to get quite right."

"I don't want to be your friend, Lucas." Her voice

CHAPTER SEVEN

LUCAS WAS TOUCHING her again. Emily didn't want him
touching her. The heat of his hands burned right through her
T-shirt, scorching her flesh, branding her with memories.

"Why are you saying these things?" she asked, hating
that her voice cracked, that she wasn't strong enough to
hide her emotions.

His thumbs stroked over her flesh, making tiny waves
of awareness shoot through her. "I'm not over you."

Something inside Emily shattered. She wasn't sure if it
was her resolve or if it was the glued-back-together pieces
of her heart. Either way the impact left her unsteady.

Oh, the times she'd dreamed of this conversation. At
times, she'd dreamed of falling into his arms, of their kissing, making love, laughing that they'd ever let anything
come between them and vowing to never lose sight of
each other again. At others, she'd lift her chin and scorn-
fully laugh at his admission, telling him that ship had
long ago sailed.

Instead of doing either, she seemed frozen in place, stiff
and cold in his heated hands.

"Emily, when I told you I wanted to be your friend, to
kiss you, I was serious." He sounded serious. His hands
gently squeezing her shoulders, turning her around to face
him, felt serious. "That is what I want. I want to be a part

of your life again, to have you be a part of my life. I didn't know that when I took the position at Children's, but I do now."

"What about what I want?" she asked, trying and failing to keep the pain out of her voice. She did not want to give this man any power over her. Feeling pain was letting him have power over her. He didn't deserve that power. He didn't deserve anything from her.

"What do you want, Emily?"

"That one's easy." There went her chin jutting forward. "For you to go away and to never have to see you again."

Silence.

"Is that really what you want?" He touched her chin, forcing her to face him, stared down into her eyes. His gaze searched hers with an intensity that made her legs no sturdier than the barely touched pudding sitting on the table. "Do you want me to resign from my position at Children's, to disappear from your life and never bother you again? Because if that will make you happy, then I'll give you that, Emily. Tell me what you want right now, and I'll do anything within my power to give you what you want."

She blinked up at him, unable to answer with words.

Because the words that would come out weren't the words that should come out.

She wanted him to disappear and never bother her again. Really, she did. That was the absolute best thing that could happen. She'd loved him more than anything in the world and he'd broken her to bits, left her devastated and alone when she'd fallen apart and lost everything. She should hate him.

"Answer me, Emily. Do you want me to go away and never bother you again? To leave Children's and never purposefully cross your path again? Just say the words, and I'll go."

"I..." She paused, her gaze dropping to his mouth. When had he gotten so close that his breath fanned her lips? When had his warm body become almost flush with hers?

"I don't want to go, Emily, but if that's what you want, I will."

She looked back up, met his cloudy gaze and opened her mouth to answer him, to tell him that, yes, she wanted him to go away, to never bother her again, to leave Children's and to never purposefully cross her path again. She did want all those things.

But none of that came out and whatever she'd been going to say was lost to the pressure of his mouth covering hers in a kiss.

A kiss she didn't want.

A kiss she wanted more than anything else in the whole world.

A kiss that was surprisingly gentle, almost as if he hadn't been able to not kiss her and wasn't completely sure she wouldn't push him away. His lips were soft against hers and somewhere in her mind she recognized that if she told him to stop, he would, that if she pushed him away, he'd let her. That for the moment he was giving her the power, the control, and she could do with it what she would.

Why wasn't she stopping him?

Instead, her body betrayed her, tingling all over, craving to be closer and closer to him.

This was Lucas. Her Lucas. His lips. His hands. His body. Lucas.

She was kissing her ex-husband and the world was still standing around her. Was it perhaps snowing in hell? Or perhaps pigs had learned to fly? All three seemed just as unlikely phenomena.

She needed to push him away.

But she wasn't.

She couldn't.

She needed to tell him to stop.

But she didn't. Couldn't.

She needed to not enjoy the pressure of his lips, the possessive thrusting of his tongue into her mouth.

But she did.

Oh, how she did.

Kissing Lucas had always caused hot lava to fill every inch of her.

He'd been right. She had been curious as to whether or not he could still cause her body to implode with pleasure with the slightest effort on his part.

Her fingers found their way to his nape. His hands had found their way to her bottom and were pressing her hard against his body.

His hard body.

How had that happened so fast?

She squirmed in remembered pleasure. He'd felt so good, made her feel so good physically. So completely and thoroughly satisfied. She craved that satisfaction, that ultimate pleasure that having him inside her had given so many times in the past.

Her head fell back and he trailed kisses down her throat, sucking gently at her skin.

"You feel so good."

She did feel good. She felt good that he was kissing her, touching her. That he wanted her.

But those weren't things that should be making her feel good. He was her ex-husband. They were no longer married, were no longer anything to each other except for painful memories.

So why wasn't she stopping him?

Because sex with Richard hadn't achieved more than

a meager orgasm and she wondered if she'd imagined the mind-blowing meltdowns she'd had at the ministrations of this man's mouth, hands and body.

She hadn't imagined a thing. Just Lucas's kisses, his hands, had her on the brink of volcanic eruption. She wanted that explosion, that release, even if it wasn't real.

She wanted him for an orgasm. The kind that made her want to wrap her legs around his waist and cling as tightly to his body as she could as wave after wave of pleasure shook her.

She'd let him give the pleasure she knew was his to give. She'd take his kisses, his touches, his body inside hers. She'd demand he give her more and more until he lost control and they both saw stars.

This time she was under no illusions of grandeur or love or happily-ever-after.

Lucas cupped Emily's bottom and molded her against where he throbbed. His lips tasted the sweetness of her throat, his tongue nipped into the groove of her collarbone.

She wiggled, grinding her body against his, and he almost swore.

He'd had sex since their divorce. Not once had he felt this heat, this burning. Not even at the pinnacle. They'd not even removed a single item of clothing and he was bursting at the seams. For Emily.

His Emily.

With her, the burn had been about so much more. It had been a heated look, a light stroke of her finger across his skin, an accidental bump of her body against his, and he'd lose focus of everything except taking them both so high they'd never fall back to the ground.

But they had fallen back to the ground and it had been

a rough fall. One that had left Emily in constant tears and him feeling helpless to dry them.

He pulled back, cupped her face and made her look at him. "We have to stop."

Her eyes widened, then filled with anger. "No. You are not going to do this to me. You aren't going to be the one to push me away. Not this time."

The second she'd spat the words at him, regret had filled her face. She'd revealed things she hadn't wanted him to see. Things he suddenly needed to see, to understand.

"What do you mean?" He hadn't pushed her away. He'd wanted her. Always. He'd just not been able to bear the sadness he'd caused her.

"Never mind." She went to pull away, but he held her to him.

"No. I'm not leaving until you tell me."

Her body stiffened, but she didn't fight to get loose. "Then you'd best pull up a chair and make yourself comfortable, because you're in for a long wait."

Why did he feel as if he'd handled this all wrong? Maybe he was destined to always do things wrong with Emily, to always upset her and make her unhappy. Yet she was the only woman he'd ever wanted to do things right with.

"Emily, I want you."

She laughed, but it was a humorless sound that could have just as easily come from a wounded animal who'd just been kicked. "Yes, I can tell by you saying we have to stop after making me think you wanted to have sex with me."

"I do want to have sex with you."

"Would you please make up your mind? Your indecisiveness is killing me."

"I'm not being indecisive. I'm trying to do the right thing."

"Toying with my emotions by seducing me with your kiss, then pushing me away, that's your idea of doing the right thing? You really are a sick one, aren't you?"

He raked his fingers through his hair. "I guess you might see it that way, but hear me out."

"I'm all ears."

"There is nothing better I'd like to do than push you up onto that countertop and kiss you until you scream with pleasure." His hands dropped to her waist, caressed her there, as if he considered making good on his suggestion.

"But?"

"But I didn't come here for sex, Emily. I came here tonight because I wanted to be with you, because the thought of eating alone, or even with someone else, when I could be with you just wasn't acceptable. I'm here tonight because I needed your company and no one else's would do." His hands moved to her hips, pulled her flush against his hard body and worked her shirt free from her pants. "No one else has ever done. Just you."

His words were aphrodisiacs to her tortured mind and body.

"Maybe we should have just stuck with sex the first time around," she said, arching her pelvis against him and running her fingers along his shoulders.

"Maybe. Certainly, I don't want marriage again." His hands slid beneath her shirt, lighting fires in the wake of his fingers trailing over her skin. "That isn't in my future."

"You think I want marriage to a selfish jerk like you again? Wrong."

Had she really just tugged his shirt out of his waistband while calling him a selfish jerk? Was she really going for his belt?

"You're sure this is what you want?"

She got his belt buckle loose, undid the snap of his pants, his zipper. "What do you think?"

He groaned as her hands flattened against his abdomen, then moved to his hips and pushed downward on his pants. "I'll make it good for you," he promised.

"You better." He always had. From the very first time, he'd made sure she enjoyed what was happening between them.

She always had.

Emily's breath came in short, hard pants. Her heart raced. Her body was coated in a glistening sweat.

She remembered exactly why she'd allowed to happen what she'd just allowed to happen.

Sex. Good sex. Great sex. Out-of-this-world sex.

If anything, Lucas had been even better than she remembered.

He'd stripped her of her pants, her shirt, kissed every inch of her body, lingering in key places until she'd begged him for more, done her on the counter, on the kitchen table, hard against her refrigerator until they'd both orgasmed. She was pretty sure they'd permanently dented the stainless-steel door.

Now she was a sweaty mess. Naked. And wondered what she'd done.

As much as she probably should, she didn't regret having sex with Lucas.

If anything, she wanted to thank him.

She'd thought she'd lost the ability to do the things her body had just done.

She hadn't. No way, she hadn't. With Lucas, she'd felt like a sex goddess, like the queen of phenomenal sex, like a fiery siren who gave as good as she got.

"Thank you," Lucas breathed into the curve of her neck. "Thank you, Emily."

"No." She shook her head and began separating her body from his. "Thank you."

She picked up her clothes from the various places they'd landed in their fevered removal, but she didn't rush to re-dress. She didn't want him to think she was self-conscious in front of him. She wasn't. He'd seen her naked and flushed with the afterglow of sex many times before.

She'd just had sex for the sake of sex and for no other reason. Should she feel guilty or cheap?

"You were amazing."

She flicked her gaze his way. He was smiling, looking arrogant and proud and satisfied. She'd done that. She'd put that look on his face, had given as good as she'd gotten. She knew she had, that he'd been right there with her all the way right up until they'd climaxed in a loud, guttural cry.

"So were you," she admitted, starting to feel claustro-phobic as the implications of what they'd done hit her. They'd just had unprotected sex.

What had she been thinking?

What had he been thinking?

Obviously neither of them had been thinking.

Panic built within her chest. So much so that she needed him gone, needed time to think, to process what had hap-pened between them. She was on the pill, but what if some-thing went wrong and she got pregnant?

She couldn't. She just couldn't. What if…?

"I need you to leave while I go take a shower." Even to her own ears her voice sounded panicked, high-pitched.

Confusion replacing the satisfaction on his face, his brows veed together. "Huh?"

"I'm going to take a shower." She tried to sound calm. She didn't want him to know how shaken she was by their having had sex. By the fact that, since Lucas didn't know she was on oral contraceptives, he had just risked getting her pregnant, something he'd meticulously made sure to never risk while they'd been married.

She met his gaze and didn't so much as blink as she stared him down. She couldn't or the tears she was fighting might spill free. "Be gone from my apartment when I get out of the shower."

CHAPTER EIGHT

CASSIE BELLOWS'S NIGHT NURSE reported that the child had cried in pain most of the night. They'd given her medication, but even in her sleep tears had fallen.

Emily's heart twisted as she took report on the little girl. She hated the thought of the child in so much pain that she'd cried even during sleep.

"I called Dr. Cain and he'll be by this morning to check on her. He plans to get her into surgery this week."

Lucas was coming by.

Of course he was coming by. He worked there. She worked there. They'd see each other, behave professionally as if they hadn't had sweaty kitchen sex the night before, and they'd be polite.

Only, when Lucas came in, he wasn't polite. He was irritated. With her.

He should be grateful that she wasn't a wide-eyed innocent who wanted marriage, children and happily-ever-after as she'd been when they first met.

Children. Emily's breath caught and for a moment a wave of dizziness almost overtook her. Why hadn't Lucas mentioned birth control the night before? Why hadn't she thought to ask him? Why hadn't he worn a condom? He was a wealthy man, one whose parents had accused her of trying to trap him.

If only they knew the truth. If only Lucas knew.

"When was Cassie's last dose of painkiller?" he practically growled.

Emily leaned in and pointed to the computer screen.

"Right there." She tapped the screen, pulling up where the medication was recorded. He was still fairly new. Maybe he truly hadn't known. Then again, Lucas was a quick study. She would guess he knew more ins and outs of their computer system than she did after being there for years.

He studied the screen, then frowned. "I want to increase her dose." He named the quantity.

She made a mental note. "With her next dose due when?"

"Now. Give the medication," he ordered. "I don't want Cassie in pain. I'm taking her to surgery early in the morning. Even if she stays sedated most of the day, that's preferable to her crying in constant pain. I'd do surgery today if I could have gotten an operating suite and team approved." His look said he wasn't very happy that he'd been unable to. Perhaps that was why he'd been irritable when he'd joined her.

"Cassie's status changed a great deal overnight."

Looking stressed, he nodded. "As much as I hate to expose her to more imaging, I've requested an MRI brain scan that I want done stat. Whether they want to approve it or not, the operating room staff may have to find me a suite and staff today."

Part of her couldn't believe she was having a normal work conversation with the man she'd had crazy hot sex with the night before. Then again, they'd had normal conversations after having phenomenal sex in the past. So why it seemed odd to her now she wasn't sure, just that it did.

"About last night," he began, and she cringed. So much for her previous thoughts.

She shook her head. "You don't need to worry. I'm on birth control, so let's not have this conversation. Especially not at work."

The fatigue etched on his face earlier returned. "That's not what I wanted to talk about, although it probably should have been. Still, you're right. This isn't the time or place."

"Agreed." As far as she was concerned, there never would be a time or place for that conversation.

She'd rather chalk that one up to rebound sex or curiosity sex or just "spur of the moment because Lucas was hot" sex.

Right or wrong, this time she'd keep her head high rather than drowning in a thousand pitiful tears.

Sure, she'd had a moment of questioning herself when she'd walked into her kitchen, prepared to straighten up the mess from their meal only to find he'd already done so. She'd done the majority while she'd been cooking their meal, but he'd loaded their dishes into the dishwasher, wiped down the countertops and table, and her kitchen had looked as if he'd never been there.

"I'd ask you to dinner so we could talk about last night," he interrupted her thoughts, "but I may be tied up in the operating room."

"You really think something emergent has happened?" She wasn't going to bother to acknowledge how his comment affected her heart rate or her pretense of calm. Nor would she tell him that she thought their seeing each other again outside of work was a bad idea.

"With the changes in her vitals and pain level? It'll surprise me if her test doesn't come back showing something different."

"What do you suspect?" After all, the brain tumor had been there for months and months with only gradual changes in her neurological status. Cassie's condition shouldn't have changed so drastically from her tumor.

"If I didn't know better, I'd suspect a bleed. But the tumor shouldn't have caused that. She's fallen several times prior to her admission, but she's had imaging that didn't show any evidence of a bleed or fluid buildup." His words seemed to be brainstorming as much as telling her his thoughts.

As much as she didn't want to share any kind of connection to him, she liked the insight to how his mind worked, liked that she could tell he was open to any ideas she might have.

"A bleed seems the most logical explanation for a sudden change," she agreed.

"I need to get the kid into surgery, get that tumor out and find out what the unknown is."

She recalled his talking about unknowns in the past. There were the known unknowns and the unknown unknowns and the latter were the ones that in his profession were the killers. Hearing him say the word swamped her with a wave of nostalgia that she quickly shoved aside.

No more nostalgia allowed. None. Only...

She stared at him a few minutes, at the concern on his face. He sincerely cared about Cassie and her outcome.

Not that he was an uncaring person, but when he'd been in medical school, he'd seemed removed from his patients, more as if they were just case studies and diagnoses, not real people. It had struck her when she'd walked in on him doing the puzzle with Cassie. Never in the past could she have imagined him working on a puzzle with a child. Now he fretted over what was going on beneath the surface with the girl's health. He was worried about what her unknown was.

He cared. He truly cared about his patient.

The same as he cared about Jenny and had looked so protective of the child. Emily had liked that look. Which she didn't like. Because the less she liked about Lucas, the better.

They'd had their shot, hadn't worked, and the things that had torn them apart were all still there. They weren't meant to be and to let herself get caught up in the spell just being near him again wove would only lead to heartache for her.

She didn't want to think Lucas had a soft side. A vulnerable, caring side.

It was much easier to think of him as the one who'd given up on their marriage and no longer wanted her. The one who hadn't had a heart.

If she saw him as a person with a heart, didn't that mean she had to wonder what it had been about her that had caused him to push her away?

Lucas had known. Of course, in this one instance, he wished he'd been wrong.

Then again, at least seeing the pocket of fluid on Cassie's brain explained why his functioning patient from the day before had gotten into serious trouble overnight. Most likely she had a slow hemorrhage from one of her falls related to her poor balance. The poor kid couldn't seem to get a break.

He scrubbed his hands, gloved up and proceeded to the operating table where Cassie Bellows was anesthetized.

Sometimes, it still awed him that he was a brain surgeon. Him. A spoiled rich kid who'd never had any real responsibilities until he got to medical school.

Once there, he'd done just fine except for the short period of time he'd been with Emily. During that time, he'd had a neurosurgeon mentor pull him aside and tell him he'd best get his act together or he was going to make a mistake that could be detrimental to his patients' lives and Lucas's career.

One thing he'd always known was that he didn't want to follow in his financial guru father's wealthy footsteps. He'd wanted to follow his own path and life calling, to make a positive difference in the world. When in high school a classmate had suffered TBI from a football injury, Lucas had become fascinated with the boy's care and known that was what he wanted to do with his life. Perhaps living off his parents' money while achieving that hadn't been making his own way in many people's eyes, but, until Emily, Lucas had never questioned his right to do so. It was what he'd grown up expected to do.

Emily had made him feel guilty for living an easy life. Wasn't that what his parents wanted for him? What they'd worked to give him? Should he have refused their help, left his trust funds untouched and struggled? What purpose would that have served? He was an only child, his parents loved him, and they'd not understood Emily's aversion to their help, especially since they'd been so suspicious of her motives. Still, other than with educational expenses, he'd abided by the rules Emily had set about taking money from his parents.

He still didn't agree with Emily, but time had given him the ability to at least have a better understanding. Perhaps she'd wanted him to have a better understanding of who she was, of where she'd come from, to where they had more insight into each other's world.

Either way, it had been his inability to juggle a depressed new wife along with his other obligations that had been the big problem, not his parents' money.

He'd tried to stop Emily's tears but had only seemed to

make them worse. Being around her, knowing he'd caused her unhappiness, had left him feeling impotent. When he'd catch glimpses of her at the hospital, she seemed fine. Only around him did the waterworks start. So he'd stayed away more and more, focused on the things he had control over and hoped his wife would kick out of her depression.

Instead, she had started talking babies almost nonstop.

He'd full out panicked. What little time he'd had away from studies, he'd spent away from her and the longing he could see in her eyes for something he simply couldn't give her. Not at that point in their marriage, which was something she hadn't seemed to understand or accept. He knew people managed a lot more than what had been on his plate, but, for him, he'd already felt he was halfway doing too many things.

What if her depression had gotten worse? What if she hadn't been able to deal with a baby and he'd had to take on that load, too? He'd have made it work, but he'd worried about the effects on Emily. Which had affected him. Affected them. They'd grown further apart. He'd wanted to make Emily happy, had tried to. Instead, she'd gone into deeper despair and refused to seek help.

He'd failed on all counts.

Here he was scrubbing up for surgery and distracted from what he was doing by memories from the past. He needed to put Emily out of his head. Far, far out of his head until he finished with Cassie's surgery.

Which proved a little more difficult than he would have thought when he walked into the surgical suite. Despite the fact he could see only her green eyes beneath her surgical gear, he immediately recognized her. Emily was in the operating room.

What was she doing there and why?

* * *

Emily had started out in the operating room at Children's. It had been the only job opening when she'd applied. She'd been desperate to escape working with Lucas every day and had taken the first offer that had presented itself.

Which made her recognize the irony of her volunteering to go into the operating room with him this evening. Truly, she'd come full circle.

She'd had only an hour left on her shift. The hospital had been scrambling to put together a team for the operating room, and before she'd been able to give better thought to it, she'd volunteered to work overtime and assist.

Since Jenny had remained stable, and Cassie was her only other patient, getting the okay for Emily to go into the surgical suite had been an easy process and one the hospital had appreciated her doing.

Now that she was here, watching Lucas drill a hole into the child's skull, she wondered if she'd been too hasty.

As gruesome as some of the surgeries she'd assisted in were, that aspect didn't bother Emily. She knew what they were doing was to Cassie's benefit and without the procedure the child's odds of survival were poor.

If she did survive, the longer surgery was delayed, the higher the risk of permanent brain damage.

It was watching the precision and expertise with which Lucas worked that was getting to her. Her gaze kept wandering to him.

She performed her job duties with remembered ease, always there to hand him what he needed, to assist in any way, along with the others assisting with the procedure.

When Lucas located the tiny hemorrhage that was causing so many problems, when he got the bleed stopped, he sighed in relief. He looked up, sought her gaze, and although she couldn't see more than his eyes, she saw so much.

The relief, the fear that had been eased. He'd cared about Cassie, cared that he took good care of her. She wasn't a number or a case study. She was a child who'd been assigned to his care. He took that seriously.

Emily was glad.

So glad that she smiled at him. Not that he could see her beneath the mask, but maybe he knew because she'd swear he smiled back even though she couldn't see his mouth beneath the surgical mask, either.

What was happening? She did not want to feel any kind of bond with Lucas. Not physical, not emotional, not professional, not any.

Yet, at this moment, she felt as if time had never passed and she was looking into the eyes of the man who'd stolen her heart rather than the one who'd broken it.

When her doorbell rang later that night, Emily wasn't surprised by who was on the other side of her viewer despite the late hour.

Nor was she truly surprised by the fact she opened the door to let him in.

"I know it's almost midnight, but…" he said, stepping inside, looking tired and a bit forlorn, as if he wasn't sure he should be there, but that he hadn't been able to stay away.

She understood.

So when he took her in his arms and kissed her, she kissed him right back. Why not? It was just sex. Really, really good, hot sex. Or so she kept telling herself because no way would she let herself consider for even the remotest possibility that she could be falling back under Lucas's spell.

He kissed her, held her, breathed her in as if he was

starved for everything about her. She understood. She felt the same.

They made it to her bed, remembering the condom this time, and reached just as high heights as they had the night before. When they'd climaxed and Emily lay there trying to catch her breath, Lucas stroked his fingers over her lower back, tracing the dip right above her buttocks.

He was so good, such a perfect lover. Only, he wasn't her lover. Not really. He was a man she was having sex with whom, if she wasn't careful, she would end up being destroyed by again. She couldn't let herself fall into the trap of thinking they had a second chance. To do that would be foolish and asking for trouble.

Within minutes, his breathing evened out and she realized he'd dozed off. Panic hit her. She rolled over onto her side to face him and shook his shoulders. "You can't go to sleep. You have to leave."

"I know." But he didn't open his eyes.

He'd looked so tired when he'd arrived that she felt guilty. It was long after midnight.

But she couldn't sleep with Lucas. She couldn't snuggle up next to him and close her eyes and drift off into sleep, expecting to wake next to him. For one, what if he was gone when she woke? How devastating would that be? But even more important, what kind of expectations would her heart attach to waking next to Lucas? To sleep next to the man she'd once thought she'd spend the rest of her life sleeping next to, to wake next to the man she'd once given all her love to, was just too intimate. She couldn't do it.

With more gusto, she shook him again. "Lucas, you need to get out of my bed. You can't stay here."

His eyes opened and he frowned.

"Why not? What does it matter?" Lucas asked, yawning as he stretched in her bed and looked way too perfect as the covers slipped low on his waist.

Fighting to keep her gaze trained on his face, she assured him, "It matters."

"Why?"

Why? Such an innocent question, but the answers ran much deeper than she could ever elaborate.

"I don't want you here," she answered as simply as she could. Perhaps a grand oversimplification, but she didn't want him there.

"You wanted me here a few minutes ago," he reminded her, rolling onto his side and grinning sleepily at her.

"That was just sex."

Lord, she hoped what they'd shared was just sex on her part. She couldn't go through another round of heartbreak. She'd barely survived the first time.

Just sex. The words rankled Lucas. Just sex. He didn't want anything permanent. So just sex should be fine. So why did her claim irritate him?

What he did want was her friendship back. He'd always been able to talk to her, to share his thoughts, to tell her things that had happened throughout the day. Right up until they'd gotten married, that was. Then their communication skills had gone missing. Eventually, they'd been leading completely separate lives.

How had that happened between him and the woman he'd been so crazy about?

He reached out and ran his fingertip over her bare hip. She was beautiful. Ethereal even. "You're sure you don't want me to stay?"

"Positive." She climbed out of the bed and handed him his underwear to prove her point.

"Have you eaten?"

She nodded. "I heated up something when I got home."

He saw the hesitation on her face, the battle that took place prior to her asking, "Did you?"

He shook his head. "I'm starved."

Her shoulders stiffened and again war waged within her. "There's a twenty-four-hour Chinese takeout that's pretty good on the corner."

Sitting up on the side of the bed, he nodded. He could take a hint. She really did want him to leave.

"Or I could heat up some leftovers from last night."

"Liver, broccoli and asparagus after midnight?"

She nodded.

What was wrong with him that he'd rather eat his three least favorite foods in the early-morning hours than go get Chinese takeout?

"Okay, sounds good." He wasn't lying. The thought of spending more time with her did sound good.

Because he wanted more from Emily than just sex.

He always had wanted more from Emily than just sex.

He wanted her in his life.

Just this time, they wouldn't make the mistake of marriage.

Why had Emily offered to heat up leftovers for Lucas? She berated herself over and over as she pulled plastic containers from her refrigerator.

She should have made him leave. He was a big boy. He wouldn't have starved. He'd obviously been feeding himself for the past five years just fine without her.

He'd been doing just fine on a lot of things without her.

Because his body was honed to a lean muscle machine. He'd always been fit, but he'd taken his physique to a higher level.

Which she'd thoroughly appreciated when it came to

the man's endurance and stamina. He was a truly phenomenal lover.

Not because of his body, although that was certainly easy on the eye. No, it was what he did to her body, how he looked at her as if she were the most desirable thing he'd ever seen, as if he couldn't kiss her, touch her, be inside of her nearly enough if he spent the rest of his life trying. It was in the combination of desperation, awe and tenderness in which he touched her. As if she were precious and he couldn't quite believe he was with her, touching her. Those were the things that made him a phenomenal lover.

He made her feel special.

He had before, too.

Which was how she'd ended up giving him her virginity despite the fact she'd intended to wait until marriage. An outdated view, she knew and openly admitted, but she'd thought it a gift she'd wanted to save for her husband.

She'd been as desperate for consummation as he'd been and they'd never even discussed marriage on the afternoon he'd surprised her by coming by her apartment earlier than expected. She'd been reading a nursing magazine and he'd walked in, kissed her, and even before they'd gone to her bedroom, she'd known she wasn't going to stop him that time as she had before. She'd known she was desperately in love with him and wanted him to be her first even if she'd known he was wildly out of her league.

He'd proposed a month later and they'd married the month after that. Everything had been rushed, but it had been what Lucas had wanted and she'd been so ecstatic that she'd just gone along for the ride.

In hindsight, she realized she should have known better.

They'd been as different as night and day.

"What are you thinking about?"

She spun toward his voice. "Why?"

"Because you've been standing there opening and closing that plastic lid over and over for the past five minutes."

"Oh." But she didn't tell him she'd been thinking about them. She probably didn't have to. After the past two nights, he probably had a pretty good idea what weighed on her mind. "I don't like you, you know."

"That's what you were thinking about?"

"I don't want to date you," she added, ignoring his question.

"Okay." He didn't argue.

"Our having sex again is a very bad idea."

"Probably."

She swapped the bowl in the microwave out for the one she held. "I don't like you."

"You've already said that."

"I just wanted to make sure we were clear."

"Why don't you like me, Emily?"

"Because…" Because he'd broken her heart into a zillion pieces that had never completely fit back together no matter how she'd tried. Because he was so freaking perfect and she was just her. Because… "You're my ex-husband. I'm not supposed to like you."

"Says who?"

"Says everyone."

"Since when did you listen to what everyone says?" he challenged.

"Don't act like you know me. I've changed a lot the past five years."

His gaze skimmed over her from her face down her T-shirt, gym shorts, and then over her legs to her bare feet. It was all she could do to hold her toes still rather than shuffle her feet at his inspection.

"You haven't changed that much."

"Maybe not on the surface, but inside I've changed

a lot." The microwave dinged, indicating the bowl was heated, but she didn't remove it, just stared at him, refusing to let her gaze waver. "I'm not an innocent kid anymore that it's easy for some smooth-talking man to come along and take advantage of."

"Is that how you saw me back then? As a smooth-talking man who took advantage of your innocence?"

Did she? Not really. "You were definitely more experienced in the ways of life than I was."

"A rock was more experienced in the ways of life than you were."

She wasn't sure if she should be offended or not.

"Good thing I decided to go out and get a life." She turned, took the bowl out of the microwave, grateful the dish was still warm. "I'll let you take out however much you want. You may need to throw your plate back into the microwave for a few minutes, though."

"Why did you open your apartment door, Emily? For sex?"

Why did he think she'd opened the door?

"We have nothing in common, have no desire to build a future together, no history we want to repeat. The only thing we have between us is good sex. Of course sex is why I opened my apartment door. Now, hurry up and finish your food so you can leave. I'm tired and scheduled to work tomorrow."

Her words sounded so logical, so like she believed them. If only she did. If only when she looked at him she didn't long for things that would never be.

CHAPTER NINE

CASSIE WAS STILL in a medication-induced coma when Emily took report the following morning. She was grateful the child didn't seem to be in pain or suffering. Her poor mother, on the other hand, was a wreck when Emily checked on the girl.

"When will she wake up?" the woman asked from where she sat next to Cassie's bed.

"That depends on a lot of things. For right now, Dr. Cain believes it's in her best interest to keep her unconscious to give her more time to recover from her procedure."

"She's not going to know anything, is she?"

A scary question, because the increased intracranial pressure from the bleed had only complicated things that were already complicated enough.

"There's really not a way to know at this point. I do know Dr. Cain is very hopeful that she won't have lost any major body function or thought processes."

"She might not know who I am when she wakes up," Mrs. Bellows cried. "Do you know how horrible that will be if my baby wakes up and doesn't know who I am? And this isn't even it. Once she recovers from this, she'll still have to have the tumor removed. Life is so unfair."

Cassie's mother began sobbing. Emily stopped what she was doing and held her, letting her cry on her shoulder.

"Dr. Cain is an excellent neurosurgeon. From everything he said, he views the surgery as a success. Let's wait and see how Cassie is when she wakes up before we borrow trouble," she soothed. "She's going to need you to be strong for her."

Who was she to tell this woman to be strong? She'd never dealt with a child who had to have brain surgery. She'd never gotten to deal with a living, breathing child at all, which wrenched her heart with a grief she rarely let rear its ugly head. Sometimes she felt so inadequate at her job. Sometimes she wished she had the power to instantly heal her patients.

"I know she is going to need me," Cassie's mother agreed. "I want to be strong, but this is hard."

"I can only imagine," she answered honestly. "All Cassie's vitals held during the night and this morning, too. Everything is stable. That's a blessing."

The woman nodded. "I'm just being impatient, wanting her to wake up and be normal."

"Hopefully, that's exactly where she will be soon."

Both women jumped at the voice joining their conversation.

"Dr. Cain."

"Lucas," Emily said at the same time, then corrected herself. "Dr. Cain, we didn't hear you come in."

"I see that." He smiled empathetically at Cassie's mother but didn't look at Emily. "How's our girl this morning?"

"The same as last night when you stopped by about two."

He'd come back to the hospital after leaving her apartment? Did the man sleep? While they'd been married, she'd often wondered how he pulled the long hours he did, how he got by on so little sleep.

"Thank you for that, by the way," Mrs. Bellows continued. "You sitting with me meant a lot."

Not only had he stopped by, but he'd stayed and sat with Cassie's mother. Why? Seemed she asked that question a lot where Lucas was concerned these days.

She stared at him, taking in his dark navy scrubs that did little to hide his abundant sex appeal. His dark hair was ruffled, whether by the wind or from running his fingers through the silky tufts she wasn't sure.

She'd run her fingers through his hair the night before. She'd… No, she was not going to go there.

What little sleep he'd gotten the night before must have been in the doctors' lounge. Why?

"If there's nothing you need from me, Dr. Cain, I'm going to check on my other patient," Emily said, needing to get away from him, away from her questions.

"Sorry I went all boo-hoo on you," Cassie's mother apologized, rising from her chair and giving Emily a quick hug.

"Not a problem." She hugged the woman tightly, then didn't wait for Lucas to say anything, just exited the room as quickly as she could without causing a commotion.

"What have you been up to? Because you look guilty as sin," Meghan pointed out the moment Emily stepped into the hallway.

With a backward glance toward Cassie's room, she shushed her friend. "Nothing."

"Right. That's why your cheeks are all flushed and your eyes have a light in them that I never saw Richard put there."

"Shh!" she repeated. "I don't have a light in my eyes unless it's tears from how much my heart hurts from what my patient and her family are going through."

"Sorry, I heard about Cassie's brain bleed and how you

volunteered as a surgical nurse last night near the end of your shift." Meghan's gaze cut back toward Cassie's room. "He's in there, isn't he?"

"I've no idea where Richard is." She purposely misunderstood. She didn't want to talk about Lucas, not even with Meghan. "I told you we ended things."

"I wasn't referring to your pharmacist and you know it."

Emily sighed. She should have known Meghan wouldn't let her get away with that one. Still, at least she'd bought a few seconds to collect herself a little.

She grabbed her friend's arm and walked her away from Cassie's room. "Yes, I know who you mean, and yes, he is in there, and no, I don't want to talk about him."

An "I knew it" smile spread across Meghan's face. "You had sex with him, didn't you?"

"What?"

Meghan gave her a no-brainer look. "Don't bother denying it, because I know you did. I've never seen you look so twitterpated."

"I am not twitterpated. If that's even a word."

"Sure it's a word. Didn't you ever watch that kids' cartoon with the deer?"

She frowned.

"And you, my friend, are twitterpated."

"If that means I'm aggravated at you for making wild accusations, then yep, I am."

"I note you said wild and not false."

Knowing she was fighting a losing battle, she just shrugged and stared at her friend.

Meghan's mouth dropped open and her eyes sparkled with animation. "You did. You had sex with Dr. Cain. Was he as awesome as he looks like he'd be?"

Would the floor please open up and swallow her now?

"I'm not answering that and would you please whisper? I don't want anyone to overhear you."

"You don't have to answer." Meghan looked as if she might burst with excitement. Seriously, had her friend disliked Richard that much? "I can tell by your face."

Emily glanced around the busy hospital hallway. "This is not where we should be having this conversation."

"Then let's go have dinner together after we get off work this evening. You can tell me everything."

Emily didn't meet her friend's eyes.

"You can't, can you? Because you're seeing him?"

Emily shrugged again. "We don't have any specific plans."

"But you're hoping you'll see him?" Meghan guessed again.

"I suspect I will."

How ridiculous was she being? She was not going to go home and wait around in hopes that Lucas would show up for another round of sex. She just wasn't.

Yet that was exactly what she'd been thinking when she'd not agreed to Meghan's suggestion.

"Let's do it," she said, unwilling to start the "sitting around waiting on him" bit. She'd been there and done that years ago. "Where do you want to meet?"

Meghan arched a brow. "You're sure?"

"Absolutely."

How pathetic was Lucas that he was knocking on Emily's apartment door hoping to be invited back into her bed?

Pretty pathetic.

So why was he still standing there?

Because he was crazy about her.

He hadn't meant to fall for Emily again, but he was hooked. If he hadn't realized before, when she'd thrown him out the previous night he had realized how much he wanted to stay. How much he wanted her to want him to stay.

And not just for sex.

Are you home? he texted, leaning back against her apartment door frame and wondering at his current state of sanity, or lack thereof.

Nope, came her almost instant reply.

She wasn't home. At least she hadn't been ignoring him.

Where are you?

On a date.

On a date? His stomach knotted.

With the pharmacy guy?

Nope. We broke up. This date is a lot hotter.

You're on a date with yourself?

He was trying to tease her into telling him who she was with, trying to curb the jealousy surging through his veins.

Not hardly.

Lucas gripped his phone in his hands a lot tighter than he should. Emily was on a date and was being vague about who she was with. How could she be on a date after having sex with him the night before? The night before that, too?

Then again, he had no claims on her. Just a strong desire to be with her and the inability to stay away.

My date says you should join us.

Lucas blinked at his phone.

Your date wants your ex-husband to join you?

Doesn't know about you. No one does, remember?

How could he forget? She'd completely erased all traces of him from her life. Which he supposed was what he'd done with her, too. Yet he didn't like that their time together had been completely obliterated.

You should tell him, he suggested, trying to squelch his jealousy.

Not a him.

Not a... Why did relief flood him that she wasn't with another man just hours after being with him? Because he wanted her.

All of her.

Just for him.

I'm with Meghan.

The pretty brunette nurse who worked on the pediatric neuro floor who'd been with Emily the night of the fundraiser. He'd seen her around the hospital and always made a point to say hi.

Where are you?

She told him the name of a club a couple blocks away.

I'll be right there.

* * *

"He's on his way," Emily stage-whispered to Meghan, leaning across the bar table to give her friend a pleading look. "Now what?"

"Now you get to have some fun with Dr. Yummy Tummy."

"How do you know his tummy is yummy?"

Meghan giggled. "Well, isn't it?"

Yes, Lucas's stomach was pretty yummy. Pretty cut. Pretty six-packed.

She sighed. "I shouldn't have invited him here."

"Why not?"

"Because it's our night."

"Emily, I love you, hun, but you've not been with me since we got here."

"Huh?"

"Don't think I haven't noticed that you've checked your phone every two minutes, and when he finally texted, you almost passed out with relief."

Her shoulders sagging, she squished up her nose. "I did, didn't I?"

Her friend nodded. "So tell me about him. Besides the obvious."

"The obvious?"

"That he's hot and has the hots for you."

"Obviously, I have the hots for him, too," she admitted, wondering at how much she should tell Meghan. She and the woman had instantly hit it off when Emily had started at Children's and their friendship had grown over the years. She loved Meghan, but telling her, telling anyone, about Lucas made her nervous. Still, she needed an objective opinion and there was no one she trusted more than Meghan.

"Obviously." Her friend laughed, taking a sip of her drink.

Emily followed suit, taking a small sip of her diet soda and a huge leap of faith. "I used to be married to him."

"What?" The loud music and dim lights did nothing to hide Meghan's shock.

Emily swirled the contents of her glass. "He's my ex-husband."

Meghan looked floored. "Dr. Cain is your ex-husband? The one you were devastated by when you started at Children's? The one who it took you years to get past and start dating again? That ex-husband?"

Toying with the tiny straw in her drink, Emily nodded. "Yep, he used to be all mine."

Which sounded an awful lot like she wanted him to be all hers again, because, seriously, she could have just said "yes, that ex-husband," right?

She didn't want him to be all hers again. Did she?

She couldn't. To want that would be begging for heartache and tears.

Only…

Meghan let the implications sink in. "Did he know you worked at Children's when he accepted the position?"

"He knew. He said my being there was his only hesitation with accepting."

Meghan's forehead wrinkled. "I don't understand. Why would he buy your date at the auction if you were what made him hesitate on accepting the position?"

"Because he's here to torture me." Okay, so that was an exaggeration, but being near Lucas, kissing him, having sex with him, all of it was torture because she knew it was temporary.

Meghan's brow arched. "Seriously?"

Emily took another sip of her soda. "Actually, I don't really understand why he bought my date. He says he wants for us to get along and not be awkward at work, but he didn't have to win my bid if that's what he wanted. I've never been able to resist him long."

"Maybe he didn't think you'd ever let him close enough without the forced time together."

"Maybe. Regardless, he's close enough now. Too close." What had she done? "Meghan, what am I going to do when we quit having sex?" Quit having sex because, really, she couldn't call it dating. They'd gone out to eat at Stluka's, she'd cooked for him, and they'd had sex twice. That didn't exactly qualify as boyfriend/girlfriend. She didn't want Lucas to be her boyfriend. She'd been there, done that and had the divorce papers to prove it. "The last time he and I got involved, I ended up leaving my job. I love my job at Children's. I'd prefer not to change jobs every time he shows up in my life."

Meghan shrugged. "Then don't change jobs."

If only it were that simple.

"You don't understand what it was like after we split and I had to go to work knowing I'd see glimpses of him there…" Her voice trailed off. She'd dreaded each and every day. Had wondered how he could see her and not know the great loss within her. The grief and suffering she felt every moment of every day and seeing him going on about his life had only added to her pain and loss. She'd quickly known she couldn't continue working there and had turned in her notice. Starting work at Children's had been a godsend.

"I knew you had been married before, but you never wanted to talk about it, so I never asked." Meghan winced, then took a sip of her drink. "I remember how sad you looked when you first started. The first time I ever saw you, I wanted to hug you and beat the crap out of who-ever had hurt you."

"Our friendship was formed on pity?"

Meghan shook her head. "Our friendship was formed based upon the person you are being someone I came to love. You're a great friend, Emily."

"Even though I never told you about Lucas?"

"I wish you'd felt you could tell me, but I understand why you didn't, why you wouldn't want to talk about him at all. He hurt you a lot, didn't he?"

Lucas had hurt her a lot, but what had come later had hurt so much more. Still hurt so much. One never got over that kind of hurt, she supposed.

"I guess in some ways we hurt each other."

"Are you sure getting involved with him again is a good idea? I mean, he's superhot and all, but aren't you afraid you'll end up getting hurt again?" Meghan reached across the bar table and touched Emily's hand. "Maybe we should leave before he gets here. I don't want to see you hurt."

She shook her head. "I'm not going to let him hurt me again."

Her friend didn't look convinced. "How are you going to stop him?"

Emily lifted her chin a notch. "Because this time I'm the one in control. I'm the one telling him to leave instead of the other way around."

Meghan blinked. "He told you to leave?"

Unable to give voice to that particular memory, Emily nodded.

Meghan stared at her as if she'd lost her mind.

Possibly, she had. But when her gaze collided with that of the man who was making his way toward their table, she admitted that rational thought didn't matter because she wanted him too much to stop this craziness.

From the moment he'd bought her bachelorette date, her fate had been sealed. Maybe from the moment she'd first met him, her fate had been sealed. Lord knew that even though she'd convinced herself she could be happy and content with a man like Richard, deep down she wondered if she would have been. Would anyone other than the man intently making his way toward her table do?

"He's here."

"You want me to leave?" Meghan offered, suddenly looking nervous.

Emily grabbed her friend's hand. "Please don't. Make me show some restraint, because when I look at that man, I just want to rip his clothes off with my teeth."

Meghan looked toward him and groaned. "Emily, a lot of women want to rip that man's clothes off with their teeth when they look at him. No offense, but he's easy on the eyes to say the least."

He was easy on the eyes. Clothed and unclothed.

She sighed. "What am I going to do?"

"What do you want to do?"

"I've already told you what I want to do. That's the problem."

Meghan grinned, then made a chomping motion.

Emily rolled her eyes but smiled at her friend.

"Why not? Obviously, he's good at what he does. Just so long as you stay in control and remember that he's bad for you regarding anything but physical gratification, why not use him for good sex?"

Why not indeed?

Other than that she'd never been the kind of girl to have sex just for the sake of sex.

Well, not until now.

Now that was exactly what she had been doing, right? No matter what lay in the recesses of her heart, she knew she and Lucas had no future. Yet she'd had sex with him the past two nights. She'd have a torrid affair with her ex-husband, let him rock her world, then she'd send his butt home night after night because to allow him to stay would change the dynamics of their relationship. She'd keep everything neatly within the physical rather than the emotional.

"Hello, Dr. Cain," Meghan greeted as he joined their table. She motioned to one of the tall bar chairs next to the table. "Have a seat."

CHAPTER TEN

LUCAS PULLED UP a chair to Emily and Meghan's table. Both women stared at him in a way that made him wonder if he had something stuck between his teeth or had developed a huge zit on the end of his nose.

First running his hand across his face, just in case, he motioned to the bartender and ordered a cold one.

When he turned back, both women were still staring.

"Am I missing something?"

"What makes you ask that?" Emily asked, taking a drink from the glass she held.

"You two are making me nervous."

"Who—us?" Meghan hooked her arm with Emily's, then laughed. "Then again, we get that a lot." She winked at Emily. "That we make men nervous."

Emily snorted. "Yep. All the time. Every time we come here, in fact."

He took in the two friends. Meghan was a pretty woman, but Emily was beautiful. So much so that just looking at her made his heart hiccup.

"Two beautiful women, I'd say you do make men nervous," he agreed.

"But not you?" Emily asked, watching him over the rim of her glass.

She made him nervous as hell. He knew the devastation this woman could cause in his life. The devastation of wanting so desperately to make her happy and not being able to.

"Should I be nervous?"

"Definitely." This came from Meghan. "And so should that delicious guy who keeps smiling at me from the bar. You two have fun. I'm going to go see how nervous I can make him by asking him to buy me a drink."

Emily and Lucas watched Meghan sidle up to the bar and indeed ask the guy who'd been staring at their table to buy her a drink.

"He looks happy to oblige."

The guy did, ecstatic even.

"Do you want something else to drink?" Lucas offered.

"No. I'm good. Haven't finished this one yet." She held up her glass that was about a third full still. "I imagine I always will be a lightweight, so much so that this is soda."

He'd figured that.

"You still go out and party with the crew every chance you get?"

He thought about her question. He did go out on occasion to hang with his friends. Those times were further and further apart and not at all since he'd joined the staff at Children's. Not that the gang didn't still get together routinely, but that he just had other things he preferred doing.

"I still see them," he admitted, not bothering to explain further.

"I imagined so."

Something in her tone had him studying her a little closer. "Did you not like my friends, Emily?"

Her cheeks pinkened. "I never said that."

She didn't have to. The truth was written all over her

lovely face. "You rarely wanted to go with me. It never occurred to me that it was because you didn't like my friends."

"Drinking and partying was never my thing."

True. She hadn't ever seemed to enjoy attending parties or hanging with his friends. He'd hoped she'd eventually relax around them. She never had.

"What was your thing?"

She hesitated a moment, then whispered so low he read her lips more than heard her. "You."

Her answer humbled him. He'd been such a fool. How could he have had her in his life, had her love and affection, and lost it? Of all the things he'd ever failed at, losing Emily topped the list.

He shouldn't have married her to begin with, and he sure shouldn't have divorced her once he had.

"I made a lot of mistakes, didn't I?"

Glancing away, she shrugged. "We both did."

"I didn't appreciate what I had, Emily."

She stared into her almost empty glass, then took one last sip. "Most people don't until they lose something."

"True." He didn't know what to say. He hadn't appreciated it that he'd gotten to wake up next to her each morning, that he'd gotten to go to sleep next to her at night. That at any point in between he could call her and hear her lovely voice tell him she loved him.

"Let's dance," she suggested, placing her now empty glass on the tabletop.

"Okay." Any excuse to have her in his arms would do.

He held her close, loving the way she fit next to his body, loving the way when he breathed in her sweet vanilla scent filled his nostrils.

They danced the slow song, then several upbeat ones

that put a sexy sheen to Emily's skin. One that he wished he'd caused from other movements of their bodies together.

"Hey, guys, I'm outta here." Meghan interrupted their dancing. "I've got to be at work bright and early in the morning."

Emily hugged her friend goodbye. "You want me to walk with you to your apartment?"

Meghan shook her head. "I'm fine. You stay and have fun."

"What about you?" Lucas asked. "You want to stay here for a while or are you ready to go to your apartment?"

"I'm not on schedule tomorrow."

"Does that mean you want to stay?"

She met his gaze, her lips slightly parted. "What do you want, Lucas?"

For her to say his name until they were both satiated. To hold her in his arms and wake up beside her and do it all over again. Day after day. Night after night.

Where the thought came from, Lucas didn't question. Just that his whole mind filled with the overpowering response.

"Whatever you want is fine, Emily. Just so long as I get to be with you."

Emily frowned at Lucas's answer. Why, she wasn't sure. Just that it was sweet and she didn't want sweet from him.

She wanted to keep him neatly compartmentalized.

"Let's go back to my apartment."

"If that's what you want."

"That would be why I suggested it," she snapped, then instantly felt bad. He hadn't done anything wrong. She knew that. "Sorry."

"Are you okay, Emily?"

"Fine." But she was lying. To herself. To Meghan. To

him. She might want to stay in control of her feelings for Lucas, but to think that was what she was doing was just downright hilarious.

She laughed. Then again.

"How many of those did you have?"

Not realizing what he meant at first, she thought of the empty soda glass she'd left on the table. "One."

"Lightweight," he accused, one corner of his mouth tugging upward.

"I'm not drunk. I told you, it was soda."

"I'm glad."

"Why?"

"Because I wouldn't have sex with a drunk woman."

"Not ever?"

"Never. Where's the pleasure in that?"

"Is that what sex is about to you?" she asked. "Pleasure?"

"Pleasure plays a big role," he admitted, his fingers tracing over her lower back. "What's sex about to you, Emily?"

"Pleasure. Nothing more," she immediately answered, refusing to give the question more thought. "Just pleasure."

Which she was feeling with her body pressed up against his. When was the music going to change back to something upbeat?

"Yet you were having sex with a man who didn't give you physical pleasure," he pointed out.

Her feet stilled. "I never said Richard didn't give me physical pleasure."

Nor did she recall telling him she'd been having sex with Richard, although maybe she had.

"Did he?"

She frowned. "You don't hear me asking about the women you've been with since our divorce, do you? You have no right to ask me about Richard or any other man."

"Have there been others, Emily?" he asked, whether he had the right or not. His body had stiffened against hers, as if he were bracing himself for her answer.

She was tempted to lie, to say that there had been dozens, many men who shamed him as a lover. But she'd never been much on untruths.

"No." She didn't elaborate.

"I'm glad."

Frustration ran up and down her spine. She pulled back to glare at him. "Really? You're glad that in the past five years I've had one lover besides you? How absolutely selfish is that when I've no doubt you've had dozens of women."

"There haven't been dozens of women, Emily." He closed his eyes, took a deep breath. "I'll be the first to admit I have no right to feel jealous of any man touching you—I gave up that right—but, Emily, I do. The thought of you being with anyone other than me rips me up inside."

"Don't say that."

"Why not?"

"Because we both know that whatever this is between us right now, it's temporary, and I don't intend to spend my life alone. There will be other men, Lucas. Someday. Maybe I'll get lucky and meet someone who can give me all the things I want first thing after you, but, if not, then I'm okay with having a few hot affairs first."

"No."

"No?"

He let out an exasperated breath. "What is it you want from a man, Emily?"

"From you or from some other man?"

"Both."

"From you, sex."

He nodded as if he knew that was going to be her answer.

"From other men?" She shrugged. "Someday, I want to meet a man whom I can have a good life with, a couple of kids, go to parent-teacher meetings and soccer games, that kind of thing."

Kids. Her heart squeezed. Would she ever have children? Did she even want to risk pregnancy again? What if she couldn't carry a pregnancy to full-term?

"You deserve that."

Oh, Lucas. If only…

"I know. I do," she agreed, wondering if there was ever a way to repair the hurt once so much had piled up on a person.

"But not with me?"

Her breath caught. "What are you saying, Lucas? You don't want those things. You don't even want kids."

He frowned. "I never said I didn't want kids."

"Sure you did," she reminded him, her fingertips curling into her palms. "When I mentioned having a baby, you shut me down real fast."

"We'd only been married a few months, Emily. You were just starting your nursing career. I was finishing up my fellowship. We were still figuring out married life. You were unhappy and I was stressed. The last thing we needed was a baby."

"Then I guess it's a good thing we didn't have one." She pulled away, unable to stand being in his arms another minute, unable to suppress the memories she never let rise to the surface. Memories she'd done her best to forget altogether.

Blindly, she made her way through the crowd on the dance floor toward the exit. She needed air.

When she stepped outside the club, she gulped in big breaths of air laced with the smell of hot dogs, pretzels and whatever else the street vendors had going.

Her heart pounded in her chest and her lungs couldn't get enough air. Why hadn't she just not answered his text? That would have been for the best. Instead, they'd gone down a conversation path she'd never wanted to take.

"Emily?"

Why had he followed her? She'd known he'd follow her. Of course he would. He'd come to the club because she was there.

She didn't open her eyes.

"Emily?"

"Go away, Lucas."

"No."

She opened her eyes. "You told me you'd leave if I asked you to."

"That was before."

"Before?"

He paused, seeming to search for the right words. "What happened back there?"

"What do you mean?"

"Your skin went green, and if I didn't know better, I'd have thought you were going to be ill. You told me you didn't have anything but soda. That shouldn't have made you sick. So tell me, what happened in there?"

"There are some things we just shouldn't talk about."

"So you were okay talking about our past lovers but not your perception that I didn't want children? Your false perception, I might add."

"No, I wasn't okay with talking about our past lovers or my perceptions. I'm not okay with any of this."

She pulled away and started walking down the street in the direction of her apartment. Her building wasn't far.

"I don't want to fight with you, Emily. I never wanted to fight with you," Lucas said from beside her just outside her apartment door.

"Odd, that's what we seem to do best."

"That's not what we do best."

"Then too bad we can't just stay naked all the time, eh?"

"Well, it's a safe bet to say you'd win every argument if that were the case."

She shook her head. "Don't make light of this, Lucas."

He touched her face, running his fingers along the edge of her hair, then cupping her nape. "I'm sorry, Emily. For whatever it was I said wrong inside the club, I am sorry. For every mistake I ever made where you are concerned, I'm sorry. Forgive me."

She wasn't sure she could if she wanted to, but that didn't stop her body from melting against his when he pulled her inside her apartment and kissed her.

CHAPTER ELEVEN

CASSIE BELLOWS REGAINED consciousness at some point during the night.

Apparently, Cassie's nurse had called Lucas, because he was there and in Cassie's room when Emily arrived at the hospital and took report from the night nurse.

"He's in with her right now. Has been for a while. He's such a great doctor. He's going to be a great father someday."

Emily's heart squeezed so tight in her chest that she thought she might pass out. She didn't respond to the nurse's comment. There was no need. Amy was still going on and on about Dr. Cain's many fabulous features.

"I bet you were ecstatic when he bought your TBI basket."

"Ecstatic," she agreed to keep Amy from digging deeper if she told the truth about how she'd felt about Lucas buying her basket. She liked Amy but wasn't close enough to the woman to be sharing intimate details of her life. She still felt a little nervous that she'd told Meghan about who Lucas was. She didn't want her friend's pity should things go wrong.

"How a good-looking guy like him hasn't been snapped up by some smart woman is beyond me."

"Looks aren't everything," she mumbled under her breath, not really meaning for Amy to catch her words.

"Yeah, but that man is the total package. Looks, intelligence, sense of humor, compassion and money. A girl could do a lot worse."

Ugh. How did she end up in this conversation?

"I suppose."

"Hey, all I'm saying is that if it were me he'd paid that much money to go to dinner with, I'd make sure he got his money's worth." Amy waggled her brows suggestively. "You should at least think about it. I heard you and the pharmacist broke up."

Gossip sure spread fast.

"We've already gone on our dinner date."

"And I definitely got my money's worth."

She hated how Lucas did that, walked up behind her and joined into conversations she was having. But she supposed if she was going to talk about him, he had a right to join in. Not that she'd wanted to talk about him, but it seemed she couldn't escape doing so.

Amy blushed at being caught. "Hi, Dr. Cain. We were just talking about you."

"I heard." His smile reached his eyes. "All good things, I hope?"

"Absolutely." Amy laughed a little flirtatiously. "Is there anything else to be said?"

His gaze met Emily's, as if challenging her to speak up. She kept her mouth closed.

She might have lots of negative things to say, but since she'd been having mind-blowing sex with the man, she really didn't think she had the right to point out any flaws.

"Did Amy tell you the good news?" His gaze searched Emily's. "Cassie woke up during the night."

"She mentioned that. She also mentioned you came to

the hospital after she woke up and that you've been with her since."

As in, she knew he'd come here when he'd left her place, and when had he slept? Because, as handsome as he was, Emily noted the fatigue around his eyes and it pulled at her heart.

"She's going to be fine from the bleed." He sounded genuinely happy about the news. "No lasting damage that I can tell from the increased intracranial pressure."

"That's wonderful."

"I'll be taking her back to the operating room soon to remove the tumor. Just as soon as she's strong enough to withstand another surgery."

Emily nodded.

"She's going to feel like a new person when I'm finished."

"No doubt." She met his gaze. "Did you need for one of us to do something for you, Dr. Cain? Because Amy needs to finish giving me report so I can go check on my patients this morning."

It didn't surprise Emily when Lucas showed up again later that day. She was in Cassie's room and had just finished helping her mother sponge bathe the little girl. They'd just settled her back into her clean hospital bed.

"Hi, Dr. Cain," Cassie said, smiling at him despite the bandages around her head. "Are you…going…to take my blood?"

He shook his head. "You're safe from me sticking you."

"Good, because…I feel…a lot better." She truly was doing better, but one only had to listen to her speech, watch her hand and arm movements, to know that there were still serious health issues.

"I see that." He smiled back at the child. "Your color is a lot better than when I was here this morning."

"Momma says…I can…go to the playroom…soon…if I keep…getting stronger."

"Hopefully, you'll be strong enough very soon."

He ran through a check on Cassie's cranial nerves, making her smile as he asked her to make the different facial expressions at him. He puffed his cheeks out, waggled his eyebrows, smiled, frowned, furrowed his brow and gritted his teeth back at her with each check, eliciting a giggle from his patient and a smile from Cassie's mom.

He really was great with Cassie. Amy had been right. Lucas would be a great father. If only… No. Emily absolutely positively was not going to let her mind go there.

Even if her mind had been going there on and off since he'd first shown up at Children's. How could it not have?

Still, some memories were best never resurrected.

Some parts of the past she just couldn't deal with.

Not ever again.

Having lived through them the first time had almost killed her.

"Will you please go to dinner with me tonight?"

Emily bit the inside of her lip. She didn't want to date Lucas. She wanted… She wasn't sure what she wanted. Just that she was scared of going to dinner with him. She'd had fun with him at the club, dancing, but overall that experience had just left her feeling raw. Everything about being near him left her feeling vulnerable.

"I promise I won't bite."

Her gaze cut to his. "Yeah, I've heard that before."

His lips twitched. "Promises not to bite when I'm in bed don't count."

"Says who?"

"Me?"

Despite her misgivings, she laughed. "You're the final authority on biting?"

"I probably don't have near enough experience to be the final authority, but if you want to volunteer for me to practice nibbling on, I'm all for upping my game."

"I'm sure you are."

"But I'd like to take you to dinner first."

"Why?"

"I enjoy being with you and want to spend time with you."

She enjoyed being with him, too. Naked, no problem. That was easy to categorize into just sex. But spending time with Lucas with her clothes on? That wasn't so easy to justify away from work.

"I'd like to take you to this little French bistro off Broadway. They have this fresh-baked bread that just melts in your mouth."

"And straight onto my hips."

"Your hips are perfect, Emily."

His compliment came out as sincere and not one meant to puff her up. She liked that. Liked that he sounded as if he truly believed what he said.

"But they won't be if I indulge in fresh-baked bread," she pointed out, trying not to get too elated that he'd said her hips were perfect. He made her feel perfect. When he looked at her, touched her, with such awe, how could she not?

He'd always done that in the beginning, made her feel good about herself, made her feel as if she was the only woman in the world and the center of his existence.

"I promise to make you burn every single carbohydrate before the sun comes up."

She rolled her eyes. "I know what will be coming up before the sun."

He grinned. "You know me so well."

Yes, she did. And yet she didn't. Not anymore. He'd changed in the years they'd been apart. He was more mature, more stable these days, more caring and aware of others around him. Then again, he was five years older, a man in his thirties. Of course he'd matured.

"Does that mean you'll give me the privilege of taking you to a late dinner for two?"

She sighed, then nodded. It wasn't as if she could say no. Even if she could, all she'd do was think about him and hope he showed at her apartment. What would be the point of saying no? "But only if you promise to make me enjoy every second of carb-burning."

His grin was lethal. "Was there ever any doubt?"

No, that, Emily never doubted.

Emily's menu hadn't had prices, but she didn't need dollar signs to know she was in a restaurant way out of her price ballpark. Part of her wanted to question Lucas about wasting so much money on taking her to eat at such a place when she'd have enjoyed grabbing a pretzel dog and walking around Times Square to people watch just as much.

Well, almost as much.

She had to admit the cozy candlelit booth with just the two of them was nice. Perhaps a bit too over-the-top romantic for a divorced couple. Then again, most divorced couples weren't having hot sex every night, either.

Or maybe they were. What did she know about such things other than that Lucas got to her physically as much as he ever did? The absence of the golden band he'd slipped onto her finger so long ago hadn't changed that one bit.

Not really.

"You got quiet. Should I be worried?"

"I was thinking about when you put my wedding band on my finger." Automatically, her thumb brushed across the empty spot. She'd never been much of a jewelry person, and these days she chose not to wear any rings unless it was a fun, chunky costume piece that complemented whatever she was wearing.

His expression tightened. "What about it?"

She shrugged. "Not really anything specific. I was just thinking about you doing so."

"Do you still have your rings, Emily?"

Wondering if she should admit such craziness, she nodded. "I thought about selling them, but there just seemed something weird about doing so. I guess keeping them is just as weird."

"I've still got mine, too."

"You do?" Why did that surprise her? Why did some deep part of her rejoice that he'd held on to his wedding band? It didn't mean anything that he'd kept the ring. The only thing that meant anything was the legal divorce document that had torn away any meaning the ring had once held.

He nodded. "Like you, I've thought about getting rid of it but never have."

"We were too young," she mused.

"That's what everyone said." His gaze met hers. "But the truth of the matter is that I was older than you are now."

Her eyes widened a little. "You were, weren't you?"

Not that she hadn't known, just that she hadn't thought about it. He'd seemed much younger at the time than she currently felt. Maybe because he'd still been working on his education and had still lived in his parents' home.

"I'd led a pretty sheltered life up until I got to medical

school," he admitted, echoing her thoughts. "It was harder work than I'd anticipated."

"You always made excellent grades." She knew he had. She'd seen the academic awards he'd won throughout his college and pre-college years.

"That was easy. Medical school not so much so. I struggled a lot more than I let people see."

Odd, she'd never thought of him as struggling. Then again, by the time she'd met him, he'd been doing his surgical fellowship. Maybe she'd missed a lot of the struggling times.

"A lot more than I let you see," he added, squashing her theory.

"I remember you studying and looking up stuff on patients, but you seemed to blow through it with ease."

"Because I'd rather be playing with you than studying."

What he was saying sank in. "If I made your education more difficult, I apologize. I never wanted to interfere with any of your dreams."

He started to speak but didn't as their waiter showed up with some of the bread Lucas had bragged about.

"Mmm, this is worth every thigh jiggle," she admitted after the first buttered bite.

Lucas didn't say anything, and when she looked up and met his blue gaze, his eyes were dark. "You're beautiful, Emily. If I failed to tell you that back then, let me constantly remind you now. You. Are. Beautiful."

Where had that come from? She'd been blabbering on about food and jiggling thighs and he was proclaiming her beautiful? What was up with that?

"So are you." Because what else could she say? That once upon a time he'd made her feel like the most beautiful woman on the planet? That once upon a time when he'd looked at her she'd known he thought her the most beautiful thing he'd ever seen and she'd thought she'd be his forever?

That once upon a time she hadn't been able to look at him without bursting into tears because she'd been pregnant with his baby and he'd no longer wanted her or their child?

Lucas loved to watch Emily eat. Always had, but he'd forgotten. When she'd stuck the piece of bread in her mouth and licked her fingers, he'd sincerely thought about asking for a lick himself. Her eyes had filled with heaven, her face had relaxed in pleasure, and her sounds of enjoyment had only added to his longings.

But it was more than the physical.

With Emily, it always had been more.

He enjoyed her. Watching her. Listening to her. Talking to her. Touching her, and not just in a sexual way, although there was always that. Life just seemed better with Emily.

A lot better with Emily.

Then again, the problem had been her unhappiness, not his.

"You're making me nervous," she said, drawing his gaze back to hers.

He took her hand into his and brought her fingers to his lips. He pressed a kiss there. "You have no reason to ever be nervous around me, Emily."

"Right." She pulled her hand away and tucked it under her leg. "Because you're as harmless as a hungry lion."

"Perhaps, but I'd never intentionally hurt you. Despite what you may believe, I always wanted to make you happy."

But he hadn't been able to make her happy, had hurt her, and the truth of that hung in the air between them.

* * *

How had Lucas convinced Emily to go for drinks at the top of a hotel with a revolving restaurant so they could view the New York City night skyline?

It wasn't as if she hadn't lived here her whole life. She knew what the city looked like. She'd guess most everyone in the restaurant were tourists except them.

"You guys need anything?" their waitress asked. There was a one drink minimum, but they'd both ordered bottles of water rather than anything alcoholic.

Just being with Lucas made her feel drunk.

Or maybe it was the slowly turning restaurant.

But she doubted it. The room turned at a pace where you didn't realize you were even moving until you started watching the buildings around you.

"Admit it, this was a good idea."

She fought to keep her gaze from going to his no doubt smug expression. "I suppose."

"What would you have rather done?"

He sounded as if there was nothing she could say that would top what they currently did. She had to admit, the evening had been nice, talking with him had been nice even, but she wasn't admitting those things.

"Gone back to my place?" she suggested.

"My bad. You win." He stood, pulled a money clip from his front pocket and tossed a bill onto their table.

"Lucas." She laughed, tugging on his arm. "Sit down."

"But you said…" Grinning, his eyes full of mischief, he sat back down.

"We're here now. I want to see if I can see the Statue of Liberty from up here."

"I was told that you once could, but new buildings have gone up since this one was built and have blocked the view."

Disappointment filled her. "Oh."

"I'd take you there if you want to see Lady Liberty."

"I've been before." On an elementary school field trip, they'd taken the ferry out to the island and toured the statue. She'd been in total awe of the size and magnificence of such a gift symbolizing freedom. She'd often wondered if any country had given another such a glorious present.

"Sometimes things are better the second time around."

She hesitated only a moment before agreeing. "I guess we could go. It has been quite a few years since I visited."

"I've never been."

She looked at him in disbelief. "What?"

He shrugged. "It's not that big of a deal. I've just never been out on the island."

"Which means you've never gone up in the statue, either?"

"No."

"Well, that's just sad."

A wry smile played on his lips. "There goes my image of a childhood full of privilege."

"Oh, that image is still there," she didn't hesitate to point out. "Now, I just wonder how many educational gaps were there, too."

"Educational gaps?"

"Things like trips to the Statue of Liberty. Poor, poor Lucas."

"I've been to the Eiffel Tower, does that count? It's French, too."

The Eiffel Tower because he truly did come from a background of privilege. He'd once told her that the year after he'd graduated from high school he'd "backpacked" Europe with some friends, whatever that had meant.

The farthest from home she'd ever been was New Jersey.

She'd never really had a reason to leave New York. Everything she'd needed was here.

Maybe someday she'd travel and see some of the world's more exotic cities. She loved the night lights, the excitement of big cities with lots of people from every walk of life within close distance. She loved the access to so many different cultures and restaurants and shops and…

"Maybe I could take you there someday."

"To the Eiffel Tower?" Her eyes widened. "Why would you do that?"

"Don't sound so shocked, Emily. Why wouldn't I want to take you to Paris? You'd love the city, the food, the people."

Good grief. Had he been reading her mind or what?

"Paris is a long way from New York."

"Not that far."

"Just a hop, skip and jump over the ocean," she mused.

"I was serious when I offered to take you."

"Thank you, but I'll pass."

"Why?"

"Because women don't go to Paris with their ex-husbands."

"Perhaps they should."

"Why?"

"To sit by the Seine, drink a cup of coffee and watch the sun rise. To visit the Louvre and so many other fascinating places. To eat a superbly cooked meal with a view of the Eiffel Tower while the sun sets."

"As if I'd want to get out of bed that early in the morning while on vacation." Anything to throw her focus anywhere but on what he was saying because he made her want to do all the things he said. With him. The harsh reality was that, despite their little sexual interlude, if she ever did see Paris, it wouldn't be with Lucas. And now if she ever did, she'd be battling the images he'd just put in her mind.

She bit the inside of her lip.

"Yet again, you do make a valid point," he agreed. "Perhaps we'd skip the early-morning sitting by the Seine and just watch the sun come up from our hotel-room bed."

She took a drink from her water.

"I should have brought you to Paris for our honeymoon."

"I couldn't have enjoyed our honeymoon any more if you'd brought me to Paris, or London, or any other exotic locale you can think of."

"Because Atlantic City is the most romantic city in the world?" he teased.

"That weekend, it was perfect," she answered in all honesty.

His gaze searched hers, but for what she wasn't sure. She didn't say anything and for the longest time neither did he. When he did, his words were poignant.

"I believe you may be right about that, Emily. That weekend was the best of my life."

"Cheap hotel, cheap food, playing on a crowded public New Jersey boardwalk and beach… I doubt that, but we did have a good time."

His brows veed. "Why you can't believe me, I don't understand, but, yes, we did have a good time."

Memories of that weekend shook her, and when she looked at him, she knew he was flooded with similar ones. Did he also wonder how something that had been so perfect had gone so wrong?

"I'd like to take you back to your place and make love to you now, Emily Stewart."

She wasn't going to argue. She wanted that, too.

Perhaps, if she was honest, she'd admit she'd never stopped wanting him to do that.

Then his words hit her. He hadn't said he wanted to go have sex with her.

He'd said he wanted to make love to her.

No. She shouldn't read anything into his words. That was all they'd been. Words.

They'd be having sex. Not making love.

At least, Lucas would.

More and more, Emily questioned exactly what it was she was doing with Lucas.

CHAPTER TWELVE

WHEN THEY GOT to her apartment, Lucas undressed her slowly, kissing and caressing each newly uncovered area of her body.

By the time she stood in only her panties, she ached for him, but he wasn't finished with his sweet torture.

"How come I'm the only one with my clothes off?" she demanded, tugging at his shirt.

"Because you're the one who's exquisite."

"You're good with the lines, Lucas. Keep them coming and you're liable to get lucky."

"I'm definitely getting lucky. Actually, I already have. I'm here with you."

"See, that's what I mean with the lines. Good job," she praised as she undid his shirt buttons and pushed the material aside to reveal his chest. She groaned at the masterpiece she unveiled. "It should be illegal to cover that up."

He laughed. "Good thing it's not. I'd freeze during winter."

"A frozen Lucas. I'd have a lick of that."

"I'd let you and imagine I'd thaw pretty fast with your hot mouth anywhere near me."

She bent, kissed his belly, felt him suck in his breath, saw the goosebumps that covered his skin. She'd done that. Her touch. Her kiss. Sure, maybe he reacted to lots of women, but right now, at this moment, he was with her and it was her touch he craved.

She craved to touch. To kiss. To lick. To taste every inch of him.

So she did.

When neither of them could stand more, he positioned himself above her, paused, stared at her with so much emotion in his eyes that she felt overwhelmed. What was he waiting for?

"I've missed you, Emily. So much." Rather than giving her what she ached for, he kissed her mouth. A kiss way too sweet for the heat of the moment.

A kiss way too sweet for her peace of mind.

His gaze locked with hers, he moved his hips, giving her what she needed, what they needed.

Rather than the frenzy of their previous matings, he kept his pace slow. When she'd try to increase it, he'd resist. When she gripped his buttocks, urging him faster, deeper, he took her hands into his and held them above her head, locking them into place by his hand over her wrists. She didn't really try to escape. Why should she when the heat was rising inside her thighs, when warmth swirled in her belly, building?

His gaze still locked with hers, he built her higher until she went so high there was nowhere to go but over the edge.

So she fell.

Further and further, she floated downward.

He let her float, but not all the way down. Instead, he moved and took her up, up, up again.

And again.

Chest heaving, Lucas collapsed onto the mattress next to Emily. Her chest rose and fell. Her lips were swollen from his kisses. Her body flushed from his loving. Her hair fanned out around her in messy, just-had-wild-sex disarray.

He'd never seen anything more erotic. He'd never seen anything more beautiful.

"You need to get dressed," she told him, her voice breathy. "So you can go home before it gets any later. I have to work tomorrow."

Then there was that.

"I don't want to go, Emily."

"I don't want you to stay."

Which was a hard pill to swallow.

"Why not?"

"We aren't dating, Lucas. We aren't moving toward a relationship with each other. We're using each other for sex. Nothing more. For you to stay in my bed, to actually sleep beside me, implies an intimacy we don't have."

"What if I want that intimacy with you?"

"This isn't just about what you want."

"I realize that, but—"

"No buts, Lucas." She climbed out of the bed and grabbed his underwear off the floor and tossed it at him. "Here."

"What are you afraid of, Emily?"

Rather than climb back into bed, she opened a dresser drawer and pulled out an oversize New York Knicks T-shirt and put it on. "With you? Everything."

That had him pausing with his boxer briefs halfway up his thighs. "After what we just shared, how could you possibly be afraid of me?"

"That was sex."

He shook his head. "You keep telling yourself that, Emily, but we both know that wasn't just sex. Never was. Never will be."

Panic filled her eyes. "That's all it can be."

"Why? I want a relationship with you, Emily. I want to be the man in your life. The man you fall asleep next to and wake up beside."

The thought of her sinking back into depression, of him stealing her happiness, terrified him, but maybe they could have a relationship that built upon the good between them.

She stood beside the bed watching him, but she looked ready to run if he so much as moved toward her. "I won't ever marry you again."

"Nor would I ask you to. Marriage is where we messed up."

"Marriage is where we messed up?" She shook her head as if trying to process what he meant. "How did marriage mess anything up?"

"You were so sad after we got married, Emily." He didn't know how else to answer her question, but obviously marriage had ruined their relationship.

"We are what messed up our relationship, Lucas. Me and you. We would have fallen apart whether we had been married or not. We may have phenomenal sex, but we were never destined to be together."

"You're wrong."

"You think we were destined to be together?" she scoffed.

Did he?

"I think there's something between you and me that we don't share with anyone else."

"It's called sexual chemistry."

"It's more than sex."

She rolled her eyes. "How's this for irony? The woman is trying to keep sex as just sex and the guy is trying to attach feelings to the physical."

He shrugged. "The truth doesn't change regardless of how we label it."

"The truth? The truth is that you shouldn't be here, that we are divorced and should start acting like it."

What she was saying sank in.

"You don't want to see me anymore?"

"I never wanted to see you to begin with, Lucas. I was fine, just fine, until you came back into my life with all your potent sex appeal and fancy orgasms."

That had him stopping, grinning a little despite their conversation. "I gave you fancy orgasms?"

She threw her hands into the air.

"Sorry, but a man likes to hear that he gave his woman orgasms, and when she calls them fancy, he definitely wants to hear more."

Her hands went to her hips. "I'm not your woman."

There was that.

"You used to be."

"In the past. Doesn't matter anymore. The past is gone."

"The past is never really gone. It's the culmination of all the past that makes up the present."

That one earned him another eye roll. "Oh, don't go spouting your Harvard Philosophy 101 at me."

"Are you purposely trying to fight with me, Emily? Because I refuse to fight with you. If you want me to go, I'll go. But not without you knowing that it's not because I want to go. What I want is to be with you and to sleep with you in my arms."

She sank onto the edge of the bed and stared at him. "You're crazy."

Yeah, he was.

"About you." With that, he leaned over and kissed her forehead. "Good night, Emily. Sweet dreams."

A couple of weeks later, Emily was on duty when Kevin Rogers was admitted. He was a four-year-old pedestrian who'd been a hit-and-run victim. According to eyewitnesses, a taxi driver had driven up on a sidewalk while glancing down at his cell phone, hit the boy, then disappeared quickly.

The boy had been admitted with multiple fractures and traumatic brain injury. The emergency-room physician had given him poor odds of surviving.

The CT of his head had shown active brain bleeds. If he wasn't taken to surgery to relieve the pressure and stop the bleeds, he'd be dead before midnight. If he did manage to survive, he'd likely have permanent damage from the increased pressure on delicate brain tissue.

Probably because Emily had volunteered when Cassie Bellows had needed emergency surgery, Emily's charge nurse had informed her she was being shifted over to the operating room to assist Dr. Cain along with the rest of the assembled surgical team.

"But I have patients," she reminded her, not wanting to go back into the operating room with Lucas.

"Meghan and Amy are down to one patient. I was going to have to send one of them home. I'm going to reassign Jenny and Cassie to them and send you to the OR rather than someone having to be called in."

What the nurse manager said made perfect sense. But Emily fought the urge to beg the woman not to make her.

Although she opened her apartment door to Lucas night after night, she tried to avoid him as much as possible at the hospital. She didn't want others to see how he affected her. She didn't want others to associate them together.

She didn't want to deal with the aftermath at work when things fell apart.

Been there, done that, had ended up leaving the job.

Whereas during Cassie's surgery Emily had been as-signed care of Cassie, this time she was assigned to directly assist Lucas.

Which meant she'd be right beside him.

Which meant there was no avoiding him.

Which meant she'd have to touch him, albeit through sterile gloves and under harsh lights and circumstances.

She was still mentally bemoaning having to assist Lucas while she scrubbed up. It wasn't that she didn't enjoy being in the surgical suite. She'd enjoyed the time she'd worked there, but she'd missed direct patient care.

She entered the surgical suite, made sure she had everything Lucas would need on her tray and winced a little on the inside at how tiny the boy looked on the hospital bed when he was wheeled in.

A sterile decked-out Lucas followed him into the suite and the surgical team jumped in to try to save the little boy.

An hour into the procedure, Emily was dabbing sweat from Lucas's forehead and studying the exhaustion showing on his face.

An hour later, he still meticulously worked, doing all he could to stop the tiny bleeds in the boy's brain.

By the time Lucas finished, Emily's heart hurt for him, but because of the others in the room, she didn't say anything, didn't offer comfort.

The surgery had gone past the end of her shift, so she performed the rest of her duties, cleaning her area, changing back into her own scrubs from the hospital-issue surgical scrubs, then clocked out.

Prior to heading home, she went by to check on Jenny and Cassie and was pleased to find them stable.

She swung by a take-out shop and picked up enough food for two. Who knew if Lucas would have eaten when he came by later that night?

Only, as the clock minutes ticked by, Lucas still hadn't shown at close to 1:00 a.m. Unable to stand it anymore, worried about where he was, but not wanting to wake him if he had just gone home to sleep, she texted him.

Where are you?

Within seconds her phone sounded with a texted reply and relief spread through her body.

Outside your door.

What? She got out of bed and practically ran to her living-room door, peeped through the viewer and undid the chain and dead bolt.

"Why didn't you knock?"

"I left the hospital and had just gotten off the elevator when your text came through."

"Oh."

"Did you miss me?"

She could lie. She could tell him she hadn't. But he looked so exhausted, so much as if he needed her to tell the truth, that she did.

"Yes."

"Good." That was all he said. Good. Then he stepped inside her apartment, waited while she relocked the door and safety chain, then took her in his arms.

"What took you so long?"

"Kevin Rogers died."

Emily's breath caught. The little boy had died?

"Oh, Lucas!" She winced, then wrapped her arms around him. "I'm sorry. You did all you could."

"Did I?"

His question caught her off guard. "Of course you did. I was next to you all those hours you searched for bleeds, making sure you stopped each one."

"Obviously, it wasn't enough."

She hugged him. "You aren't God, Lucas. You can't heal what's too broken to mend."

"I know that, but that little boy shouldn't have died. He was too young to die."

"Age has nothing to do with injuries. You know that."

He swiped his hands through his hair. "Is it okay if I take a quick shower? I headed straight here and I'm a mess."

She nodded. "Have you eaten?"

He shook his head.

"Lucas, you've got to take better care of yourself. You don't sleep. You don't eat. What am I going to do with you?"

"Let me shower, then I'll show you exactly what you can do with me."

"I'm going to heat you up something to eat while you shower. After you've eaten, we can discuss whatever you want to show me."

"Deal."

The shower had turned off long ago, but Lucas still hadn't joined her in the kitchen, where she'd heated up the left-over takeout she'd brought home.

She'd put on hot tea and sipped on a cup while she waited.

Bless him that he'd taken the boy's death so hard. That, she understood. Didn't she feel a similar responsibility for each person she took care of?

She'd had patients die over the years. When you took care of the seriously ill, death happened.

No doubt Lucas had lost patients in the past, too, but something about Kevin Rogers had clearly gotten to him.

She glanced at her cellular phone, noting the time. He'd been in her bathroom for a long time. Was he okay?

Intent on knocking on the bathroom door to see if he needed anything, she went to her bedroom and stopped just inside the room. Lucas lay on her bed, his hair damp, nothing on but a towel about his waist, and he was out cold.

"Lucas?"

No change in the even rise and fall of his chest.

"Lucas?" She had to wake him. He couldn't stay.

Only, he still didn't stir. Could she really wake him and send him away when he was so completely exhausted?

She winced.

She didn't want him to sleep in her bed.

But she couldn't bring herself to wake him.

She walked back into the kitchen, put away the food, flipped off the lights, stared at her sofa for long minutes contemplating how comfortable it would be, then sighed.

She didn't have to work tomorrow, but she didn't think she'd sleep a wink on the sofa, either.

Lucas wasn't the only one exhausted.

With her heart pounding and her insides shaking, she went back into the bedroom, studied the sleeping man in her bed.

A man she'd loved. A man she'd hated.

A man... What was it she felt for him now?

She didn't love him. She didn't hate him.

What was this feeling inside her? Definitely, she felt something. Sexual chemistry as she'd claimed? Yes, she felt that, but there was more.

Looking closer, she noted the redness around his eyes.

Dear Lord. He looked as if he'd been crying.

Emily swallowed the knot that formed.

Had he cried in the shower over Kevin Rogers's death?

Her heart tightened to where she couldn't breathe.

Forget the sofa. She crossed the room, turned off the lamplight and snuggled up against a man she suddenly wanted to comfort and protect from the whole world.

Not a feeling she welcomed. Not a feeling she wanted. But she hugged him and fell asleep with her arm wrapped around him all the same.

CHAPTER THIRTEEN

Lucas woke just as light began streaking into the room. A room he'd never seen bathed in the colors of sunrise.

Emily's bedroom.

She'd let him stay the night after they'd had sex.

He frowned. Actually, she'd let him stay even though they hadn't had sex. Emotionally and physically exhausted from Kevin's surgery, then death, he'd lain down meaning to catch only a few minutes of shut-eye to get a second wind and he'd passed out.

Occasionally, a patient got beneath his skin and just got to him. The boy and the utter loss in his parents' eyes when he'd met with them had done so. He'd wanted to be the hero, to repair what he'd known going in might not be fixable. He'd failed and that hadn't been an easy pill to swallow.

Why hadn't Emily awakened him and sent him home?

It was what he'd have expected. Only, she hadn't. She'd crawled into the bed next to him and at some point they'd gotten under the covers. Currently, her backside was spooned up against him and he held her close.

He took a deep breath, catching a faint whiff of vanilla.

Emily.

His Emily.

He kissed the top of her head and realized there was nowhere in the world he'd rather be than holding her.

His ex-wife.

Closing his eyes, he buried his face in her hair and held her close. He wasn't scheduled with patients today, wasn't on call at the hospital. Emily had worked the past three days. She should be off today, too.

If she'd let him, he'd spend the day with her doing whatever she wanted to do.

Until then, he'd count his blessings.

Even on her days off work, Emily tended to wake bright and early. This morning had been different. She'd been snuggled against a hard male body and she'd slept hours later than she usually did.

Then again, so had Lucas.

She twisted around to look at him. His eyes were closed, but she wasn't sure if he was asleep or awake.

"Good morning, Emily."

Awake. Heat infused her face. "Morning."

His eyes opened and he smiled and whatever embarrassment she'd been feeling at getting caught looking at him disappeared.

"Sorry I passed out on you last night."

"I guess you were tired."

"I guess I was. Thank you for not throwing me out."

"We both know it was probably a mistake in letting you stay."

"How do you figure?"

"Sleeping together is too intimate."

"Sex isn't?"

"Sex is…sex."

"Make no mistake, there is shared intimacy when having sex, Emily."

"I know that. You're not understanding what I mean."

"Actually, I probably do. You want to keep distinct boundaries that everything between us is only physical."

"Exactly," she agreed, smiling, glad he understood.

"It's not going to work."

Her smile faded. "Why not?"

"Because I want more than physical with you."

She scooted away from him, sat up and pulled her knees to her. "I can't be friends with you, Lucas. I just can't."

"Why not?"

"Too much has happened between us for you and me to be friends."

"We can be lovers, but not friends?"

"I get the feeling you're laughing at me. Whether you understand or not, I'm serious."

"I know you are and I don't mean to tease you, Emily."

"Sure you don't."

"Okay, so maybe I do a little. I always enjoyed teasing you. Like the time I…" He launched into a story about when she'd met his best friend.

"How is Hank?"

"Still same old Hank."

"Does he know you're working with me?"

Lucas nodded. "He knows."

"And?"

"And nothing."

"He didn't warn you that you were crazy or question why you were taking a job that would force you to see your ex-wife day after day?"

"No, he didn't."

"Why is that?"

"Good question, and one you'd have to ask him."

"I doubt I'll ever see him again."

"We could go out with him and his wife tonight."

"Hank is married?"

"Two years ago. His wife just found out she's pregnant a few months ago."

Pregnant. Emily's empty uterus spasmed. Lucas almost sounded envious, but she knew better. Or maybe she didn't. He'd said she'd been wrong about his not wanting children.

Was that what had driven him to seek her out? That his best friend had settled down and Lucas realized he was the odd man out?

The possibility seemed hard to fathom, but just his being there, having taken a job at Children's, telling her he wanted to have a relationship with her, his ex-wife, all of it was hard to take in.

"Do you think we'd have kids by now if we hadn't divorced?"

Lucas's question gutted her as surely as if he'd stabbed her. She leaped out of the bed. "It's too early in the morning for questions like those."

Not glancing his way, she rushed into the bathroom, shut and locked the door. She slid down to the floor and cried tears she refused to let have sound no matter how badly her body shook.

From the time Emily had emerged from the bathroom, Lucas knew something was different.

There was a hollowness to her eyes, a blankness to her facial expression that told a deeper story.

Plus, she hadn't met his eyes a single time. Not even when he'd cupped her chin and tried to get her to.

She was shutting him out and he felt the gap between them widening with every breath she took.

She was going to end things. In his gut, he knew she was.

A desperation hit him.

He didn't want Emily ending things between them.

He needed her.

A heavy realization to make.

He needed his ex-wife.

"I'm going to call the hospital and find out what Kevin Rogers's funeral arrangements are. I feel I should go."

Staring into her cup of coffee, Emily nodded.

"Will you go with me, Emily?"

She glanced up, looking like a deer caught in the headlights. "Why?" Her voice squeaked.

"I'm not good at funerals, and especially not a kid's."

"I—" Her expression pinched. "Lucas, we really don't need to be spending so much time together."

He'd known it was coming, but her words still punched at him.

"Please go with me."

Her inner turmoil was palpable in the room, but in the end she nodded. "If you want me there."

"I want you there." He needed her there, at his side, where she belonged.

Because Emily belonged beside him.

And he belonged beside her.

The tortured scowl on her face said now wasn't the time to go spouting off about past feelings he'd realized weren't in the past, but present at this very moment.

"What would you like to do today, Emily? I'd really like to spend the day with you."

Did Lucas not hear anything she said? Hadn't Emily just said they didn't need to be spending so much time together?

Yet she'd agreed to go to a funeral with him. Because the memory of how he'd looked when he'd shown up at her apartment, at how his red puffy eyes had looked even in sleep, had left her unable to do anything other than be there.

She hated that.

She hated how entangled he was becoming in her life. If she didn't put a stop to it, every aspect of her life would soon be taken over by him. Then what?

She knew.

If she let Lucas invade everything, when he moved on to the next phase of his life, she'd be a devastated wreck as she'd been five years ago.

Only, she wouldn't. Not this time.

She was stronger. She'd picked herself up, rebuilt a life for herself even after suffering horrendous blows. She was a survivor, and no matter what he did, she would survive. Plus, she didn't have crazy hormones influencing how she thought, causing a constant flow of tears.

But she wasn't so masochistic as to continue to let him worm his way into her very being.

She needed time away from him.

"I have other plans today, Lucas." Actually, she really did. She was taking a bus to Brooklyn to visit her parents.

Then again, her mother might take one look at her and know Lucas was back. That wouldn't go over well. Maybe she'd bail on her parents and spend the day running errands or something.

"Can't you change them?"

She shook her head. "I can't."

"I'd hoped to take you to visit the Statue of Liberty."

"Tempting, but no, thanks. I'm going to my parents'."

He winced. "I guess I wouldn't be a welcomed addition."

"Not if I want to keep my father out of jail."

"That bad?"

Her parents had never thought she should marry Lucas,

didn't believe in divorce, but had comforted her after the demise of her marriage and the aftermath. Lucas showing up on their doorstep would be that bad.

"You divorced his baby girl, what do you think?"

Despite fear her mother would see right through her, Emily opted to still go see her parents. Her mother eyed her suspiciously, but, other than to ask her if she'd changed her hair, she hadn't pried.

Emily hadn't stayed long for fear she might break down and spill everything. Her mother had been there during that awful time after she'd left Lucas. Her poor mama didn't deserve to have those worries put on her, so Emily kept silent, hugged them bye and headed out.

That was when she caught sight of the majestic lady standing tall in the Hudson Bay.

Without really questioning herself, she bought a ticket and rode the ferry out to the island, poked around, read facts and wished she'd been able to reserve in time to go to the top.

"Emily?"

She spun, surprised to see the man she'd said goodbye to that morning standing near the base of the statue. "What are you doing here?"

"I mentioned bringing you here this morning, remember?"

Yes, she remembered. "I said no, thanks."

"Yet we're both here." He gave a whimsical look, as if he couldn't believe she was there. "I decided to go for a walk to clear my head. I ended up buying a ticket, riding in the top of one of those tour-bus things and taking a ferry here."

"You rode on top of one of those tour buses?" She couldn't picture him having done so.

"Yep." He reached in his pocket and pulled out a receipt. "I even have proof."

"Why?"

"Someone accused me of having educational gaps. I filled in quite a few as the tour guide informed me where all the celebs live in Manhattan."

"I'm not sure riding in one of those tour buses counts as filling in educational gaps."

"Believe me, gaps were filled during that experience."

She narrowed her gaze. He was smiling, looked more relaxed and rested than she'd seen him look in days.

"Maybe I need to take a ride, too."

"I'd buy you a ticket."

"I can buy my own ticket," she immediately said.

"I know, but sometimes I'd like to buy you things, Emily, and surely a bus ticket isn't something you'd find offensive."

"Fine." She pressed her lips tightly together and smiled. "Let's go ride on top of a bus."

The ferry ride back to Battery Park was uneventful. They stood outside and the mist of the bay probably kinked Emily's hair, but she didn't care.

When they arrived, Lucas bought her a bus tour ticket, and they took seats at the back. It wasn't crowded, so it was only the two of them on the back row of five seats. They took the middle ones and Lucas immediately took her hand into his.

Emily was tempted to pull away but didn't want him to question why she did so when it was just holding hands and they'd done so much more over the past few weeks.

Yet his big strong hand laced with hers seemed to signify so much that wasn't real. Would never be real.

The more she didn't acknowledge that, didn't deal with that, the harder all this became.

A half hour later, Lucas squeezed her hand and grinned. "Admit it. This is fun."

"Exhilarating," she said halfheartedly. Actually, she was enjoying the tour but kept battling that she'd ended up spending the day with him anyway.

He laughed. "Tell me what you really think."

She rolled her eyes. "Fine, the weather is great."

It was. Not too cool. Not too hot.

"The company is great, too."

"And so modest."

"I meant that you were great company, Emily. Not me."

"You're not so bad."

"But you don't really want to be with me."

No, she didn't. Yet she did.

"You have to admit, our being together is pretty crazy."

"Crazier things have happened than you and me getting back together."

Back together? Where had that come from?

"We're not back together, Lucas."

"Maybe we should."

She shook her head. "No, we shouldn't."

"Why not?"

"Because…" She struggled to come up with a verbal answer, but a thousand reasons floated just beyond her tongue's reach. She knew they did.

"It's not something we have to decide at this moment, Emily. But I've told you a dozen times how much I want you in my life. You need to think about what you want."

"I can't do this, Lucas. I thought I could, but I can't."

Had she really just said that while on top of a tour bus with a bunch of tourists? Sure, the closest ones were a few seats up, but this wasn't a place for a private conversation.

Concern darkened his face. "You're getting motion sick?"

"Us, not the tour bus." Although, suddenly she couldn't do that anymore, either. Fortunately, the bus pulled over to a stop. Emily stood and headed to the front of the bus and the stairs that would lead her out of it.

She took off walking down the street, glad they were in a part of the city she recognized and that wasn't too many blocks from where she lived.

"Emily, please don't leave me like that."

He'd followed her. Of course he'd followed her. Had she really thought he wouldn't? Had she even wanted him not to?

She was the problem. Her and her mixed-up emotions.

She wanted him, but she didn't want him. Hadn't her crazy emotions been a problem before, too? She'd not been able to stop the tears, to control the mood surges that had caused her to pick fights with him. Her hormones had been all over the place. She didn't want to remember, didn't want to think about the past, about her relationship with Lucas and how everything had fallen apart. About why everything had fallen apart.

Berating herself and her weakness where he was concerned, she kept walking without answering him.

He grabbed her arm, halting her. "What's wrong, Emily? Talk to me. Please talk to me."

Now fighting tears that she had no idea where they came from, she shook her head, pulled loose and resumed walking.

He stayed beside her but didn't try to stop her again.

When they reached her building, she turned to him.

"I'm sorry, Lucas. I feel I'm an emotional wreck these days and I just… I just had to get off the bus." She didn't say *and away from him*, but the words dangled between them.

He studied her. "I've done this to you, haven't I?"

She shrugged. "I'd be lying if I said I was expecting you to show back up in my life. I wasn't prepared for a second emotional roller-coaster ride with you. I don't want to do this anymore. I want my normal, calm life back."

"You were happier before I came back into your life?"

"Yeah, I was," she said and meant it. At least, she thought she did. At the moment, everything was swirling in her mind. "Continuing this only spells disaster for me and I want off the ride before we crash."

CHAPTER FOURTEEN

LUCAS HAD CONSIDERED skipping out on Kevin Rogers's funeral but in the end had opted to attend.

Currently, he sat in a church pew, listening to the pastor doing the funeral service recite accounts of the little boy's life and how he'd been a blessing to his parents.

Surprisingly, Emily sat next to him. She wore a pretty black dress that was classy and made her eyes sparkle like emeralds.

He wasn't holding her hand and was acutely aware of that fact. For that matter, he was acutely aware of the fact that he'd not seen her or spoken to her or kissed her or made love to her for the past two days. He'd done his best to avoid her, to give her what she wanted. He'd stayed away.

She'd been waiting on the steps when he'd arrived at the church. She'd looked tense, as if she didn't want to be there.

She could have not shown. Not Emily. She was always one to fulfill her responsibilities.

Despite how uncomfortable she'd appeared, she'd also taken his breath. Lord, he missed her.

Only the memory of her depression, knowing that he'd caused her sadness, had given him the power to honor her request of staying away. Still, he'd struggled, had wanted to take her in his arms and demand she tell him what it was about him that caused her to hurt inside so much.

Was that why he'd stayed away all these years? Because he'd watched a bubbly young woman turn into a sad, depressed shell of herself and he'd blamed himself?

He should have talked to her back then, explained how he felt, enlisted her parents' help in getting her depression treated. He'd have gone to counseling with her, would have done whatever it took.

Emily deserved a good life, a happy life. If she felt he was a complication she didn't need, that she was happier without him, he'd leave her alone.

Maybe he'd even leave Children's because having to see her would be torture knowing he could never have her.

He'd hate to leave Children's, but he wouldn't submit Emily, or himself, to having to see each other daily. Nor would he submit himself to having to see her meet and fall in love with someone else.

She wanted a husband, kids, a family.

He wanted those things, too. With Emily.

With Emily, the thought echoed through his mind.

He glanced over at her, thinking he'd just sneak a quick look, but frowned at what he saw.

Emily was crying.

Not tears of a nurse who'd just met a young child once in a surgical suite, but real tears that were ripped from her heart.

Past memories of tears rocked him. Memories of not knowing what to do. Of being helpless to ease her tears.

He wrapped his arm around her shoulders and pulled her closer, hugging her in an embrace he hoped would comfort.

Her tears worsened and Lucas felt lost.

Hadn't her tears always left him feeling lost?

* * *

Who would have dreamed that Emily would someday be sitting in a church with Lucas attending a funeral service for a child?

Not her.

She'd known today was going to be difficult, but she'd not felt right about not attending after she'd said she would. She'd braced herself. But she'd not been prepared for the onslaught of tears that had hit her as she listened to the pastor extol the boy's life and how blessed his parents had been to have him for four years.

Anger flared inside her at the man beside her for not loving her enough to want her to stay. Anger at fate that the baby she'd loved and wanted had been snatched away, too.

Anger mixed with grief so intense she thought she might shrivel up and die.

She wanted out of the church.

Lucas hugged her to him.

She didn't want his hug. Didn't want his comfort.

"Do you want to leave?" he whispered close to her ear.

She shook her head.

Not that she didn't want to leave. She did. Just that she wasn't sure her legs would hold her. If she collapsed to the floor, that would cause a scene at the boy's funeral. She wasn't willing to risk that.

"Emily?" Lucas whispered, obviously not understanding. He couldn't understand. Guilt hit her. But why feel guilty? There had been nothing to be gained by telling him. Knowing would have only possibly hurt him, too. Despite all her pain, she hadn't wanted Lucas to hurt.

She'd kept the pain all to herself.

Shaking her head, she held up her hand, silencing him.

His expression was worried. His arm tightened around her body.

The glass house Emily had been living inside for the past five years cracked, then shattered all around her as grief she'd kept buried burst free and let loose an explosion of emotions.

The funeral service ended and Lucas let out a sigh of relief. Had he known how upset attending was going to make Emily, he'd never have asked her to go with him.

He felt horrible that he'd subjected her to the funeral and helpless as she'd silently sobbed.

Had she never been to a funeral before? Perhaps not. He'd only been to a handful. His grandparents. A few family friends. A few patients. None had ever affected him the way Emily mourned for a child she hadn't known. Maybe that said something about the way he viewed life, viewed death. Or maybe it was more a sign of how she viewed those things. Emily had a big heart, always had.

"Excuse me," she said. She stood and made her way out of the chapel without a backward glance.

Watching her go, Lucas still battled confusion. Losing a patient was hard, especially such a senseless death as the young boy's had been. At least the hit-and-run taxi driver had been caught and arrested.

No matter how he tried, Lucas couldn't understand Emily's quiet sobs. He'd spent most of the service trying to figure out why she was so upset, but kept coming up with more questions.

Then again, he'd never understood her tears.

That she was gone from outside the church entrance didn't surprise him.

She'd told him to leave her alone, and he would. But he needed to make sure she was okay from the emotional beating she'd endured during the funeral.

His heart ached. How was he supposed to ignore how

her body had silently shaken with tears? How was he supposed to walk away with that having been the last time he'd touched her?

He needed to tell her how he felt. Even if it was only for her to laugh and reject him and tell him to leave, he owed it to Emily and to himself to tell her everything.

That was when he saw her, standing several hundred yards down the street. Apparently, she'd taken off walking, then decided to wait on a taxi when she'd recalled how far away they were from her apartment.

Even from the distance, he could tell she still cried.

He flagged down a taxi, got inside and then had the driver pull over to pick up Emily.

She got inside and pulled the door closed.

Lucas told the driver the address to Emily's place. She glanced up at him, obviously startled to see him inside the cab. Had she been so upset that she hadn't realized he was there?

She swiped at the tears running down her cheeks. "How do you just show up wherever I do?"

"This time it was intentional," he admitted. "I had the driver pull over to pick you up."

She turned away from him and pretended to stare out the window, but he suspected she really did so to hide her tearstained face.

"I'm taking you home, Emily," he told her, keeping his voice gentle but firm. "Then you and I are going to talk. I'm going to tell you a few things I've discovered about me, you, and about us. You're going to tell me what upset you so much at that funeral. When we're through talking, I'll leave and I'll turn my notice in at Children's, if that's what you want. For that matter, I'll leave Manhattan if you think the city isn't big enough for the both of us. But prior to my stepping out of your life forever, we are going to talk."

* * *

Lucas was so wrong if he thought Emily was going to tell him why she'd started bawling and hadn't been able to quit.

So very wrong.

What would be the point of telling him after all this time? There was nothing he could do to change the past. Nothing good could come out of telling him. Only more pain.

Pain she already lived with.

Pain she wasn't even sure he'd feel.

Or that she hadn't believed he would feel for so many years. Now she wasn't so sure.

Having seen him with Cassie, Jenny, with his other patients, she had to question what she'd always believed. Over the years, she'd convinced herself that Lucas would have been glad their baby had died. It was how she'd dealt with the loss of him and their child.

Sitting next to him in that church, listening to that boy's funeral, that conviction had been buried.

Lucas wouldn't have wanted their baby to die.

That she'd ever believed so to begin with had been hormones and perhaps a coping mechanism to deal with her grief over losing her husband and her baby so closely together.

She'd needed him at the last funeral service she'd attended. He should have been there, but hadn't.

Despite her grief, she recognized he couldn't have been there even if he'd wanted, because he hadn't known about the small service only three guests had attended. Emily and her parents.

She choked back more tears at the memories, at the overwhelming sense of loss. "I was pregnant."

Dear God, had she really just said that out loud in the

back of a taxi two blocks from her apartment? Talk about inappropriate. Talk about bad timing.

Lucas's face went ashen. "I didn't hear you, Emily."

Now was her chance. Just tell him it was nothing. That she hadn't even spoken. That what he thought he'd heard, then dismissed as having been wrong, had indeed been incorrect.

"I was pregnant," she repeated a little louder than her first whispered admission. She turned away from him, unable to bear his confused expression, and stared blankly out the taxi window.

What was wrong with her? She couldn't stop crying and now she couldn't stop saying things she shouldn't be saying.

She didn't need to be looking at Lucas to feel his tension, to know that his entire body had stiffened.

"When?" If she hadn't known who was sitting in the back of the taxi next to her, she wouldn't have recognized his voice. He sounded distant, removed, like a stranger.

He was a stranger. Five years ago, he'd told her to leave, she had, and then he'd divorced her. Five years in which they'd had no contact whatsoever. Just because he'd jumped back into her life and into her bed didn't mean a thing.

Not a thing.

Except that once again she was crying.

She turned, met his gaze and spoke low but clearly. "When you told me the very last thing you wanted was for me to have your baby."

Lucas stared into Emily's tear-streaked, puffy face.

She'd been pregnant.

His baby had been growing inside her.

He'd told her he didn't want her to have his baby.

She'd already been pregnant.

Understanding of so much from the past hit him. Understanding of her silent sobs at the funeral.

She'd been pregnant, but there was no baby.

His insides crumbled. "What happened to our baby?"

Emily's face paled to a ghostly white. Her mouth dropped open, but she didn't speak. Her face contorted in pain and guilt hit him that he asked, yet he had to know.

"I'm sorry." He felt as if that was all he said where Emily was concerned. *I'm sorry. I'm sorry. I'm sorry.*

He was sorry.

So very sorry.

"I didn't know you were pregnant, Emily."

"I know." Her voice was a broken sob and she reached for the taxi's door handle, no doubt preparing to jump out the moment the taxi stopped outside her upcoming apartment building.

Lucas reached in his pocket, pulled out a twenty and tossed it up to the driver through the window as he followed Emily out of the car.

She went inside the building and he followed her, unable to leave, but not sure he had any right to be there.

Yes, he did have a right.

She'd been pregnant with his baby. He deserved to know more, to know the details of what had happened to their child.

Without a word, they rode up the elevator together, then she unlocked her apartment door and he followed her inside.

She tossed her over-the-shoulder handbag onto her sofa, then turned to face him. Tears streaked down her face still, gutting him. How many tears had he caused her to shed?

"Tell me what happened."

She shook her head. "It was a long time ago. I never should have said anything. You don't need to know."

For the first time a spark of anger hit him. She'd been pregnant with his baby and hadn't told him. Now she was telling him he didn't need to know about their child because it had been a long time ago?

"I'm not leaving until you tell me." His voice broke as he spoke. How did he convey that he felt grief over the loss of a child he hadn't even known about until minutes before? That he felt grief that she'd dealt with that loss by herself when he should have been there. "You should have told me years ago."

"Why?"

"Because I deserved to know." Had he really? He wasn't sure. But he should have known. He should have been able to look at her, his wife, and have known his baby was growing inside of her.

"How did it happen?"

Her eyes narrowed defensively. "I didn't get pregnant on purpose, if that's what you're asking. I know that's what your parents would have thought if they'd known, but we always used protection. Always."

She'd talked about having a baby so often, hadn't he worried that was what she'd do? Hadn't he quit coming home for fear that she'd purposely get pregnant? Instead, she'd already been pregnant and had wanted him to show some sign that he might be happy about the news. He never had, and she hadn't told him that it was already a done deal.

Was that why she'd cried all the time? He'd thought her depressed. Had she really been suffering from extreme pregnancy hormone mood changes?

His short spark of anger dissipated. "I meant, how did our baby die?"

She paced across the room, paused, her back to him. "I started bleeding and it wouldn't stop. The obstetrician at the emergency room said my hormones were really out of line, that it had only been a matter of time before I miscarried as my body was rejecting the pregnancy. There was nothing they could do."

"How far along were you?"

"Five months."

Lucas's feet went out from under him and he sank onto the sofa. Five months. His wife had been five months pregnant and he hadn't known.

Five months. How was that even possible?

Sure, he'd stopped having sex with her for fear she'd get pregnant, but shouldn't he have noticed something different? Or had he been so busy trying not to look at her that he'd failed to see the obvious?

"I didn't know."

"I never thought you did. Although I could see the difference in my belly, I hadn't gained any weight overall. When dressed, it was easy to hide."

Why hadn't she gained weight? Perhaps the stress of a strained marriage? Perhaps all the tears she'd cried?

"I'm sorry, Emily." There he went apologizing again. "I should have been there."

She didn't correct him. Nor should she. He should have been by her side in that emergency room.

"Were you alone when it happened?"

"I went to my parents after I moved out of our apartment." She shook her head. "I'd felt bad all week but thought it was from what was going on between you and me. When I started gushing blood, my mother called the ambulance. She stayed with me."

"She probably hates me."

"You're not her favorite person."

"I imagine not." He tried to let it sink in. Had Emily not miscarried, he'd be a father. He'd have a five-year-old kid. Would she have told him if she hadn't miscarried?

"I had to threaten my mother that I'd never speak to her again to keep her from going to give you a piece of her mind."

"I wish she had." Because then he would have known.

Then what? What would he have done differently? Would he have gone to Emily and comforted her?

"The last thing I wanted was more drama."

Which explained why she'd just accepted his ridiculous divorce papers that he'd expected her to show up at their apartment and throw back in his face. Despite her depression, he'd expected her to fight for their marriage, to fight for him. When she hadn't and he'd realized she wasn't going to, he'd felt a devastation unlike any he'd ever known. Pride had helped him replace hurt with anger.

As with much of their marriage, he'd reacted on hot emotion when he'd filed for divorce, but, as stupid as he'd been, he'd never expected their marriage to end. He'd thought receiving the divorce papers would send Emily home, would snap her out of whatever was bothering her, would cause her to admit she had a problem and needed help. Instead, she'd signed the papers, rid her life of him and never looked back. She'd not wanted anything else from him. She'd just wanted to forget he'd ever been a part of her life and she'd moved on as if he'd never existed in her world.

He'd been the one with a problem, the one who'd needed help.

She'd given birth to a five-month-old baby.

"Did we have a son or a daughter?"

She hesitated and for a moment he wondered if she was going to tell him anything more, but then she sighed and looked so gutted his insides twisted.

"A daughter."

He'd had a daughter. A daughter whom he'd never gotten to see or hold or even fantasize about.

"They wouldn't let me see her," Emily said, her tortured words invading his thoughts, making him ache with the pain he heard in her voice.

"I wanted to," she continued. "I wanted to hold her, but they wouldn't let me."

Lucas got off the sofa, went to Emily and wrapped his arms around her while she cried. He shed tears of his own.

"You're a much better person than I am," he told her long minutes later.

Not speaking, she shook her head. "I've held that in for so long. I can't believe I told you."

"You should have told me long ago."

"Why? What good can come out of you knowing? Nothing."

"At least now I understand why you signed the divorce papers."

"You told me to leave, then sent me divorce papers. Did you think I wouldn't sign them?"

"In the middle of an argument, I told you that if you were that unhappy being married to me, you should leave. You left."

She closed her eyes. "How could I stay when you wanted me to leave?"

"I never wanted you to leave." He disentangled himself from where he held her. He needed to process the things that had happened, the things he'd learned and how he felt about those things, how he felt about Emily, about himself, about the fact he'd had a child he never knew about. "I just couldn't be what you needed me to be at that point in my life. You were crying all the time, so moody, I felt I could never do anything right, could never make you happy. Between my fellowship, my mom's grief over my grandmother's death, the financial constraints you insisted upon, the stress of wanting to be a good husband, I just wasn't coping well. When, between crying bouts, you started talking about wanting a baby, I choked. I already felt like a failure. How was I supposed to add in daddy duties?"

"I guess it's a good thing you never had to."

"No, Emily, that isn't a good thing. Not at all. Had you been upfront and told me you were pregnant, I would have wanted our baby."

"How could I have told you I was pregnant? Your parents were already accusing me of being a gold digger, warning you that I'd get pregnant on purpose. You were drifting further and further away from me and the more I tried to pull you back, the further away you slipped."

"I wasn't slipping away, Emily. I was staying away because I didn't want to make you pregnant."

She stared at him. "What do you mean?"

"I was afraid you'd intentionally get pregnant."

"I'd never have done that."

"I know that. Now. At the time, I was stressed and was hearing from all sides how I'd rushed into marriage and how you'd be quick to want to start a family so you'd have a permanent tie to my family's wealth."

"I never wanted money from you."

"No, you never did." He raked his fingers through his hair. "I'm sorry, Emily. For making you so sad, for everything I ever did wrong."

"Me, too."

Lucas wasn't sure how long he stood at Emily's window, staring down at the street below. When he turned, she sat on the sofa, watching him with her red-rimmed eyes.

He'd done that. He'd put that deep hurt inside her. He'd pushed her away and she'd lost his baby. No wonder she'd changed hospitals to get away from him. No wonder she'd not wanted anything to do with him when he'd first shown up at Children's.

He'd hurt her in ways that couldn't be easily forgotten, couldn't readily be moved beyond. The fact that she hadn't told him she was pregnant, that she'd kept something so significant from him during their marriage, caused pain he'd not easily forget or move beyond, either.

Tonight, he needed to hurt, though, to feel the pain and let it cut at his very soul while he came to grips with the past, with the loss of a baby daughter he'd not even known about.

Emily had said too much had happened for them to ever have a second chance. He hadn't understood that before.

Now he did.

CHAPTER FIFTEEN

EMILY POKED HER HEAD into her patient's room. Her heart swelled at what she saw.

Cassie Bellows awake and, although still groggy and sleeping more often than not, holding her mother's hand.

"How's she doing this morning?"

Cassie's mother smiled. "She woke up several times during the night but seems a little stronger each time she wakes up."

"That's what the night nurse told me during report. She said Cassie was doing great."

The girl's mother nodded. "Dr. Cain says everything went as perfectly as it possibly could have when he removed the tumor. Now we just have to wait and see how successful the surgery really was or wasn't."

Dr. Cain. A man Emily hadn't seen for three days.

Three days in which he'd just disappeared from her life.

But not life in general because he'd been at the hospital each day, had done his rounds, had transferred Jenny, who was steadily improving, to the orthopedic surgical floor for further correction of her limb injuries. He'd scheduled Cassie for surgery and performed the surgical excision of her tumor early the day before.

Cassie had done great. Emily had checked on the child

before she'd gone home from her shift but had made sure to carefully avoid Lucas.

If he didn't want to see her, she wouldn't put herself in his path. Not intentionally.

She didn't fool herself that she'd be able to avoid him altogether, not with them working at the same hospital. She'd toyed with updating her résumé but had nixed the idea. She loved her job at Children's and wasn't leaving. If her being there made him uncomfortable, he could leave. He'd said he would if that was what she wanted. Was it? No, she wanted him to have the opportunity to pursue his dreams, to do his research. Children's provided him with that opportunity.

They were both better off without each other.

If only she could convince herself of that.

She had five years ago. She'd convinced herself that he was a horrible person who hadn't wanted her or their baby.

That belief had been a balm for her pain and helped her move forward.

This time she knew better. She knew that her pregnancy hormones had prevented rational thought, that she'd blamed him for things that had perhaps been as much her fault as his.

Lucas was a good man, a good doctor. They'd both been immature and had made mistakes then and now.

Not that telling him about their baby was a mistake. The mistake had been not telling him immediately when she started suspecting she might be pregnant all those years ago, letting her hormones, and fear of what others thought, of what he might think, drive her thoughts to irrational limits.

But he'd already started acting so distant and some-how she'd known he wouldn't be happy with her news even before she'd started hinting about a baby. Still, she should have told him.

"Her vitals are looking really good," she told Mrs. Bellows, knowing the woman was waiting for a response of some type.

The woman nodded. Emily checked Cassie's reflexes, pleased when each one responded appropriately.

"Her neuro check is right on target."

Cassie's eyes tracked everything Emily did as she quickly assessed her patient. That the girl's eyes didn't leave hers was a great sign.

By the time Emily finished her examination, Cassie had dozed back off.

Mrs. Bellows bent over the bed to kiss Cassie's cheek. "Dr. Cain said he'd wean her off the ventilator today if she continued to hold her own."

Dr. Cain. Dr. Cain. Dr. Cain. Maybe Emily would have to rethink the whole staying at Children's thing. Listening to his patients and their families extol his virtues didn't rank high on her list of things to do if she wanted to keep her sanity.

Not that she didn't understand Mrs. Bellows's admiration of Lucas. Emily did. He'd saved Cassie's life when he'd stopped the bleed and he'd given them hope that Cassie was going to be okay when he'd removed the brain tumor.

"She is. I bet he'll be by this morning and give the order for the ventilator to be discontinued. My guess is that he only left it in overnight as an extra precaution."

The woman nodded, then glanced down at where her hand was laced with Cassie's.

"She squeezes my hand in response to my questions," the woman assured her, sounding ecstatic by the simple communication.

Emily smiled. A mother's love was a beautiful thing.

Something she'd never allowed herself to really embrace. Not before telling Lucas about their baby. She had been a mother. She had loved her baby.

Telling Lucas about their daughter had healed areas of her heart she'd thought incurable.

"I asked if she knew who I was and she gave me the funniest look and tried to nod her head, then squeezed my hand. I asked her to squeeze it twice if she knew." Mrs. Bellows's voice choked up. "She squeezed it twice."

Feeling a little choked up herself, Emily patted where mother's and daughter's hands were linked. "She knows you."

Emily was sure the child did. She'd seen the recognition and love in Cassie's eyes when she'd looked at her mother.

"She really didn't wake up much yesterday but has been awake several times during the night and this morning. She never lasts long, but each time I see her eyes, it's enough to reassure me that my baby girl is still in there. But we won't really know much until the ventilator is out and we see how she responds to simple tasks."

Emily knew that it was possible Cassie would have reverted to the skill levels of a much younger child from the trauma of having part of her brain excised. Or that she might have suffered permanent damage and lost ability to stand, or walk, or talk, or so many things.

But so far every indication was that the girl's surgery had been a huge success. Emily prayed that trend continued.

"I'll be in and out checking on her, but if you need anything, don't hesitate to call me to her room."

Emily turned to leave the room and found Lucas standing in the doorway. She wasn't sure how long he'd been watching her and Cassie's mother. She supposed it didn't really matter.

She opened her mouth to speak, but nothing came out.

If he'd wanted to say something, the same thing must have happened, because he just stood there, staring at her as if trying to see inside her head.

Feeling a fool, she stood next to Cassie's bed as if paralyzed.

"Dr. Cain," Mrs. Bellows greeted him, her face lighting up at seeing him. "You just missed Cassie being awake."

"I'm sorry I missed her," he answered, dragging his gaze from Emily's.

Dear Lord, he looked good. So good her heart ached.

He'd been her husband, her lover, her best friend, and now...now she supposed he was her colleague and that would be the only link they maintained.

Sadness filled her, but she wouldn't cry.

No, she'd focus on what she had shared with Lucas, celebrate the good, put the bad behind her and move forward with her life.

She could do this.

But at the moment, she didn't feel so strong.

She excused herself from the room and left Lucas to talk with Mrs. Bellows and check Cassie.

It was what she needed to do.

She had another patient she needed to check.

She had a heart she had to start trying to piece back together. Again.

Lucas stood outside Emily's apartment door, wondering if she'd let him in.

He assumed she'd gone home at the end of her shift, but maybe not. He'd seen her talking with Meghan prior to leaving the hospital. It was possible they'd gone somewhere.

If so, then what? He'd been sitting in his office, thinking

about Emily, about the past, about the present, about life. He'd kept arriving at the same conclusion. The accumulation of the past made up the present and his future, and nothing in the past, present or future mattered without Emily.

He'd headed to her apartment, not sure what he was going to do, what he was going to say, just that he had to go to her.

He didn't have time to debate within himself further because Emily opened the door and stared at him.

"What do you want?"

"You."

She grimaced. "Let's not do this. I can't handle it."

"You want me to go?" Lucas's heart pounded in his chest. Was she sending him away before he'd even gotten started spilling his heart to her?

"If you come in, we both know what will happen."

He raked his fingers through his hair. "I'm not here for sex."

"But you just said…"

"You asked me what I wanted and I told you."

The apartment door next to hers opened. A head peeked out to see who was in the hallway.

Lucas gave Emily's neighbor a reassuring smile. "Let me come in, Emily."

Emily sighed, then stepped aside. She walked over to her sofa and sat down. She picked up a throw pillow, put it in her lap and toyed with the tasseled fringe. "Sit down, please."

Lucas sat on the sofa but kept a good distance between them. He didn't want to be distracted by her nearness. He needed a clear head to tell her all the things he'd done the past couple of days.

"I checked on Cassie before I came here. She is doing great off the ventilator."

"You could have texted to tell me that," she said.

"I could have, but there's a lot more I need to tell you, Emily. Things that have nothing to do with Cassie or the hospital."

She didn't say anything, just held on to the pillow in her lap and waited.

"I've done a lot of thinking over the past couple of days," he continued. "I stayed at my parents' the other night after I left here, had breakfast with them and did a lot of talking."

"You told them about our baby? Did they think I'd gotten pregnant on purpose to try to take your money?"

Lucas sighed. "I told them. Not once did either of them say anything about you getting pregnant on purpose, Emily. They couldn't help but question you in the beginning with how quickly we met and married. There are a lot of women who marry for money."

"I didn't."

"I know that." He did know that. Maybe during prideful moments he'd let his thoughts go there, but he'd never believed Emily had married him for financial reasons. She'd loved him and had simply wanted to be his life partner. "My mother was devastated by the news you'd been pregnant and miscarried, that she may have played a role in you feeling you couldn't tell me. She wanted me to tell you how very sorry she is that the two of you never got close, that she wasn't there when you lost our baby."

A sob broke free from Emily and she swiped her eyes, covered her mouth as she whispered, "I'm sorry."

"You have no reason to be sorry, Emily. You didn't do anything wrong. My mother knows that. I know that."

"That's not true. I did a lot of things wrong. I—"

"Emily," he interrupted. "I need to finish telling you this while I can."

She folded her shaking hands over the pillow. "Okay."

"I wasn't scheduled with patients that morning, so after I left my parents, I went to your parents."

Her head jerked around to him. "You went to my parents?" she gasped. "Why?"

How could he not have?

"I needed to talk to them."

"About?"

"You. Me. Them. Our baby. Our marriage. Your depression. Everything."

"And?"

"And I'm sorry I never took the time to know your parents when we were married. They are good people."

Emily visually searched him over, possibly looking for battle wounds. There weren't any. At first he'd thought perhaps there would be, but Emily's parents had sat on their sofa, sour expressions in place, and listened to what he'd had to say.

When he'd left, Emily's father had shaken his hand, and her mother had reluctantly given him a hug. He could only hope this conversation went as well as that one.

"I can't believe you went to my parents' house." She didn't say because he'd never been there before. She didn't have to. He'd been too busy to go with her to her parents' during their marriage. He'd barely juggled visiting his own, he'd justified to himself at the time.

"Why did you go there, Lucas?"

"Because there's no way for the air to be cleared between you and me without clearing the air with them."

Her forehead wrinkled. "Why does any of this matter now?"

"It matters a great deal."

She stared at him with confusion and devastation burning in her green eyes. "I don't understand."

No, he supposed she didn't. Neither had her parents. Not until he'd told them how he'd never gotten over Emily, had never stopped caring for her, that he hadn't understood her depression, that he hoped to win her heart back, and wanted their blessing, that this time around he hoped to do things right. He'd told them he realized he didn't deserve forgiveness or second chances, but he prayed they'd give them anyway, that he prayed Emily would see beyond the past and see the man he was now, the man who had learned so many life lessons. He was sure there were many more he'd learn over the years, but he wanted Emily by his side as he faced each of those challenges.

He'd told her parents all that and more. Had told his parents that. Now he'd tell the only woman who'd ever stolen his heart.

"I love you, Emily."

Emily's ears roared and her throat thickened to where breathing felt impossible. "What did you say?"

"I love you. I always have. I always will."

Tears prickled her eyes. Why was he telling her this now? Why had he gone to her parents? Why was her heart swelling to where she thought it might burst free from her rib cage?

"I love you, too, Lucas." She always had, always would. Once she'd told him the truth, her anger at him had eased, had given way to so much more, to the truth. She loved Lucas.

She'd just never expected him to feel the same.

He moved next to her, tossed her pillow to the side and took her hand into his.

She trembled. Her hands. Her body. Her very being.

"I want to be a part of your life, Emily. I knew it after I took the job at Children's and saw you again. I just didn't understand the reasons why it was so important I be near you."

Lucas wanted to be a part of her life. Wasn't that what he'd been the past few weeks?

"I couldn't stop thinking about you, dreaming about you," he continued. "I wanted a second chance with you."

Her hand still trembled within his, but she didn't pull it away. His was trembling, too.

"I messed up when we got married, Emily. I was immature, selfish, stressed with school, stressed by my grandmother's death and how my mother wasn't dealing with that. I was distracted by life, and I lost the most important thing that's ever been mine."

She just stared at him blankly.

"You."

"You never owned me."

"Sure I did. You gave yourself to me, just as I gave myself to you. Unfortunately, I was a fool who didn't see what a prize having you was. I married you for all the wrong reasons, Emily."

Her body tensed. "I wasn't pregnant when we got married."

"No, I didn't think you were and that wasn't what I meant. I married you for my convenience."

Emily didn't understand. She gazed at him in confusion, waiting for him to elaborate.

"I wanted to have you with me when it was convenient for me. I wanted to have all my old life, but to have you there when I wanted you there. I was an idiot who didn't deserve you. I probably still don't, but I want to be a part of your life all the same."

Emily digested what he'd said. Their marriage hadn't just fallen apart because of mistakes he'd made. She'd made plenty of them, too. She'd been so intimidated by his family, so hurt by their thoughts that she'd only become involved with Lucas because of money, that she'd automatically bristled at anything to do with them or money. She'd reacted similarly to his friends. She'd isolated herself from his life outside their apartment. And then, when she'd gotten pregnant, her mood swings had gotten bad, her paranoia over her lack of fitting in had grown, her ability to rationally think things through where he was concerned had failed.

"The one thing I got right, Emily, was you. I love you. I have from the beginning. That never changed. Not through the tears I never understood. Not through the fights. Not through the divorce that never should have taken place. Not through the years that have passed." He squeezed her hand. "I resented the power you held over me."

Ha. She'd been a leaf floating in the wind, at mercy to drift whichever direction he blew.

"I was powerless."

"You may not have known it, but you had all the power where I was concerned. Stop and think about it. I abided by your rules, Emily. You said we had to live in your tiny apartment, so we did. You said I couldn't use my trust fund, so I didn't. I had a thousand demands on me from the hospital, from school, from my parents and from you. I felt as if I was going to snap. Every time we were together, all you'd do was cry, then we'd fight. The more we fought, the more I justified pulling away from you."

She pulled her hand free and scooted away from him. "You wanted to put our marriage on hold until a more convenient time?" She shook her head. "Why are you telling me this now? Any of this?"

"Because to move forward all the past has to be dealt with."

"Too much has happened for you and I to move forward."

He moved closer to her, took her hand back and gently held it within his. "I hope you don't believe that, because I don't. Not anymore."

Did she?

"I was pregnant, Lucas. I was pregnant and alone and you weren't there." She hadn't meant to say the words, wasn't even sure where they came from, but from somewhere deep, dark inside the words had leaped out, revealing her innermost pain.

"I wish I had been, Emily. If I'd known, I would have been at your side." His hand tightened around hers. "When I came home and your things were gone, I couldn't believe you'd left me. Stupid pride kicked in. I called a lawyer and set the divorce into motion. For what it's worth, I never thought we'd go through with it."

"You filed for divorce. Of course we'd go through with it."

"I thought you'd tell me where I could stick my divorce papers. It's what I wanted you to tell me."

"I got the papers on the day I came home from the hospital from losing our baby. I just looked at them and felt so defeated. I signed them and put them in the return envelope to your lawyer. My mother warned me to wait, that I wasn't thinking straight and should talk to someone before I just signed them, but I didn't have the energy to wait or fight."

"I'm sorry, Emily. I made so many mistakes, so many things I wish I could do over, but I can't. All I can do is make sure I learn from the past and never make those same mistakes again."

"I'm sorry I was so adamant about not using your trust."

She bit the inside of her lip. "I was intimidated by your money. I thought if you lived within my world, we'd be okay, but that if we tried to live within yours, I'd stick out like a sore thumb and everyone would know what a fraud I was."

His eyes softened. "You weren't a fraud. You were my wife."

"I was a kid who got caught up in a love affair that she wanted to believe was a fairy tale. I realized I was too idealistic a month in. By the time I discovered our birth control had failed, I knew we'd jumped too fast."

"Emily, I don't regret having married you. I just regret our divorce."

"Me, too."

"Which brings me to why I'm here. I want to spend the rest of my life loving you, cherishing you and making up to you every stupid and wrong thing I ever did."

"No." She shook her head.

"No?"

"I don't want you trying to make up for the past. The past is done, over." Her heart ached. "I won't have you with me out of guilt."

"Woman." He pulled her to him on the sofa. "How many times do I have to say I love you before you'll understand?"

"Understand what?"

"I'm not here out of guilt. I'm here out of love. Out of a need to spend my life with the woman I want to be with above all others. The woman who I want to give everything I am to now and for forever."

He sounded like a marriage vow. The thought pinched her heart, because she knew that wasn't the case.

Could she do it?

Could she have an affair with Lucas until he tired of her and walked away?

Would he walk away?

Staring into his eyes, she wasn't so sure he would. But she didn't want just an affair. She wanted everything. She wanted to believe in fairy tales and dreams come true.

She wanted to believe in Lucas.

"I'm here to beg you to consider spending your life with me, Emily."

Was she going to refuse him? Lucas held Emily's hand within his, held his breath, prayed she felt the way he believed she felt, that too much negative hadn't happened between them to drown out all the good.

So many emotions danced across her face that he couldn't read her thoughts.

"What are you saying, Lucas?" she asked. "That you want to have an affair with me?"

An affair. He'd poured his heart out to her and she thought he was asking for sex still?

"If that's all you're willing to give me, then, yes, I'll take an affair. A lifelong one."

She stared at him, caution and the beginnings of hope in her eyes. Hope he planned to nurture for the rest of her life.

"What is it you want me to give?"

Her question was an easy one for him to answer. One he could answer with all certainty and the knowledge that Emily was his soul mate, the other half of him, the woman he wanted to wake up next to and go to sleep next to, to have her belly swollen with his children, to grow old next to, to look back on their life together and know that each step along the way had served a purpose, to teach them what was important, what was worth fighting for, what they should hold on to with all their might and hearts.

"You," he answered with his heart shining in his eyes. "Forever."

"I already did that," she reminded him, causing his heart to skip a beat. "You've always had me, Lucas. My heart, my body, all of me."

"Emily…"

"I love you, Lucas. I never stopped."

He kissed her, hard and on the mouth. "I don't deserve you."

"If this is going to work, then we have to forgive each other. Which means you do deserve me. You are a wonderful man. A wonderful doctor. A wonderful lover. A wonderful friend."

"I'd like to be a wonderful husband and father, Emily."

Emily couldn't believe her ears. "You want to get married again?"

He gave a low, nervous laugh. "This isn't how I had this part planned."

"What part planned?"

"I came here to convince you that I loved you and wanted us to be together. To talk about your depression and what went wrong between us. I'd hoped with time you'd learn to trust in our love, in us, and then I planned to propose."

Eyes wide, heart pounding, she stared at him. "You did?"

Smiling, he nodded. "I was going to take you up in the Statue of Liberty, get down on my knee and ask you to be my lady forever."

"I'm not sure if that's the sweetest thing I've ever heard or the corniest."

"I did have a plan B if that didn't work."

"What was that?"

"I was going to whisk you off to Paris and ask you at

the Eiffel Tower. If that didn't work, I'd come up with a plan C."

"Seriously?"

He nodded.

"So, really there's no incentive for me to agree."

"Only that you'd get to put this back on my finger." He reached into his pocket and pulled out a golden band.

Emily's breath caught. "You really want to get married again?"

"I do, and this time I want to do it right."

"Right?"

"I want you to walk down an aisle to me with our parents and friends there. I want to take you on a honeymoon to wherever you want to go—"

"Even if I said Atlantic City?"

His eyes glimmering, he nodded. "Even if you said Atlantic City."

"I don't need fancy weddings or fancy trips, Lucas."

His smile told her all she needed to know. He lifted her hand to his mouth and kissed her fingertips.

"Just fancy orgasms?"

"That and a fancy pediatric neurosurgeon husband. I'll be the envy of all my coworkers. They think he's pretty awesome. I agree."

"You'll marry me?"

She took his wedding band out of his hand and clasped it tightly in hers, lifting it to her heart. Rather than answering him, she rose from the sofa, went to her bedroom and returned with something she held out to him.

His eyes glassy, he looked at what she held, then met her gaze as he took the rings into his hand and closed his fingers around them.

"We've wasted five years being apart. I don't want to wait a minute longer."

"I can't believe we're even thinking this," she mused.

"I can't believe we ever let each other go."

"Never again."

"Never again," he repeated, taking her hand into his and kissing her fingertips. "I know there will be ups and downs. There are in every relationship, but I'll fight for you, for us, until my dying breath, Emily."

As she stared into his eyes, all Emily's old hurts melted away and happiness took their place.

Happiness that she knew was going to last ever after this second time around.

* * * * *

If you enjoyed this story, check out these
other great reads from Janice Lynn

WINTER WEDDING IN VEGAS
NEW YORK DOC TO BLUSHING BRIDE
FLIRTING WITH THE DOC OF HER DREAMS
AFTER THE CHRISTMAS PARTY...

All available now!

SEVEN NIGHTS
WITH HER EX

BY
LOUISA HEATON

Published in Great Britain 2016
By Mills & Boon, an imprint of HarperCollins*Publishers*
1 London Bridge Street, London, SE1 9GF

© 2016 Louisa Heaton

ISBN: 978-0-263-91513-6

Our policy is to use papers that are natural, renewable and recyclable
products and made from wood grown in sustainable forests.
The logging and manufacturing processes conform to the legal
environmental regulations of the country of origin.

Printed and bound in Spain
by CPI, Barcelona

Dear Reader,

The only times I have bumped into my ex-boyfriends—
only two, I promise!—I have managed to ignore them
completely. Rather successfully, too, whilst pretending I
was having a fabulous time, laughing and chatting with
my friends. I have never been in a situation where we
were forced to spend time together, and if I had I don't
think it would have gone very well!

Beau and Gray have to spend a week together, and I
wanted to explore what would happen when two people
who have completely different versions of past events
meet and have to get along. Have to rely on one another
for their very survival. Would the past get in their way?
Would they be able to overcome their difficulties, their
prejudices and their hurt and allow the other person
back inside their heart?

It was fun to explore this possibility—and to place the
story in one of my favourite destinations in the whole
world. The glorious Yellowstone National Park. I do
hope you enjoy their adventure!

Happy reading!

Louisa xxx

To my husband, Nick, who offered to take me
to Yellowstone Park as a research trip.
(But we never did get there…sigh…)

Books by Louisa Heaton

Mills & Boon Medical Romance

The Baby That Changed Her Life
His Perfect Bride?
A Father This Christmas?
One Life-Changing Night

Visit the Author Profile page
at millsandboon.co.uk for more titles.

Praise for
Louisa Heaton

'I adored this book. The characters were refreshing and
the story line was emotional and tugged at my heart.'
—*Goodreads* on
A Father This Christmas?

'*The Baby That Changed Her Life* moved me to tears
many times. It is a full-on emotional drama. Louisa Heaton
brought this tale shimmering with emotions.'
—*Goodreads*

CHAPTER ONE

WOW! THIS PLACE is amazing!

Dr Beau Judd drove her hire car into a vacant space outside the Gallatin Ranger Station in Yellowstone National Park. Silencing the engine, she looked out of her window and let out a satisfied sigh.

This was *it*. This was what she'd been looking for. A return to nature. The vast open expanses of the American wilderness. Huge sweeping plains of golden-yellow wild flowers, ancient stone outcrops, forests of pines and fir trees, beautiful blue skies and the kind of summer weather that people back in the UK could only dream of.

She grabbed her guidebook and flipped through the pages, determined to take every moment that she could to learn about where she was. Those golden flowers—bursting skywards like mini-sunflowers—what were they called? Beau flicked through to the flora and fauna section of her book and smiled.

Balsamroots. Perfect.

Her gaze fell to the text beneath the picture and her smile widened.

Native Americans would often use the sap of this plant as a topical antiseptic.

Now, wasn't *this* what she was here for? To learn? And that plant was a perfect start to her new learning experience on the Extreme Wilderness Medical Survival Course. She'd spent too long cooped up in hospitals, on wards, in Theatre. Standing for hours, operating in the depths of a patient's brain, gazing for too long at X-rays or imaging scans, stuck in small rooms passing along bad news, living in a sterile environment, never seeing the sky or enjoying the fresh air.

Her *life* had become the hospital. She'd even begun to forget what her flat looked like. There'd been too many nights spent sleeping in the on-call room, too much time spent with patients and their families, so that she hardly saw her own. Hardly had any friends apart from her work colleagues. Hardly saw anyone she cared about at all.

This next week would all be about Beau reclaiming *herself*. Getting back to grassroots medicine. Getting back to hiking—which she'd used to love, but she hadn't worn a set of boots for years. Not unless they had a heel anyway.

She was one of the top neurologists in England. Had spent years building up her reputation, skill set and repertoire.

Now was the time to take some time out. For herself. Regroup. Do what she loved. Learn and hike in some of the most beautiful country on the planet.

Beau got out of the car and sucked in a lungful of fresh mountain air. Then she popped the boot so she could get her backpack out. She'd bought all new kit—tent, clothes, equipment, walking poles. All colour-coordinated in a gorgeous shade of red. *Matches the hair*, she thought with a smile as she tied a bandana around her head to keep her long auburn hair off her face.

The first day's hike started today. She wanted to be ready. She didn't want anyone having to slow down because of her. Here she would make friends—hopefully for life—and with this experience under her belt perhaps she could start thinking about doing that season at Base Camp, Everest. Her ultimate goal.

She slung the backpack over her shoulders, adjusting the straps, then closed the boot, locked it. Lifting her sunglasses, she strode over to the ranger station, ready to check in and meet the other hikers. Hopefully she wasn't the last to arrive. She'd left Bozeman a whole hour earlier than she'd needed to, but still… She'd find out when she got inside.

It took a moment for her eyes to adjust to the interior of the log cabin, and then she noticed the receptionist standing behind the counter.

'Hi, there! I'm Dr Judd. I'm here for the Extreme Wilderness Medical Survival Course.'

'Welcome to Yellowstone! And welcome to Gallatin. Let me see here…' She ran a finger down a checklist. 'Sure. Here you are.' She ticked Beau's name with her pen. 'The others are waiting in the back. Go on through and help yourself to refreshments. They'll be the last you'll see for a while!'

Beau smiled her thanks and headed over to the door, from where she could already hear a rumble of voices in the next room.

This was it. The moment everything about her life would change! She would enjoy great new experiences. Get back to the basics of medicine and enjoy some survival training.

Plastering a huge smile on her face, she opened the door and scanned the room of faces, ready to say hi.

The smile froze on her face as she realised who was in the room with her.

A man whom she'd hoped *never* to see again.

Gray McGregor.

How was he even *here*? In this small ranger station? In Yellowstone Park? In America? What the heck was he doing? Why wasn't he back in Scotland? In Edinburgh, where he was meant to be?

This had to be some sort of double. A doppelgänger.

We all have one, right?

The smile left her face and unconsciously she let her hand grip the door frame to keep her balance, wrong-footed suddenly by the shock of seeing him. Her centre of gravity was distorted by the backpack, but also by this imposter—the image of the man who'd broken her heart—standing in front of her.

Of all the parks in all the world, he has to be in mine.

The real Gray she'd not seen for… She thought quickly, her mind stumbling as much as she was, over numbers and years that suddenly wouldn't compute. Her brain had flipped in a short circuit. Frozen. The ability to add up basic numbers was beyond her at this terrible moment in time.

And the clone just stood there, the smile that had been on his face before he'd become aware of her presence disappearing in the same way that clouds covered the sun. His eyes widened at the sight of her, the muscle in his jaw clenching and unclenching.

It is *you.*

The noise in the room quietened as the other backpackers sensed a change in the atmosphere, but then rose again slightly as they all pretended not to see.

It was all flooding back! All of it. The day she'd dressed in white *for him*. The hours spent getting her hair done at home, giggling and laughing excitedly with her hairdresser. Then the hour spent with the beautician, getting her make-up looking perfect. Putting on *that dress*, attaching the veil, taking hold of her bouquet and glimpsing herself in the mirror before the photographer had been allowed in to take pictures.

The joy and excitement of the day had been thrumming through her veins as with every picture taken, every smile she gave, every pose she stood for, she had imagined walking down that aisle to be with him. Anticipating the look on his face, the way he would smile back at her, the way they would stand side by side in front of the vicar...

Only, you weren't there, were you, Gray?

The *heartache* this man had caused...

He looked a little different from the way she was used to seeing him. Back then he'd been fresh-faced, his dark hair longer and more tousled. Today his hair was cut shorter than she remembered, more modern, and he had a trim beard that was as auburn in colour as her own hair. And he was staring at her with as much shock in his own eyes as she was feeling.

But I'm not going to let you see how much you hurt me!

Deliberately she tore her gaze from him, tried to ignore her need to hurry to the bathroom and slick on a few more layers of antiperspirant, and walked over to one of the other hikers—a woman in a dark green polo shirt.

'Hi, I'm Beau. Pleased to meet you.'

She turned her back on him, sure that she could feel his gaze upon her. Her body tensed, each muscle flooded with more adrenaline than it needed as she imagined his gaze trailing up and down her body.

Resisting the urge to turn around and start yelling at him, she instead tried to focus on what the other hiker was saying.

'...it's so good to meet you! I'm glad there's another woman in the group. There's three of us now.'

Beau smiled pleasantly. She hadn't caught the woman's

name. She'd been too busy trying not to grind her teeth, or clench her fists, whilst her brain had screamed at her all the horrible things she could say to Gray. All the insults, all the toxic bile she had once dreamed of throwing at him...

All the pain and heartache he'd caused...she'd neatly packaged it away. Determined to get on with her life, to forget he'd ever existed.

What was he even *doing* here? Surely he wasn't going to be on this course, too?

Of course he is. Why else would he be in this room?

Months this trip had taken her to plan and organise. Once she'd realised that she needed a change, needed to escape that cabin fever feeling, she'd pored over brochures, surfed the Net, checking and rechecking that *this* was the perfect place, the perfect course, the perfect antidote to what her life had become.

It was far enough away from home—from Oxford, where she lived and worked—for her to know that she wouldn't run into anyone she knew. Who did she know anyway? Apart from her family and patients? And her colleagues? How many of *them* had planned a trip to Yellowstone at the same time as her? None. The chances of *him* doing the same thing, for the same week as her... Well, it had never even crossed her mind.

Why would it? She'd spent years forcing herself to not think of Gray McGregor. The damned Scot with the irrepressible cheeky grin and alluring come-to-bed eyes!

Eleven years. Nearly twelve. That's how long it's been.

Eleven years of silence. Why had he never contacted her? Apologised? Explained?

Like I'd want to hear it now anyway!

Outwardly she was still smiling, still pretending to listen to the other hiker, but inwardly... Inwardly a small part of her *did* want to hear what he had to say. No matter how pathetic it might be. Part of her wanted him grovelling and on his knees, begging for her forgiveness.

I'll never forgive you, Gray.

Beau straightened her shoulders, inhaled a big, deep breath and focused on the other hiker—Claire. She was talking about some of the trails she'd walked—the Allegheny, the Maah Daah Hey.

Focus on her, not him.

'That's amazing. You walked those trails alone?'

'Usually! I think you can take in so much more when you've just got to entertain yourself.'

Was he still looking at her? Was he thinking of coming over to speak to her? Beau stiffened at the thought of him approaching.

'What made you come on this course?' she asked.

'Common sense. A lot of walkers I meet on trails are… shall we say, *older* than me? And when I was walking the Appalachian, this guy collapsed right in front of me. In an instant. I didn't know what to do! Luckily one of his group was an off-duty responder and he kept the guy alive until the rescue team arrived. You never know when you're gonna be stuck in the middle of nowhere with no medical assistance!'

Beau nodded.

'What about you, Beau? What made you come on this course?'

'I just wanted to get out and about, walking again. Somewhere beautiful. But somewhere I can still learn something. I want to work in the hospital tent on Everest at some point.'

'Oh, my Lord! You're braver than me! Are you a nurse, then?'

'A doctor. Of neurology.'

'My, my, my! You'll no doubt put us all to shame! Promise you won't laugh at my attempts to bandage someone?'

Beau didn't think she'd be laughing at anyone. The mood of her trip had already changed. Just a few moments ago she'd been carefree and breathing in the mountain air, assuring herself that she'd made the right decision to come here. But now…? With Gray here, too?

She would make him see that she was not amused by his presence. She wasn't *anything*! She had no energy to waste on that man. He'd been given more than enough of her time over the years and her life had moved on now. She was no longer the heartbroken Beau whom he had left standing at the altar. She was Dr Judd. Neurologist. Recommended by her peers. Published in all the exclusive medical journals. Award-winning, innovative and a leader in her field.

She would have nothing to do with him this next week, and if he didn't like her cold shoulder, then tough.

Beau slipped off her backpack, put it to one side and went to make herself a cup of tea at the drinks station. It would probably be the last decent cup of tea she'd experience for a while, and she didn't want to miss having it. They had time before they set out.

She kept her back to the rest of the room, studiously ignoring Gray.

He would have to get used to it.

Yellowstone National Park. Over three thousand miles away from his native Edinburgh. He'd travelled over the North Atlantic Ocean, traversed mile upon mile of American soil to make it here to Wyoming, this one small spot on the face of the *whole planet*, and yet… And yet somehow he had managed to find the one small log cabin in the huge vastness of a national park that contained the one woman he could not imagine facing ever again.

Why would he ever have expected to find her *here*? This wasn't her thing. Being outdoors. Hiking. Roughing it in tents and having to purify her water before drinking it. Beau was an indoors girl. A five-star hotel kind of girl. Life for her had never been about struggle and survival. This should have been a safe place to come to. The last place he would have expected her to be. Wasn't she a hotshot neurologist now? Wasn't she meant to be knee-deep in brains somewhere?

Seeing her walk into the room had almost stopped his heart. He'd physically felt the jolt, unable to take in oxygen. His lungs had actually begun to burn before he'd looked away, breaking eye contact, his mind going crazy with questions and insinuations as heat and guilt had seared his cheeks.

You broke her heart.

You never told her why.

You deserve to suffer for what you did.

And he *had* suffered. Hadn't he?

If only she knew how much he longed to go back and change what happened. If only she knew how much he'd hated himself for walking away, knowing what it would do to her but unable to explain why. If only she knew of how many nights he'd lain awake, thinking of how he could put right that wrong...

But how to explain? It was easy to imagine saying it, but actually having her here, right in front of him... All those things he wanted to say just stuck in his throat. She'd think they were excuses. Not good enough. Was she even in the right frame of mind to want to talk to him?

Beau had turned her back. Begun talking to another hiker. Claire, he thought she'd said her name was.

He took a hesitant step forward, then stopped, his throat feeling tight and painful. He wouldn't be able to speak right now if he tried. She clearly wanted nothing to do with him. She was ignoring him. Spurning him.

I deserve it.

Other people in the room were milling about. Mixing, being friendly. Introducing themselves to each other. Gray allowed himself to fall into the crowd. Tried to join in. But his gaze kept tracking back to her.

She still looked amazing. Her beautiful red hair was a little longer than he recalled, wavier, too. She'd lost some weight. There were angles now where once there'd been curves, and the lines around her eyes spoke of strain and stress rather than laughter.

Was she happy in life? He hoped that she was. He knew she was successful. Her name had been mentioned in a few case meetings at work. He'd even suggested her once for a family member of an old patient. His own work in cardiology didn't often give him reason to work with neurology, but he'd kept his ears open in regard to her. Keen to know that she was doing okay.

And she was. Though she had to have worked hard to have got where she had. So had he.

He watched from a distance as she mingled with the others, placing himself in direct opposition to her as she moved. The room was a mass of backpacks, hiking boots, men slapping each other on the back or heartily shaking each other's hands as they listed their posts and achievements to each other. Two women at the back of the room sat next to each other, their backpacks on the floor as they sipped at steaming cardboard cups. The last taste of civilisation before they hit the wilds of America.

But all Gray could concentrate on now was Beau. And his own overwhelming feelings of regret.

Would simple words of apology be enough?

Would telling her about the many times he'd picked up the phone and dialled her number even be adequate? Considering that he'd never followed through? He had always cancelled the call before she'd had a chance to answer. And all the emails he had sitting in his 'Drafts' folder, addressed to her, in which he'd struggled and failed each time to find the right words... The times he'd booked to go to the same medical conference as her, hoping to 'accidentally' bump into her, but had then cancelled...

She'd just call me a coward. She'd be right.

He had been afraid. Afraid of stirring up old hurts. Afraid of making things worse. Afraid of hurting her more than he already had...

Time had kept passing. And with each and every day that came and went, it had become more and more difficult to make that contact.

What would have been the point? He could hardly expect forgiveness. Or reconciliation. An apology would mean nothing now. He'd broken things so irrevocably between them. How could he fix them now? He had nothing to offer her. Not then and certainly not now. He was broken himself. And even though he'd known that, years ago, he'd still asked her to marry him! He'd forgotten himself and what he actually was in the madness of a moment when he'd felt so happy. He'd believed anything was possible— got carried away on the *possibility* of love.

But he didn't expect her to understand that. They'd come from two separate worlds and she'd known nothing of his family life. Of what it was like. He'd deliberately kept her away from his poisonous family. Kept her at a safe distance because she was so pure, so joyful, so full of life, believing in happy-ever-after.

She still wasn't married. And that puzzled him. It had

been all she'd ever wanted back then. Marriage. And children. It was what she had thought would complete her. After all, she'd said yes to his proposal and then just weeks later had started talking about children.

That was too much. That smacked the reality right back into me.

That was when the full force of not having thought through what he'd done had come to the fore. That was when he'd realised he couldn't go through with it.

For a man who was an expert in hearts, he'd sure been careless with hers.

And it had almost killed him to know that he was doing it.

The tea wasn't great. But she kept sipping it, swapping hands as the heat from the boiling hot water burned through the thin cardboard cup.

She was beginning to get over the shock and was now feeling calmer. She could even picture in her mind's eye dealing with him quite calmly and nonchalantly if he decided to speak to her. She'd be cool, uninterested, dismissive.

That would hurt him.

Because Gray liked to be the centre of attention, didn't he? That was why he'd done all that crazy adrenaline-junkie stuff. He'd passed it off as doing something for charity, but even then he'd wanted people to notice him, to say he was amazing or brave. That was why he'd done Ironman competitions, bungee jumps, climbed mountains and jumped out of planes. *With* a parachute, unfortunately.

He had always succeeded. People had *always* clapped him on the back and told him he was a great guy and he'd thrived on that. Had lived for that, doing more crazy things despite her always begging him not to. Had he listened? No.

So her ignoring him? Choosing not to notice him? That would have to sting a little.

Gray was an attractive man. Usually the most attractive man in a room. And he wasn't just a pretty face, but a brilliant cardiologist, too—getting his papers published in the most prestigious medical journals, trying out new award-winning surgeries, being the toast of the town.

He could at least have had the decency to fail at *something*.

And not once had he called, or apologised, or explained. Even his family hadn't had a clue—not that they'd spoken much to her. Even *before* the wedding. Perhaps that had been a clue?

Beau risked a quick glance at him, feeling all the old hurts, all the old pains, all the grief that she'd tried so unsuccessfully to pack away come pouring out as if they'd had the bandages ripped from them, exposing her sore, festering wounds.

She swallowed hard and looked away.

I will not *let him see what he's doing to me!*

A rage she had never before experienced boiled over inside her and she suddenly felt nauseous with the force of it. She turned away from him, her hand trembling, and took another sip of her tea. Then another. And another. Until her stomach calmed and her hand grew more steady.

She let out a breath, feeling her brain frazzled with a million thoughts and emotions.

This course was meant to be an enjoyable busman's holiday for her. Could she do it with him here?

There's thirteen of us, including the guide. Surely I can just stay out of Gray's way?

Beau had been looking forward to this adventure for ages. This was the moment her career and her life would take another direction and lead her to places she had never dared to go.

She'd thought about it carefully. Planned it like a military exercise. She'd excelled in her hospital work and was top of her game in neurology. Other neurologists who felt they could do no more to help their patients would suggest *her* as the patient's next course of action. She was very often someone's last chance at life.

And she excelled, knowing that. She lived for it. The staying up late, the research, the practice, the robotic assistance that she sometimes employed, the long, *long* and challenging surgeries. The eye for detail. The precision of her work.

Awards lined her office walls at home in Oxfordshire. Commendations, merits, honorary degrees. They were all there. But this…

This was what she craved. A week of living by her wits, experiencing medicine in the wild, using basic kit to attend to fractures, altitude sickness, tissue injuries, whilst hiking through some of the most stunning scenery on the planet.

Forget technology—forget the latest medical advancements. There would be no security blanket here. No modern hospital, no equipment apart from a few basics carried in a first aid kit and what she could find around her.

It was perfect.

Even if *he* was here.

High grey-white mountains, lush expanses of sweeping green and purple, firs and shrubs, thickets of trees hiding streams and geysers. It was a vast emptiness, an untamed wilderness in all its glory, and *she* would try to beat it. No. Not beat it. Work *with* it, around it, adapt it to her needs so she could succeed and get another certificate for her wall. Another trophy so that she could think about applying for Base Camp, Everest. So she could work at the hospital there.

That small medical tent, perched on the base of one of the world's greatest wonders—that was her real aim. Her next anticipated accomplishment.

And there was no way she was going to let all that be ruined by the one man she'd once stupidly fallen in love with and given her heart to. The one man who had broken her into a million pieces. Pieces she still often felt she was still picking up.

She was still trying to prove to the world that she *did* have value. That she was the best choice. The only choice. His rejection of her had made her a driven woman. Driven to succeed at everything. To prove that he'd made a mistake in his choice of leaving her behind. To prove her worth.

Because I'm worth more than you, Gray. And I'll prove it to you.

'Yellowstone National Park is a vast natural preserve, filled with an ecosystem and diverse wildlife that, if you're not careful, is designed to kill you.'

Mack, the ranger leading their group, tried to make eye contact with each person standing in the room.

'There is danger in the beauty of this place, and too many people forget that when they come here and head off-trail. They're so in awe of the mountains, or the steaming hot geysers, or the dreamlike beauty of a wild wolf pack loping across the plains, that they forget to be *careful*. To look where they're going. We are going to be traversing land millions of years old, trying to be at one with nature, but most of all we are here to learn how to look after one another with the minimum of resources. Yes, this could be done in a classroom, but...' he paused to smile '...where would be the fun in that?'

There was some laughter, and Gray noticed Beau smile. It was exactly the way he remembered it, lighting up her blue eyes.

'Each of you will be issued with a standard first aid kit. When you receive it, you need to check it. Make sure it's all there. That's *your* responsibility. Then we're going to buddy up. The buddy system works well. It ensures that no one on this adventure goes anywhere in the park alone and that there is always someone watching your back.'

The likelihood of Gray being paired up with Beau was remote. And he certainly wasn't sure if it was something he wanted. But he caught her glancing in his general direction and wondered if she'd thought the same thing. Probably.

Mack continued. 'Today we're going to be hiking twelve miles across some rough terrain to reach the first scenario, where we will be dealing with soft tissue injuries. These are some of the most common injuries we see as rangers, here or at the medical centres, and we need to know what to do when we have nothing to clean a wound or any useful sterile equipment. Now, one final thing before we buddy up... We will *not* be alone in this park. There are wild animals that we're all going to have to learn to respect and get along with or stay out of their way. I'm sure you all know we've got wolves and grizzlies here. But there are also black bears, moose, bobcats and elk, and the one animal that injures visitors more than bears...the American bison.'

He looked around the room, his face serious.

'You see one of those bad boys...' he pointed at a poster on the wall behind him '...with his tail lifted, then you know he's going to charge. Keep your distance from the herds. Stay safe.'

Gray nodded. It wasn't just bison he'd have to watch out for, but Beau, too. She didn't have horns to gore him with, but she certainly looked at him as if she wanted him dead.

She was angry with him, and for good reason. He had walked away from their wedding and it had been one of the hardest things he'd ever done. Knowing that she would be left with the fallout from his decision. Knowing that he was walking away from the one woman who'd loved him utterly and completely.

But life had been difficult for him back then, and there was a lot that Beau didn't know. All she'd seen—all he'd *allowed* her to see—was the happy-go-lucky, carefree Gray. The cheeky Scot. But the man she'd fallen in love with hadn't existed. Not really. It had been a front to hide the horrible atmosphere at his home, the problems within his own family: his father's drinking, his mother's depression, the constant fights…

Gray's parents had *hated* each other. *Resented* each other. His mother had been trapped by duty with a man she detested. With a man who had suffered a tragic paralysing accident on the *actual day* she'd decided to pack her bags and leave him.

Being in the same house as them had been torture, watching and listening as they had systematically torn each other apart. Each of them trapped by marriage. An institution that Gray had vowed to himself *never* to get involved with.

'Love fades, Gray. Once that honeymoon period is over, then you see your partner's true colours.'

He could hear his mother's bitter words even now.

So why had he ruined it all by proposing to Beau? He hadn't wanted to get married—ever! And yet being with Beau had made him so happy.

The day he'd proposed they'd been laughing, dancing in each other's arms up close. Her love for him had been beaming from her face, her sapphire eyes sparkling with joy, and he'd wanted... He'd wanted that moment to last for ever. The words had just come out.

Will you marry me?

'We've got one hour before we're due to depart, so take this time to check your pack, check your first aid kit, use the bathrooms, freshen up—whatever you need to do before we set off. Let's meet back here at one o'clock precisely, people.'

Mack headed out of the room and a general hubbub began as people began to talk and check their bags and equipment.

Gray had already checked his bag three times. Once before he'd set off from Edinburgh, a second time when he'd arrived in America and a third time when he'd first arrived at the park. He knew everything was as it needed to be. There was nothing missing. Nothing more he needed to do.

Technically, he could relax—and, to be quite frank, he needed a bit of breathing space. He headed outside to the porch of the ranger station and sucked in a lungful of clean air before he settled himself down on a bench and took in the sights.

It was definitely beautiful here. There was a calmness, a tranquillity that you just didn't find inside a hospital. Hospitals were clean, clinical environments that ran to a clock, to procedure, to rules and regulations. As busy as a beehive, with people coming and going, visitors and patients, operations and clinics.

But here...here there was peace. And quiet. And—

The door swung open with a creak and suddenly she was there. Alone. Before him. Those ice-blue eyes of hers were staring down at him. Cold. Unfeeling.

He got to his feet, his mouth suddenly dry.

'I think it's time I made some rules about the next week.' She crossed her arms, waiting for his response.

'Beau, I—'

'First of all,' she interrupted, holding up her hand for silence, 'I think we should agree not to speak to each other. I appreciate that circumstance may not always allow that, so if you *do* speak to me, then I'd prefer it was only about the course. Nothing else. Nothing personal.'

'But I need to—'

'Second of all…you are to tell no one here what happened. I will *not* become the subject of idle gossip. And thirdly…when this is over, you will not contact me, you will not call. You will maintain the silence you've been so expert at keeping for the last eleven years. Do you understand?'

He did understand. All too keenly. She wanted nothing to do with him. Which was fair enough. Except that he felt that now she was here, right in front of him, this week might be his chance to explain everything. Forget a pathetic phone call or a scrappy little email. That had never been his style. He had seven days in which to lower her walls, get her to accept his white flag of truce and ask her to listen to him.

But he didn't want to become the subject of gossip, either. He didn't want to fight with her. Nor did he want to share so much that she found out about his injury. But time would tell. They had a few days to cool down. They'd get to talk. At some point.

'I do.'

Her lip curled. 'You see? That wasn't too hard to say, was it?'

Then she pointed her finger at him, and he couldn't help but notice that her hand was trembling.

'Stay out of my way, okay? I want nothing to do with you. *Ever.*'

He nodded, accepting her rules for the time being, hoping

an opportunity would present itself to allow a little bending of them.

They would have to talk eventually.

Beau checked her first aid kit against the checklist—gloves, triangular arm bandage, two gauze pads, sticking plaster, tape, antiseptic wipes, small scissors, one small saline wash, a safety pin. Not much for a medical emergency, but she guessed that was part of the challenge. The other part of the challenge for her was going to be a mental one.

Ignore Gray McGregor.

How hard could it be?

She retied her hiking boots, used the ranger station bathroom and then grabbed something to eat, forcing herself to chat pleasantly with some of the other hikers. No one else had a medical background, it seemed, apart from her and Gray. The others were experienced walkers, though, used to long treks and mileage, so she hoped they could all learn something from each other.

At one o'clock precisely Mack came back into the room, followed by another ranger. 'Right, everyone, gather round. I'm going to issue the buddy list. Now, remember, your buddy is more than just your friend. They're your safety net, your lookout, your second brain. You don't go anywhere without your buddy, okay?'

He awaited assent from the group.

'Now, we've tried to divvy everyone up equally and pair people with similar interests, so here goes.' Mack picked up his list. 'Okay, let's see who we have here. Conrad and Barb—you guys are married, so it makes sense to buddy you guys up... Leo and Jack—you guys are both from Texas... Justin and Claire—you guys mentioned you've met before, walking the Great Wall of China... Toby and Allan, both ex-Forces personnel...'

Beau shifted in her seat. There were only four of them left to name: her and three guys, one of whom was Gray.

Please don't pair me with Gray!

But what did she have in common with the other two? They were brothers, and surely Mack was going to pair brothers. Which meant... Her heart sank and she began to feel very sick.

'Dean and Rick—brothers from Seattle, which leaves our UK doctors, Beau and Gray. Welcome to America, guys!'

Beau couldn't look at Gray. If she looked at him, she'd see that he was just as horrified as she was about this.

Was it too late to change her mind and go home? Go back to the hotel in Bozeman and stay there for a week?

No! You've never backed away from anything!

Looking around the small room, she saw that everyone was pairing with their buddy, shaking hands and grinning at each other. Reluctantly she let her gaze trickle around the room until she locked eyes with Gray. He looked just as disturbed as she was—uncomfortable and agonised—but he seemed to be hiding it slightly better. She watched as he hitched his backpack onto his back and came across the room to her, looking every inch the condemned man.

Staring at him, she waited for him to speak, but instead he held out his hand. 'Let's just agree to disagree for the next week. It should make this easier.'

Easier, huh? He had no idea.

She ignored his outstretched hand. 'Like I said, let's just agree not to talk to each other *at all*. Not unless we have to.' Her voice sounded shaky, even to her own ears.

'That might make things difficult.'

'You have no idea what *difficult* means.' She hoisted her own backpack onto her shoulders and tightened the straps, turning away from the muscle tightening in Gray's jaw.

'I think I do, my lass.'

Her head whipped round and she glared at him. 'Don't call me that. I am *not* your lass. You know nothing about me now.'

'You want me to talk to you like you're a stranger?'

'I don't want you to talk to me at all.'

'I'm not going to be silent for a week. I'm not a monk.'

'Shame.'

'Beau—'

She glared at him. *Don't say another word!* 'Let's get going...*buddy*.'

He took a step back, sweeping his hand out before him. 'Ladies first.'

Beau hoped her stare would turn him into stone. Then she followed Mack and the others out of the ranger station.

CHAPTER TWO

BEAU MARCHED ALONG at the front of the pack, as far away from Gray as possible. She knew he would be lurking at the back. She walked beside Barb, her nostrils flaring and her nails biting into her palms.

She was beginning to get a headache. Typical! And it was all *his* fault. And she had no painkillers in her first aid kit. No one did. She had to hope that it would pass soon. The whole point of this course was to make her think differently. To use what was around her to survive.

Beau thought that she already knew quite a bit about survival. About not giving up when everything was against her. About not allowing herself to succumb to the void.

Since the day Gray had left her standing at the altar, she'd become a different person. Stronger than before. Driven. Her eyes had been opened to the way men could hurt her.

And to think that I solemnly believed that he wouldn't do that to me.

She'd allowed herself to feel safe with Gray. Secure in the knowledge—or she'd thought so at the time—that he loved her as much as she loved him.

Beau ground her teeth. Perhaps she'd been naïve. Perhaps she'd been cocky. She'd told everyone back then how Gray was her soulmate, her one true love. That he was the most perfect man and she was so lucky because he wanted *her*. There had been one time she remembered sitting in the kitchen with her mum, waxing lyrical about how wonderful he was, how happy *she* was and how she couldn't believe she'd found a man who wanted all the same things she did.

Her mum had listened and smiled and rubbed her arm and told her daughter how happy she was for her. How this was what life was all about. Finding love, settling down, creating a family of your own. That it was all any-one needed.

Beau had almost not been able to believe how lucky she was herself. But she'd believed in *him*. Almost devoutly. Her faith in their love had been undeniable, and when Gray had asked her to marry him, she'd been the happi-est girl in the world.

She'd thought no one could be happier than her. She'd thought she was going to marry the man she was head over heels in love with and that they would have children and a brilliant life together, just as her parents had done. They'd be strong together, united, and when the time came for them to be grandparents, their love would continue to grow. It had all been mapped out in her mind's eye.

But then he'd destroyed everything she'd believed in and she hadn't even got an apology! Not that it would mean much now. Too much time had passed. The time for an apology had been eleven years ago. Not now.

But there was nowhere for her to escape him here. They were stuck together. Buddied up, for crying out loud! She must have tutted, because Barb turned to look at her as they slowly marched up a steep, rocky incline.

'Mack mentioned you're a doctor?'

Brought back to reality, she tried to push her anger to one side so that she could speak politely to Barb. 'Yes, I am.'

'Do you have a specialty?'

She nodded and smiled. 'Neurology.'

'Ooh! That sounds complicated. They say there's so much about the brain that we don't know.'

'Actually, we know a good deal. Technology has advanced so far nowadays.'

'You know, I think I saw a documentary once where there was a brain operation and they did it with the patient wide awake! I couldn't believe it! This poor man was having to identify pictures on flash cards whilst the surgeons were sticking God only knows what into his brain!'

Beau smiled. 'It's called intraoperative brain mapping.'

Barb shuddered. 'Have you seen it done?'

'I've done it. I'm a surgeon.'

'Ooh! Con—you hear that? Beau here's a *brain surgeon*!' Barb grabbed her husband's arm to get his attention and Conrad nodded at Beau.

'Well, let's hope we don't need your services during this next week, Doctor.'

She laughed, a lot of her anger gone. The married couple seemed nice. They were both middle-aged, though Conrad's hair was already silvery, whereas his wife's perfectly coiffed hair was dark. They reminded her slightly of her own parents. Happily married, easy in each other's company and still very much in love.

Despite everything, it made her smile. 'How long have you two been together?'

Barb glanced at her husband. 'Thirty-five years this August.'

'Wow! Congratulations.'

'Thank you, dear. I have to say it's been wonderful. We've never had a cross word and we've never spent more than a night apart.'

'How do you do it? Stay so happy, I mean?'

'We pursue our own hobbies, but we also make sure we follow an interest together. Which is why we're doing this. We both love walking and seeing the country. Though last year Con had a few heart issues, so we thought we'd come on this course. Combine an interest with a necessity. Sometimes you can be out in the middle of nowhere and it can take hours before you get medical attention. We both thought it a good idea to get some medical basics under our belts.'

Beau nodded. It *was* a good idea. For a long time she had thought that basic first aid, and especially CPR, ought to be taught in schools. So many more people would survive accidents or sudden turns of events in their own health if everyone was taught the basics.

'Good for you.'

'What made *you* come on this course? This kind of stuff must be old hat to you.'

Beau looked across the plateau they'd reached, at the glorious sweeping plains, a patchwork of green, grey and purple hues, and the mountains in the distance. The open expanse. 'I got cabin fever. Needed to get back to nature for a while.'

'And the other doctor? The Scottish one? It looked like you two know each other.'

There was so much she could have said.

Why, yes, I do *know that lying, conniving, horrible Scot...*

'Briefly. A long time ago. We haven't seen each other for a while.'

Barb peered at her, her eyebrows raised. 'Parted on bad terms, did you?'

She smiled politely. 'You could say that.'

'Aw...' The older woman patted her arm. 'Life's too short for holding on to anger, honey. When you get to our age, you learn that. Our son Caleb, bless his heart, always jokes that Con and I are *"on the coffin side of fifty"*!' She laughed out loud. 'And he's right—we are. People waste too much time being angry or holding on to resentments and it keeps them stuck in one place. They can't move forward, they can't move on, and they lose so much time in life, focusing on being stuck in the sad when they could be focusing on being happy.'

Beau appreciated what Barb was trying to say, but it didn't help. There was still so much anger inside her focused on Gray. Suddenly she realised that until she heard some sort of explanation from him, she didn't think there was any way for her to move forward. She knew an apology wouldn't help—not really. But maybe she'd like to hear it, see him wriggle about on the end of his hook like the worm that he was.

Gray McGregor owed her *something*, and until she heard it, she wasn't sure what it was. But she wouldn't let it bother her. She told herself she didn't care. Even if she *was* still trapped in the past when it came to Gray. She might have grown up, found herself a stellar career and proved to her peers that she was one of the top neurologists in the country, but in her heart she was still a little girl lost. Hurt and abandoned.

Her heart broken in two.

And there was only a certain Scottish cardiologist who might be able to fix it.

Gray replayed in his mind his recent words with Beau. He kept his gaze upon her, walking far ahead of him, wondering how she was feeling.

Those dark auburn waves of hers bounced around her shoulders and gleamed russet in the sunshine. He could see her chatting amiably with Con and Barb and wished

she could be as easygoing with him. It would make the
next week a lot easier for both of them if they could put
the past in the past and just concentrate on enjoying the
hike and the medical scenarios.

But the sweet, agreeable Beau he'd once known seemed
long gone, and in her place was a new version. And this
one was flinty, cold and dismissive.

He wasn't sure how to handle her like that, and he'd
already been feeling enough guilt about what he'd done
without her laying it on thick to make him feel worse.

I know I owe you an explanation.

So many times he'd thought about what he needed to say
to her. How he intended to explain, to apologise. Always,
in his own mind, the conversation went quite well. Beau
would listen quietly and attentively. Most importantly, she
would understand that the decision not to turn up at their
wedding had hurt him just as much as it had hurt her.

But now he could see just how much he'd been wrong.
Beau would not sit quietly and just listen. She would not
be understanding and patient.

Had *he* changed her? By walking away from her, had
he changed her personality?

So now he chose to give her space. Letting her walk
with Barb and Conrad, staring at the back of her head so
hard he kept expecting her to rub the back of it, as if the
discomfort of his stare would become something physical.

And he worried. There was strain on her face, a pallor
to her skin that reinforced the brightness of her freckles
and the dark circles beneath her eyes.

Surely *he* wasn't the cause of that? Surely she'd just
been working too hard, or for too long, and wasn't getting
enough sleep? He knew she worked hard. He'd kept track
of her career after medical school. She was one of the top

neurologists in the country—maybe even in the whole of Europe. That had to take its toll, right?

But what if she's ill?

A hundred possibilities ran through his mind, but he tossed them all aside, believing that she wouldn't be so silly as to come out on a trek through the wilderness if she was ill.

It had to be stress. Doing too much and not eating properly.

He hadn't seen a ring on her finger. As far as he was aware, she wasn't married, and the hours she worked would leave hardly any time for dating. Unless she was seeing someone at work? There was always that possibility...

He shifted at the uncomfortable thought and tugged at the neckline of his tee shirt, feeling uneasy. Hating the fact that the idea of her being with someone else still made him feel odd.

Yet she was never mine to have. I should never have let it get so far in the first place. I was wrong for her.

'Here you go...have a pull of this.' Rick offered him a small flask. 'It'll keep you going. Always does the trick for me at the start of a long hike.'

Gray considered the offer, but then shook his head. 'No, thanks. Best to stick to water. That stuff will dehydrate you.'

'What do you think I've got in here?' Rick grinned.

'It's a whisky flask, so I'm guessing...alcohol?'

'Nah! It's just an energy drink my wife makes. It's got guarana in it. It's good for you!'

Gray took the flask and sniffed at it. It smelled very sweet. 'And how much caffeine?'

'Dunno. But it tastes great!'

He passed it back without sampling it. 'Do you know

that some energy drinks can trigger cardiac arrest even in someone healthy?'

Rick stopped drinking and held the flask in front of him uncertainly. 'Really?'

'If you consume too many. The high levels of caffeine mixed with other substances can act like a drug, stimulating the central nervous system to high levels when consumed in high doses.'

'You're serious? I thought all that pineapple and grapefruit juice was *good* for me.'

'It can be. Just don't add all the other stuff. Do you know for sure what's in there?'

Rick shook the flask, listening to the swish of the liquid inside. 'No. But she spends ages in the kitchen making it for me and it always seems to help.'

Gray grinned. 'I'd stick to water, if I were you.'

'How do you know all this?'

'I'm a cardiologist. I've operated on a fair few people who've ended up in the ER because of too many energy drinks.'

Rick began to pale. 'Wow. You think something's good for you…'

'Sorry to be a party pooper.'

'Nah, you're all right.' Rick tipped the flask upside down and emptied the juice out onto the ground. 'Doesn't make sense to carry the extra weight, does it?'

Gray looked up at Beau and considered all the extra emotional weight he was carrying. 'It doesn't. It doesn't help you at all.'

They'd been walking for a steady hour, and by Beau's reckoning—not that she knew much about these things—they'd walked about three miles into the park, all of it uphill. Her calf muscles burned and she was beginning to feel sore spots within her new hiking boots. She hoped she wasn't getting blisters.

The hillside had produced a plateau, a wide expanse of grasslands, and eventually they'd passed through a grove of lodgepole pine trees—tall and slender, the bark looking almost white from a distance, but grey up close.

Mack stopped them as they got near. 'You'll see a lot of these throughout the park. They're a fire-dependent species, and the seeds you can see, once fallen, provide a natural foraging source for grizzlies as we pass into fall. So you see this tree, then you look for the bear that goes with it. Luckily there isn't one here today.'

He smiled as everyone looked at each other and laughed nervously.

'But this is one example of always needing to be prepared. If you're walking in a new area, know the ecology, the flora and fauna—it can help you stay safe. Today there's no reason not to know. The Internet can tell you in an instant. There are books. Read. Research. It could save your life. Medically, indigenous tribes have used the lodgepole pine for many ailments—they steam the pine needles and bark to help with lung issues, and they also use it for bronchitis, fever and even stomach ache treatments. You can make a pitch from the pines and use it as a plaster for infections, burns and sores.'

Beau looked up at the canopy of the tall tree and was amazed. Working in a hospital, with the technology and advancement that came in the present day, it was easy to forget that all medicine originated from the use of plants, trees, shrubs and flowers. But it was important and not to be forgotten. She got out her compact camera from her pack and took a picture.

Mack walked them on and the plateau soon began to dip down towards a narrow rocky stream. The sound of running water was refreshing in the day's heat and Mack encouraged them all to take in some liquid refreshment and eat a small snack.

Beau perched on a large stone and nibbled on a flapjack she'd brought, avoiding Gray's glance and hoping he would stay away from her for a while longer.

Irritatingly, he sat down opposite her.

'How are you enjoying this so far?' he asked in his lilting Scottish burr.

'It's wonderful. Especially when I don't have to look at *you*.'

He glanced down at the ground. 'There's no need to attack me all the time, Beau. I feel bad enough as it is.'

'Good.'

He let out a heavy sigh, looking out across the stream bordered by rocks and grassy banks. 'I suppose you want me to go away?'

She didn't look at him. 'Or just be quiet. Either would do.'

He pulled some trail mix from his pack and offered it to her. 'Nuts?'

She glanced at him to see if he was making fun of her or being insulting. 'No. Thank you.'

'You know you're stuck with me, hen?'

She put away her flapjack, annoyance written all over her face, and refastened the buckles on her backpack. 'I'm not a hen.'

'Sorry, lass.'

She stood up and heaved the pack onto her back. 'Wow. An apology. You *do* know how to make them, then?'

Gray looked up at her, squinting in the sun. 'Aye.'

'*And...?*'

'And what?'

'Where's my *real* apology? The one you should have made eleven years ago?'

He cocked his head to one side and pulled his sunglasses down over his eyes. 'I'm saving it.'

'Saving it? For what?'

He looked about them before getting to his feet and leaning in towards her, so that his face was up close to hers. It was unnerving, having him this close. Those moss-green eyes staring deeply into her soul and searching. His breath upon her cheek.

'For when you're actually ready to listen. There's no point in me trying to explain whilst you're like this.'

'I'm not sure it's important, anyhow. Too little and too late.'

'And that proves my point.'

He walked away to sit down somewhere else.

Beau began to breathe again. Their brief conversation had unsettled her. Again. Plainly the way she was reacting to him was not working. Open hostility towards Gray was like water bouncing off an umbrella. It made no difference to him at all. He quite clearly was not going to apologise to her unless she got herself together.

Irritating man!

Most irritating because she was stuck with him for a week!

She had to be realistic. They were here. Together. And, worst of all, they were *buddied up* together. She knew from the itinerary for the trip that there would be paired activities where they would have to work with each other away from the main group. Orienteer themselves to another part of the park. Which meant time alone.

They had to start working together. Whether she liked it or not.

She turned to look for him and saw him standing with

Mack, chatting. Beau headed over and plastered a charming smile onto her face. 'Excuse me, Mack, could I have a quick word with my buddy here?'

'Absolutely. Glad you're here, Gray.' He slapped Gray on the arm before walking away.

Gray looked at her curiously. 'Yes?'

'You're right. We need to be working together for this next week and, as buddies, we need to be strengthening our working relationship. I'm not prepared to fail this course, and with that in mind I'm willing to put our past to one side in the spirit of cooperation and...peace. What do you say?'

She saw him consider her outstretched hand. Saw the question in his solitary raised eyebrow, saw the amiable smile upon his face before he reached out and took her hand.

A charge shot up her arm as her hand tingled in his. The strange yet all too familiar feel of his hand on hers was electrifying and thrilling. Her instinct was to let go. To gasp for oxygen. To rub her palm against her khaki trousers to make it feel normal again. But she did none of these things because her gaze had locked with his and she'd stopped breathing anyway.

Who needs oxygen?

Gray's leaf-green eyes bored into hers with both an intensity and a challenge, and Beau felt as if she'd been pulled back through time to when they'd first met on a hospital rotation.

They'd been so young, it seemed. All the students had been fresh-faced and eager to learn, eager to start their journeys. The girls smartly dressed, professional. The boys in shirts and ties as yet unwrinkled and sweat-free.

She'd noticed him instantly. The gleam in his eyes had spoken of an ambition she'd clearly been able to see. And had held a twinkle that had spoken of something else: his desire to stand out, to be noticed, to be cheeky with their lecturers. The way he'd pushed deadlines for work, the way he'd risked failing his assessments—that side of him that had been an adrenaline junkie, carefree and daredevilish.

His mischievous, confident grin had pulled her in like a fish to a lure and she'd been hooked. His attitude had been so different from anyone she already knew—so different from that of any of the men in her own family. He'd been that breath of fresh air, that beam of light in the dark, that sparkling, tempting palace in a land of dark and shadow.

He'd shaken her hand then and introduced himself, and instantly she'd heard his soft, lilting Scottish burr and been charmed by it. The very way he'd said her name had been as if he was caressing her. He'd made her feel special.

She'd not wanted to be dazzled by a charming man. Not at the start of her career. But family, love and marriage were high on her agenda and she'd desired what her parents had. A good, steady partner, with a love so deep it was immeasurable. Beau had had no doubt that she would find it one day.

She just hadn't expected to find it so soon.

Gray had stuck to her side and they'd worked together, played together, studied together and then, after one particularly wild party, slept together. It had seemed such a natural step for them to take. He'd filled her heart with joy. He'd made her feel as if she was ten feet tall. Every moment with him had been as precious as a lifetime. She'd wanted to be with him. She'd wanted to give him everything—because that was what love was. The gift of oneself.

And he hadn't disappointed her.

Afterwards, as she'd lain in his arms, she'd dreamed about their future. Wondering about whether they would get married, where they might live—not too far from her parents, not too far from his, so their children would have a close relationship with each set of grandparents—and what it would be like to wake up next to him every day for the rest of their lives together.

She'd liked the way he acted differently with her—calmer, more satisfied, considerate. *Relaxed.* He'd been a hyperactive buzzing student when they'd met, full of beans and so much energy. He'd exhausted her just watching him. But when he was with her, he wasn't like that. As if he didn't need to be. And she had found the side of him that she could fall in love with…

Gray smiled now. 'I hear you. Cooperation and peace. Seems like a good start to me.'

Beau chose not to disagree with him. It was already looking as if it was going to be one very long week ahead, and this adventure was going to be uncomfortable enough as it was.

I'm letting go of the stress.

So she smiled back and nodded.

Mack suggested that they all get going again, if they were to get to the first scenario and have enough extra time to pitch their tents for the evening.

They walked through scrub brush, conifers and thick deep grass. The overhead sun powered down upon them and Beau stopped often to drink and stay hydrated. At one of her stops Gray came alongside and waited with her.

'How are your parents?'

Beau fastened the lid on her water bottle. It was getting low. Hopefully there'd be a place to refill soon. 'Not that they're any of your business any more, but they're good, thanks.' She answered in a clipped manner. 'Yours?'

No need for her to go into detail. What could she say? That they hadn't changed in over a decade? That they still went to church every Sunday? That they still asked after him?

'They're fine.'

'Great.' These personal topics were awkward. Perhaps it would be best if they steered away from them? Gray's parents had always been an awkward subject anyway. She could recall meeting them only a couple of times, and one of those occasions had been at the wedding! They'd been a bit hard to talk to. Gruff. Abrupt. Not that keen on smiling. She'd babbled on *their* behalf! Chattering away like a radio DJ, musing on life, asking and answering her own questions. She'd been relieved to leave them and go and talk to others, and had just hoped that they'd liked her.

They'd turned up to the wedding anyway. Mr McGregor in his wheelchair, his face all red and broken-veined.

They trekked a bit further. Beau snapped pictures of columbines and hellebores and a herd of moose they saw in the distance. Then Mack brought them into a large clearing that had a stone circle in the centre.

'Base Camp Number One, people! I'll teach you later how to safely contain your campfire, but first we're going to get working on our first medical scenario—soft tissue injuries. As I said before, these are some of the most common injuries we get here in the park, and they can be minor or major. A soft tissue injury is damage to the ligaments, muscles or tendons throughout the body, so we're looking at sprains, strains and contusions. This sort of damage to the body can result in pain, bruising or localised swelling—even, if severe, loss of function or blood volume.' He looked at each of them with determination. 'You do *not* want to lose either. So what can we do out here with our limited kit? Gray? Care to enlighten us?'

'Normally you'd follow the PRICE protocol—protection, rest, ice, compression and elevation.'

'Perfect—did you all hear that?'

The group all murmured agreement.

'Now, unless you're in the North or South Pole, you aren't going to have any ice, so you might have to skip that step, but can anyone think of an alternative?'

Beau raised her hand. 'If you have a sealable bag, you could fill it with water from a stream and rest that over the injury.'

'You could. What else might happen with a soft tissue injury? Someone without a medical degree care to hazard an answer?'

No one answered.

'You'll need to stop any blood loss. And you have minimum bandages in your first aid kit. So, I want you all to get into your pairs and have one of you be the patient, with a lower leg injury that is open down to the bone from knee to ankle. The other partner needs to use whatever they have to hand to protect the open wound. *Go!*'

Beau looked up at Gray. 'Doctor or patient?'

He shrugged. 'Ladies' choice. You choose.'

She smiled. 'Then I think I'll have to be the doctor.'

Gray nodded and plonked himself down on the ground, then looked up at her, squinting in the sun. 'Can you help me, Doctor? I've got a boo-boo.'

CHAPTER THREE

SHE WATCHED AS he reached forward to raise his trouser leg and tried not to stare.

His leg was thick with muscle and covered in fine dark hair, and she swallowed hard, knowing she would have to touch his skin.

Distracted, Beau opened her first aid kit and tried to concentrate. For an open wound she'd have to use the gloves, the saline wash to clean away any dirt in it, two gauze pads, the triangular arm bandage, tape and maybe even the safety pin. Almost all of the equipment in her first aid kit.

She looked up at Mack, who was wandering through the group, watching people's ministrations. 'If we use all of this on one wound, Mack, that only leaves us plasters, antiseptic wipes and scissors for the rest of the week.'

Mack grinned back at her, mischief in his eyes. 'So what do you want *me* to do? You're out in the field—technically I'm not here. You two need to survive. You need to bandage his wound.'

'Because of blood loss and the risk of infection?'

'So what are you going to do?'

'Use it.'

Mack grinned again.

'But that doesn't leave us much if there's going to be another injury.'

'Well, if you didn't clean the wound properly or stop the bleeding, what would happen to your patient?'

'He could lose consciousness. Or it could become septic.'

'So you have your answer.' He walked on, pointing things out to others, showing some of the less well-trained how best to use the triangular arm bandage.

Beau squatted beside Gray and considered his leg. 'Okay, I'll flush the wound with saline first.' She put on the gloves and cracked the end of the small container, allowed the saline to run down Gray's leg, watching as the rivulets separated and dribbled along his skin.

'You could use drinking water, too.'

'Yes, but keeping you hydrated would be a strong reason to save as much water as possible, in case I can't light a fire to boil some more.'

He nodded and watched her.

'Gauze pads next, along the shin line.'

'Should I yell? How much acting do they want us to do?'

Beau gave a small smile. 'Whatever you feel comfortable with, I guess.' She looked around her and picked up a short thick stick, proffered it towards his mouth. 'Do you want to scream?' She grabbed hold of his shin and calf muscle and deliberately pushed her thumbs into his pretend open wound.

He grimaced. 'I might have to dock you points for being a sadist.'

She grinned as she pulled open the packing around the triangular arm bandage, then gently and delicately draped it over his shin and tied it as neatly as she could behind the leg, creating some constriction to prevent blood loss, but not making it too tight to restrict blood flow.

'How's that, Mr Patient?'

'Feels great. I can sense survival already.'

'Good.'

'You *do* have a gentle touch.'

'You see? There's a lot you don't know about me.'

She sat back on her haunches and looked around the rest of the group to see what everyone else had done. Justin and Claire hadn't used their gauze pads, but everyone had used the arm bandage.

Mack was nodding his head in approval as he walked amongst them. 'Good. Good. You've successfully treated the wound—but what do you need to be aware of whilst you wait for recovery or help?'

Beau raised her hand. 'Whether the patient can still move his toes—and look for signs of infection, too.'

'And how would we know there are signs of infection without undressing the wound?'

Again, Beau answered. 'Signs of fever, pallor, increase of pain in the affected limb, loss of function, numbness, unconsciousness, rapid breathing.'

Mack nodded.

Gray leaned in and whispered, 'Still the teacher's pet?'

She glanced at him. 'I like to learn. I like to know that I'm right.'

'Still, you're a doctor. You need to give the others a chance to answer a few questions. Perhaps they'd like to learn, too?'

She almost bit back at him. *Almost.* The temptation to answer him sharply was strong. To tell him to mind his own business, let him know that he couldn't tell her what to do. But she was also mindful that she'd agreed to a truce and, not wanting more confrontation, she nodded assent.

Mack continued to walk amongst the group. 'What would you do if blood began seeping through the bandage?'

Beau almost answered, then bit her lip as she felt Gray shift beside her. *Let someone else answer.*

'Would we replace the bandage?'

Rick answered, 'No. We could tear strips of clothing and add it on top of the bandage.'

Mack nodded, smiling. 'Good. Okay. You all did quite well there. Now, let's think about setting up camp—and then we're going to tackle recovery position and CPR.'

Gray began to remove the bandage and then rolled his trouser leg down.

Beau watched him, then gathered up the bits and pieces they'd used. 'What shall we do with these, Mack? There aren't clinical waste bins out here, either.'

'We'll burn them on the fire once we get it going.'

Right. She supposed that seemed sensible. All the others were starting to get out their tents and equipment, so Beau turned to her own backpack. This was the part she'd been dreading. Putting up a tent. She'd never done that before.

All part of the learning experience.

'Look at you. Reading the instructions like a real Boy Scout.' Gray appeared at her side.

'I like to be prepared. Proper planning prevents poor performance. I'm not like you. Spontaneous. Off the cuff. I like to know what's happening. The order of things. I don't like surprises. You should know that.'

He shook his head. 'I disagree. I think you take risks, too.'

'Me?' She almost laughed at his ridiculous suggestion. 'I don't take risks!'

'No? Who chose to come on the Extreme Wilderness Medical Survival Course on an active supervolcano?'

Beau opened her mouth to speak but couldn't think of anything to say.

'And the Beau I know wouldn't do any of this if it wasn't part of some bigger plan—am I right?'

She closed her mouth, frustrated.

It was so maddening that he could still see right through her.

Gray hadn't brought a tent like everyone else. He had a tarpaulin that he'd propped up with a couple of walking poles, spread over a hammock that he'd attached to two sturdy tree trunks. It took him a matter of a few minutes to get his pitch all set up, and once he was done, he was eager to get his boots off and relax.

But he couldn't concentrate.

Beau was opposite him, on the other side of the campfire, trying—and failing—to put up her tent. She was *inside* the tent now, and he could hear her muttered cursing.

After one particularly loud expletive he chuckled and went over. 'Er...knock-knock?'

There was a pause in the muttering and angry swearing and eventually her head popped out of the tent. Her face was almost as red as her mussed-up, statically charged hair. *'What?'*

Gray knelt down beside the tent entrance so that he was level with Beau's face. 'Do you want a hand?'

She looked at him, her brow creased with frustrated lines. 'From *you*?'

'Tent erection at your service.'

He watched as she blushed deeply before looking at everyone else around the camp, who all seemed to be managing at a reasonable rate compared to her.

'You know, I could have just let you get on with it. I'm being kind here. Offering a branch with pretty little olives on it.'

She bit her lip. 'Okay. But this is the only kind of erection I want from you.'

He smiled. 'Okay.'

She nodded and crawled out, huffing and puffing, standing tall and then letting out a big sigh as the tent collapsed onto the ground beside her like a deflated balloon. 'It was meant to do that.'

He managed not to laugh. 'Of course. Have you…erm… ever put a tent up before?'

She pursed her lips before answering and he tried his hardest not to focus on the fact that she looked as if she was awaiting a kiss.

'No. I've never camped before. But I read the instructions and it looked quite simple.'

He held out his hand. 'Give me the instructions.'

Beau pulled them from her back pocket and handed them over. They were folded up and creased.

Gray thanked her, pretended to look at them briefly and then threw them onto the campfire.

'Gray!' She stared after the instructions open-mouthed as they were eaten up by the orange flames. She turned back to him.

'You don't need the instructions. Tents are easy.'

'Oh, *really*? Easy, huh?'

'Absolutely.'

'Well, be my guest.' She looked around for a seat but after finding none just sat on the ground with her arms and legs crossed. She looked smug, almost as if she expected him to fail and become as frustrated as she'd been when she'd tried.

Gray grabbed the poles he needed, from where Beau had laid them out on the ground in logical order and size, and instantly began threading them through fabric tubes and forming the outer shell of the tent.

He heard her curse and tried not to smile at his own smugness when he saw the look on her face. He picked up the pegs and pinned the tent to the ground. Within minutes he had it ready.

Wiping his hands on his trousers, he turned to her with a happy smile. 'There you go. The best erection in camp.'

'How did you...? Where did you...?' She sighed. 'How...?'

Gray shrugged. 'A gentleman never tells.'

She cocked her head to one side and smiled. 'I'm not asking a *gentleman*.'

'Ouch!'

'Come on...how did you do that so fast?'

He considered the tent briefly before he replied. 'I've got one of these.'

She looked at his tarp. 'But not on this trip?'

'I prefer the bivvy and tarp during the summer months.'

'Okay. Well, thank you very much. I appreciate it.'

He could tell that it had taken her a lot to thank him. He simply smiled and let her get her equipment into the tent, even helped her roll out her sleeping bag. Once they were done, they both stood there awkwardly, staring at each other.

Gray felt so tempted to tell her everything there and then, but something inside told him that now was not the right time. Beau was still suspicious of him. Trying to show that she was indifferent to his presence. Which obviously meant she was still angry. Perhaps he would talk to her in a few days. Give the shock of them both being here a chance to pass away. Give her time to cool down and be receptive to what he had to say.

Perhaps if he showed her during this course that he was a good guy—reliable, dependable, someone she could trust with her life—then maybe by the end of the week she'd be much more amenable to hearing what he had to say. And they could put the past to rest.

Mack made his way over. 'Hey, Gray, you're rostered for cooking duties tonight. Feel like running up a culinary masterpiece with some beans?'

Cooking? He didn't feel confident about that. And not for other people! Not if they wanted to stay alive. He could perform heart transplants or bypass grafts or even trans-myocardial laser revascularisation—but cook up something tasty? That was edible? That didn't require its film to be pierced and to be shoved in a microwave?

'Er…sure, Mack.'

Beau stood watching him now, her arms crossed, one hip thrust to the side and a grin on her face.

'Problem, Gray?'

Of course she would remember his fear of the kitchen. When they'd been together, Beau had done all the cooking after his one disastrous attempt at a beef stroganoff had resulted in a weird brown splodge on their plates that had tasted, somehow, of nothing.

He'd never learnt from his mother. The kitchen had been her domain—the one place she'd been able to escape from the men in her family and know they wouldn't disturb her. The mysteries of the kitchen and its processes had always eluded Gray, but that had always been fine with him. The hospital had a canteen, and when he wasn't there, he ate out.

'Maybe.'

'I thought you'd camped before? Whatever did you eat?'

'I brought army ration packs. They were self-heating. I didn't have to do anything.'

'Okay…what ingredients do you have to work with?'

Beau headed over to the bags Mack had pointed out

and rummaged through the ingredients. There were butter beans, tomatoes, potatoes and a small can of sardines.

'That's not a lot for thirteen people,' she said.

Mack grinned. 'Well, this *is* a survival course. Be thankful I'm not making you forage for ingredients. Yet.'

Beau's face lit up. 'Of *course*!' She disappeared into her tent and came back out holding her guidebook on Yellowstone. 'This will tell you what we can eat. We could get some of the others to forage for foodstuffs and add them to the pan. You stay here and chop up the potatoes. Leave the skin on, Gray—the most nutritious part of the vegetable is just under the skin.'

'Is that right?' He was amused to see her so energised. It reminded him of the sweet Beau he'd used to know so well. 'Are you chaining me to the kitchen sink?'

She shrugged. 'Stops you running away.'

Then she headed off to clear her plan with Mack and gather some of the others to help find food.

He watched her. Asking Mack for advice on foraging and safety. Organising people. Arranging them into teams. Showing them what they might be able to find. One pair was dispatched to gather more firewood. Another pair to collect water for purifying.

She was in her element.

Gray sighed, sat down by the potatoes and grabbed a small, short knife, ready to start chopping.

Considering she hadn't even been able to bring herself to even look at him earlier today, they had already taken huge steps towards bringing about a ceasefire. Maybe soon they could have those peace talks they so desperately needed.

While everyone waited for dinner to cook, Mack began teaching the recovery position.

'If you come across a casualty who is unconscious and breathing, then you'll need to put them into the recovery position. Anyone tell me why?'

Beau's hand shot into the air and Gray smiled.

Mack looked for someone else to answer, but when everyone looked blank, he allowed her to. 'Yes, Beau?'

'Rolling a patient onto their side stops the tongue from blocking the airway and also helps prevent choking in case of vomiting.'

'That's right. Beau, perhaps you'd like to be our pretend patient?'

She nodded and went over to the ranger and lay flat on her back on the pine-needle-covered ground.

'Before we put the patient into the recovery position, what should we check for?'

'Check breathing again?' suggested Conrad.

'You could. But let's assume she's still breathing. You'll need to check to make sure there's nothing in her pockets that will jab into her when we roll her over. So, things like car keys, pens, pencils, sticks—things like that. We should also remove the patient's glasses and turn any jewelled rings towards the palm.'

He demonstrated by sliding a ring round on Beau's hand.

'There's also a little poem you can remember to remind yourself of what you need to do here. *"Say hello and raise my knee, then take my hand and roll to me."'*

He placed Beau's hand palm-up by her face, as if she was saying hi, and then grabbed her trouser leg and raised the knee of the opposite leg, so that her foot was downwards on the forest floor. Then he grabbed her other hand, put it by her face and, using the trouser leg of the raised knee, rolled Beau over onto her side, adjusting the hand under her face to open the airway.

'Simple. Okay, tell me the poem.'

'"*Say hello and raise my knee, then take my hand and roll to me.*"'

'Good. You need to keep repeating that to yourself. It'll stand you in good stead. Always remember to position yourself on the side you want the patient to roll onto. Now, what if your patient is pregnant?'

'You'd need to roll them onto their left side,' said Gray.

Mack nodded. 'Absolutely. Why?'

'Less pressure on the inferior vena cava.'

'Thank you, Gray. Now, I'd like you all to get into your buddy pairs and practise this. Take turns at being the patient. Off you go.'

Gray stood over Beau and smiled. 'Want to stay there?'

'If I must.'

He knelt beside her and awkwardly patted her pockets. He hadn't expected to be *touching* Beau. Not like this. Not holding her hand in his and laying it by her face. It was too much, too soon.

Talking to her he could handle. Joking with her and keeping the mood light he could handle. But this enforced closeness…? It reminded him too much of the past, when touching her had been easy and pleasurable and had made her eyes light up.

Not now, though. Now she lay stiffened on the floor, uncomfortable and gritting her teeth. Was it that awful for her? Him being this close? Was she hating every second of it?

Once she was in the recovery position, she leapt up and brushed herself down. 'My turn.'

Disarmed, he lay down and closed his eyes, not wanting to see the discomfort in *her* eyes, not wanting to make this any more difficult for her than it plainly already was.

Beau got him into the recovery position quickly. 'You're all done.'

He got up and brushed off the pine needles and they stood there awkwardly, staring at each other, not knowing what to say.

Clearly the activity had been difficult for both of them and Gray couldn't stand it.

'I'll just check on the food.' He went over to the cooking pot and gave it a stir. It didn't look great, but it did smell nice. Mack had shown Beau and the others where to find some small bulbs of wild garlic, and they'd added that to Gray's dish.

He glanced through the simmering steam at Beau and began to wonder just how the hell he was going to get through this week.

Mack got everyone up. 'Okay, folks, that's it for today. The rest of the evening is your own. Gray is our chef this evening, so let's all keep an ear out for him ringing the dinner bell.'

Gray had no idea when it would be ready. Claire came over and asked, and when he shrugged, she stuck the small paring knife into the potatoes to check.

'Seems good to me.'

'Yeah? I'd better dish up, then.'

Gray served them all a portion that was quite meagre, even with the additions. It actually tasted nice, which was a surprise. The others made satisfactory noises whilst eating it anyway, so he could only hope they weren't just being polite.

Afterwards Gray was ready for bed. His foot was starting to trouble him and he ached in places he hadn't been expecting. Not to mention that his nerves were still on edge from the recovery scenario.

He had to get around the way it felt when he touched

her. He had to forget the softness of her skin, the smooth creaminess of it and the knowledge that he knew exactly how the rest of her felt.

It would feel so good to caress her again.

He sneaked a glance at her whilst she was talking to Dean and Toby. He saw the twinkle in her eyes, her joyous smile. Heard her infectious laughter. She looked relaxed, as if she was enjoying herself.

I want her to be that way with me.

Later, Gray and Beau carried the pile of tin dishes down to the creek and laid them beside the shallow running water, trying to rinse them in the darkening light. Beau was struggling for the right thing to say. How could she start a conversation with the man she'd once thought she'd known inside out…?

But he started it instead. 'I'm glad we're both making the effort to try and get along.' He paused to glance at her. 'It's good.'

'It's easier than trying to ignore you.'

He smirked. 'I'm in joyous rapture about that.'

The dishes rinsed well in the stream, and Beau figured the small particles of food that were getting rinsed off would hopefully feed some of the fish or wildlife further downstream.

'Your cooking has improved.'

A smile crept across his face. 'A compliment? I'll take it.'

'No, really. It was a nice dinner. Considering.'

'Considering it was cooked by me?'

She nodded and laughed.

He smiled at her, as if pleased to hear her laugh again. 'Thank you. I'm just glad everyone was able to eat it without choking. No one's been taught the Heimlich manoeuvre yet.'

She laughed again, her gaze meeting his, and then suddenly she wasn't laughing any more. She was caught by the deep mossy stare of his eyes, the longing she saw within them, and by her own fear as old feelings came bubbling to the surface.

She stood up abruptly. 'We ought to head back. It's dark. Who knows what's out here with us?'

He stood, too. 'Yeah, you're right.'

The deepening shadows around them just served to make his eyes more intense as he looked at her. She could feel old urges reasserting themselves, and memories of how easy it had once been to be with this man—how she'd loved him so much she hadn't thought there was anything left of her own soul that was just her.

Beau bent to gather the dishes. Gray helped, and both of them were careful not to touch each other before they headed back to camp. Walking a good metre apart.

CHAPTER FOUR

SHE'D COME A long way since her arrival at the ranger station that morning. If anyone had told her that by the end of the day she'd be sharing a meal with her ex-fiancé and washing dishes by a stream with him—whilst *smiling*—she would have told them that they were crazy. No chance.

But she had. And now she sat across from him, with the campfire crackling away between them as night fell, catching glimpses of his face in the firelight.

He was still the same old Gray. Slightly more grizzled, slightly heavier set than before, but still with the same cheek, the same nerve. The other hikers all seemed to like him. But he'd always had that effect on people. Dean and Rick, the brothers from Seattle, were currently seated on either side of him, and beyond them everyone seemed to be listening to the story Gray was weaving.

He was a born storyteller, enamoured of holding everyone's attention. It was probably why he'd chosen cardiology, she thought. Heart surgeons always seemed to act as if they were the best. Because without the heart the body wouldn't work at all.

Well, Gray, without a brain the heart doesn't stand a chance, either.

That was the difference between them. She could see that now. Beau had always been the steady influence—the thinker. The planner. Everything meticulously detailed. Whereas Gray had always been the rash one, the passionate one, the spontaneous, carefree daredevil.

Initially she'd been excited by those qualities in him. His indifference to planning the future, his studies, his life. She'd loved the way he could get excited about one thing and then develop a passion for something else entirely further down the line. How he could be thrilled by new technologies, new inventions, new medicines. Whereas *she* had always been cautious—researching new methods, new techniques, checking the statistics on their success, talking to the people involved about their experiences, making sure everything was *safe* before she considered using anything in her work.

Beau did not like surprises. Especially unpleasant ones. And Gray had caused her the most unpleasant surprise in her life so far by not turning up to their wedding. A wedding could be planned in advance, carefully thought-out, with alternatives arranged, waiting in the wings, to prevent any last-minute hitches. You planned the day meticulously so that you didn't have to worry about it running smoothly, so that it *just did*. And on the day itself you were meant to just turn up and go with the flow. Put on your dress, do your hair, do your make-up, smile for the camera and *enjoy*.

And because she'd planned her wedding so well, she'd not expected anything to go wrong at all. She'd been naïvely blissful, secure about her feelings for her husband-to-be, anticipating the joy that their marriage would bring, knowing the happiness they already had was growing and growing with every day.

So when he hadn't shown up, it had felt as if she'd been punched in the gut! A blow that had come out of nowhere. And her heart…? It had been totally broken.

And then the questions had flooded her mind. Why

had he abandoned her? Had she been wrong? Had it all been one-sided?

Looking at him now, adored by his fellow hikers, she still found it hard to tell herself that he had actually just left her there. Without a word. Without a hint of concern.

Had there been signs in the days *before* the wedding that he'd planned to run out on her? She couldn't recall. He had seemed a little distant occasionally, when she'd gone on about the arrangements, but weren't all grooms-to-be like that? Surely it was the bride's prerogative to go overboard when planning her perfect day?

The pain had been incredible. It had made her doubt their love. Made her doubt *herself.* She'd spent weeks worrying that there was something wrong with *her.* That she was lacking something—that there was something Gray needed and couldn't get it from her.

But what? She was a nice person. Clever. Kind. Friendly. Loving. She'd never been shy in showing him her affection. Their sex life had been great! *Hadn't it?* Of course it had been. No man could make a woman feel like that and then say things were lacking in that department.

He hadn't said much in the days leading up to the wedding, she supposed. He hadn't said much in regard to their marriage, or his hopes and dreams, so she'd talked about hers, hoping to draw him out. But he'd never said anything. Just smiled and looked…nervous.

Beau poked at the campfire with a long stick and watched as the embers collapsed and spat heat upwards and outwards, tiny flecks of flame bursting forth and disappearing into the night sky above. The dark blue of the night revealed the sparkle of stars that she could never have hoped to see from her home town of Oxford. Even from the hospital roof you couldn't see a sky such as this.

The vast openness of Yellowstone made her realise that

there was so much she wasn't used to seeing. Or noticing. It made her aware that she wouldn't know if something else was out there until she made the time to look for it.

Was there something about Gray that she'd not known about?

She glanced up at him once more and caught his gaze upon her through the heat of the orange flames. He looked pensive, and he rubbed at his jaw before he turned to answer Rick, who'd asked him a question.

He looks weary.

She wasn't used to seeing him look worn down. He'd always looked sprightly. Ready for anything. Raring to go.

Had today done that to him? Had *she*? She didn't like how that made her feel, how uncomfortable she suddenly was, and her stomach squirmed at the notion.

Perhaps there was more to this situation between them? Something she'd not been aware of because she'd never thought to look for it. Was it something obvious? Was it staring her in the face? Like the stars—always there, but not always seen?

Was I so wrapped up in the wedding that I forgot to focus on us?

Beau threw her stick into the fire and watched as it got swallowed up by the flames. She knew with certainty now that this week was going to be one hell of a learning experience.

And not the kind that she'd been expecting.

Beau had spent an uncomfortable night in her tent. Before the trip she'd bought a decent one, and a groundsheet, a sleeping mat and a sleeping bag, and had thought that would be enough for her to get a decent night's sleep. But the ground had been hard and unforgiving and she'd tossed and turned, worrying about being away from her patients, being here with Gray—not to mention the possibilities of insect invasion—before she'd finally fallen into a broken sleep at about five o'clock in the morning.

Unfortunately Mack had woken them all up around seven by banging a tin bowl with a rock right by the entrance to her shelter, and she'd woken blearily, feeling as if her body was bruised all over.

'Okay, okay… I'm awake,' she'd moaned, rubbing her eyes and blinking thoroughly until they seemed to operate correctly.

Now she sat up, stretching out her back muscles and rolling her stiff shoulders and noting, with some small satisfaction, that her tent had not filled with ants overnight. *Perhaps it's safe to sleep on the ground after all?* Then she pulled herself from her sleeping bag, put on a fresh set of underwear, the clothes she'd worn yesterday, and put her hair up into a ponytail and unzipped her tent.

'Morning, Beau.'

Gray was already up, looking freshly groomed, his eyes bright and sparkly.

She groaned. Used to her normal schedule, Beau was not a morning person. She needed a good-sized mug of coffee, a Danish pastry and a blast of loud music in her car to wake her properly before she got to the hospital, and she guessed she wouldn't get that here.

She peered gloomily at the pot that Barb was in charge of. 'What's for breakfast?'

'Oatmeal.'

'Porridge? Great,' she replied without enthusiasm.

It wasn't exactly a buttery, flaky pastry delight, but never mind. It would have to do. She warmed her hands over the fire and then ducked back into her tent to grab her toothbrush and toothpaste. She stood and cleaned her teeth and rinsed her toothbrush with the last of her bottled water.

'I've got a pot of boiled water cooling down already,' Barb said when she returned. 'Have you got your purifying tablets?'

'I've got a filter.'

'Brilliant.'

Beau was quite pleased with her state-of-the-art filter. It meant that she could collect water from any source, pour it through, and all protozoa and bacteria would be removed, including giardia and cryptosporidium, the two biggest causes of infection in water. It saved having to boil water and wait for it to cool before it could be put into containers. It had been one of her new purchases, thoroughly researched and tested, and she'd even looked up reviews from previous customers to make sure it was the best for the job.

After she'd put her toiletries away, she stretched her back once again and took in the view. Now that she was more awake, she could appreciate where they were. High up on a mountainside, on a grassy plateau, surrounded by nature, with not a building, a towering spire nor a frantic cyclist in sight. Just clear blue skies, promising the heat of another day, the sun, a gentle warm breeze and the bright, cheery sounds of birdsong lighting up the morning.

'It's gorgeous, isn't it?'

'It certainly is.'

Gray smiled down at her, making her jump. She sat up. 'What are we doing today?'

'Mack said we need to cover CPR, as we missed it last night, and then we're heading higher up to cover altitude sickness.'

She nodded. 'Right. How far up do you think we already are?'

'Four or five thousand feet?'

'And altitude sickness sets in at…what? Eight thousand or more?'

'Depends on the climber. Could be now.'

'Mack won't want to take us up that far, will he?' she asked, feeling the pain in her calf muscles from yesterday's climb.

'No, I won't,' Mack answered as he came out of his tent. 'It's a survival course, not a medical experiment.'

She smiled at him. 'Glad to hear it.'

Barb gave the oatmeal a stir. 'This is done. Everyone hungry?'

Everyone nodded and grabbed their metal dishes to receive a small helping of breakfast before sitting down around the fire to eat quietly.

Porridge wasn't her thing, but Beau ate it anyway, and Justin and Claire offered to get everything washed up before they packed up camp.

They soon covered the CPR training—how to do it effectively without defibrillators. Two breaths to thirty compressions in two rounds, before checking for signs of life—breathing, pulse rate, chest rise and fall. Mack showed them all how to find the right spot on the chest for compressions. How to place their hands. What sort of rhythm they needed and how fast. Showed them that even if they did it properly they might hear ribs break—which made everyone cringe at the thought!

Then there was a short break before Mack showed them how to put out the fire safely, and once they'd packed up their tents and equipment, they all set off once again on the next hike.

Gray fell into step beside Beau and she noticed that he was limping.

'Blisters?'

He didn't quite meet her gaze. 'Er...no. Not really.'

'How did you sleep?'

'Well, thanks. The hammock was great.'

'Lucky you. I barely got forty winks before Mack's alarm. The ground mat I bought felt as thin as tissue paper.'

He smiled. 'That's why I brought a hammock. Off the ground is better. Even the most comfortable bed is on legs.'

'The voice of experience?'

'Most definitely.'

Mack led them up a stony trail. Like a line of ants they began their ascent, and in the early-morning warmth they were all soon puffing and panting, stripping off layers as they got higher and higher. Beau focused on one point— the shirt of the person in front. Her mind was blank of everything as she simply concentrated on putting one foot in front of the other. Plodding on, climbing bit by bit, until they reached a lookout high on the side of the mountain.

Mack indicated a rest stop by dropping his backpack to the floor. 'Let's take an hour here. Get fluids on board, and then we'll start our next lesson from this beautiful viewpoint.'

Beau slipped off her backpack and used it as a seat as she took a drink of water from her bottle. She was hot and sweaty, totally out of breath, and the muscles in her legs *burned*. She stretched her legs out in front of her and counted her blessings.

This was what she had come here for. To find nature. To escape the confines of the hospital. When had she last climbed anything? She didn't even climb stairs any more— she changed floors at the hospital by using the lift, and the same at home. Her flat was on the sixth floor and the lift worked perfectly every time she needed it. She *needed* this sort of workout. Blowing away the cobwebs on muscle groups that she ought to have been using. Using her body and not just her brain. Breathing in this fresh, crisp mountain air and feeling alive!

She watched a large bird, far out above the canyon,

circle effortlessly in the air. 'Now, *that's* the way to climb to new heights.'

Gray squinted up at the sky. 'I wonder if birds get altitude sickness.'

'Or have a fear of heights. Can you imagine?'

'We humans think too much. We worry and fret, build our anxieties on imagined threats. If you think about it, animals have it easier.'

She took another drink of water. 'What worries *you*, Gray? You never struck me as a worrier.'

He stretched out his legs. 'I worry about lots of things. I just choose not to show it.'

Leo came over and rested against the rocks next to them. 'You're a surgeon, though, aren't you? You can't show your patients that you're worried. They'd have no confidence in your abilities if you did.'

Gray nodded. 'That's right. It's a strength not to wear your heart on your sleeve. Patients need to see that you're confident and sure.'

But Beau was thinking about their past. 'And what if you're *not* sure about something?' she asked, her face curious. 'Do you talk to them about your concerns? Do you ever share your doubts so they know the full picture?'

It was obvious he knew she wasn't just referring to his work. 'I always let my patients know the full picture. They always understand the risks. Letting them know about dangers and possibilities doesn't stop you from being confident.'

'But what if you're *not* confident in an outcome? What then?'

He stared at her, long and hard. 'Then I don't proceed.'

She nodded, her face stony. 'You don't move forward?'

'No.'

Leo looked between the two of them, clearly puzzled

at the tone of the conversation and at the way they were looking at each other. He took a bite from his trail bar. 'Looks like Mack's about to start the next lesson.'

He was right.

Mack gathered them all round. 'Okay, I'm sure that as we made the climb up here we all noticed we were getting a little out of breath. Now, imagine being like that all the time…not being able to breathe, feeling like there isn't enough air, struggling to take in enough oxygen. How do you think that's going to affect you on a day-to-day basis?'

Rick put up his hand. 'You'd struggle.'

Mack nodded. 'Too long in too high an altitude, without a period of adjustment, can affect thinking skills and judgement calls, and it leads to hikers and climbers taking risks. Luckily here in Yellowstone we don't have the extreme elevations that provoke serious cases of altitude sickness, but we do have heights over eight thousand feet, and as soon as you go beyond this number, you'll start to see symptoms. Now, can anyone tell me what those symptoms are?'

Beau was itching to answer, but she thrust her hands in her pockets and bit her lip to stop herself from speaking.

Conrad suggested an answer. 'Dizziness?'

'That's one. Can you give me another?'

'Nausea?'

Mack nodded. 'Most people complain of a headache first. They get nauseous, feel exhausted. Then they might be short of breath, might get nosebleeds, muscle weakness. So what do we do to alleviate the condition?'

Beau gritted her teeth, let Mack continue.

'We descend. Height creates the problem, so going back down to where it's easier to breathe solves it. People *can* adjust, though. This is why on mountain climbs—and specifically when tackling Everest and those sorts of places—climbers ascend and then come down for a bit. Then they go up again—then down. It's a back and forth dance. Two steps forward, one step back. It acclimatises them to the new altitude. It allows their bodies to get used to the thinner air.'

Everyone nodded.

'The air itself still has oxygen at about twenty-one per cent. That doesn't change as you go higher. What *does* change is the air pressure, and that's what causes altitude sickness. Unfortunately we can't tell who will succumb. Some of you may even be feeling it now.'

He looked around at them and Claire raised her hand and mentioned that she had a headache.

He nodded once. 'So we start to head down. Let's go!'

They all got to their feet and slung on their backpacks wearily. The air did seem thinner. Everything seemed so much sharper up high. But the trail Mack led them down quickly led them into a beautiful green valley where they had to wait for a herd of moose to pass by.

Beau got out her camera. They were magnificent animals! As tall as she was, heavyset, with brown-black coats and long, horse-like faces. There was one with huge cupped antlers, and he stood there proudly as his herd passed the hikers, heading for a crop of willow trees, where they stopped to graze.

She took shot after shot, excited by getting her first close-up with an animal she hadn't a chance of seeing in the wild in the UK, and when she finally put her camera away, Gray smiled at her.

'What?'

He laughed. 'You're still the same.'

She shook her head, disagreeing with him. 'I'm older. Wiser, I hope.'

'I grant you that…but you still have that joy in you

that I saw all those years ago. You always saw the joy and goodness in everything.'

'That's my problem. I *thought* I saw it in you once, but…I was wrong.'

He stopped walking and sighed. 'You weren't wrong.'

'Then why did you hurt me so badly?' She stopped to look at him directly. The others were ahead. They couldn't hear.

Gray looked down at the ground. 'That wasn't my intention. I was trying to stop you from being hurt further down the line.'

He passed her and began to walk to catch up with the rest of the group.

Beau watched his retreating form and felt the old hurt and anger begin to rise. She pushed it down, refusing to show him that he could still press her buttons.

She hurried to catch up, too, and as she passed him, she muttered, 'Just for your information…it didn't work.'

Gray stopped and stared after her.

They walked for a few more hours. They passed through rocky canyons, small copses and grassy open plains. They followed the Gallatin River, passing a few men who stood in it in waders, fly-fishing, and giving them a wave.

Gray could feel the weariness in his legs—particularly his left leg—and ached to stop and stretch out, but he said nothing, preferring to soldier on.

They were all alert and on the lookout for bears, knowing that these mammals were keen on fishing themselves, but they saw none, and Mack soon led them off the popular trail and deeper into wilder country.

Just as Gray was feeling the familiar pinching pain in his left calf that told him a cramp was about to set in, he heard crying and groaning. His ears pricked up at the sound and his doctor radar kicked in. Someone was afraid and in pain. And then suddenly, there before them, in a clearing, were three people lying on the ground with blood everywhere.

Adrenaline shot through his system. The cramp was forgotten as he raced past the others in his group with Beau to attend the casualties before them.

There were two men and a woman. First he needed to assess them all, find out who was in the most medical danger, and he knelt by the first patient—the woman—who lay on her back, clutching at a bleed in her thigh, hopefully not her femoral artery. Out here, a bleed like that could be fatal.

'Lie back! Can you tell me what happened?'

He went to check the leg, already pulling off his belt so that he could create a tourniquet, and then he noticed that there was no wound. No tear in the fabric. And the blood was fake. He looked up at the others, to see Beau looking confused, too.

Mack knelt down beside him, grinning. 'Pretend patients! The wounds aren't real, but you might come across people on your travels with serious injuries. I want you to work in groups of four. Each group take a patient. Assess the injury, ascertain what happened, and then I want you to tend to that patient. We'll feed back to the group what we did and why. Gray, you work with Beau, Conrad and Barb. Jack and Leo—you're with Dean and Rick. The rest of you, tend the third patient.'

Gray had already got fake blood all over his hands and he let out a huge breath. *Thank goodness it's not real!* It had really got his own blood pumping, though.

Beau knelt beside him and Conrad and Barb gathered round.

'Barb and I will let you two take the lead, Doc,' said Conrad. 'We're sure you know more than us.'

'Maybe, but you need to learn. Let's see what our "patient" can tell us.' He looked down at the woman on the ground. 'Can you tell me what happened to you today?'

'We were camping when we were attacked.'

'By animals?'

'No, some lads came into our camp. They were drunk and waving knives around.'

Gray nodded. He'd actually been in a similar situation once before, hiking in the Peak District. A group of rowdy teenagers had wandered into his campsite, drunk and disorderly, and had become very threatening. Luckily he'd managed to talk them down and send them on their way—but not before one of them had tripped over his guy rope and broken his nose.

'Was your leg injured with a knife or something else?'

'I'm not sure.'

He nodded, then looked up at Conrad and Barb. 'What do you think we should be thinking about doing here?'

'Stopping the bleeding?' Barb suggested.

'Good. How?'

'We could apply some pressure? Raise the injured limb?'

He nodded. *Good. They knew some basics.* 'What else? What if it was an arterial bleed?'

'Pressure and a tourniquet?'

'Good—but you'd have to be quick. Arterial bleeds spurt, and with force. The area around the wound will get messy quickly and the patient can lose a large amount of blood in a short time. What else do we need to do?'

Conrad and Barb looked blankly at each other. 'We're not sure, Doc.'

Beau smiled at them. 'Once you've dealt with an arterial

bleed, and it appears to be under control, you need to do two things. Find a way of getting more help, but also look for further injuries. Too many people assume that if a patient has one major injury that's all they have to look for. But patients can quite often have more possibly fatal injuries, so you need to assess your patient properly once the bleeding is stemmed and under control.'

'What if the bleeding doesn't get under control?'

'Then your patient could go into hypovolaemic shock. If they don't get help, they'll die.'

Barb paled slightly and Conrad put a comforting arm around his wife's shoulders. 'That's terrible.'

Gray showed the couple how to check for further injury, and how they could assess their patient's level of consciousness, then Mack gathered them all together.

The three 'patients' stood and had a bit of a stretch, grinning.

'Okay, so what did we all learn?'

Gray gave a brief rundown on what they'd covered with Conrad and Barb. One group had dealt with a venous bleed to an arm; the other had dealt with what had looked like a simple contusion—or bruising—to the abdomen.

Mack focused on this last one. 'Who else thinks that this was just a simple case of bruising?'

Beau put up her hand.

'Yes, Beau?'

'There could be internal bleeding. A bruise is the definition of an internal bleed, in fact.'

'So what could happen to our patient if this is ignored as a minor injury?'

'He could die. There are multiple major organs in the abdomen, all at risk—the liver, the spleen, the pancreas...'

'Dangers of internal bleeding, please?'

'Exsanguination—possibly a tamponade on the heart.'

'Which is…?'

'A closure or blockage. Fluid collects around the heart, between the organ and the pericardial sac, and surrounds it, applying pressure and preventing it from beating.'

Mack looked at the group. 'Do we all see how different injuries—even ones that *seem* minor—can have devastating effects on a patient?'

The group nodded and agreed.

'And can we all agree that when you've been hiking for a long time—when you're exhausted, maybe sleep-deprived, hungry or starved of air, perhaps in a dangerous situation—how easy it might be to miss something important when assessing a patient or to make a mistake?'

Again there were murmurs of assent from them all.

'Out in the wilds you need to be on your game. You need to see the present danger, but you also need to be looking three steps ahead. Keeping your wits about you. Not making avoidable mistakes. Now…the likelihood of getting help immediately can be small. You might find yourself on your own, needing to get help and having to overcome obstacles to find it. Everyone get ready—I'm about to show you how to cross a river safely. Without a bridge.'

Gray raised his eyebrows. Surely everyone was exhausted? They'd hiked miles today and barely eaten. Though he guessed this was all part of the package. Trying to replicate the environment people might find themselves in and show them how easy it was to make a mistake.

He knew all about mistakes.

He'd made plenty.

He fell into step beside Beau and found himself drawing into himself. As always, when he focused on medicine he could exclude every other worry or emotion in his head—

but when he wasn't, and real life had an opportunity to take residence, there was nothing to distract him.

Beau's presence had shaken him. With her here, he couldn't ignore what he'd done any more. Every time he looked at her it was a reminder of the pain he'd caused, even though at the time he'd told himself he was doing it to save her greater pain in the long run.

Beau had had aspirations for their future. It wasn't just going to be marriage for them—it was going to be a whole life together. Children. Grandchildren. *Great*-grandchildren. That was what she'd seen for them when she'd said yes to his spur-of-the-moment proposal.

She hadn't just said yes to him, but yes to all that, too. She'd seen years ahead of them, spent happily in each other's company as they went on holidays or had romantic weekends away, had picnics in the park, ice creams on the beach. She'd seen cosy chats, the pair of them snuggled under a quilt, holding hands, kissing, enjoying being with each other. Snatched kisses in the hospital as they passed each other on their way to work.

She'd only ever seen joy...

How could he ever tell her that he'd seen something different? How could he tell her that if he'd married her it might have been okay to start with, but then there would have been little differences of opinion? Silences and resentment and screaming arguments. How could he say he had known how their fallouts would turn into sleeping in separate rooms? That they would go without talking for days or, if they did talk, would only snipe at each other and resent the other person for making them feel so bad? How could he tell her that he saw slamming doors and broken plates as well as broken hearts? How could he begin to tell her that he wouldn't have—*couldn't* have—brought a child into all of that?

Marriage had meant something different to them both and she'd had no idea. There'd not been any way for him to tell her that marriage for him meant torture and ruination. How could you show that sort of vision to someone who viewed everything as though the world was only full of good things? Of hope and promise and happily-ever-afters.

Beau had been the light to his dark. The sun to his shadow. She had always been better than him. She'd had such a pure outlook and he hadn't wanted to spoil her beliefs. Dilute her sunshine and make clouds cover her world.

He'd walked away that day, knowing he couldn't face marriage. That he just didn't have it in him to stay and say those vows when he didn't believe they could be true. To love and to cherish? Maybe to start with. For better, for worse? Definitely too much of the latter! Until death do us part? Why would he want to put either of them through *that*?

Marriage to Beau should have been the greatest thing, but he'd been unable to see past his dread. He'd been a child of a loveless marriage. He knew what it was like to be forgotten. Unwanted. Not loved as a child should be loved, but *used*.

He could almost feel another wound ripping across his heart at the thought of it. His love for Beau had meant he'd tried to do the decent thing. He'd wanted her to be married. Happily. To someone who could give that to her and who stood an equal chance of believing in the same possibility of happiness. There had to be a man out there who thought the same as Beau. Who wanted the same things.

And yet... And yet Beau was still single. Alone. Her career was her shining light. Her joy.

They were both in their thirties now, and Beau still hadn't any children. What was that doing to her? It had been her dream to have kids...

Gray closed his eyes wearily and rested against a tree for a moment to catch his breath. His leg—his *foot*—hurt physically. Trying to ignore it, trying to gather his mental strength, he opened his eyes to carry on—but stopped as he noticed that Beau had come to stand by him.

'Are you okay?' she asked.

He tried to gauge if she really was concerned. But the look in her beautiful eyes was enough to convince him that she was truly worried. Her brow was lined with worry. She'd even reached out her hand to lay it on his upper arm.

He nodded. ''Course. Just trying to ignore something that's not there.'

Beau looked puzzled. 'Are you in pain?'

He shrugged. 'A little.'

She tried to make him hold her gaze. 'Anything I can help you with?'

Gray let out an angry sigh. He was angry with himself. Angry at having got everything so wrong. Angry at hurting Beau. For still hurting her even now. And she was being *nice* to him. Showing care and concern when she had every right in the world to be ignoring him still.

But when he looked into her eyes, he got caught. He was trapped and ensnared by her gaze. Her concern and worry for him was pushing past his defences, sneaking around his walls of pretence and bravado, reaching around his heart and taking hold.

Hesitantly he reached up and stroked her face. 'You're so perfect, Beau.'

She stiffened slightly at his touch. Was she afraid? Shocked? But then she began to breathe again. He saw the way her shoulders dropped, her jaw softened.

She gazed right back at him. 'Just not for you.'

'But we were so close, weren't we?'

She nodded, a gentle smile curling her mouth. 'We were.'

He took a moment just to look at her. At the way the sunshine reflected off her hair, at the way the tip of her nose was beginning to catch the sun. The way the smile on her face warmed his heart...

Gray looked away. He had no right to enjoy those feelings any more. He tried to cast them aside, to stand straighter, to concentrate on the task ahead—the walking, the hiking. He couldn't start to feel that way for Beau any more. He'd only ended up hurting her in the past. He'd not been able to offer her what she'd needed then—and now...? Now he had even less. He wasn't even a whole man. He was broken. His mistake had been to think he had been whole in the first place.

He stepped past her, feeling her hand on his arm drop away as he moved out of reach. His heart sank. He had to be firm with himself. It was at moments like these when he might all too easily slip into thinking about another chance with Beau.

What would be the point? Where would it lead?

To a relationship again?

No. We'd just end up in the same place.

Gray almost let out a growl of frustration. Instead he gritted his teeth and pushed through the pain he was feeling.

CHAPTER FIVE

THE RIVER GENTLY flowed from east to west and was about twelve feet wide, with gentle ripples across its surface. On the other side their campsite waited for them, taunting them with its closeness.

They were all tired. It had been a long day—first hiking up the mountain and then their rapid descent, with the medical scenario on the way down. Beau was beginning to see how people might make mistakes with their decision-making when they were tired, hungry and sleep-deprived. It would be easy to do when you just wanted to be able to settle down and rest but knew you couldn't.

Now Mack stood in front of them, before the river, giving his safety lecture.

'Whenever you need to cross water, my advice is to always travel downstream until you come to a bridge. *That's* the safest way. But sometimes there may be an occasion where you need to cross without one, and you need to know how to do this safely. I would never advocate that you do this alone. It's always best to do this with someone else, and if possible with ropes.'

He pulled some ropes from his backpack and lay them out on the forest floor.

'Basic instructions are these—when you cross, you cross the river by facing *upstream* and slightly sideways. You lean *into* the current, because this will help you maintain your balance. You do *not* want to be swept off your feet.'

Beau glanced at the water. How deep was it? It looked pretty tame, but she guessed that there might be hidden currents, rocks beneath the innocent-looking water or even a drop in the riverbed's level.

'You shuffle your feet across the bottom. You do *not* take big steps and lift your feet out of the water. You do *not* cross your feet over, and your downstream foot should always be in the lead.' He demonstrated what he meant before turning around and staring intently at them. 'Do you all understand? Okay—practise that step on dry land.'

Beau imitated what he'd shown them. It seemed simple enough, but she could imagine that in the water it would feel different. She glanced at Gray and could see a worried look on his face. Why was he so concerned? Surely this was a thrill for him? The kind of thing he found a challenge?

'If there is a long stick available—a tree branch, a walking pole, something like that—you can use it for extra balance and to feel beneath the water for obstacles. If you find an obstacle, you'll need to put your feet upstream of it, where the water will be less powerful.'

She was getting nervous now. This was a lot more complicated than she'd thought.

'With a stick or pole, you can place that upstream, too. You move the pole first—then your feet. If the water gets higher than your thighs, and there is more than one of you crossing, you'll need to link arms and lock your hands together. This is called chain crossing. The biggest team member should be upstream, the smallest member downstream. You'll then move through the water using the same principles, parallel to the direction of the current.'

'What if it's too deep for that?'

'Then we use ropes, if available.' He began to lay out the instructions for using rope to cross water. He showed them how to anchor it, how to use a hand line, how to use a second rope as a belay and all the safety concerns involved.

It all got quite serious, quite quickly, and they were soon forging into the water to test its depth.

Considering the warmth of the day, the water felt cold, and Beau gasped as it came to just above her knees, soaking through her brand-new boots and socks and quickly chilling her to the bone. It was an odd sensation, being so cold below the knee but quite warm up top, and the sensation made her shiver and shake a little.

The water's current was deceptively strong, and she could feel it pushing and shoving hard against her legs like a persistent angry child. She was now shaking so much it was hard to tell where her feet were in the water, and feeling a rock beneath the water, she instinctively lifted up her foot to step over it, forgetting Mack's warning.

In an instant the current took her—unbalancing her, sweeping her off her feet.

She was down, with the water closing over her head in a frightening wave, filling her mouth, and she felt the cold suck at her clothes and body as the current tried to push her downstream. Gasping and spluttering, she tried to rise upwards, to find her feet and grab hold of something—anything—so that she could regain control and stand up. But the sheer coldness of the water, the disorientation she was feeling from being hungry, exhausted and sleep-deprived, meant she didn't know which way was up.

She opened her mouth to breathe, but it just filled with water. Beginning to panic, she splashed and opened her mouth even more to call for help—only to feel two strong arms grab her around the waist and pull her upwards.

'I've got you!'

She blinked and spluttered, gasping for air, wiping her wet hair from her face, and saw that Gray had her in his arms. She was pressed against him, soaking him through, but the joy of feeling her feet against the solid riverbed floor once again, and being upright and out of the cold, stopped her from feeling awkward.

She coughed to clear the water from her throat and clung tightly to him. 'Thanks.'

'You okay?'

She pulled a piece of river grass from her mouth and looked at it for a moment, disgusted, before throwing it away. The other hikers were looking at her with concern, still making their way across the river. It was then that she realised just how up close and personal she was with Gray.

Pushing herself away from him, she felt heat colour her cheeks—before she shivered slightly and recoiled at the feel of her wet clothes clinging to her body.

'I'm fine.' Why was he looking at her like that? There was far more than just concern in his eyes and it made her feel uneasy.

Anxious to get out of the water and to the campsite to dry off, she made her way across the river and clambered onto dry land with some difficulty. Her boots were full of water and her backpack had got soaked in the water, too. It would take her ages to dry everything off! Though she supposed the hot June weather might help, if she laid her things out on some rocks…

Once the others were all safely across, Gray insisted on putting her tent up for her quickly so she could get changed. As she'd suspected, everything in her pack was wet, but Claire kindly lent her some spare clothes to wear whilst her own were drying.

Mack was stern, giving her what felt like a lecture, and feeling like a naughty child, she sat by the river alone, her chin against her knees as she looked out across the innocent-looking water and thought about what might have happened.

She didn't have too long to think about it before Gray came to sit alongside her.

'How are you feeling?'

She shrugged, not willing to answer right away. Her fall in the river had disconcerted her. She *never* got things wrong. She always got things right—picked up new things quickly, learnt easily. Fording the river had shown her that control of things could all too easily be taken away from her when she wasn't expecting it. She'd thought she could handle the river—she'd been wrong.

And she'd thought she could convince herself that her feelings for Gray were those of uninterest and anger. She'd told herself that she didn't care about him any more. She'd been wrong on that count, too.

The way he'd rescued her in the river...the way she'd felt talking to him again...it was confusing. This was a man she should be *hating*! A man she should be furious with. Not even *talking* to. But being around him was stirring up feelings that she'd told herself she would *never* feel for a man again.

Gray jilted me! Rejected me!

And yet it had felt much too good to be in his arms again. Much too comfortable to be pressed up against him...much too familiar and safe and...and *right* to be that close to him again.

He'd felt solid. Sturdy. Strong. A safe haven. A certainty. And for a long time she'd tried to tell herself that Gray was an *un*certainty. An unstable individual who had always been a risk to her security and happiness.

How could she be getting this so wrong? Why was she so confused about him?

Even now, as he sat next to her on the rocks, she could feel her body reacting to him. To his presence. It was almost as if it were craving his touch again, and to be honest it was making her feel uncomfortable. It wasn't just the discomfort of being in someone else's clothes, or the knowledge that she'd made a mistake in the river and might have drowned, but also the discomfort of knowing that the chapter in her life which concerned Gray was not as closed as she'd once thought it was.

Somehow he was breaking back in and opening that door again.

'I was really worried about you.'

She didn't want to hear that from him. 'Don't be.'

'I saw you go under. I… My heart almost stopped beating. You just disappeared under the water like you'd been swallowed up by a beast.'

She could hear the pain in his voice. The fear. It was tangible. Real. She had no doubt he meant every word he said.

But I can't allow myself to react to him. Gray's no good for me.

'But you caught me, so everything was all right in the end.'

She refused to turn and face him. She couldn't. If she did turn—if she did see the look in his eyes that she knew to be there—she would be lost. She needed to fight it. Fight *him*. And her reaction to him. Her desire to feel him against her again. It had to go.

She stared out at the water, cursing its calm surface, knowing of the torrent below.

'If you had been swept away—'

'But I wasn't! I'm okay.'

She glanced at him. Just briefly. Just to emphasise her words—she *was* here, she *was* safe. Then she turned back to the river, her stomach in turmoil, her whole body fighting the desire to turn and fling herself into his arms again.

He didn't speak for some time and she could sense him looking out at the river, too.

'Are you cold? Would you like my jacket?' he asked eventually.

His jacket? The one that would carry his scent? What was he trying to do? Drown her in *him* instead? How would she even be able to *think*, wrapped in its vast depths, with the echo of his warmth within them?

'No, I'm good, thanks,' she lied.

'You're still shivering.'

'I'm not cold. It's just…just shock. That's all.'

'Well, shock isn't minor, either. We need to keep you warm, hydrated. Come and sit by the fire—we can get some hot tea into you.'

'Honestly, Gray, I'm fine.'

It was killing her that he was trying to take care of her. It would be easier if he left her alone for a while. Allowed her to gather her thoughts. To regroup and rebuild those walls she'd built for the past eleven years. Because somehow, in the last few hours, they'd come crumbling down and she felt vulnerable again. Vulnerable to *him*. And that was something that she couldn't afford.

'Come and sit by the fire, Beau. I insist.'

He grabbed her by the arm and gently hauled her to her feet. His arm around her shoulders, he walked her over to the fire and sat her down on a log next to Barb. Then he disappeared.

Just as she thought she could relax again, he came back. She tensed as he wrapped a blanket around her shoulders.

'How's that?' He rubbed her upper arms and knelt before her, staring into her eyes.

He was close enough to kiss.

She tried not to think about it—tried not to look down at his mouth, at those lips that she knew were capable of making her shiver with desire. She tried not to notice the way he was looking at her, the way the lines had increased around his green eyes, the way his beard emphasised his mouth—his perfect mouth—the way his lips were parted as he stared back at her, waiting for her response.

I could just lean forward...

She closed her eyes and snuggled down into the blanket. *No.* She couldn't allow herself to do that. It was wrong. *He* was wrong. What the *hell* was she doing, even *contemplating* kissing him?

Beau scrunched up her face and gritted her teeth together before she opened her eyes again and looked directly back at him. She nodded to indicate that she was fine, but she wasn't.

She was fighting a battle within herself.

And she really wasn't sure, at this moment in time, which side would win.

Rick was next on the rota to make a meal, and Mack provided him with a small amount of rice and some tins of tuna. It wasn't great, but it was protein and carbohydrates—both of which they all badly needed—and despite its blandness, despite the lack of salt and pepper, they all wolfed their meal down, hungry from restricted rations and exhausted from the long, tiring day.

Except for Beau.

She toyed with her food, pretending to eat, but in reality she was just pushing it round her dish, trying to make it look as if she was eating.

Gray sat next to her, put down his dish. 'You need to eat.'

'I'm not hungry.'

'You've had a shock. You need to eat for strength. You're too thin as it is.'

She could hear in his voice that he was concerned about her. Could hear that he had good intentions. But she didn't want to hear them from him. She didn't want to be reminded that he cared, because if she acknowledged that, then she would need to accept that *she* still cared about *him*, too.

'I'm fine.'

'No, you're not. You're hardly eating and you're as thin as a stick of rock.'

She sucked in a breath, trying to not get pulled into an argument. 'Honestly, Gray—just leave it, will you?'

'Beau, I care about—'

She stood up and cast off the blanket and walked away from the campfire, aware that everyone would be wondering what the hell was going on, but not having the energy or the inclination to explain. Irritated, she stamped over to the riverbank and checked to see if her clothes had dried on the rocks.

Luckily for her they were almost dry, the heat of the sun having done its work, and she scooped them up and headed to her tent to get changed. Clambering in, she turned and zipped up the tent beside her, shutting out the outside world before she collapsed on the ground, trying her hardest not to cry.

How dare he show me that he still cares? Does he not understand what that is doing to me?

Just a couple of days ago, safe in her work environment, if one of her colleagues had asked her how she felt about Gray McGregor, she would have been able to answer calmly and easily that he meant nothing to her any more. That she hardly ever thought of him, and that if she did, it was only because of a vague curiosity as to what he might be doing now.

That would have been true. But *now*?

Now she felt all over the place. Confused, upset, *disturbed*.

I wanted to be in his arms! I wanted to kiss *him!*

She'd only been with him for two days. Two days into a week together! What on earth would she be like at the end of it? Beau had thought she was strong. She'd thought—she'd assumed—that she was resolute in her feelings towards the man. That those feelings wouldn't change…that she'd be able to carry on with her life and every day would be the same as the one before it. Just the way she liked it.

Only, Gray being here had changed everything.

She pulled off the clothing that Claire had let her borrow, and as she sat there in her underwear, she heard Gray clear his throat outside her tent.

'Ahem…knock-knock?'

Just hearing that lilting Scottish accent, purring away so close to her, sent shivers of awareness down her spine.

Gritting her teeth, she pulled her tee shirt over her head and retightened her ponytail. 'Yes?'

'I've come to see if you're okay.'

Growling inwardly, she lay flat to pull herself into her khaki cargo pants and zipped them and buttoned them up before she yanked open the zip to her tent and stuck her head out.

'I'm fantastic.'

His head tilted to one side and he raised a questioning eyebrow. 'You sound it.'

'Good. Then maybe you'll leave me alone.'

'So you're angry with *me*?'

She scuttled out from within her tent and stood up, straightening her clothes. 'Yes—and don't say that I don't have good reason.' She knew she sounded petulant, but she didn't care.

'I'm sorry. I didn't realise that asking if you were all right was a capital offence.'

She didn't answer him, just knelt down to gather up Claire's clothes so she could return them.

'Only if *you* do it,' she said eventually.

He shrugged and squinted into the bright sun. 'My apologies, then. I was just trying to show that I care.'

'Well, you can't.'

'Why not?'

She turned to him, exasperated, but kept her voice low so as not to share their argument with the whole camp. 'Because it's *you*, Gray. You. I put my life in your hands once before. I gave you everything and you abandoned me. And...' she raised a hand to stop him from interrupting '...just when I thought I knew where to place you on the evolutionary scale—which, for your information, was somewhere below pond scum level—you turn up here and you're nice! You're *annoyingly* nice and pleasant and charming, and then you have the nerve to save my life and make me feel *grateful*! Do you know what happened to me the last time I was grateful to you, Gray? Hmm...?'

All through her rant, all through her rage and exasperation, he'd stood there, staring calmly back at her, not saying anything. Just listening. Just being *gracious* about the whole thing, for crying out loud!

'I was just worried that you weren't eating enough.'

'That's for *me* to worry about, Gray. Not you. *I* get to worry about me. You don't get that opportunity any more—do you understand?'

He nodded once. 'Okay. If that's what you want.'

She let out a pent-up breath. 'That's what I want.'

'Okay. Well, I figured you might want this. I sneaked it

into my backpack and I was saving it for a special occasion, but...but I think you might need it more than me.'

He reached into his pocket and pulled out a chocolate bar. Not just *any* chocolate bar, but her *favourite*.

She blinked uncomprehendingly. Then she reached out and picked it up, almost not believing it was really there until she held it. Her anger—which had been simmering quietly ever since she'd stepped foot into that ranger station and seen him there—disappeared.

'I love these.'

'I know.'

'But...but you didn't know I was going to be on this course.'

'No, I didn't. But I've always bought them. Ever since...' He stopped talking and looked down at the ground. 'Anyway, you can have it. Seeing as you skipped dinner.'

He walked back to the campfire and joined the others, his back towards her.

She stared at the chocolate bar, which was slightly crumpled and soft from where it had been tightly packed into his bag, and felt her heart melt just a little bit more.

He still bought them. Even after all this time.

And I've just said all those horrible things...

Beau swallowed hard. Now she felt guilty. Guilty for being so harsh towards him just because *she'd* been feeling confused. Was it *his* fault that she felt that way? No. She should be in greater control of her feelings. Hadn't she always been before? Since he'd left her, she'd kept a rigid control over everything. Even down to making sure there were no unexpected surprises during her day. Her life had been timetabled to within an inch of its life. Knowing what would happen and when had kept her safe for so long. Had kept her from being hurt again.

But maybe...maybe surprises could be a good thing?

Maybe a little uncertainty, a little risk, was okay? Didn't babies learn to walk by falling over? They didn't expect the fall, but they learnt from their mistakes.

Perhaps I need to let myself make a few mistakes? Take a few risks? Maybe there might be a little something out there for me, too.

She peeled open the chocolate bar and took a small bite.

The next morning Mack woke them early again and began teaching them another lesson. The topic this time was fractures.

'You have to know, even as a layman, how to evaluate an injury—either for someone else in your group or yourself.'

Beau could appreciate that. She was having a hard time assessing herself right now.

'You need to consider three things—the scene, a primary survey and a secondary survey if you're to come to the most accurate conclusion and assist yourself or another hiker out in the wild.'

'What's a primary and secondary survey?' asked Leo. 'I always get confused about those things.'

'Good question. A primary survey means looking at your patient and checking for life-threatening injuries or situations. So ABC. *Airway.* Is it clear? If not, why not? Can you clear it? *Breathing.* Is your patient breathing? Is it regular? Are there at least two breaths every ten seconds? And last of all *circulation.* Is there a major bleed? What can you do to stop it? That's your primary survey.'

'And if there aren't any of those signs?'

'Then you do your secondary survey. This also consists of three things. Remember with first aid and CPR there's generally a rule of three—ABC is one set of three. Scene survey, primary survey, secondary survey is another. If you remember to check three, you can always feel secure in knowing that you've checked everything. The secondary survey includes checking vital signs, taking the patient's history into account and a full head-to-toe body exam.'

'I'll never remember it all!' declared Barb.

'You'd be surprised,' Gray said.

'Once you've checked their vitals are okay, you can ask if they have pain or an injury. Find out how that injury occurred. Does it sound like there was enough force to create a fracture? Then you check the body, feeling firmly for any pain or deformities. But remember—even if the patient seems okay, their condition could change at any moment. You need to be alert. You may miss an injury because the patient is focusing on the pain from a bigger injury. And then what? Beau?'

'Then you swap hats,' said Beau, happy to answer. 'You take off the hat that states you're treating a fracture and put on the hat that says you're treating someone who's unconscious—you put them into the recovery position. If it gets worse again, you put on the CPR hat.'

Mack nodded. 'So, now let's focus on the fractures themselves. You look for the signs and symptoms of a fracture. Gray, can you tell us what they are?'

'Inability to bear weight on a limb, disabled body part, obvious deformity, pain, tenderness or swelling, angulation or bone protruding through the skin or stretching it. The patient might also mention hearing a crack.'

'Good. Did you all get that? You need to treat all possible skeletal injuries as if they are fractures. Even if you suspect a sprain or a dislocation, treat as a fracture until proved otherwise.'

'Okay, so how do we do that with no splints available?' asked Rick.

'There's always something you can use,' Gray continued.

'You've just got to think outside the box. Splinting is correct. It stabilises the break and helps prevent movement on the splintered ends—which, believe you me, can be excruciatingly painful.'

He rubbed at his leg, as if remembering an old injury.

'If you don't splint an injury, it can lead to further damage—not just to the bone, but to muscle, tissue and nerves, causing more bleeding and swelling, which you do *not* want.'

'So what do we do?' asked Rick.

'You need to get the bones back into the correct anatomical position. Which means traction—which means causing yourself or your patient *more* pain. But you must do it—particularly if you're hours or even days from medical help.'

Claire grimaced. 'I'm not sure I could do that.'

'You'd have to. It can be upsetting, but it's best for the patient. Causing pain in the short-term will help in the long-term.'

Claire nodded quickly, her face grim.

Mack took over. 'Let's imagine a break on the lower left leg, near the ankle. This will be the most common injury you'll come across. People hiking and trekking across strange open country, falling down between rocks, not putting their feet securely down—all that contributes to this kind of injury. Claire, why don't you be my pretend patient?'

She got into position before him.

'You need to grasp the proximal part of the limb—that means the part of the limb closest to the body—and hold it in the position it was found. Then, with your other hand, you need to apply steady and firm traction to the distal part of the limb—this is the furthest point—like so.'

He demonstrated by gripping above and below Claire's 'fractured' lower leg.

'You do this by applying a downwards pull, and even though your patient may cry out, or try to pull away, you *must* slowly and gently pull it back into position. This will help relieve the patient's pain levels. Okay?'

Everyone nodded, even if they were looking a bit uncertain about their ability to do it in a real-life situation.

'Before you apply a splint, there's a rule of three again. You need to check CSM—their *circulation*, their *sensation* and their *movement*. Can you feel a pulse below the injury? In the case of this one, can you find a pulse in the foot?' He demonstrated where to find it. 'Is the skin a good colour? Or is it pale and waxen, indicating that the positioning may still be off? Does the patient feel everything below the injury? Can they wiggle their toes? If there's anything restrictive, like a tight boot or socks, you can remove it to help reposition the limb properly.'

'What if the break is inside the boot?' asked Rick.

'You leave the boot on. The boot itself can act as a splint around the ankle sometimes—it's for you to judge what needs to be done.'

'What if we do something wrong?'

'You might never know. Or the patient might get worse, in which case you'll assess and treat accordingly. You can use sticks for splints, or walking poles, backpacks, snowshoes, the straps off your packs—anything that will provide a steady and supportive purpose.'

Rick nodded. 'Okay, but when we put a splint alongside the injury, how exactly do we attach it? In the middle? Where the injury is?'

'No. Fasten the splint above and below the suspected fracture.'

'Right. And what about an open fracture? Do we bind it? Compress it?'

'No. Leave it uncovered before you splint, and if you

can find enough splints to go around the injury on all sides, that's even better. Use padding, if you need to, to prevent discomfort—torn clothing...whatever you can find. But remember to keep checking it afterwards, because the wound may cause swelling and the splinting may then be too tight. You need to assess frequently and often. Have you all got that?'

They nodded.

'Right. Now the practical. With your buddy, I want you to practise assessing for and splinting a left ankle break. Remember to do a scene survey, and a primary and secondary survey. Remember your rules of three and use the environment around you to find and locate splints. Patients—give your doctor a few surprises. I'll come round and assess when you're done.'

Beau looked to Gray. It was his turn to be the patient. But for some reason he looked extremely uncomfortable, and she wondered briefly what it was that was worrying him. He'd seemed fine just a moment ago.

Was he thinking of a way to surprise her? As Mack had suggested? If he was, then she was determined to be ready for him.

CHAPTER SIX

'MAYBE I SHOULD be the doctor for this one,' Gray suggested.

'No. You've already rescued me. It's your turn to be the patient.'

'I was the patient for the leg wound. It's your turn.'

She looked at him, feeling exasperated. Why was he getting antsy all of a sudden? Why didn't he want to be the patient? He'd get to sit down and have a rest!

Beau decided to give him 'the look'—the one that told him, *Sit down right now. I don't have time for this!*

Gray cursed silently, his lips forming expletives she couldn't hear, before he shook his head in defeat and sank down to the floor.

'Do my right ankle.'

'Mack said the left.'

'Well, I'm surprising you. I broke my right one.'

'Gray, what's the matter with you? Now, first of all the scene survey. It's safe for me to approach you…there are no hazards.' She knelt down beside him and smiled broadly. 'What seems to be the problem?'

Gray tried his best glare, but when he could see that it wasn't having any effect on her, he resigned himself to what was about to happen. 'My ankle hurts. I think I've broken it. I heard something snap.'

'Uh-huh. Which one?' She smiled at him sympathetically and saw his face soften under her onslaught of sweetness.

He let out a breath. 'My left.'

She nodded, glad he was finally playing ball. Though why on earth he'd wanted to swap ankles was beyond her. She *had* noticed that he had been limping slightly. Perhaps she was about to find out that he really did have blisters and hadn't been looking after them properly.

'Okay. So, primary survey—your airway is clear, you're breathing normally and there don't appear to be any bleeds. Do you feel pain anywhere else?'

'Only in my pride.'

She laughed, puzzled by the strange discomfort he seemed to be displaying. 'Okay…so, secondary survey. Lie back—be a good patient.'

Gray lay back on the ground, but she could see he wasn't relaxed at all. He looked tense. Apprehensive. It was odd. This was a simple scenario—he should be fine about all of this.

'Okay, and on a scale of one to ten, with zero being no pain and ten being excruciating pain, how would you rate it?'

'Definitely a ten.'

'And how did you damage your ankle?'

'I slipped. I wasn't concentrating.'

'Uh-huh. Okay, I'm going to check the rest of you and make sure there are no other injuries. Just relax for me, if you can.'

She felt around the back of his neck and pressed either side of his neck vertebrae. No reaction. Then she felt his shoulders, checked his clavicle, then ribcage.

There was plenty of reaction. In her own body!

Touching him like this, enveloping the muscle groups as she checked both his arms, patted down his hips and applied a small amount of pressure on the hip bones, aware of how close her hands were to his skin, was almost unbearable. Her hands encompassed the thick, strong muscles of his thighs, moved past his knees down to his...

Huh? What was that?

She sat back and frowned, staring at his lower leg, then glancing up at his face in question. Waiting for him to answer. To explain.

'What is that, Gray? A brace?'

Had he hurt his leg? Had he been hiding an injury all this time? What had he done to himself?

Gray sat upright and his cheeks coloured slightly. His brows bunched heavily over his eyes and the muscle in his jaw clenched and unclenched before he answered her, without meeting her gaze. 'It's a prosthetic.'

She felt a physical shift in her chest, as if her heart had plummeted to the dirty ground below, and her stomach rolled and churned at the thought that he'd been so hurt somehow. That Gray—her once beloved, powerful and strong Gray—had been hurt to such an extent that he had physically lost a part of him.

'A what?' she asked in an awed whisper, not wanting to believe him.

The word 'prosthetic' literally meant an addition. An attachment. An artificial piece that replaced a missing body part. Something lost from disease, or a congenital condition, or trauma.

She could feel herself going numb. Withdrawing, almost. If she heard his answer, it would make it even more real.

Gray sighed and lifted up his left trouser leg, looked at her directly this time. 'I lost my foot, and some of my leg below the knee.'

She stared at it. Watched as he peeled off his boot and then his sock and revealed it to her in its full glory. The shiny plastic exterior…the solid metal bar from mid-shin down to the ankle, where the fake foot began.

'Gray…'

'Please don't, Beau. Don't tell me you're sorry. There's no need to be. I can still do what anyone else does. People have climbed Everest with a prosthetic.'

'I know, but…'

'You always told me—always warned me—that I took too many risks and, well…here you are. You were proved right. I did something stupid.'

She reached out to touch it, then stopped. She had no right to touch him there. Or anywhere, really. Her hand dropped back to her lap. 'Are you okay?'

'Apart from missing half a limb?'

'How did it happen?'

He pulled his trouser leg back down. 'It's a long story.'

'I want to hear it.'

'Why? We're not together any more—you don't have to prove you care.'

'Gray—'

'Please, Beau, leave it. Just splint the ankle.'

'Are you sure? I could just—'

'Just…splint it.'

She looked at his downcast face, the anger in his eyes, and her heart physically ached for him. To see him like this—bared and open…wounded. Not the strong Gray he'd always shown the world, but having to—being forced to—reveal a weakness… Beau knew how that must be making him feel.

But it didn't matter. His prosthesis didn't make him any *less*. He was still Gray. And he was right. People today could do anything with a prosthesis. Look at all those athletes. Or any ordinary person, carrying on with life. He was still a top cardiologist. It didn't stop him from operating. It didn't stop him from saving people's lives. But how to say that to him without sounding preachy? He knew it already. Surely?

He's still the same Gray. Life tries to strike you down, and though it feels, at the time, like it's the worst thing you'll ever have to get through, like you'll never survive... well, you do get through it. You do survive. You're changed. You're different. But you survive.

She knew Gray must have gone through a period of grieving for his lower leg and foot. A part of him truly *was* missing. But he was strong. Resilient. She had to believe in that. He was *here*, wasn't he? Hiking across Yellowstone for a week. You didn't do *that* on a prosthetic unless you were determined and believed in yourself.

Beau began to look around her for something to use for splints. There was plenty of wood, but she needed to find something sturdy enough to support a joint. There were some thick pieces of wood over at the treeline and she gathered them and came back to Gray. She silently began attaching them, using the bungee cords from her backpack. She fastened them, checked to make sure they weren't too tight, then knelt back and waited for him to look at her.

'Please tell me how it happened.'

For a moment she didn't think he was going to speak at all, but then he began.

'There's a place called St John's Head on the Isle of Hoy, in the Orkneys. Have you heard of it?'

She shook her head. 'No.'

'It's considered the world's hardest sea cliff climb and I wanted to give it a try.'

She nodded. Of course he had. That was what he'd always been like. Pushing the envelope. Pushing boundaries. Seeing how far he could go.

'You're not just fighting the heights and the rock there,

but the gale-force winds, the rain, the birds dropping…' He paused for a moment to think about his choice of words. 'Dropping *stuff* on you. It's a sheer rock face, with almost no fingerholds. There's a route called the Long Hope. It's amazing. You have to see it to believe it.'

'It sounds…exposed.'

He gave a laugh. 'You have no idea. When you're up there, you feel like you're the only person in the world.'

'You went alone, didn't you?'

He nodded. 'I was trying to free climb it. No ropes, no equipment. This other guy managed it a few years ago. I'm an experienced climber—I'd done free climbing before—I thought I'd be okay.'

'But something went wrong?'

Gray nodded. 'Before I knew what was happening, I was falling. I hit the rocks below, broke my leg in three places, fractured my pelvis, had an open fracture of the ankle. Luckily I had my phone. More importantly, I had a *signal*. Mountain Rescue and the coastguard joined forces and got me to a hospital.'

'Did they try and save your leg?'

'They tried. I had three surgeries. But an infection set in and they had to amputate. It wasn't the fall that lost me my foot—it was bacteria.'

She felt sick. It was awful. Yet he'd got himself back up, carried on with his demanding work, come on this course…

'Is that why you're here? To prove to yourself that you can still achieve things?'

Gray shifted on the ground and fidgeted with the splint she'd assembled on his lower leg. 'Maybe.'

'You're still *you*, you know? Just because there's a physical piece missing, it doesn't mean you're any less than who you were.'

She was a little shocked that she hadn't realised he was

injured in this way. She'd noticed the limping, but it hadn't occurred to her that it might be something so significant. What else had she missed about Gray?

'I know that. I was mad at myself for making a mistake on the cliff. Even now I can't pinpoint what went wrong, and that irks me. But I knew if I got one of the more expensive prosthetics I could still do things like this. Still have my adventures.'

She smiled at him. That was better. The fighting spirit she knew and…

She glanced at the ground, feeling her cheeks colour. 'Go on, then—tell me. I know you're dying to. What are the specs on this thing?'

He gave a sheepish grin. 'It's got a tibial rotator, which allows the leg to rotate even when the foot is placed firmly on the ground. It also helps prevent skin irritation in the socket, where there's an extra gel padding cuff for hiking trips. The foot itself is multiaxial, so it can tilt and rotate over uneven ground.'

'Sounds top of the line.'

'It is.'

'I'm glad you're out here.'

Gray looked surprised, then reached out and laid his hand on hers, curling his fingers around her palm and squeezing back when he felt her hand squeeze his. 'Thank you, Beau. I don't deserve you. I never did.'

She didn't know what to say. He was wrong! He *did* deserve her! Even now she could feel…

Beau swallowed hard, trying to find an anchor in this sea of swirling emotions she was reeling under. She wanted to wrap her arms around him and hold him. She wanted to press him close. To feel him safe in her arms. But another part…a much smaller part…told her to keep holding back.

Told her that this was *Gray* and she was crazy even to be thinking of giving this man comfort.

Instead she concentrated on the feel of his hand in hers. Its steady strength. Its warmth. The solidity of him near her. His presence—all too real and all too confusing.

Why couldn't she have been there to help him during his time of need?

Would I have gone if he'd called me and asked?

Yes. I would have.

They sat quietly, holding hands, until Mack came along-side them to assess Beau's splinting skills and medical surveys. They dropped each other's hand like a hot coal at the ranger's approach. Only once Mack had given Beau a big thumbs-up and suggested that they swap roles did they manage to look at each other again.

Something had changed between them.

Something weird and almost intangible. Whatever it was, it had strength and influence, and Beau lay on the ground and tried to ignore the feelings raging through her body as Gray assessed her for injury and applied a splint to her left ankle. Her cheeks kept flushing, she felt hot, her stomach was turning and spinning like a roulette wheel, and she tried to tamp down the physical awareness she felt with every touch of his hands.

When Mack called for a break, and told them all to make camp and put up their tents, she hurried over to her backpack and put her tent up quickly, eager to get inside and just *hide* for a while. Gather her thoughts. Regroup her emotions. Wipe away the solitary tear that rolled down her cheek at the thought of Gray broken and alone at the base of a sea cliff.

What does all this mean?

Am I in trouble?

* * *

It was Leo's turn at the cooking pot, and he had rustled up a spicy potato dish. Gray had no idea what had gone into it, just knew that it tasted good and he wanted more. But, as always, Mack had limited the rations so that they were always just the empty side of full, burning more calories in the day than they were able to take in, so they could see how hunger might affect their choices.

Tomorrow would see the start of the paired orienteering—sending the buddied couples out into the wild on their own, to see if they could navigate to a particular spot, make it safely and deal with any issues on the way. It had been the part of the week that he'd been looking forward to the most—surviving on his own wits with just one other person. But now...now he wasn't sure.

Now Beau knew about his leg. He'd tried his hardest to hide it from her, feeling a little foolish about it at first, but now he'd come clean and she wasn't fazed at all.

But I still feel incomplete. Is it just my leg? Or is something else bothering me?

If he'd ever felt he might stand another chance with her, that feeling had died when he'd fallen from that cliff and lost that part of his leg. It had been a physical manifestation of the fact that he wasn't whole. That he wasn't the complete package. That he couldn't offer her what she wanted from life. And that realisation still hurt like hell. He might have a new bionic foot and ankle, capable of coping with any terrain thrown at it, but what about *him*? What could *he* cope with?

Beau had meant everything to him. She'd made his heart sing and he'd been able to forget all the drama and misery of his own home when he'd been with her. She had brought him comfort and repose. A soft place to fall. *She* had been his home.

But he'd ruined it. That tiny slip, that tiny lapse of concentration, and he'd blurted out the one question he'd never thought he'd ask… *Will you marry me?*

It had changed everything. Turned his happiness upside down, put a deadline on his joy. No, not a deadline— *a death sentence.* Marriage would have killed who they were. Their happiness at being in each other's presence would slowly have been eroded and familiarity would have bred contempt. Living in each other's pockets would have caused them to seek time apart, space from one another, just so they could breathe again. They would have grown to dread being in each other's company, started to hate the way they ate their food, the way they fought about who wanted to go out and who wanted to stay in, whether they squeezed the toothpaste tube right… *Every tiny thing* would have been used as a stone to throw at the other.

He'd lived it. He'd seen it. Been stuck in the middle of two warring factions—both sides of which he loved for different reasons, both sides of which he stayed away from for the same reasons…

It was a fact that children imitated their parents. Gray might try not to be like them, but he was sure little things would sneak through. Sure, he might just have little quirks that at first Beau would find amusing, and then irritating, and then soon she'd be so opposed to them she would threaten to leave him unless he changed his ways…

Marriage was only possible for people who knew what they were doing. Who were emotionally available. Who had the strength to get through it. But for him and Beau…? *No.* He was damaged goods. He'd been broken before they'd even got started.

He knew he should have spoken to her earlier, but she'd seemed so happy, so confident in their happiness. Had he been wrong to try to let her be happy for as long as she could? Not to decimate her dreams? She'd even started talking about how after the wedding she would come off birth control so they could try for a child straight away...

That had been terrifying. Being responsible for bringing another child into another potential battleground? No. He couldn't do it. He'd *been* that child and look at what it had done to him.

The problem was whether Beau would understand all this. Her world was perfect, and her parents—the strangest couple in the world, who actually seemed still to *love* each other after many years—had been a different example entirely. There were no broken marriages, as far as he knew, on her side of the family, so *some* people got it right, but...

Beau was in the dark regarding his experience. She couldn't possibly know how he felt about marriage. The fear it engendered in him. That pressure to get it right when he had no idea how.

When everyone had finished eating, he volunteered to wash the dishes in the river and noticed after a few minutes that Beau had joined him.

'Hi,' she ventured.

He glanced at her—at the way her beautiful wavy hair tumbled around her shoulders, at the way her eyes glinted in the evening sunshine. She was still the most beautiful woman he had ever met. And then some.

'Hi.'

'Want a hand?'

'I've got two of those, thanks. Do you have a foot handy?' He laughed gruffly at his own joke and carried on swirling the dishes in the crystal-clear running water.

'Only my own. I don't think you'd want one of them— they've got sparkly pink nail varnish on the toenails. But I'd give it to you if you needed it.'

She took the dishes from him as he finished and began wiping them with a towel.

'You never know. My prosthetic has got all the latest tricks and flicks, but it doesn't have sparkly pink nail polish. I think that may be the latest upgrade it needs.'

She smiled at him. 'You know, I've been thinking about your accident…'

He paused briefly from his washing. 'Oh?'

'Just wondering who…who supported you through all that.'

'I got myself through it.'

'What about your family?'

He shrugged. He'd refused to lean on them for any kind of support. 'Well…'

'Did you tell them?'

'Not at first…'

'But they *do* know?'

'They do now. I told them after it was all over. Once I'd healed.'

'Why didn't you tell them?'

He shifted his stance, switching his weight from one foot to the other. 'We aren't that close. Never were. And my mother had enough to do, looking after my dad, so…' He trailed off, not wanting to say more. He'd always protected her from the reality of his family and it was a hard habit to break.

'You know, one day you're going to have to tell me. I'm not going to let this rest.'

He nodded. 'I know. When I'm ready.'

Beau gazed at him and smiled. 'I can wait.'

Perhaps she was nearly ready to listen? He let his fingers squeeze hers, acknowledging her support. For a moment he couldn't speak. He was so taken aback that she was saying these nice things. They'd both certainly come a long way in the last few days.

'And, you know…apart from the fact that you've got a body part that will *never* wear out…you'll make a cracking pirate if you choose to put a wooden peg in its place!'

He smiled. 'Of *course*! Stupid me for not seeing the best of my situation.'

'Well, you've always been guilty of *that*, Gray.'

His smile dropped. 'What do you mean?'

She looked up at him, startled by his reaction, realising she'd said more than she should. She'd answered too quickly. Without thinking.

'Erm… I don't know… Forget it.'

'No. You meant something when you said that—what did you mean?'

Beau looked uneasy, shifting her eyes away from his. 'Just that…back then…well…you had *me*, Gray.'

Her gaze came back to his, slamming into him with a force that almost knocked him off his feet.

'I thought we were happy together. That we had something special. That our love was stronger than anything else!'

The tears beginning to run from her eyes were real. Knowing that he was still causing her pain almost ripped him in two.

He cradled her hands against his chest. 'It *was*!'

She shook her head. 'No, it wasn't. You didn't love me enough—you let your doubt, or whatever it was, tell you to abandon me. Leave me. Without a word. Not a *single* word!'

'Beau—'

'I wasn't enough for you. Our *love* wasn't enough. You focused on something else. Something that tore you away from me. And do you know how that made me feel? *Worthless!'*

He pulled her towards him, into his arms, pressing her against his chest, hoping to dry her tears, hoping to show her that she could never be worthless to him. But feeling her against him, feeling her cry, woke something in him that he'd buried deeply. Buried so far down he'd thought it could never be found again. He'd found it now, though, and it had him in its grip.

He pulled back to look at her, to make her look him in the eyes, so that he could tell her that she was the most important person who had *ever* been in his life...

But as soon as his eyes locked with hers, he was mesmerised. Her shimmering sapphire eyes were staring back at him with such pain in them that he felt compelled to take that pain away, and before he knew what he was doing—before he had a chance to think twice—he lowered his lips to hers and kissed her.

It was like dropping a lit taper into a fireworks factory. There was a moment of shock, of disbelief and wonder at what he was doing, and then—*boom!* He lost control. All those years of being without her, all those years of never allowing himself to *feel*, came crashing down and his body sprang to life. It was as if she was a life-giving force and this was the kiss of life.

His arms enveloped her and pressed her to him. He couldn't get enough of her. He *had* to feel her. All of her—against him. Her softness, her delicate frame was protected by him. Her lips were against his, and the way she gasped for air and breathed his name was like oxygen feeding his fire.

It could have become something else, something...*more*, but just as he thought he couldn't resist her, couldn't resist the desire to feel her flesh against his own, the others in the group started catcalling.

'Get a room, you two!'

They broke apart and stared at each other, shock in their eyes, both of them not quite sure how that had happened.

Then Beau walked away, pulling open the flap to her tent and darting out of sight.

Gray gathered the dishes and took them back to camp, where he received many pats on the back from the other men and some raised eyebrows from Barb and Claire, whom he glanced at sheepishly.

'Well, that explains a few things,' Barb said. 'I *knew* there was something going on between you two. Feel better now?'

He didn't answer. He wasn't sure. The kiss had been amazing. More than amazing. But what was Beau thinking? She'd said some things… Had he made things worse? Had he made things better? Surely she wouldn't be in her tent if he'd helped in any way. He wondered if he should go and talk to her.

He glanced over at her tent, but Barb shook her head. 'I'd leave her a while, if I were you. It looks like you woke something up between the pair of you and she needs time to get used to it.'

'But shouldn't I—'

'Give her space, Gray. You'll have more than enough time on the orienteering hike, alone together, to talk out any last wrinkles. For now, give her time to absorb what's happened.'

'Shouldn't I at least go over and apologise?'

She cocked her head at him. 'You're *sorry* about kissing a girl like that?'

He thought for a moment. 'No.'

Barb grinned. 'Good! The world would be a lot better

if husbands kissed their wives like that a bit more, I can tell you. Con? You listening to this?'

'Sure, honey.' Conrad, who was tending the campfire, turned and grinned at them both.

'Pah! You old romantic! Anyway, if you ever kissed *me* like that, I think I'd drop dead from the shock—and I ain't ready to go yet.' She laughed. 'But, Gray, listen to me—and listen good. You and Beau look like you have something special going on. Something deep that comes from *here*...' She pointed at her heart. 'You don't let that go. Not ever. That kind of love is the stuff that gets you out of hot water.'

He frowned. 'How do you mean?'

'You don't need no old lady telling you how to live your life, but if I had one piece of advice to give you, it'd be to tell yourself every day just *why* you love that other person. What you're grateful for. What they do to make you feel loved and special. Because if you're busy focusing on the good stuff all the time, the bad times, well...they can seem a lot easier to get through.'

He nodded to Conrad by the fire. 'Is that what you do?'

'Sure is!' Barb leaned in, speaking in a mock whisper. 'Or I'd have killed him already! The man could snore for America!'

Gray glanced over at Beau's tent. *Was* it as simple as that? Just thinking of the good things? Reminding yourself every day why you loved that person? Reliving moments like that kiss they'd just shared? *Could* it be that easy?

He didn't know. He wasn't sure he wanted to admit that it could, because if he did, then the pain he'd put them both through had been for nothing. If he believed that, then everything could have been avoided if only he'd had enough faith in his love for Beau being stronger than any day-to-day drudgery trying to ruin it all.

Did I ruin our lives because I didn't think I was strong enough? No. I thought I was protecting her. Protecting me. I couldn't bear the idea that she could ever hate me.

But hadn't that happened anyway?

Gray rubbed his hands over his face and groaned. Why couldn't this be easy? A case of two plus two equalling four? Why did life have to have so many twists and turns, dead ends and multi-car pile-ups?

He stared at the entrance to Beau's tent, willing her to come out.

CHAPTER SEVEN

THERE WAS ANOTHER breakfast of porridge the next morning. Beau had suffered a long, uncomfortable night, having stayed in her tent for most of the previous evening, only coming out when Claire and Barb had called for her. She'd grabbed her toiletries bag and hurried away with them, her head downcast, ensuring she didn't make eye contact with Gray.

They'd kissed!

And she'd forgotten how wonderful kissing Gray had been. Her feelings had been all topsy-turvy, her heart hammering, her pulse pounding and her brain bamboozled and as fragile as a snowflake above a firepit as she'd fought to decide whether she should continue with it or fight him off. But it had been too delicious to stop.

I certainly didn't fight him off!

No. She'd breathed his name, gasped it, making those little noises in her throat that now made her feel so embarrassed as she thought of them. Had he heard her? *Of course he had!* He would have had to be deaf not to, and there was nothing wrong with his hearing. Or any of his other body parts...

She tried not to recall the sensation of him pressed hard against her.

And now I'm sitting here, around a campfire, eating

porridge that's as difficult to swallow as week-old wall-paper paste, trying not to look up and catch his eye. What am I...? A mouse?

She gritted her teeth and looked up. He was opposite, talking to Mack in a low whisper, and by the way Gray was pointing at his leg, she assumed they were discussing his prosthetic. Or maybe the accident that had caused it? She supposed Mack must have known about the prosthetic beforehand. Health and safety—these were the all-important buzzwords everywhere these days. Surely Gray had *had* to declare it beforehand? He might not have been allowed on the course otherwise.

Gray glanced over and caught her gaze, smiled.

Quickly she looked away. This was going to be awkward. Today they would be splitting up into their pairs for the orienteering challenge, after one final lesson around the campfire with Mack. She and Gray would be alone together. Just the two of them. Hiking through Yellowstone to a pre-approved grid reference, where apparently there would be a checkpoint to collect supplies before they headed to another grid reference, where they would find the ranger station. They would have to talk. There would be no escape for either of them.

And we're hardly going to be able to get through it in silence, are we?

Silence would be nice after that kiss. Preferable, actually.

No, forget that. Not coming on this trip would have been preferable.

But she had. So had he. And they'd kissed. And it hadn't been one of those polite kisses you gave at family gatherings, either. That polite peck on the cheek for a family member you hadn't seen for a few months.

It had been hot. Passionate, searing, breathtaking, goosebump-causing...

He had to have felt something, too. A reawakening. A refiring of something that had once burned so hot. That *unfinished* feeling between them... That entwining of souls—the kind of feeling that was so intimate it touched your heart.

Beau knew she had to get a grip. Take control. Let Gray know that, yes, she acknowledged something had happened between them, but that was all it could be—*something*. An undefined moment. And there was no need to explore it further. She had to make it very clear that they should leave it alone and get on with finding their way back to civilisation, thank you very much.

The situation they were in was so intense. It was risky. People got close to each other in this kind of situation because that was what happened in a high-pressure moment. It created a false reality. And when life returned to normal afterwards, the feelings just weren't there...

He *had* to know that this didn't mean anything for them. She'd come on this course alone and, damn it, she was going to leave it alone, too. There would be no need for further contact. She wouldn't be exchanging telephone numbers or email addresses with him. He would go back to Edinburgh and she would return to Oxford and life would continue. Everything in its neat little box, the way it always had been. In *her* control.

The reason the kiss had happened in the first place was because the whole thing had got *out* of her control. This wasn't reality.

But something *had* changed between them, and she'd learnt more about him in the last few days than she'd ever known before. She knew that there was so much more to understand about her enigmatic ex-fiancé. And that wasn't all. Though she hated to admit it, her lips still tingled from his kiss.

Her senses had gone into overdrive since, and though she'd been huddled in her tent, preferring to believe that she'd caught some sort of strange disease and was suffering from a weird kind of fever, she'd been aware of exactly where Gray was outside her tent. Whenever he'd come close or walked by, she'd known. Whenever he'd spoken during that evening, she'd frozen, just so she could listen to what he said. Her body had ached for him.

Ached!

She hadn't wanted someone this badly since…

Since Gray.

If she could have, she would have groaned out loud, but instead she shoved in another spoonful of the dreadful porridge. She filled her mouth with the soft mush just to stop herself from crying out.

Are you kidding me?

She sat there, miserable in her silence, staring at Gray, all rumpled and tousled opposite her, wanting both to kiss him and beat her fists against his chest in equal measure.

'Okay, everyone. Last-minute stuff before I send you off in your pairs out into the big, wide world. You remember what I said about the big animals in the park, yes?'

They all nodded.

'Well, now you need to know about the smaller beasts. They may be lighter than a two-thousand-pound bison, but they can still knock you off your feet if you're not careful.'

'Such as…?' asked Claire.

'Snakes, for one. There have only been two recorded snakebites in this area, and your main culprit is the prairie rattlesnake. You'll find her in dry grasslands and the warmer river areas. You all know what a rattlesnake looks like? Sounds like?'

Again, they nodded sagely.

'You hear that rattle—you head in the other direction. You give her a wide berth. Usually they rattle to warn you, before you get too close, but not always—so be on your lookout when you walk.'

'Are they always on the ground?' asked Gray.

'Mostly. But they have been known to climb trees, or rest in crevices between rocks, so always check your surroundings. There may be the rare occurrence of a snakebite, and a rattler bite will inject you with plenty of nasty stuff—hemotoxins that cause the destruction of tissue. If you don't have a reverse syringe handy—which you don't—you need to keep your patient calm and still, and wrap the affected limb tightly. Apply a splint and get yourselves some medical help as soon as possible.'

'Shouldn't we attempt to suck out the poison with our mouths?'

'Technically, it should be safe to suck out the venom if the person doing the sucking doesn't have an open wound in their mouth. Poisons only affect you if you swallow them. But we're not dealing with poison here—we're talking *venom*. Venom is toxic only when it's injected into the lovely soft tissues of the human body and its rich bloodstream. So if you suck out venom from a snakebite, you *should* be okay—but we don't advise it any more. My advice? *Don't do it.* The human mouth isn't that clean, either, and you're just as likely to introduce bacteria into the wound and do as much damage as the snake did.'

He looked at their sombre faces.

'Walk with a stick when you're out in the wilds alone. You can tap the ground before you, and if there is something you've missed, the stick is more likely to get attacked before you.'

'And that stick will come in handy for a river crossing— let's not forget!' said Conrad.

Everyone smiled and the sombre mood was lifted.

'The next thing is stating the obvious—you need to keep an eye on your buddy. Heat exhaustion and dehydration can set in quickly. This time of year it's hot—you're sweating constantly and you'll need to keep up your fluid intake and stay out of the midday sun for as long as is possible. Beau, do you want to let people know the signs?'

She coloured, feeling Gray's eyes upon her, and her answer, when it came, was not given in her usually confident voice. 'Erm…you might feel weak, thirsty. When you go to the loo, your urine might be only a little amount, deep in colour, or it might even hurt to try and pass water… Erm…'

Gray helped her out. 'You might feel drowsy, tired, dizzy, disorientated. Faint when you try to stand. These are all signs of it getting worse. You must keep putting the fluids in, even if it means stopping to purify water. Water should be your top priority.'

Mack nodded. 'Then there are the mosquitoes, the leeches, the spiders, the ticks. These could all just be minor irritants, but long-term might lead to other problems. Tick bites, especially, could lead to Lyme disease.'

'Ooh, that's *nasty*. My cousin has that,' Barb said.

'I know you've all got bug spray, and some of you have citronella. These are all good repellents, but you need to check each other at every stop for ticks. If you get one, don't just try to pull it out. You need to remove them by twisting them out with tweezers or proper tick removers.'

He smiled and stood up.

'Right! Let's pack up camp, douse the fire, and then

I'll hand out your coordinates and maps. You'll each be given a different route to follow, but we should all arrive at the ranger station by Heart Lake sometime tomorrow afternoon. When we do, you can all tell me how wonderful I've been whilst you sip real drinks and eat a proper meal. Sound good?'

They all cheered, and he nodded and headed over to his own tent, started to take down the guy ropes.

Beau helped Barb wash the breakfast dishes. 'Are you nervous about heading into the wild with just you and Con?' she asked.

'No. I know he'll look after me and I'll look after him.' She looked up at Beau. 'You nervous?'

'A bit.'

'About the wildlife problem or the cute doctor problem?'

Beau blushed. 'One more than the other.'

'Oh, don't you worry, honey. That man has got your back. And maybe some time alone together is just what you two need. A romantic walk together... A campfire beneath the stars all on your own...'

'But what if it *isn't* what we need? What if we find ourselves alone and it all turns bad? What if we really hate each other?'

Barb tilted her head as she gazed at Beau. 'I don't think that's going to happen. Do you?'

Beau wasn't sure. Having the others around had provided a security she hadn't realised she'd been relying upon. Now they were all about to go their separate ways and she'd be on her own with Gray... Well, there were enough butterflies in her stomach to restock a zoo.

When the dishes were done and packed away, she headed over to collapse her tent—only to find that most of it had been done already and Gray was kneeling on the pine-needle-littered ground, putting her rolled-up tent back into its bag.

'Oh! Erm…thank you.'

'No problem. I saw you were busy, so…'

She nodded. 'I can take over now.'

She held out her hands for her things and took the tent from him, started to rearrange her pack. Keeping her back to him, she breathed in and out slowly, trying to keep her heart rate down. But it was difficult. He was so close! So near. Watching and waiting for her…ready to say goodness only knew what when they were alone.

Perhaps she could pre-empt him. Let him know there wasn't going to be a continuation of what happened yesterday. Because if there was… Well, she wasn't sure her senses and her heart would survive the onslaught. Gray was like a drug to her. She could feel that. The effect he had on her was as if she *had* been bitten by a rattlesnake! With her body turning to mush and her ability to think shot to pieces…

She had to let him know where she stood. Where *they* stood.

Beau turned and faced him, squaring her shoulders and standing her ground as if she were about to go into battle. 'Gray? You need to know that after…after last night…what happened… I… It won't be happening again. We can't let it happen. We can't.'

Try to look him in the eyes!

'But we do need to work together to get back to the ranger station, so can you promise me that you won't do anything? You know…won't provoke something of a similar nature?'

The corner of Gray's mouth turned up in a cheeky way. '*Provoke* something? What do you mean?'

Beau looked about them. Was anyone listening? She

leaned into him, closer, so that she could whisper. 'I mean the kissing! Please don't try to do anything like that again!'

Gray stared deeply into her blue eyes, searching for an answer he obviously couldn't see. But he must have heeded her words, because he stepped back and nodded. 'I won't start anything. You have my word.'

'Thank you.' She felt her cheeks flush with heat again at the relief.

'But only if...'

'Only if what?'

'Only if *you* can keep *your* hands to *yourself*.'

He turned away from her to haul on his backpack, and when he turned back to face her, he was grinning widely. He really was maddening!

'I'm sure I'll try to restrain myself.'

A few hours later they had been given their coordinates and were walking to their first checkpoint. Or so Beau hoped. Gray was the one reading the map and leading the way and she was putting her trust in him totally.

Feels familiar. And look where it got me before!

'Er... Gray? Could I just glance at the map?'

'Well, that depends...'

'On...?'

'On how often you've used a map to navigate across country.'

She let out a tense breath and glared at him. 'I made it from Oxford to Heathrow in one piece.'

'By GPS?'

'It can't be that hard! Could I just have a look?'

He handed her the map with a smile on his face. 'There you go. You're in charge.'

She nodded with satisfaction and glanced at the map. She'd expected a few place names, splodges of green for woodlands and trees, maybe patches of blue to mark out lakes and blue lines for rivers. This map *had* all of those things—but it also had other lines that went all over the place. And where were the grid references…? 1…2…3… It was all numbers!

She bit her lip, her eyes scanning the map, looking for some sort of point of reference that was familiar with their surroundings. 'Is this even the right map?'

'You have to know our longitude and latitude to start with.'

'Which is where again?'

She wouldn't look him in the eye. So he stood by her side and pointed at a small spot on the map. 'Just there.'

'And we're heading to…?'

'Over there.' He pointed again. 'Our first checkpoint.'

'Right.'

It wasn't getting any clearer. What were all those other lines? Elevation? That seemed about right…

'So we need to take this trail ahead of us until we reach this…' There were a lot of lines all tightly together. 'This high spot?'

He nodded and smiled. 'Looks like it. We should make it there by nightfall. Camp overnight and then tomorrow we need to cross another river.'

Now she looked at him, feeling the cold memory of her previous accident shiver through her body. She wasn't looking forward to that. What if it was deeper and more dangerous than the last one?

'Oh…'

'But we should be able to get to the ranger station by lunchtime. Just imagine—tomorrow we can be drinking real tea and tucking in to a restaurant meal with all of this behind us.'

'Sounds simple.'

'Should be.'

She passed him the map. 'Maybe you *should* have this.'

They'd parted company from the rest of the group—everyone with nerves and butterflies in their stomachs, everyone hugging each other, whispering words of encouragement into each other's ears before setting off—turning around occasionally until the others were out of sight.

Each pairing had been given a different checkpoint to reach, and then from that checkpoint they all had to navigate their way back to the ranger station. Nothing too arduous, but enough of a toe in the water to prove to themselves that they *could* do it, that they'd survive and, if need be, could cope with any injuries on the way.

Beau had learnt a few things on this trip so far. She'd learnt that she could cope with being around Gray. With talking to him. Being civil. They'd even got…*close*…and she'd discovered her feelings for him were still very much up in the air. He was maddening and gorgeous and frustrating and sexy and… Had she mentioned gorgeous?

He still bought her favourite chocolate bars. He'd been incredibly hurt and had survived alone. The idea of him lying there, broken and hurting, at the bottom of that remote sea cliff had been nauseating. Heartbreaking. What had he thought of as he'd lain there? Had he thought he was going to die? Had he had regrets?

Was I one of them?

Beau had never rested. Since the day he'd left, she'd pushed herself. Striving, challenging herself, working harder and harder, until the hospital had become the only thing in her life worth a damn.

But there was always a part of me missing…and that part was Gray.

She'd never had any closure. She'd never found out the reason for his disappearance.

There were a few clues now. Maybe it was something to do with his family? Had someone warned him *not* to marry her? It certainly couldn't have been anyone from *her* family. They'd all been so pleased for her when she'd announced their engagement.

Beau glanced at him as they walked, admiring the cut of his jaw, the stubbornness there in the line of his mouth, his tightly closed lips, his lowered brow as he slowly led them up an incline.

And he was doing all this with a prosthetic leg! He was amazing. He was still the man she'd known all those years ago, still challenging himself, pushing the boundaries, taking risks.

I'd be a fool to get involved with him again.

Gray held out his arm in front of her chest and Beau walked straight into it, frowning.

'Hey!'

'Shush!' He held his finger to his lips and pointed ahead through the treeline. 'Look…a herd of bison.'

Bison?

She stared hard, feeling the hairs rise on the back of her neck as the huge beasts passed them.

It was a large herd. Easily a hundred or so animals, maybe more. It was made up of mainly adults, as tall as her and Gray, with a few youngsters trotting alongside. They were thick, broad animals, with shaggy fur, some of it clumped, accentuating their humped backs as they ambled along, in no hurry at all. Several of them nibbled at the ground, others were snorting and looking around, keeping watch.

Instinctively Beau and Gray knelt out of sight by a large rock at the side of the trail. Beau's legs felt like jelly, but she drew on the reserves inside her that she always drew from. The reserves that had got her through sixteen-hour surgeries, nights on call and the all too numerous occasions when she'd had to sit at a family's bedside and deliver bad news, trying her hardest not to cry alongside her patients' relatives.

She'd had to stay strong. She'd made a profession out of it. Forcing herself to stay dry-eyed, forcing herself to stay on her feet, to answer one more patient call, to do one more consultation, perform one more surgery.

Shifting her feet, she glanced at Gray, excited at having seen these amazing animals up close. 'Should I take a picture?' she whispered.

'Does your camera have a flash?'

'I can switch it off.'

He nodded and she struggled to get her camera out of her fleece pocket. Once she'd deactivated the flash, she pushed herself up onto her knees and peered over the top of the rock. Breathing heavily, she used the zoom to focus in on one particular specimen that was snorting, using its tail to bat away flies as it scanned the horizon, alert for any danger.

'Wow...'

Back down behind the rock, she showed the digital picture to Gray and he smiled and whispered, 'It's good. But no more. We don't want them to know we're here.'

'Surely they can smell us?'

'Maybe. But I think we're upwind, so I'm going to go with no. Let's stay out of sight until they've passed.'

They sat with their backs to the rock and got some fluids on board.

Beau glanced at Gray. 'I don't suppose you've got another chocolate bar stashed away in those pockets?'

He smiled. 'No. Sorry.'

'Trail mix it is, then.' She rummaged in her pack for the small resealable bag and pulled it out, offering him some.

'No, thanks.'

She shrugged. 'More for me.' She ate a mouthful. Then another, savouring the taste of rich nuts and dried fruit, regretting that none of them was covered in chocolate. 'You know…you surprised me a lot the other day.'

He turned to her, an eyebrow raised in amusement. 'On which occasion?'

'The chocolate. That was my favourite bar. The kind you always used to buy me whenever you passed the shops on the way home from a shift. You said you still buy them. Why?'

Gray shifted on the hard ground, as if it had suddenly got a lot more uncomfortable in the last few seconds. 'Because…' He let out a heavy sigh. 'Every time I pass a store, every time I have to shop, I buy them. Eat them. They remind me…'

'Of me?'

He gave a smile. 'Of some happier times. I have this image in my head of you curled up in the corner of the sofa, your head buried in a pile of medical texts, nibbling away at a bar, one piece at a time, savouring each block before you ate the next. I don't know…it probably sounds stupid…but having them, eating them, makes me feel… closer to you.'

Beau stared at him, her heart thudding away in her chest. That was so sweet. That he still bought those bars. And for him to openly admit… She wondered if he would talk to her about his family, open up more if she asked.

But she didn't. This moment wasn't the right time. Now was the time for being honest—but not in that way. It was not the moment to bring up painful stuff that could turn all this on its head. And she didn't want this going wrong. They were heading in a good direction. Communicating. Opening up about little things. It was a start.

And she liked it. Liked talking to him. Right now they were building bridges. They were forging new pathways ahead of them and they were doing it together. That was what was important.

So instead she smiled at him. 'We're close now.'

She reached out and took his hand, squeezing it, looking up into his eyes and feeling warmth spread within her, as if her heart was opening up and letting him in again. It was scary, but strangely, suddenly, it felt so right.

Their kiss now seemed like a dream, and she began to wonder how it would feel to kiss again—but this time when she was ready for it. Prepared. Able to appreciate it properly. Even instigate it?

Perhaps she ought to take a leaf out of Gray's book? Be daring. Take a risk. Put herself out there on the ledge. Make that leap of faith.

To where, though? Where do I want us to end up? If I kiss him, what message will that send?

Gray smiled at her, then laid his head back against the stone and closed his eyes.

I could kiss him now, but...

Something held her back. She stared at him for a moment longer and then let out a breath, the tension leaving her chest, her shoulders relaxing. Now was not the time.

They continued to wait for the herd to pass. Gray with his eyes closed, resting. Beau just watching him, taking in all the details of his face, questioning her heart's desire.

After the last of the bison had gone, they forged onwards until they reached their checkpoint—a tree marked with a wooden first aid box. Upon opening it, as instructed, they found the extra 'luxuries' that Mack had promised them would be in there. They'd daydreamed about what they might be. Food? Chocolate, maybe? Perhaps even a small bottle of wine to celebrate?

But no. Upon opening the box they found a standard first aid kit, a roll of toilet paper and a tick remover.

'Great...maybe we can eat those?' Beau suggested wryly. 'What *is* the correct way to cook loo roll? You're meant to boil it, right?'

Gray smiled, then they got to work setting up camp for the night. He successfully lit a small fire that they edged with rocks and they ate a rather tasteless lentil broth, their thoughts drifting to dreams of the next day, when they would be back at their luxury hotels. Though even that dream was tempered by the sour note that by then they would have parted ways, and there was still so much they hadn't said...

Beau gazed through the flames to look at Gray. He was looking straight back at her, but this time she didn't look away. She held his gaze, thinking of how they'd once been with each other. The way he'd made her feel. How happy he'd made her. Before their wedding day anyway. She'd loved him so much.

She swallowed hard, determined not to cry over something she'd shed enough tears over. That had been then. This was now. They'd both changed and here they were, in the heart of Yellowstone Park, beneath the stars, sitting around a campfire, with just the sounds of crackling wood and distant insects, the air scented with woodsmoke and pine.

'At any other time I would say this is quite romantic.' She smiled.

He smiled back. 'But not this time?'

Now she felt awkward. She didn't know how she should reply. She wanted to keep the good mood. Keep the good feeling they had. She'd missed it. The *ease* of being with him. And she didn't want to let it go. She wished they were sitting closer. Not separated by the flames.

'Well.' She shrugged and grinned, feeling her cheeks flush with an inner heat. 'It's kind of awkward. Don't you think? If we were still together, we'd take full advantage of this moment... The stars, the campfire beneath the moon, just the two of us...'

He nodded, agreeing. 'But let's not forget that I promised to keep my hands to myself.'

She matched his nod. 'Yes, there's that, too.'

They stared at each other across the fire. Smiling. Breathing. Keeping eye contact.

Beau felt a strange awareness inside her. She could feel the weight of her clothes against her body. The tightness of the tops of her socks, her waistband digging into her stomach. She felt uncomfortable. Keen to move.

She stood up and nodded some more. 'I think I ought to go to bed.'

Gray stood, too. 'If that's what you think is best.'

'I do.'

There was a tense silence. The air was charged with a heat that did not come from the flames below.

Beau kept remembering the way he'd kissed her the other day. How it had felt to be back in his arms. That ease of being with him that she'd never felt with anyone else. He was so close now! So available. But was she brave enough to start something?

'Right, I'm going, then.'

'All right. Goodnight.' He slipped his hands into the pockets of his jacket, his jaw clenching and unclenching in the moonlight.

'Goodnight.' She stared at him, unwilling to walk away. Not really wanting to go to bed. Not alone. Anyway. 'Gray, I—'

She didn't get to finish her sentence.

Gray stepped forward, and for a brief moment she

thought he was going to take her in his arms—but, disappointingly, he didn't. Instead he began to speak.

'We need to talk.'

Beau sucked in a breath. *Okay.* This was going to be one of those moments, wasn't it? One of those life-changing moments when your path in life forked and you could choose to go left or right.

'All right.'

He reached out and took her hand, enveloping it in both of his, gazing down at them as he stroked her skin, inhaling deeply, searching for the right words to begin.

'I need to be honest with you. If anything is to…happen… between us, then we need to be honest with each other. That's what destroyed us in the past. Secrets. I *did* want to marry you, Beau. I need to say that. Right at the start. Because you *must* believe it. I did. I wanted you to be mine for ever. I wanted to know that you'd be there for me every single day of the rest of my life. I loved you. Deeply. Do you believe me when I say that?'

She searched his face, saw the intensity in his eyes, felt the way he squeezed her hand whilst he waited for her answer. Yes. She believed him.

'I do.'

'Good. That's good. The wedding…the actual day itself… that would have been easy for me. That wasn't why I left— the pressure of the day. That wasn't the bit that worried me. It was the next part I was worried about.'

'The honeymoon?'

She didn't understand. How could he have been worried about that part? She'd spent many a night with Gray McGregor and he certainly knew what he was doing. This man had made her body *sing*. He had made her cry out in ecstasy and shiver with delight. She'd used to lie in his arms and fall asleep, feeling secure, loved and cherished.

He had been her other half. The part that had made her whole. She'd never found that since. With anyone. Connections she had made had seemed…wanting. Unreal. There'd always been something missing.

'No, not that. The *marriage* part.'

Oh. Beau frowned. She didn't understand. 'Why?'

'You were right when you said that there was something about my family you didn't know. There was something… *is* something. Even now.'

She remained silent, waiting for him to explain, but she stroked the back of his hand absentmindedly, being supportive, as much as she could be, whilst he told her his story. She was apprehensive, too. For years she'd wanted to hear his explanation, and now that it was here, well… she wasn't sure if she could bear to hear it. What if it was terrible? What if it was something sad? What if all these years he'd been hurting, too?

'When my parents first met, they were madly in love. They were like us. Young. Hopelessly enchanted with each other. All they could see was a bright future ahead of them. They thought that no matter what happened they would face it together and they would be *strong*. That's what they believed.'

She smiled at the mental image, picturing it perfectly. But her smile faltered when she remembered that something had then changed.

'But…?'

'But that didn't happen. They got married, yes, but they were poor. Jobs were scarce. My mother got a job in a factory, part-time, just as she learnt she was pregnant with me. My father was working as a mechanic in a garage, fixing and tending buses for the council. He worked incredibly long hours. She hardly saw him. But he had to work to bring in the money. Especially when she stopped working to have me.'

She nodded, understanding their financial struggle. Even though it wasn't anything she'd experienced herself, she had seen it in others. 'It must have been difficult for them.'

This was all new information for Beau. She'd known almost nothing about Gray's family. Just that his father was in a wheelchair, paralysed from the waist down, and that his mother hardly spoke, her face for ever shut in a pinched, tight-lipped, sour way. Their early years together sounded like a tough time.

'It was. And I was a difficult bairn. Mum found it hard to cope. Dad couldn't help—he was always at work. When he got home late each evening, he was exhausted, barely having enough energy to eat before collapsing into bed each night.'

She squeezed his hand.

'Mum begged him to help more at home, but he had no time. He was afraid that if he took time off work he'd lose his job, and they couldn't afford that. She started taking in sewing and ironing to earn a few extra pennies, and they simply began living separate lives. I had colic. I barely slept, apparently. Crying all the time and nothing would soothe me. My mother felt like a single parent. They became true ships that passed only in the night.'

She felt his pain but wondered what this had to do with *their* relationship. 'What happened?'

'I don't know… My mum would bad-mouth him to me all the time. Say that he was useless, that he was a waste of space. He wound her up. The way he was never there. The way he irritated her when he *was*. The way he never lifted a finger to help her at the weekends. She even suspected there might be something with another woman. The receptionist at the garage. I didn't know if he was having an affair, but my dad would go on at me the same way. Say that my mother was a harridan, a nag, that she couldn't leave a hard-working man in peace.'

Beau felt uncomfortable. How awful that must have been—to be stuck between two warring parents. The two people you relied on and loved most in the whole world.

'Their verbal battles sometimes got physical. He didn't hit her or anything, but they both threw things. The soundtrack to my childhood was yelling and hearing ceramics hitting the walls. I even ended up at the doctors once, after accidentally treading on something sharp that had been missed in the clear-up afterwards.'

He let out a deep breath and his face brightened just slightly.

'That was where I began to love medicine. It was the only place where I'd been tended with real care and compassion.'

His eyes darkened again.

'My parents hated each other. Despised each other. The slightest thing would set them off. A look. The way the other one chewed their food. Whether they snored. Anything. And I was left as a go-between. Used like some pawn in a battle that I didn't understand. Then one day my mum decided she'd had enough. She packed her bags and waited for him to come home so she could tell him she was leaving.'

Beau was shocked. 'Without you?'

He nodded. 'The time he should have been home came and went. She got furious because she thought he'd gone to the pub with the other woman, spending money we couldn't spare on booze, and said that he was preventing her from giving him the performance of a lifetime. She'd planned on telling him once and for all how he was a good-for-nothing husband and she was leaving, But then the phone rang. He'd had an accident. A bad one.'

Beau felt sick. 'The one that paralysed him?'

He nodded again. 'A bus had come off a raised ramp and rolled over him, crushing his spine and pelvis. I'll never forget the look on my mother's face as she heard the news. Shock…disbelief…and then a deep sadness. Resignation. We went to the hospital, but he was in surgery. The nurses were very good to me—loving, caring. It was there I decided I wanted to be like them. Nothing like my parents. I wanted to become a doctor. We learnt later that Dad was paralysed.'

Beau could picture it all. The shock of the accident. The complete one-eighty that Gray's mother must have had to do…

'And then your mother felt she *couldn't* leave?'

'That's right. She unpacked her things whilst he was in the hospital and I've never seen a sadder woman since. They just get on with things now. She helps him. Cares for his him. But they barely talk. They just exist in the same house. Despite what had happened, what they'd gone through together, they've become more separate. Their marriage has become a prison. Each is saddled with the other for eternity. And to think they once loved each other so much…'

He couldn't look at her, his eyes downcast, lost in the painful past.

She was silent for a moment. Taking it all in. What had happened to his parents was awful. The way their relationship had crumbled under tough times. The accident… The paralysis… The way his mother must have felt obligated to stay… The way his father must have felt, stuck with a nursemaid wife he could barely tolerate speaking to…

'That's horrible, Gray. And I can't believe I'm only hearing about it *now*. Why didn't you tell me before?'

He looked at her then, sadness in his eyes. 'I've *never* known them to be happy, Beau! Not *once* can I see, in any part of my memory, either one of them smiling, or laughing, or being happy! I grew up in a dark, stormy world, full of crazed arguments, broken china and tense silences you'd need a machete to cut through! I loved being at school because I was *away* from them. I stayed away from home as much as I could because it was the only way I could be happy—without *them* dragging me down, dragging me into their battles. And when I met *you*…my sweet, beautiful Beau…I couldn't believe that a man and a woman could be so happy together! You were a breath of fresh air to me—the first hint of spring after a lifetime of bitter, endless winter…'

She could hear that he was trying to explain how he'd felt when he'd met her…but he'd *left* her. Surely it couldn't be true that their perfect future had been ruined because of what had happened to his *parents*?

'But, Gray, how could you have left me because of *them*…?'

Beau stared up at him, tears burning her eyes. Her hurt, her humiliation from all those years ago came flooding back again. The pain was fresh once more. All those years she'd thought there'd been something wrong with *her*. Something she'd been lacking. Something missing that had made him walk away. Maybe into the arms of another woman? And she'd racked her brains, trying to think of how she could have been *more* so that he would have stayed. Had pushed herself ever since, trying to prove that he'd been wrong to walk away and give her up.

'Gray, I'm sorry your parents had an awful time, but it hurts to see that you let that impact *us*. So your parents gave you a bad example…? Mine gave me a *great* example of what marriage could be.' She smiled through her tears. 'They still do. After all this time. Are you saying that my experience of *my* parents' marriage is wrong? *Why* couldn't you believe in a happy marriage? With their example?'

He shook his head. 'Because your family was the exception to the rule. Everywhere I looked I saw married couples barely getting along. Couples who had nothing to say to each other after many years. Couples who could only talk about their children. Couples who did things separately. Who took time apart, holidayed on their own. Couples who looked like all joy of life had left them.'

'You thought that would happen to *us*?'

She almost couldn't believe it. His parents' story was tragic, and she felt for him that he had been trapped in it. But that had been his parents' pain. Not *theirs*. She and Gray had been happy. Strong.

'I feared things would end up that way. Because I couldn't be honest with you about this before we got married, so what you saw in me was a lie. I was a lie. *We* were a lie. We wouldn't have survived! I accept the fact that leaving you at the church like that was a cowardly thing to do, and I should have turned up to tell you to your face that I was leaving. But at the time I was so racked with guilt, so broken in two at knowing that I *had* to walk away from you—away from the woman I truly loved so that I didn't take her into a tortured future—that I wasn't thinking clearly. So I'm sorry I left you at the altar, Beau, but if I hadn't, then you would have left *me*. At some point.'

'I would *never* have left you.'

Tears flowed freely down her cheeks now. His pain was so raw. His suffering so real she couldn't imagine how he had managed to keep it so contained. And how had she not known? How had she not noticed?

'I should have pushed for more. I should have made you tell me back then. We could have avoided this.'

'We couldn't. Because we were based on a fantasy. *You* thought we were perfect.' A pained look crossed his face. He didn't want to hurt her. 'We *weren't*. I couldn't tell you because you didn't want to hear it. You didn't ask about *me*. All you could see was the romance and the fun and the laughter.' He stared hard at her. 'You didn't want the reality of me. You were so caught up in the wedding preparations you couldn't see what was right in front of your eyes.'

Her cheeks were wet. She could feel the drips of her tears falling from her jawline. 'What? Are you saying that I...I *failed* you somehow? That I didn't listen? That I didn't give you the chance to tell me what you needed to say?'

It hurt to think he might believe that. *Had* she been at fault?

'I wasn't ready, Beau. I had doubts. A real fear as to what awaited us in the future.' He sighed heavily, as if worn down by the argument. 'I wanted to love you for ever, Beau. I really did. But I knew it couldn't happen. Unless we were honest. You weren't ready to hear that, so I walked away.'

She looked out across the plateau at the mountains in the distance, now dark with greying shadow as the sun set. The sky was filled with glorious tones of orange and pink. It all looked so pretty. So wonderful. But how could this sunset be so beautiful? So warm? There were blooming flowers in the distance. The crackle and pop of burning wood and the scent of woodsmoke drifting past them. The last of the day's bird chorus slowly fading to nothing.

Was she also to blame for their relationship failing in the way that it had? And if that was the case, didn't she need to take some of the responsibility for everything that had gone wrong? For the fact that what they'd had in the past had all been *fake*?

She pulled her fleece jacket around her. 'I loved you. That part was real…'

She looked away, her bottom lip trembling. She feared that maybe he'd never loved her. That their relationship had never been what she'd thought it was. She tried to pull her hands free of his, tried to separate herself from him, acknowledging that she had somehow always imagined things wrongly. That their past relationship had been some sort of dreamworld she'd been living in. Had she been deluding herself that he loved her?

But Gray wouldn't let her get away. He held on tight, pulling her back and making her look him in the eyes.

'I loved you, too. More than *life*! And I refused to put you through that. I refused to let us go blindly into the future with you thinking that everything was fine when I knew that it wasn't.'

'Our love was real?' Her bottom lip trembled.

He nodded and pressed his lips to her forehead before looking down at her. 'It was. I couldn't lie about that.'

'But—'

'Beau, look at me.'

She looked up at him with eyes glistening from salty tears, with her heart almost torn in two by the heartbreak of knowing that she'd caused him pain and that she'd kept him *silent*. Unable to tell her what he needed. She so badly wanted to put that right. So she would listen to him now. Hear what he had to say.

'Yes?'

He stared deeply into her eyes, as if searching for something. 'We had something special, but it wasn't our time then.'

'Is it our time now?' she asked, with hope in her heart.

Gray swallowed, cupping her face, his hands so tender, warm and soft, and then he took another step towards her, breathing heavily, lowering his head until their hungry lips met.

She sank into his embrace. Against his hard, solid body. Tasting him, enjoying him, her hands up in his hair, grasping him, pulling him towards her, desperate for his touch. Remembering, recalling *this*—how good it had always felt to be with him. How special.

Their past was forgotten in that instant.

She *needed* Gray. Had missed him so much it was painful. But now he was back in her arms and it felt so good. She didn't want to let him go. She wanted to enjoy the moment, and to hell with the consequences, because right now she needed this. *Him.* It didn't matter what he'd said. All that pain he'd shared. Because *this*—this was what was important. Being with him. Reconnecting.

Her fingers fell to the hemline of his top and she began to lift it, to pull it over his head, so that her hands could feel the touch of his skin, his broad shoulders, his taut chest, that flat stomach she remembered so well. His sleeve caught on his chunky wristwatch and she had to give it a yank, but then it was gone, discarded.

For a moment she just looked at him, taking in the beauty of his body, the solidity of his muscles, his powerful frame, and then she was pulling off her own top, kissing him again as he unclipped her bra in a fervour. She wriggled her arms so it would fall to the forest floor. Gasped as his hands cupped her breasts and brought them to his lips. So in need for the feel of his hot lips against her skin.

The touch of his tongue tantalised her, causing her to gasp and bite her lip. She felt as if she was on fire. Her whole body a burning ember. A delicious liquid heat seared from her centre right through her body, inflaming every nerve ending, every sensation, every caress, stroke or lick, driving her insane with need.

'I want you, Gray.' She made him look at her as she spoke, wanting him to know in no uncertain terms what she wanted him to do.

He stared back into her heavy eyes and nodded, then took a step away from her.

She almost cried out, fearing that he was going to stop, leave her in her fevered state, that he was going to humiliate her just as she'd laid herself bare.

But no. He was grabbing a groundsheet, a blanket, and then he took her hand and pulled her towards it.

Hungry for him, hungry for more, she moved to him and felt the core of her burning with need as his fingers began to unbutton her trousers. Hurriedly she kicked off her boots, then her trousers were cast aside, and she hopped from one foot to the other as she removed her socks, before throwing herself back into the safety, security and heat of his embrace.

She wasn't cold. It was a perfect summer's evening. The air on her body felt like a lover's caress in itself, and there was something thrilling about that. As Gray lowered her gently onto the blanket, his hand drifted up the length of her thigh and then delicately began to stroke the thin lace of her underwear before reaching down to feel the heat between her legs.

Yes! Touch me there...

She breathed heavily, her eyes open, gazing upwards at the stars, as she felt his fingertips drift lazily over her body, felt his gaze roaming the expanse of her nakedness, his lips tenderly kissing the underside of her breast, then her waist, her belly button.

And then… Then his mouth drifted downwards, towards the lace, towards the place she wanted him the most.

Beau closed her eyes, her hands gripping his hair, and gasped.

They slept under the same canvas that night. Naked, entwined, they lay together, his body wrapped around hers, until sleep and exhaustion claimed them.

Gray woke first. He was glad. It gave him a chance to put his prosthetic back on. Beau hadn't really seen him without it yet, and after what they'd shared last night, he didn't want to spoil what had happened with the sight of his stump over breakfast.

He'd grown used to it. Accepted it. But still, sometimes when he saw it, he remembered what his leg had looked like before, what it had felt like to be whole, and he hated the reminder.

He could spare Beau that, at least. Hadn't he shown her enough last night? He'd hurt her with his words. With his confession. He knew it deeply. He'd seen it in her eyes. She'd started to question herself. Look back. He'd hated seeing her pain, but maybe now, after last night, they could move forward?

Their relationship had died a death before because he'd never been honest with her about his family. About his fears of what might happen to them if they married. But last night…last night had been *amazing* and he wanted that to continue. For them to be together again. He and Beau were a good match.

His finger gently swept up the length of her bare arm and he smiled as she groaned slightly and shifted in her sleep, pressing her body against him.

The length of her, naked and warm, was nuzzled into

him, and he looked down at her face, soft in repose against his shoulder.

Why had he ever listened to that infernal internal voice? To the voice of logic and reason that had kept niggling away at him? Telling him it would all go wrong, that they would end up behaving exactly like his parents' in a toxic marriage.

Thinking of his parents made him remember his father at his stag party, when he'd said, 'You'll regret it. You mark my words, son, you're about to ruin both your lives...'

He grimaced, refusing to hear those words again. He was not going to let thoughts of his father's bitterness ruin what he had at this moment. This perfect moment—holding the woman he had once loved so much in his arms.

Could we start again with a clean slate?

His heart agonised over the possibility.

But he didn't have long to argue with himself.

Beau blinked open her eyes and smiled as she looked up at him. 'Morning.'

'Good morning. Sleep well?'

'I did. The first time in ages. You?'

He nodded. He *had* slept well. And he was in no doubt that it was down to being with Beau. He didn't want to move. Didn't want this moment to end. Could they possibly lie here for ever?

'Would you like breakfast?'

She smiled and gave him a brief kiss. 'Depends what's on the menu.'

He laughed and pulled her onto him, feeling his body spring into life for her once more. 'I think I could possibly find something a bit more interesting than oatmeal.'

Beau grinned. 'Really? I—' She stopped, tilting her head at a funny angle. 'Can you hear that?'

He wasn't sure he wanted to listen to anything. But to

humour her he remained silent and tried to listen. He could hear birds singing and... He squinted and sat upright, his hands still holding Beau to him. Was that...*snuffling*?

'Stay here.'

He slid Beau to one side of him and pulled on his trousers and then, hurriedly, his socks and boots. Quietly he slid the zip down on the tent and looked out. There was nothing he could see in front of the tent. He popped his head back inside.

'I don't think there's anything there, but just to be on the safe side get dressed and we'll go and take a look.'

The snuffling noise was definitely there, and it sounded as if it was *behind* the tent, where they couldn't see without stepping outside.

Gray didn't think it was a mountain lion, and wolves were dawn and dusk creatures. It was now—he glanced at his wristwatch—nearly eight in the morning. When Beau was dressed and had put her boots on, he took her hand and then slowly stepped out, peering over the top of the tent.

And froze.

Behind him Beau was crouched, unable to see what was happening. 'What is it?'

'It's...er...something.'

Beau pushed past the tent flap and came out of the tent to peer past Gray. The second she saw the herd of bison she also froze, feeling her blood run cold.

Mack had warned them. Bison were dangerous. They'd seen that herd last night—they should have *thought*, should have considered that they might still be in the area. But they hadn't. They'd had...*other things* on their minds.

'Gray, what do we do?' she asked in a whisper.

There was nowhere for them to go. The bison herd filled the whole plateau around them. The only place for them to go was the cliff edge.

Where a river ran far below.

About a forty-foot drop.

Gray turned slowly to look at her. 'The tent won't protect us, and these animals can be dangerous.'

'Perhaps they don't even know we're here!'

Gray glanced over and caught the eye of a bull, which peered at them, snorting through its nose. Was he the leader of the pack?

Gray watched in silent dread as the tail of the bison began to rise.

'It's going to charge!'

'What?'

'We need to jump.'

'Please tell me you're joking.'

'Nope.'

He grabbed her hand in his and made a quick run to the cliff edge, where they stopped to look over at the drop.

It was dizzyingly high. Precipitous. And he could feel the pull of gravity as he looked over the edge. He was used to heights. To climbing. To the risk of a fall. But Beau wasn't, and he needed her to jump without hesitating.

A quick glance back at the bison told him it was starting to head their way. Without doubt the animal was going to charge them. Protect its herd. There was nowhere else to go.

'On three…'

'Gray…' She gripped his arm in fright.

'One…two…*three*!'

He held her hand tight and took a leap off the edge, feeling her jump with him, hearing her scream filling the air as they fell, with the water rushing up to meet them.

CHAPTER EIGHT

HER SENSES WENT into overload. Her scream was whipped away by the passing air as she looked down at the terrifying sight of the water rushing up to meet her.

She was falling fast. The air rushed past her mouth before she had time to inhale, her stomach was rising into her chest cavity, and her limbs were flailing madly, trying to find something—anything—to grab on to in mid-air. But of course there was nothing. It was terrifying.

I'm going to die!

The river that had at one point seemed so far away was getting disturbingly close, and then suddenly, *splash*! Her body hit the water, which smacked her in the face as if she'd just been hit by a heavyweight boxer, making her gasp. Water flooded her mouth, her nostrils, her ears, as she struggled against it. Her body stung from the impact, every nerve ending screaming, but somehow there was an even more important agony she had to contend with—the need for oxygen.

It hurt to look about under the water, and all she could see beside her and below were dark shadows, whereas above her there was light. Sparkling sunlight glittering on a surface that didn't seem that far away. She began to swim, her lungs stretched to breaking point.

And just when she thought she wouldn't make it, just

when she thought the surface of the water had just been a mirage, she broke the surface, coughing and spluttering as she gasped for air and tried not to swallow more water.

Inhaling deeply and quickly, wiping her wet hair out of her face, she trod water, turning and twisting, trying to get her bearings.

Where was Gray?

He suddenly popped out of the water next to her, his hair plastered over his forehead, looking for her, and he gave a relieved smile when he saw she was right next to him. 'You okay?'

'I'm all right. Are you okay?'

He nodded and looked up. 'Can you believe that? We did it!'

She blew water from her lips and nodded. Yes, they had done it. And now she was treading water in her clothes and the water was colder than it looked.

She could see a bank further downstream, where they'd be able to crawl out and get on dry land, and she pointed at it. 'Over there.'

She tried to swim, trying to remember how to coordinate her limbs for the breaststroke. The current wasn't too strong and she made it easily, clambering from the water like a sodden sheep, the weight of her clothes dragging her down, cold and shivering.

Slumping onto the ground, she turned to wait for Gray, who crawled from the water beside her before flopping onto his back and letting out an exhausted breath.

Beau swallowed hard and lay back against the dirt, exhausted. There was probably mud getting in her hair, but she didn't care.

I jumped off a cliff!

'I can't believe we did that.'

He turned to look at her and grinned. 'Well, we did. You did great.'

Her gaze drifted to the clifftop, where their camp had been. 'All our things are still up there.'

Gray nodded and let out another sigh. 'But the most important thing is down here. With me.'

She met his gaze and smiled, and then she rolled towards him and planted a kiss on his lips. 'Thank you.'

'What for?'

'Saving our lives.'

'I made you jump off a cliff.'

'Yes. But as we are *not* currently a bison's breakfast, I'd still call that a save.'

Gray frowned. 'I don't think bison *eat* people.'

'Maybe not, but they sure as hell can flatten you if they want, and I don't know about you, but I quite like to have my body in full working order.'

Gray looked away and then sat up, running his hand down his left leg towards his prosthetic.

Oh. I shouldn't have said that. I didn't think.

She bit her lip. 'Sorry.'

'It's fine.' Gray got to his feet, testing it out. 'Still works.'

She stood up beside him, looking around them. The river flowed downstream away from them and on either side were gorse bushes and trees and mountains rising high. 'Are we lost?'

He looked at her briefly before turning, scanning their surroundings for himself. 'I don't think so. If I remember correctly, Heart Lake is fed into by this river. If we follow it we should make it back to the ranger station in a few hours.'

She nodded. 'Okay. Should we try and find water, or do you think we can make it without?'

'It's getting warm, but we should be fine if we keep a steady pace.'

She bit her lip and he reached out a hand to grab hers.

'Hey, we'll be fine.'

Beau hoped he was right.

Gray trudged on, leading the way. Apart from being hungry and thirsty, he wasn't sure what to feel. Last night had been bittersweet. He and Beau had become close again last night! And though he'd loved every second of it, he still wasn't sure they'd resolved anything by this morning. Kissing her, then making love to her, had distracted their thoughts, and though he had wanted to lie in her arms for many more hours, enjoying that blissful moment when it had seemed the rest of the world had stopped turning, he'd been well aware that the issues between them were still there.

Jumping off that cliff with her, her hand in his... He remembered with a cold shudder how it had felt to hit the water, to feel his prosthetic weigh him down. He had struggled to swim, to get to the surface. Beau had let go of him and for a moment—a brief, terrifying moment—he'd thought she'd been swept downstream. Until he'd broken the surface and seen her there next to him. Safe.

But only just. How could he look out for Beau when he could barely survive himself?

If he had a magic lamp and he could make a wish, then he'd wish for a long, happy life with Beau. No doubt about that. But...

What could he offer her now? He'd told her the truth at long last, there was that, so they had honesty now—and, yes, there was still that intense heat between them. But relationships had to be more than just sex. There had to be trust, intimacy, love, compassion. There had to be give and take. Compromise. Teamwork. They had to be a unit. A solid couple. He had to feel as if he could protect her and love her in the way she deserved. In the way she wanted. She *needed* that happy-ever-after, but was he the man who could give it to her?

Did he deserve another chance with her?

They didn't live near each other. They each had a career in different parts of the country. They each worked really long hours. Beau had her family in Oxford—his were in Edinburgh. What did he have to give Beau apart from their painful, disappointing past? And although she'd said his leg didn't bother her, it *did* bother him. He wanted to be perfect for her. Whole. If she took him on, she'd be taking on his leg. The phantom pains he still got…the possibility of getting early osteoarthritis in his good knee because of the amputation. She had to accept that he was disabled—like his father.

Did she deserve that? Want that? There were so many men out there who had all four functioning limbs and hadn't hurt her in the way that he had. Men who hadn't let her down.

He didn't want to burden Beau the way his own mother had been burdened—with a disabled man whom she'd grow to resent.

He knew that she wanted him. He'd seen it in her eyes. In the way she'd listened to him reveal his soul and the way she'd looked as they'd made love. She had feelings for him still—he could see it. And he couldn't deny the way he was feeling about her.

The only problem was he wasn't sure if they should pursue it. Because if they gave things another go and it all went wrong, the heartache of losing her again would be too much.

Not worth going through for anything.

Perhaps walking away would be the kindest thing after all?

Around them Yellowstone Park was glorious, dressed in its summer colours: bright blue skies, wispy white clouds drifting past, trees adorned with many greens, from the darkest pine to the lightest willow, blue-white columbines attracting butterflies of every shape and size amongst the yellow cinquefoil flowers like buttercups.

They ambled through the landscape together, breathing heavily under the oppressive heat, until around midday, when Beau had to stop and sit down. Collapsing to the floor, she sucked in oxygen, exhausted. She was as thirsty as anything, her mouth dry as dust.

When had she *ever* felt this spent? She'd been on her feet for only a few hours. She'd had much longer shifts in hospital. But at least then she'd had access to drinks. The river trickling alongside them almost seemed to mock her. All that water…

All that campylobacter. All that giardia. Drink that and you certainly will be in hospital. With sickness and diarrhoea.

She swallowed and tried not to think of a nice cold glass of iced water. Instead she decided to focus on something much better. The fact that she and Gray had grown close again. That they'd overcome the barrier of their past. Gray had shared his concerns and fears. They'd made love under a starry sky and she'd slept in his arms and felt happy again for the first time in an age.

After everything, it seemed things were going *right* for her with Gray, and she'd thought she'd never be able to say that. *Ever.* Yet here they were. Together. Supporting each other, protecting each other, looking out for each other.

This was what couples did. They worked as a team. They were strong. United.

Her feelings for him were very strong. She still loved him. She knew it in her heart. She'd been struggling against it ever since she'd walked into the ranger station just a few days ago. Her love for him had never gone away and he was the only man who could make her feel this way.

Last night had been a revelation. A new chapter for them both. She'd been grateful for his honesty. For his making clear that which had been blurry. Explaining the pain. Explaining his reasons for walking away.

It had hurt to feel that she'd been to blame for some of it, but truth sometimes did hurt. She'd listened to it, acknowledged it. Accepted it. *Some of it was my fault.* But then they'd slept together and he'd held her in his arms, and she'd felt so good to be there. She just *knew* she could never let that go again.

'Do you think there's much further to go?'

He ran a hand through his hair. 'Couple of miles, maybe. Not far.'

'We might run into the others soon. They might have water! You know…if they didn't have to jump off a cliff.'

He smiled at her. 'Maybe.'

'I'm glad I'm here with you, Gray. Doing this. It wouldn't have been the same without you. Us meeting again. Getting close again. Opening up. It's been good for us, don't you think?'

Gray nodded and looked about them. 'Ready to go again?'

She stood and slipped her hand into his, surprising him. 'I'm ready.'

He said nothing, just started to walk.

Then, within the hour, they met some familiar faces.

CHAPTER NINE

BARB AND CONRAD waved to them and they hurried over to meet up with the older married couple, who both looked quite fresh and not at all trail-weary.

The two women hugged and the men patted each other on the back—until Barb frowned and looked at them both. 'Where's your gear?'

Beau grinned at Gray. 'A bison took it.'

'Oh! Really?'

'We woke this morning and we were surrounded. One started to charge and we had to jump into a river to escape.'

Barb looked at her husband. 'You weren't hurt? Con, get these people some water.'

But Con was already doing that, and he handed over their flasks to let them both take a long, refreshing drink.

'Oh, wow—that tastes so good!' Beau wiped her mouth and handed it back, but Con waved it away.

'You keep it. We're nearly back to the ranger station. Look over there—through the trees. See that strip of blue? That's Heart Lake.'

Beau squinted and shielded her eyes—and, yes! There it was! They'd made it back, safe and sound, and their friends were okay, too.

Barb threaded her arm into Beau's and walked with her, whilst Gray walked behind them with Con.

'So how did you two get on?' she asked.

Beau smiled and nodded. 'It was good. I think it might just be okay for us.'

'Oh, honey, I'm so pleased to hear that! You two look made for each other.'

It felt good to hear someone else say that. It reinforced everything that Beau had been thinking. She'd made some mistakes in the past. She'd taken Gray's feelings for granted. Had not given him the opportunity to share how he truly felt. She'd been caught up in her romantic tale of love, of how they'd had the romance of the century, but none of it had been true. Well, almost none. They *had* loved each other. But the foundations of their relationship had been shaky.

She'd not known the full truth about her then husband-to-be, but now she did. She'd been so busy trying to have what her parents had that she hadn't realised that he'd been trying to steer them away from what *his* parents had.

But it's settled now. We're nearly back to civilisation. We can make this work. Somehow.

She supposed they'd have to travel to see each other at first. Maybe one of them could try to get a job in the other's hospital. There was always a need for a good neurologist or cardiologist. Then, being close, they could work on just being together again. It was scary—being back with Gray, taking a risk—but it felt *right*. As if she was home.

The brain had two hemispheres and there were connections—neural pathways that connected the two, making the brain a whole so that it worked to perfection. Being separated from Gray had been like having only one hemisphere. She could survive, but there were deficits. She'd known something was missing. That she wasn't whole.

Now they were coming back together and everything was slowly becoming *right*.

The rest of the group began to emerge from different directions as they got closer and closer to the ranger station. Seeing each other's faces brought comfort and joy, and when they were all back together again, they walked into the ranger station with the biggest grins on their faces. Their happiness in their joint achievement filled the room with its glow as they each told their stories—the funny moments, the scary moments. How they'd survived.

Beau listened to it all, her heart full.

As the chatter died down, Mack congratulated them all on getting back safe and sound, and after a quick debrief they all started to decamp. To gather their things and get ready to catch the minibus that would take them back to Gallatin and their own cars. Where they would all part ways.

Seeing as Beau didn't have any gear to sort through, she located Gray and waited for him to end his conversation with Toby and Allan. The guys were promising to keep in touch.

Afterwards, when they'd left, he turned to her and smiled. 'You okay?'

'I'm good! I'm great, actually. Looking forward to getting back to my hotel and changing my clothes. Taking a hot shower. I thought that maybe you'd like to join me?'

It was forward, she knew, but she wanted this good feeling to continue. To make sure he knew they could work on this relationship and make it succeed this time. Now she knew what he had feared, what he'd worried about before, they could move on.

But Gray's face was blank. 'I'll be heading back to my own hotel. I've got a flight to catch tomorrow and I'd like to get some rest.'

Oh.

'Are you sure? I thought that we—'

'This isn't what you deserve, Beau.' He lowered his voice and moved her away from the others. '*I'm* not. I can't love you the way you want me to. I think it's best if we close the door on what we had and just move on.'

Beau stared at him, feeling sick. Was he really saying this? But they'd shared so much!

How could I have read you so wrong?

Gray walked away from her once more, his feet leaden, his heart weary. Every step he took became more and more painful as he increased the distance between them.

It was tempting. So tempting to turn around and go back to her, give her what she wanted, but he couldn't. He needed to get away from her. Create some space. He couldn't think when he was this close to her. He couldn't think when she looked at him like that. With *love* in her eyes.

It was like stepping back in time. Right back to where they started! Surely she could see that he was doing this for both of them?

'*Gray!*' She grabbed his arm and spun him round. 'What are you *doing*?'

'We're still in the same place. It's eleven years on, and we're in a different country, but we're still stuck in the same place!'

'No. It's different now.'

'Is it? You still see the sweetness and light in everything. Despite what I've told you. Despite knowing I can't protect you. Can't love you the way that you need. Can't offer you anything but a disabled partner who sure as hell doesn't deserve a second chance.'

'It won't be that way—'

He pulled his arm free. 'Please, Beau! I can't think when

you touch me! I can't think with you around. It's too much. Believe me, it's better this way.'

'For who? For *you*? Because it isn't easy for *me*!'

'I just…need some space. Please, Beau, will you let it go? I can't be who you need.'

She looked up at him with sadness. 'Who are *you* to know who I need?'

He couldn't speak then. He couldn't reply. He couldn't *think*. Seeing the tears fall from her eyes was so hard. But what could he do? The feelings that had resurfaced when they'd made love had shaken him. He wasn't prepared for this! He'd expected to apologise, he'd expected her to listen grudgingly, but so much else had happened. Emotions were getting involved again—love and longing, hurt and pain. He couldn't see what he needed to do.

Gray needed her to go.

Gritting his teeth, he turned his back on her and waited for her to walk away.

He hadn't sat next to her on the bus. It had been like a slap in the face. Instead he'd walked past her and gone to sit at the back with Dean and Rick.

So she'd sat there alone, behind the driver, trying her hardest not to turn around and look at him in case everyone else saw the heartbreak on her face.

Where had it gone so wrong?

They'd talked. They'd made love. That night had been exquisite. The sensations he had made her feel had made her…euphoric. He'd been tender, caring, passionate. They'd lain together afterwards, entwined. He'd smiled at her that morning, had kissed her—he'd seemed fine. They'd jumped off that cliff. Survived the fall without injury. Got out of the river without being swept away. They'd both been so happy and exhilarated at what had happened, and then...

He'd gone a little quiet on the trek back—but then again, they both had! They'd been thirsty. Talking had just seemed to make her mouth drier. But whilst she'd allowed herself to think everything was different, had got carried away with imagining the glorious future they could have, he'd been thinking...what?

'I'm not what you deserve. I can't love you the way you want me to.'

How was it *his* choice to decide what she deserved? She deserved *him*! He was her soulmate. Her better half. Her match. In every way. She *needed* him.

She loved him.

Did I do it again? Did I get carried away with a romantic fantasy?

Maybe he was right. Maybe he *could* see right through her. Perhaps he was right not to rush into anything? Could he see that she was falling into old habits?

'I can't love you the way you want me to.'

She just wanted to be loved by *him*. He was the only man who would do. Who would fulfil the need she felt every day. To be touched by him. Loved by him. Held in his arms. She'd had eleven years to realise she wouldn't be able to find that with anyone else. Not the way she felt when she was with Gray. That sense of completeness.

When he got off the bus, if he left without her, he would be taking her heart with him.

Beau wiped away a tear and looked out of the window.

The minibus trundled along the park's roads, past sights they hadn't seen. Glaciers. Geysers. She saw some elk, and high above some birds circling on the thermals in the blue skies. The raw beauty of the place hurt her eyes. It was too beautiful to look at when she felt so ravaged, so she closed her eyes and laid her head against the window, allowing the motion of the vehicle to rock her to sleep.

She dreamed. She dreamed that she was in the water again, after the jump, and that she'd just exploded to the surface, gasping for air, looking about her for Gray. Eventually his head popped up out of the water, further downstream, and though she called for him, though she waved to show him where she was, he simply got washed downstream, disappearing from sight...

She woke with a jerk, sitting bolt upright, aware that people were getting off the bus. Looking outside, she could see the car park of the Gallatin Ranger Station, and over to her right her rental car. Had it been only five days since she'd parked it there? So much had happened...

Beau stood up, determined to speak to Gray, to not let him get away without a word as he had once before. She turned around to face the back of the bus, where he'd been sitting.

He was gone.

She looked out at the others, still gathering their bags from the bus's storage compartments, but he wasn't there, either.

Beau clambered down the steps and grabbed Barb's sleeve. 'Where's Gray?'

'I think he went into the ranger station, honey. You have a good sleep?'

She didn't answer. She raced for the station, blasting through its doors and scanning the room, then darting past the receptionist into the room in which she'd first seen him. He had to be there! He had to be with Mack or someone.

But the room was empty.

She shot back outside to check the toilets, but they were

empty, too. Desperate now, she headed back to the receptionist. 'Has Gray McGregor been in?'

'He collected his car keys just a few minutes ago. I
think he's gone.'

No!

She darted outside, aware that the others were looking at
her strangely, but not caring. All that mattered was finding
Gray. She couldn't see him in the car park and there was
no car leaving. Had he already left? Had she missed him?

As Rick passed her, she grabbed his arm. 'What hotel
was Gray staying at? Did he mention it?'

'Sorry, Beau, he didn't.'

'But he gave you his number? To keep in touch?'

'Yeah, but it's a UK number.'

'Not his mobile?'

'His cell? No, sorry.'

She almost cried out. How could this be happening?
How could he do this to her again?

She stood in the middle of the car park for ages. Con and
Barb picked up their car and waved to her as they passed
by, as did the others. She stared at nothing. Thought of
nothing but her loss as the cars drove past her, some toot-
ing their horns.

She didn't move until her bladder began to scream at
her. Only then did she slowly plod over to the bathroom
and relieve herself, before going into the station and col-
lecting her car keys and belongings.

The luxury of the car felt wrong. The leather seats,
the air conditioning. That new car smell. It all seemed so
false. So manufactured. She'd become used to nature in
that short week. The fresh, warm air. The smell of pine—
real pine. Not that stuff that was made in a factory and
created from chemicals.

She started the engine and entered the address details

for her hotel into the GPS system, began to drive. She drove almost on autopilot, getting back to her hotel, barely remembering the drive at all.

When she'd checked in to her room, she dropped her keys onto the dresser and turned on the shower, shedding clothes in slow motion, feeling as if she was moving through thick treacle, stepping under the warm spray and closing her eyes, trying to feel nothing. Trying not to think.

But it all became too much.

And she sank into the corner of the shower and began to cry.

His hotel room was a world away from the last week's experience. Had it really been just a week? The room, though familiar, looked empty—dry of life. Not real. A false environment. A place that was meant to make him feel as if he were at home, but was so false it almost made him feel sick to be there.

Home was where Beau was.

It always had been. And it had ripped him apart to walk away. Again. But how could he throw himself into their relationship? He loved her. With all his heart and more. But he wasn't *right* for her. If they tried to make it work, one of them would have to give up their career at their current hospital and move. That bit might not be so bad, but what about when the thrill of being back together again wore off? What happened when reality sank in? What if they decided to have children?

He couldn't do it.

All that time, all those eleven years he'd spent away from her, he'd struggled to feel satisfied or happy with anything. And finding Beau again, in Yellowstone, of all places, had made him realise just what he'd been missing.

She had always had his heart. From that very first day

when he'd spotted her at medical school—that gorgeous, long-limbed, elegant woman with the flaming red hair— his breath had been taken from him. He'd tried to use his old, familiar chat-up lines and they'd had no effect on her. She'd laughed them off, almost disappointed by his attempt at using them. And so he'd tried a different tactic.

He'd been as genuine as he could. He'd listened to her. Studied with her. Helped her revise. He'd been content with just *being* with her. Basking in her glow. Enjoying the warmth that she'd created in his cold, empty heart. The first time he'd kissed her... Well, that had been something else!

After that he'd been unable to tear himself away from her. Beau had been his bright star, his happiness. His joy. His deep love. He'd never known it was possible to love another person so much. Whenever they'd been apart, he'd thought of her. Whenever he'd been on a day shift and she on a night shift, and they'd met like ships in the dawn of the early morning, their time together had been too short. Bittersweet.

Sometimes they'd meet in the hospital cafeteria and just drink coffee silently together. Happy to be next to each other. They hadn't needed words. They hadn't needed grand gestures to show the other how much they meant to them. They'd just been happy to *be*. Sitting opposite each other, holding hands.

He refused to end up hating her. His heart, his logical brain, told him he wouldn't do that to himself. They'd met again. Cleared the air. Shared a wonderful few days together. And it was best to leave it at that. With good memories. Ending on a high.

So why do I feel like this?

His heart physically ached. He was fighting against

the urge to throw caution to the wind and go and find her again. To feel her in his arms just one more time…

But what good would it do? It would hurt them each and every time they had to part ways.

But what if it could work?

The devil's advocate part of his brain kicked in. Presented him with images of them happy together, surrounded by a brood of happy, red-haired, green-eyed children. Mini-versions of him and Beau. Having the kind of marriage people dreamed of.

Some people managed it, didn't they? He'd read about them in the news. Couples celebrating fifty, sixty, seventy years of marriage and giving their advice for a long, happy marriage:

Never go to bed on an argument.

Enjoy each other's company.

Be honest.

Be realistic.

It was that last one he'd held on to. Surely he *was* being realistic? Over fifty per cent of marriages *failed*, and those couples that stayed together he knew were doing it for reasons other than love. They didn't want to be alone. They were staying together for the sake of the kids. It was a habit they couldn't break. It was too expensive to separate…

Which of them were *truly* still in love?

It was hard to admit that he was afraid, but he knew he was. Afraid of hurting Beau. Afraid of having her hate him. Afraid of having her resent him. Afraid of her looking at him the way his mother looked at his father…

He sat on the end of his hotel bed and held his head in his hands.

Trying to convince himself he was doing the right thing.

It didn't help that there was a voice in his head screaming at him that he was doing the *wrong* thing.

He needed some space.
He needed some calm time.
He needed to *think*.

She'd kept herself busy—reading books, magazines, the newspapers. Watching television. Well...telling herself she was reading. Telling herself she was paying attention to the screen. All so she didn't think about Gray.

It wasn't working.

He was in her thoughts constantly, and her mind was churning with all the possibilities. Perhaps he'd done a good thing for them both by walking away. Because what if he was right? What if they *were* doomed to a future of having one of those relationships where people put up with what they'd got because the alternative was too terrible?

Being alone...

I'm alone now, aren't I? And it sucks!

He was wrong. They were stronger than that. Their love was stronger than that. Because it had lasted for the eleven years they'd been apart—always there, burning away quietly in the background and then roaring back into full flame when they'd met up again.

There was no point in fighting it. When she got back to the UK, she would go to Edinburgh. She would find his hospital and she would wait in his surgery until there was time for him to see her. He *would* see her. He would do her that honour. And it didn't matter if he listened and then told her he couldn't do it, she had to at least *try*. He had to know that she wanted to be with him. Had to know how much she loved him. Wanted to be his partner, his lover, his soulmate. She was all those things already—it was just that he was refusing to see it!

Could she convince him that there was another kind of future for them? Let him know that there was an alternative?

That they could be happy, like her parents? People who had such a deep love for each other were strong enough to get over any day-to-day upsets. Get through the rigours of life. People *succeeded* at marriage! Those couples who were determined to make their vows mean something. Who solved their problems before they became big issues. It was impossible to get through a marriage without there being ups and downs, but it *was* possible to do it without hating each other—and they had a love strong enough to do so.

He needs to know that I won't give up on him this time.

He'd shocked her, and there'd not been a chance for her to say what she needed to say. Well, he'd had *his* chance. And soon, back home, she would have hers.

The plane home was delayed by two hours, so Beau waited in the airport lounge, sipping coffee and finally— *finally!*—able to get her hands on a beautiful, flaky, buttery Danish pastry. She could almost feel herself salivating at the thought of it, but when it arrived, when it came to eating it, she found it difficult. Dry. Cloying. Tasteless.

She left it, pushing her plate away and swallowing the last of the coffee. Just as she was doing so she heard the boarding call for her plane.

She'd got an aisle seat and she settled down, anxious to get her feet back on British soil, where the air would be refreshingly damp and chill and the only animal likely to make her jump out of the way would be her neighbour's overenthusiastic Red Setter.

She sensed rather than saw Gray arrive. She'd not even been looking at the passengers getting on the plane, but she'd felt someone brush by and suddenly she *knew* who it was. The cologne, her awareness of his proximity—it all pointed to the one man she'd thought she'd never see again.

'Gray...' She almost choked on his name as she stumbled to her feet. It was so unexpected to see him here. On *her* flight.

'Beau. You're looking well.'

He looked washed out. As if he hadn't slept. His eyes were reddened and there was a paleness to his skin, despite their days in the American sun.

'I am. Thank you. You're on *this* flight?'

She winced. What a stupid question! Of course he was!

'Row J.' He pointed to his row, unable to take his eyes off her, then reluctantly moved on. The passengers behind him were getting impatient that he was blocking the aisle.

Beau sank back into her seat, her heart racing, thudding in her chest. She closed her eyes and tried to take a deep, steadying breath. This was it. Her chance. Her opportunity to speak to him. Eight hours' worth of opportunity, before they touched down in the UK. No need to track him down—no need to chase after him. Fate had given her this gift.

She was suddenly afraid. Her stomach felt cold, solid, like a block of ice. Fear was pinning her limbs to her seat.

This is one of those turning points in life, isn't it? Do I want to give us another chance? I really do!

She really wanted a spot of Dutch courage.

Where are those flight attendants when you want them?

Beau blinked and thought of what her life would be like if she didn't go and talk to him. It was too horrible to imagine. She'd be alone again. Driven only by work. Her life empty. Feeling as if she was waiting for something that never came. In limbo. Her life on pause. And though she loved her job, she knew she loved Gray McGregor more. She *needed* him. More than she needed oxygen.

She closed her eyes and tried to breathe.

CHAPTER TEN

THEY'D BEEN IN the air for an hour before she finally got up the nerve to go and talk to him. An hour of letting her stomach churn, of gripping her armrests till her knuckles turned white, before she finally unclipped her seat belt and got up out of her seat. Her legs were like jelly, her mouth drier than a desert.

Instantly his gaze connected with hers, and she saw him suck in a deep breath, too.

Good. He was just as nervous as she was.

If it goes wrong, then fine. I'll just walk away, sit back in my seat, and I'll never have to see him again. But what if it goes right...?

Unsteadily, she walked down the aisle and stopped by his seat. The two chairs next to him were empty.

'Mind if I take a seat?'

'Be my guest.' He got up so she could sidle past him, and waited for her to sit before he sat down himself.

She sat in the window seat, so that there was a gap between them. She didn't want to be too close. She had no idea how this conversation was going to go.

'How have you been?'

He glanced at her, then away, his jaw muscles clenching. 'Okay, I guess. You?'

This was her opportunity. Her chance to tell him how

in torment she'd been since he'd left her at the minibus. Since he'd crushed her heart by telling her that he didn't deserve a second chance with her.

'Not bad.' She paused. 'Actually, I've been…thinking.'

He raised an eyebrow. 'Thinking?'

She nodded quickly, her blood zooming through her veins, carried along on a jet stream of adrenaline. 'About you.'

'Oh?'

He wasn't making this easy for her. But maybe he was afraid, too? She saw him swallow. His Adam's apple bobbing up and down as he thought for a moment. Was he anticipating what she was going to say? She could see fear and doubt playing across his face as he sought to find the best way to remain calm whilst she said whatever she had to.

But she was impatient. Nervous. 'You don't have to say anything. I'll speak first. I think that I should.'

He met her gaze and stared. For just a moment. The intensity in his eyes made her temperature rise and her heart pound. 'Okay.'

How to start?

'I'm sorry, Gray. I'm sorry that I wasn't there for you before. That I didn't make you feel that you could talk to me. I'm sorry for the way I treated you when we met again. I'm sorry that it's taken this long for me to be able to see what was wrong. And where the blame lay.'

'Beau—'

'Let me finish.' She smiled, her mouth trembling with nerves. 'I need to say this. Because if I don't say this right now, then…then I'll never be able to say it, and I think we owe it to each other to be honest.'

It was hard not to cry, too. She'd worked herself up so

much that the need to say everything, to get everything out so that he'd hear how she felt, was just overwhelming.

He stared at her, his feelings written across every feature. The concern in his eyes...the tenseness in his mouth...that beautiful mouth. His tight jaw...

'I loved you. I *still* love you. I always have and I always will—whether you allow me to do so or decide you never want to see me ever again. I love you. I think we could work. If you gave us a chance, I think we really *could*. We know who we are. We've put everything out there. Nothing's hidden.'

She reached for his hand and took it in hers, clasping it tightly, hoping he wouldn't be able to tell how much she was shaking.

'I know about your leg and it doesn't bother me. It doesn't stop you from being *you*. I know about your family. What you went through. I know that you think marriage is some sort of prison, but that's not how *I* see it. I see it as a journey.' She laughed nervously and hoped he would laugh, too. 'Yes, I used the J-word!'

He smiled. But he seemed too far away. He still wasn't quite with her. So she got out of her window seat and into the seat directly next to him.

She looked at their entwined hands and felt her barriers breaking down. She wanted this so much! But she was afraid of getting her heart broken again, and now her fear was making her hesitate.

'I want to be with you, Gray. Married or not. I don't need a perfect man. I don't need someone who will never argue with me or grow frustrated with me, because that happens anyway. But what I *do* want is *you*. Gray McGregor. Faults and all. We can do this. We can get it right this time—I know we can—because we both care enough to get it right, and...'

She almost ran out of words. Almost. She looked into his green eyes for inspiration and saw them smiling back at her. She fought back her tears.

'You told me that I deserved someone who could love me the way I want to be loved. You told me that you didn't deserve a second chance with me. But…but you're the one that I want to have loving me. You're the only one who can love me the way that I want. *I'm* the one who deserves a second chance with *you*! Can't you see that? I love you, Gray McGregor. Can't you love me, too?'

Gray brought her fingers to his lips, closing his eyes as he sucked in a breath and inhaled the aroma of her skin before he began to speak.

'I used to fear that our being together would turn us into different people who couldn't stand to be near each other… but being *away* from you makes me miserable. Sadder than I've ever been in my life. When I fell from that sea cliff and lay on the rocks waiting for help, all I could think of was you. I thought that if I died, then at least it would take me away from the torment of not being with you. But now we have this second chance and…and I *want* to take it. I *do*! I thought… I thought that I didn't deserve another chance and so I walked away again. Just for a moment. I needed to get my head straight. I needed to know that I was thinking clearly about us. That I'd rid myself of all that old clutter, that old pain I used to carry inside. I used to hide behind it. Using it as an excuse. Believing it—allowing it to twist me into this man who was too afraid to be with the woman he loved in case it all went wrong. But…'

He smiled at her and wiped a tear from her soft, soft cheek.

'I know what love is. I know that it's what *we've* got. Something special. We're a team, you and me. We always have been. We've shared our fears, our hopes. Our love. You know everything about me and you still love me anyway. Do you know how amazing I find that?'

She nodded, her tears turning to tears of happiness.

'I got off that bus and I had to drive away. Being around you…I couldn't think straight. But back at the hotel I could. I told you that I was scared of what might happen to us, but that was wrong. I was running away from love because I'd never truly felt it. Not until you came along. And suddenly everything was moving too fast! Marriage? Talk of having kids?'

He shook his head at the memory.

'My mother didn't want me. My father barely knew me. I was just a messenger boy. A pawn in their horrible game. And whilst I loved you, *wanted* to be with you, I was terrified of doing so in case I got it all wrong. I didn't know how to be loved like that. So strongly. Living apart from you, just dating you, I could hide from that. Disguise it. I thought that if we got married it would expose me for the fraud that I was. It wasn't you. It wasn't us. It was *me*. But now I know I'm stronger. You *make* me stronger. All that we've been through tells me we can do this.'

A stewardess came by with her trolley, offering drinks, but Gray waved her past.

'I accused you of not living in reality, but I was doing the same thing. I was living in a future that hadn't happened. We have no idea of how this will go, but I think— I *know*—the two of us will make it the best it can be. The strongest it can be. And…and I know that I love you, too. That I'm miserable without you. That my life is *nothing* without you in it.'

'Gray…'

'Fate threw us back together, but even if it hadn't…I would have found you anyway. I can never be apart from you again.' He smiled, his face warming with the strength of it, happiness gleaming from his eyes. 'Beau, you are the most beautiful woman I know. The strongest woman I know and I want you in my life for ever. Will you do me the honour of making me the happiest man in this world and marrying me?'

'*Marrying* you?'

Did I just squeak that? Since when do I squeak?

He nodded. 'I want to marry you, Beau. I want you to be my wife. I want us to be together through good times *and* bad. In sickness and in health. Till death do us part. Dr Beau Judd, my beautiful neurologist…my other half…'

A kiss.

'My soul…'

Another kiss.

'My heart…'

And another.

'Yes!' She nodded, grinning like an idiot and not caring. He loved her! *Loved her!* It was real this time. 'Yes! Yes! *Yes!* I will. Are you going to kiss me properly now, or just keep staring at me?'

'I'd like to kiss you.'

He leant forward and their lips met.

This was it. Their first kiss on the path to true love. His lips were warm and soft, and they caressed hers so expertly that she felt like a molten ball of fire. Her insides were liquid. Her hands scrunched tightly in his hair and she pulled him against her and kissed him back as if her life depended upon it.

And it did.

She knew she was nothing without this man. She had a home, a career and a family. She should have been content with just those things. But having Gray in her life made everything so much better. Brighter. Riskier, yes, but brighter.

She stroked his face, feeling the softness of his fine beard beneath her fingertips. 'I love you so much.'

He reached for her other hand and kissed her fingertips. 'And I love *you*. We made it off that clifftop—we can make it on solid ground.'

Joy beyond measure was hers. Her happiness scale exploded and blew off its top as she sank into Gray's arms and accepted his love.

But he shifted slightly, reached into his pocket and pulled out a small velvet box. 'I can't believe I had a whole other speech planned for when I tracked you down in the UK. It wasn't very good, but…everything's worked out bonny in the end. You said yes. So…this is for you.'

She took the box and glanced up at him. He looked nervous. It had to be a ring. He'd bought her one before and it had been stored in her jewellery box for too many years. Now she was getting another. But this one *meant* something more.

Beau opened the box. Inside lay a beautiful diamond set in a platinum band. It glittered and caught the light against its velvet nest and she beamed a smile through her happy tears.

'It's gorgeous.'

Gray took it from the box and then took her left hand, sliding it onto her finger. It was a perfect fit.

She kissed him again. As his fiancée. A perfect kiss. A loving kiss.

'I love you, Beau,' he whispered in her ear.

And she whispered back, 'And I love *you*, Gray Mc-Gregor.'

EPILOGUE

SHE WAS READY. Her hair was done. Her make-up was done. The dress fitted perfectly. She picked up her small posy of peonies and made her way downstairs, to where her father waited for her, dressed in smart tails and holding a top hat.

'How do I look?' he asked.

'Very handsome.' She smiled.

'You don't think I should have gone with a kilt, like Gray?'

She shook her head. 'No one but Mum needs to see *those* knees, Dad.'

He reached for her hand and let out a steadying breath. 'The car's here. Are you ready?'

There were nerves and excitement in her stomach. Her heart was pounding and her mouth was dry with anticipation. But, yes, she was ready.

'I am.'

Outside, all her neighbours were standing and watching, and there were a few 'oohs' as she came out and they saw her dressed in white.

A silver-grey car, sleek and exclusive, adorned with white ribbons, awaited her, and a chauffeur in a grey suit and cap stood by the open back door, smiling as she approached.

She waved at her neighbours, at the people who'd witnessed her devastation before, knowing they were truly happy for her. That finally she was getting her dream come true. And as they drove to the church, she clutched her father's hand tightly.

'Nervous?'

She nodded. 'A bit.'

'He'll be there, you know.'

'I know he will.'

She wasn't nervous about that at all. She could tell that this time it was different. Gray was a completely different man, a completely different groom-to-be this time. Eager to join in with wedding arrangements, making his own suggestions, telling her how he'd like the day to go. He'd been just as excited for the day as she had. There'd been no doubt. No cold feet. At all.

Just excitement. Just joy at finally getting the day— the *marriage*—they both wanted. Had both dreamed of. The marriage that they knew was now within their reach.

Everyone else was waiting at the church. Her mum had travelled earlier on, with the bridesmaids. All the rest of her family were there, most of them already inside. As she got out of the car, she saw Gray's mother and father go in, too.

The photographer wanted some pictures before she went in and dutifully she posed, her excitement building, her desire to see Gray as she walked down the aisle becoming almost unbearable.

She wanted to see his face. She wanted to hold his hand. Say her vows. Promise to be his for evermore.

The music began and she lowered her veil and took one last deep breath. She'd been here before. She'd just never got this far.

She took her father's arm and nodded.

I'm ready.

And then the doors were open, the congregation stood and she began her walk down the aisle.

She saw Gray at the other end. Beaming with joy as the wedding music soared, almost crying at the sight of her as she walked down the aisle towards him. She could hardly take her eyes off him. He looked so handsome in his red-and-green kilt, his black jacket and brilliant white shirt. Those green eyes were smiling as she drew close, and he reached out to take her hand from her father's.

'You look so beautiful,' he said.

She couldn't speak, she felt so happy. She just took his hand and smiled shyly at him.

As the music died down, the vicar came to stand in front of them and began the service.

Beau and Gray made their vows. Gave each other a ring. And were soon declared husband and wife.

'You may kiss your bride.'

Gray smiled, lifted up her veil and pulled her towards him for their first kiss as a married couple.

After they'd signed the register, they headed outside for more photos, and when they were standing in the glorious sunshine, waiting for the photographer to organise them into another pose, they kissed some more.

And then they heard an American voice interrupt them. 'Er...guys, I think we told you to get a room!'

Beau laughed and turned to see all their American friends from the Yellowstone trip—Mack, Conrad, Barb and the others. All there. All happy to be sharing their wedding day.

'Don't worry. We will,' said Gray. 'Later.'

'Who'd have guessed it would be the honeymoon suite, though?' asked Mack.

Barb looked at Beau and winked. 'Oh, I think we knew. Deep down, we always knew.'

Beau smiled and then kissed her husband.

* * * * *

If you enjoyed this story, check out these other great reads from Louisa Heaton

ONE LIFE-CHANGING NIGHT
A FATHER THIS CHRISTMAS?
HIS PERFECT BRIDE?
THE BABY THAT CHANGED HER LIFE

All available now!

MILLS & BOON®

MEDICAL ROMANCE™

THE ULTIMATE IN ROMANTIC MEDICAL DRAMA

A sneak peek at next month's titles...

In stores from 6th October 2016:

- **Waking Up to Dr Gorgeous** – Emily Forbes *and* **Swept Away by the Seductive Stranger** – Amy Andrews

- **One Kiss in Tokyo...** – Scarlet Wilson *and* **The Courage to Love Her Army Doc** – Karin Baine

- **Reawakened by the Surgeon's Touch** – Jennifer Taylor *and* **Second Chance with Lord Branscombe** – Joanna Neil

---

Just can't wait?

Buy our books online a month before they hit the shops!

www.millsandboon.co.uk

Also available as eBooks.

MILLS & BOON®

EXCLUSIVE EXCERPT

Luci Dawson's house-swap to Sydney starts with a surprise when she discovers she's sleeping in a gorgeous stranger's bed! Dr Seb Hollingsworth could be exactly what she wants this Christmas…

Read on for a sneak preview of
WAKING UP TO DR GORGEOUS
the first book in the festive new Medical duet
THE CHRISTMAS SWAP

Luci was pretty sure by now that it wasn't a burglar, but there was still a stranger in the house.

She needed to get dressed.

She switched on the bedside light and was halfway out of bed when she heard the footsteps moving along the passage. While she was debating her options she saw the bedroom door handle moving.

OMG, they were coming in.

'You'd better get out of here. I've called the police,' she yelled, not knowing what else to do.

The door handle continued to turn and a voice said, 'You've done what?'

When it became obvious that the person who belonged to the voice was intent on entering her room she jumped back into bed and pulled the covers up to her chin, grabbing her phone just in case she did need to call the cops.

'I'll scream,' she added for good measure.

But the door continued to open and a vision appeared. Luci wondered briefly if she was dreaming. Her heart was racing at a million miles an hour but now she had no clue whether it was due to nerves, fear, panic or simple lust. This intruder might just be the most gorgeous man she'd ever laid eyes on. Surely someone this gorgeous couldn't be evil?

'Don't come any closer,' she said.

He stopped and held his hands out to his sides. 'I'm not going to hurt you, but who the hell are you and what are you doing in my room?' he said.

'*Your* room?'

THE CHRISTMAS SWAP includes WAKING UP
TO DR GORGEOUS by Emily Forbes
and SWEPT AWAY BY THE SEDUCTIVE
STRANGER by Amy Andrews

Available October 2016

www.millsandboon.co.uk

Copyright ©2016 by Emily Forbes

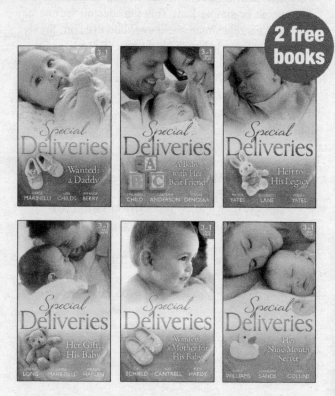